CW00420824

Orphan's
Gift

RENITA D'SILVA

The Orphan's Gift

Bookouture

Published by Bookouture in 2020

An imprint of Storyfire Ltd.
Carmelite House
50 Victoria Embankment
London EC4Y 0DZ

www.bookouture.com

ISBN: 978-1-78681-652-8
eBook ISBN: 978-1-78681-651-1

For my brother Stephen – warm, witty, irreverent, kind, generous, brilliant – and for his glorious stars: my nephew Jaisal and niece Eila

Epigraph

I hold it true, whate'er befall;
I feel it, when I sorrow most;
'Tis better to have loved and lost
Than never to have loved at all.

'In Memoriam A. H. H.'
Alfred Lord Tennyson (1809–92)

Prologue

Wonder

*

Alice

Momentous

Alice's life changes on a perfectly ordinary afternoon in the midst of a perfectly ordinary week.

Later, she will wonder: did she have any inkling of what was to come that drowsy, jasmine-and-dust-tinted afternoon?

She will look back at the day, her actions – the same as every other day, talking, listening, playing with and helping the children – and wonder, did she have a premonition, a hunch that something momentous was poised to happen?

No, she will decide.

She had absolutely no inkling that her orderly world with its everyday routines was about to tilt on its axis; that this day, which seemed like any other, was anything but.

She is in the little room off the nursery, which passes for her office, catching up on paperwork while the children have their afternoon siesta, when there is a knock at her door.

And with it, although she doesn't know it then, events are set in motion that will completely, irrevocably, inevitably alter the course of her life.

Janaki

One Moment

It takes so little to change a life.

The whisper-soft sigh between one breath and the next – that's all it takes to devastate the life you have so carefully constructed.

All it takes to pay for the happiness that is more than your due.

All it takes to balance the giant account sheet monitored by a punishing God who keeps a tally.

Janaki's stomach spasms, her body reacting to what she has just heard before her mind can make sense of it.

Around her the world goes on, a woman's low, throaty laughter clashing discordantly with the plaintive mewl of a kitten; two men arguing, each louder than the other; a child sucking the juice from a mango, his chin spattered yellow with syrup, attracting flies; a woman carrying pails of water, one in each hand, while balancing another expertly on her head, the bangles adorning her wrists chiming a merry tune, glimmering saffron and marigold in the dancing sunshine that falls in gilded streaks on the dust by the doorway against which Janaki is slumped.

All it takes is one moment for happiness to transform into tragedy, for everything to go to nothing, for life to never be the same again.

All it takes is one moment.

PART 1

....

India

Love

Chapter 1

Alice

1909

Missing

When Alice wakes, she knows immediately that all is not right; there's something vital missing.

She looks around her at a world pixelated by the mosquito net that drapes her cot. The windows are open and moist air laced with cinnamon, frying onions, caramelised sugar and cardamom drifts in through the mesh screen that keeps insects at bay. She is hot, sweaty, but that is not what distresses her. It is the sound of laughter, warm and unconstrained, just beneath her window. Now the chuckles, which she imagines as bright rainbows, stop and natter begins. She cannot take any more. She opens her mouth and screams...

'*Arre,* Missy Baba, why the upset?' Ayah laughs, gathering Alice to her, twirling her around.

And even though Alice is comforted, that dark, fathomless upset of being left out, abandoned, which had squeezed her heart – the notion that the world was turning, people going about their lives having forgotten all about her, the fear so vivid she can still taste it, salty bitter – returns in remembered sobs that come as hiccups now her wailing has quieted.

Alice breathes in Ayah's soothing smell – the tang of perspiration, jasmine from the creamy white flowers circling her bun, and sweet rose from the joss sticks she burns to the gods religiously every morning and evening – and peers around her shoulder.

Searching. Searching…

Where *is* her friend?

Ayah reads her mind even before she can formulate the word 'Raju'.

'Your first word,' Ayah likes to say, her voice warm. 'Not Mother, Father or even Ayah, but Raju. I was worried when your mother handed you over to me as a baby that my own baba might be jealous. But when Raju saw you crying, he started up as well, and when I soothed you, he grinned and clapped his hands. You were a newborn but you squinted up at him then and, I swear, you smiled. That was it, Raju's little face lit up with joy and after that, you were inseparable.'

Raju, always waiting outside her room for her to wake in the morning, always beside her, Alice's loyal companion until she goes to bed at night – today being a puzzling exception – laughs out loud when Ayah recounts this story.

Alice's friend's mirth is like the explosion of colourful bubbles that time Ayah filled the bucket with water by the tamarind and mango trees, and Alice tipped the entire cake of soap into it. Bubbles had risen, bright and profuse, holding shimmering rainbows within them. Raju and Alice had toddled after them, swatting at the bubbles. Ayah, having fished the soap out of the bucket, the cake now just a fine sliver, had been too charmed by their joy to tell them off.

'Raju is ill. He's with my sister. I couldn't risk you getting his fever,' Ayah says now.

Alice's upset, briefly appeased by Ayah's arms, erupts again.

She is lost without her playmate and counterpart.

In all her four years, she cannot recall a day when Raju has not been beside her, keeping her company. He looks after her, cares for her. He understands her every action, reading her emotions sometimes even before she can articulate them herself…

She opens her mouth and her disappointment, her hurt at Raju not being there beside her for possibly the first time that she is aware of, manifests, once again, in heart-rending bawls.

'Missy Baba, if Raju came here in the state he's in, he'd give you his fever. It wouldn't do at all.'

But Alice will not listen, she cannot.

All she is aware of is the pain of missing her friend, his yawning absence.

'Raju,' she screams, 'I want Raju.'

Ayah takes her to the central courtyard around which the house is built, carrying her past the climbing roses, the saffron marigold smiles and the cascading profusion of bougainvillea to the well, letting Alice look inside – something she and Raju have been warned *not* to do.

'You're to steer clear of the well, it is out of bounds,' Ayah has told them sternly, her normally smiling eyes bright and sharp. 'Dangerous.'

Now, Ayah allows Alice a peek, reiterating, her voice firm: 'No doing this on your own. Ever.'

The hollow, yawning hole, seemingly endless save for a darkly glittering grin, deep, deep down – a tantalising, barely-there slither of shimmering silver – sends shivers down Alice's spine.

She is allowed to touch the rope, wet and coarse, thick brown, the pulley with the pail, half-full of glinting water. The cat, daringly perched on the rim of the well, is drinking from the pail, pink tongue darting. The washing stone beside the well glows bright navy-streaked-grey in the sunshine.

Alice caresses the moss, soft velvet, lining the well surround and marvels at its carpet-like texture, her tears temporarily forgotten.

She looks around for Raju, to ask him to feel too, and is assaulted afresh by his absence, her tears starting up again, louder.

Ayah permits her to slip and slide on the cement floor, which has been sprayed with water to cool the house. This activity usually makes her break out in giggles when with Raju, the burst of her friend's laughter too infectious to resist. But it is not much fun all on her own.

Ayah carries her high up on the seat of her shoulders so that she is almost level with the fruit trees in the compound at the back of the house, allowing her to pluck a guava and count the number of bananas in each of the crowded bunches that are weighing down the banana trees so they look like stooped old women. Past the knobbly tamarind they walk, and the green peppercorns, their pungent tang making Alice sneeze.

Ayah points out the spiky pineapples growing from little shrubs on the ground like offerings, with their juicy yellow fragrance; the prickly humps of jackfruit, the sun dazzling gold, the air a festive celebration of scents, seasoned liberally with dust. And yet, despite the rosy ripeness of the guava sweet in her mouth, Alice feels bereft.

'I want Raju,' she cries, even as the other servants – the sweeper, the ends of her sari tucked in at the waist, waging her perpetual battle against the ever-present dust; Dhobi delivering a stack of freshly washed and ironed clothes smelling of soap and sun; Mali, dirt from working the soil in the garden ingrained into the grooves of his calloused fingers, the nails quite black – all make a fuss of her.

'Why so upset, Missy Baba?' they ask. 'Look, even the sun is slipping behind clouds because you're sad.'

Alice looks up. The sun is as golden bright as ever in a blinding turquoise sky majestically free of clouds. She blinks, eyes stinging.

'Fooled you,' Mali chortles, his laughter morphing into hacking coughs. 'Made you stop crying for a minute.'

Alice starts up again, furious.

Mali goes back to his plants, still coughing. He plucks potent green chillies, elegant okra, plump *brinjals* in their resplendent aubergine coats and lanky beans.

The peacocks that frequent the compound dance around his feet, their plumes open in a theatre of winking sapphire and iridescent copper-gold.

'They make a louder racket even than you,' Ayah tells Alice, smiling at her.

But Alice will not stop until her friend is with her, as always.

'Alright,' Ayah sighs, 'we'll ask Memsahib if you can visit Raju, how's that?'

At this, Alice's sobs stall, subsiding once again to hiccups.

'And *if* she agrees, we'll go. Just for a while, mind. Raju's ill, and may not be his usual self. And if we do visit, you're not to touch him or get close to him, you understand?'

Ayah wipes Alice's face with her sari pallu. It smells of sweat and sun, onions and comfort, patience and love.

'What are we to do with the two of you, eh?' Ayah says, but she is smiling. 'Inseparable.'

Alice giggles, throwing her head to the wide sky, her tears quite forgotten at the prospect of seeing her friend again.

She takes another bite of the guava and relishes its juicy nectar, savouring the syrup.

Chapter 2

Janaki

1944

Summer Sky

Clang, clang, clang!

In the girls' dormitory, Janaki jerks awake, eyes opening to the shadow-steeped darkness vibrating with deep bronze reverberations.

The others all sleep on, seemingly oblivious to the persistent ringing of the bell.

How can they sleep through the noise?

The air in the room is hot and heavy, scented with many slumbering breaths; the sticky, sweet dreams of the girls lying side by side on mats on the floor.

Janaki gets up, softly, so as not to disturb her neighbour and best friend Arthy, although she doesn't know why she bothers. Arthy would sleep through an earthquake and wake up wondering why she was pinned down by rubble.

Janaki is grateful that she is closest to the door and that there's nobody on her right. She'd be claustrophobic, stuck in the midst of a row of girls.

'I sleepwalk, you know. You don't want to be woken by me stumbling over you, blinking and weaving like a *bhoot*,' she'd declared to the other girls, and they had believed her, allowing her the coveted spot by the door.

Sister Nandita had called her aside. 'It doesn't do to tell lies.'

'But, Sister—'

Sister's all-seeing eyes had speared Janaki. 'You don't really sleepwalk, Janaki.'

Fiddling with her clothes, Janaki had been unable to meet Sister's gaze. 'But I do need to get up in the night to use the toilet.'

'Why not say that then?'

'The others will argue that they want to as well.'

'Do you have to have the space by the door? Can't you share?'

'I… I don't like being hemmed in.'

'You can sleep by the door for a month, then you will allow others a turn, yes?'

Biting her lower lip and studiously avoiding Sister Nandita's eyes, Janaki had said, 'Okay.' But at the same time her mind had been frantically trying to come up with ways to convince the others not to claim the place by the door even when offered it. Perhaps, out of Sister Nandita's hearing, she could convince them it was haunted? Cursed?

Now, Janaki slips out of the door and into the corridor. She peers down through the railings, inhaling the metallic odour of rust, towards the entrance to the orphanage, where there is a bell that can be pulled when someone leaves a baby outside. One of the nuns – usually Sister Malli, who's the most junior and thus, always on night duty – would come to rescue it.

St Ursula's orphanage is in the middle of a busy street in the heart of the city of Jamjadpur.

'When our fellow Carmelite nuns from England started St Ursula's, this was a quiet street. But the city grew and grew, and now we are right in the centre. Along with Jamjadpur, the orphanage has grown as well. We are bursting at the seams,' Sister Shanthi had once informed Janaki as they'd sat threading jasmine together. 'The businesses on either side of us keep wanting to buy our land: the compound with fruit trees at the back and this shady area in front, with its flower bushes and vegetable patch. But our benefactors, the Carmelite nuns from England who still own this property, don't want to sell. This is the best orphanage in the city, the children here growing up well rounded and—'

'Why then, every evening, do we have to pick out worms from the flour that will be used for our porridge and chapatis the next day?' Janaki had asked, surprising even herself; usually she was quiet and rule-abiding, not daring to question the nuns even on things she privately disagreed with. But the memory of the worm she had found in her chapati at lunch prompted this unaccustomed feistiness.

Sister Shanthi had stopped weaving jasmine and had perused Janaki with beady eyes. 'You're sounding very ungrateful, Janaki. It's not like you.'

'Sister—'

'You're a thousand times better off than the street kids who don't have a roof to sleep under. They'd be grateful for *any* food, even the leftovers of those chapatis you're complaining about. That flour, by the time it arrives from abroad, is not at its best, but at least you have three meals a day which is more than can be said for—'

'I'm sorry.' Janaki had been chastened.

Smells of stewing tea and roasting vegetables, sounds of clanging utensils were wafting from the kitchen, which was directly to the left of where they were sitting beneath the mango trees, fashioning fragrant wreaths to place before holy statues in the small chapel attached to the orphanage. The other orphans were having their afternoon nap (girls and boys in their dormitories on opposite sides of the orphanage, separated by the nuns' rooms and the chapel), as were most of the nuns. Janaki did not like afternoon naps and Sister Shanthi felt the same: 'If I nap now then I can't sleep at night.'

Wanting to change the topic and Sister Shanthi's mood, Janaki had asked, 'How did I come to be here?' She never tired of hearing the story of her arrival at the orphanage, as a newborn eight years earlier, and Sister Shanthi always obliged.

'Oh, your arrival was dramatic. It was right in the middle of the riots.' Her eyes had glowed with the mellow light of reminiscence.

'What riots?' Janaki had asked – Sister's cue – although of course she knew.

A gentle breeze was stroking Janaki's face with soft caresses, like her absent mother's palms would have done, she fancied.

'The Hindu Muslim riots of nineteen thirty-six.' Sister Shanthi had sighed, her expression pensive. 'Not much has changed since then. Hindus and Muslims are *still* at loggerheads and, if anything, the violence is getting worse. They all want freedom from the British but instead of finding common ground in this, they are turning on each other. However, thankfully, at the moment at least, there's peace here in Jamjadpur.'

She had fallen silent, both she and Janaki listening to the noises outside the sleepy compound: horses neighing, carriage wheels creaking, people chattering and arguing; vendors shouting out their wares, their tones slightly desperate; beggars jangling their cans, the paltry coins rattling inside.

'The city was on fire, houses burning, corpses littering the road,' Sister Shanthi continued. 'There was so much chaos, such mindless violence. And in the midst of all this, a reedy, unmistakable cry. The mewling siren of a newborn. We didn't have the

bell at the time, you see. That was only installed later, when…'
Sister Shanthi swallowed, shadows crowding her soft honey eyes.

'When what, Sister?'

'Nothing.'

'Please tell, Sister.'

'One of the babies… He must have been left at dawn but
whoever left the child did not rattle the gate to let us know – or
perhaps they did, but not loud enough for us to hear.'

'And?' Janaki had nudged as Sister was lost in musing.

'We were busy that day, the Bishop was visiting, so we didn't
check the little nook by the gate as usual. The child must have
been sickly and it was a very hot day. By the time we found him,
later that afternoon, he was dehydrated. We… we couldn't save
him.' Sister Shanthi had sighed deeply, her eyes sparkling gold.

'Oh.' Janaki had not heard this part of the story in previous
retellings. A dip formed in her stomach at the thought of that
unfortunate boy, a stinging in her eyes.

'After that, we installed the bell.' Sister Shanthi had sighed
again. Then, shaking her head, 'Now then, I've gone off on a
tangent. I'm beginning to do so more and more nowadays.'

Yes, you are, Janaki had thought but hadn't dared to say out loud,
having learnt from experience that although *they* (or at least Sister
Shanthi) admitted their faults, the nuns did not like *you* to concur.

'Where was I?'

'The cry of a baby in the middle of the riots,' Janaki had
prompted.

'We were in the chapel praying for peace. Then we heard
the unmistakable cry of a baby in the midst of all the agonised
screams. But Mother Superior was leading the prayer and we
didn't want to…'

'Mother Superior can be quite scary,' Janaki had said with
feeling, recalling the times she had been summoned to see her

and had been made to kneel on the floor, contemplating her sins while looking up at Christ on the cross, His mild, blood-stained face smiling down at her, despite His crown of thorns.

'Then there was this banging at the gate and someone calling, "Nuns! Sisters!" Mother Superior opened her eyes and nodded at me; I went running at once.' Sister Shanthi had paused again to take a breath.

A crow cawed up among the mango trees. A blue-and-yellow-sequinned butterfly, like sun-splashed sky, landed on a maroon hibiscus flower next to Janaki.

'At the gate, a miracle,' Sister Shanti had informed her. 'The Hindus and Muslims who'd been engaged in fighting unto death were all gathered together and smiling down at you, united in admiration. You were such a beautiful baby, wrapped in a green cardigan that brought out the unusual, starry blue of your eyes. You were blinking up at the men who had, a minute before, been hell-bent upon violence, ready to commit murder. Those mercenaries were misty-eyed and when I came to collect you, one of them said, "This one's special." Once I took you in, they started fighting again, taking up where they'd left off, all traces of tenderness gone.'

Now, Janaki brings her thoughts back to the present, as she stands with her nose flattened against the iron railings, night pressing, dark and secretive with shadows.

Here and there is a golden pin-pricked flicker of light. The street outside, never quiet during the day, is now dozy with slumber, even the drunks and street dwellers out for the count.

Janaki watches as Sister Malli rubs the sleep from her eyes and opens the gate, gently cradling the bundle left in the nook, bringing it inside.

A dog whines plaintively in the alleyway behind the orphanage. A cat jumps off the low, broken wall of the compound opposite, sniffing curiously at the rubbish heaped in the ditch, spilling onto the road.

Sister Malli will take the baby to the kitchen, feed it with some watered-down milk and settle it on one of the mats in the baby room.

Janaki waits, and sure enough, a shadow unpeels itself from the wall further along the road. The woman's silhouette, face covered by a veil, is just visible as she slips into the enveloping, obliterating darkness, gently wiping, Janaki imagines, tears from her eyes.

'The mothers who leave their children here, will they miss them?' she once asked.

'Of course. Tremendously. It is because they love their children so much that they give them away,' Sister Nandita had replied. 'They feel their children have a better chance here at the orphanage than with them.'

'But...' Janaki was puzzled. How could living here with strict nuns, unyielding routine, harsh punishments for small transgressions, mealy, worm-riddled food, be better than being with family?

Sister Nandita divined her unvoiced question. 'They're at their wits' end, undone by circumstances, no proper house, not enough food to go round, no means of providing their offspring with an education.'

Janaki nodded with dawning understanding, thinking of the beggars on the streets outside the orphanage, so much worse off than her. No clothes to wear or food to eat, the mothers clinging to their children, their bloodshot eyes telling stories of desperation and heartbreak.

*

The woman stops at the end of the street, turns once, her face, Janaki imagines, watery and wistful, although all she can see is a shadowy outline.

Janaki slips back into the dormitory and lies down beside Arthy, who is snoring away, oblivious, the thick, close air tasting of sleep and haunted by dreams. She thinks of the baby downstairs, now a part of the orphanage. The mother going to wherever her home is – if she has one – heartsick but hoping, praying her child has a better life because of her sacrifice.

Janaki dreams of a woman who leaves her child by the gate of the orphanage in the middle of riots. The woman's face is in silhouette, but her shoulders are hunched and shuddering; she is wiping her face with the veil of her sari even as she sends a prayer coloured the transcendent yellow of hope against the odds to the gods.

In the nook by the gate, the child, wearing a cardigan the hue of rain-burnished fields, smiles up at the men who crowd around her, admiring her eyes, which are the startling blue of a cloudless summer sky.

Chapter 3

Alice

1909

Home

Alice clutches Ayah's hand, tight, as Ayah knocks on the door to Memsahib's room. Alice doesn't like it in there, although Ayah makes her visit twice a day when Sahib is away (for then Memsahib takes all her meals in bed). Ayah takes Alice in to greet Memsahib in the morning – after she has been scrubbed clean of the hot, flustered dreams of night and plastered with sweet-smelling talc, which she doesn't mind as long as it doesn't get into her eyes – and before bed.

'You must call her Mother,' Ayah admonishes. Alice has heard Sahib call her 'Caro', and Sahib's friends refer to her as 'the lovely Mrs Harris'. Sahib, meanwhile, is 'Robert' to Memsahib *and* to his friends. To Alice, despite Ayah's remonstrations, her parents – remote figures, barely featuring in her life – are Sahib and Memsahib.

Alice has marvelled at how a person can be different things to different people. She herself is 'Alice' to her parents, but thinks of herself as Missy Baba, and feels quite peculiar when she is introduced as 'Miss Harris' or sometimes 'Miss Alice Harris' to Sahib's friends.

'What is Raju's other name?' she once queried to Ayah.

Ayah was puzzled.

'You *know*, like mine is Miss Harris.' Alice was frustrated with Ayah for not understanding.

Ayah hooted with laughter, spitting out the *paan* she was chewing, Alice jumping out of the way of the foul red liquid just in time.

'Missy Baba, you're a delight.' Ayah swooped down and gathered Alice in her onion-and-cumin-scented arms.

Alice scowled at Ayah. 'I wasn't joking.'

'Raju's *other* name is Mr Kumar,' Ayah said, smiling, her mouth stained with *paan* juice. 'Although I can't see when he will have cause to use it.'

Alice doesn't like having to speak in English with her parents. Hindi is the language of her heart, the tongue she learnt at Ayah's breast, the vernacular of Ayah's lullabies and Raju's soothing, the servants' gossip and arguments, the lingo in which Mali converses with his beloved plants, the language of Alice's dreams. Alice enjoys conversing in Hindi, its musical cadences more familiar than the clipped, crisp language she has to use when speaking to her parents. Although she sees Sahib even less than she does Memsahib – most days, he is gone before she is awake and returns home after she is in bed.

Alice has a vivid memory of Sahib – or is it a dream? She's not quite sure. All she knows is that it is bright and colourful and feels very real. She conjures it during those rare times when Sahib is home before her bedtime and his stern, preoccupied face causes her stomach to dip in fear.

In her memory/dream, she's looking up at Sahib, so tall as to block out the sun.

'Are you as tall as the sky? Does your head touch the clouds?' she asks.

And this is where she questions her memory and is convinced it is a dream, for Sahib laughs, his chuckles like warm stones tumbling on glass, like thunder rumbling. She cannot recall ever hearing Sahib laugh or even seeing him smile except in this vibrant dream-memory.

Now he is bending down, his eyes twinkling at her. 'You can decide for yourself.'

And then he is lifting her, oh so high! It's as if she is flying!

'You're *not* as tall as the sky,' she declares. 'But you *can* see for miles.' Awe and wonder burnish her voice bright rainbow.

Sahib sets her down, still smiling. 'Go and find your nanny, Alice.'

Nanny? For a moment Alice is nonplussed and then she realises Sahib means Ayah!

'She's *Ayah*, not Nanny, and you can call me Missy Baba,' Alice corrects imperiously. She has always associated 'Missy Baba' with warm affection, and now that Sahib is being so friendly and kind, she's decided he can call her so too.

But...

A stormy scowl steals the remnants of the smile from Sahib's face.

'Your name is Alice – Missy Baba is what the servants call you for you are their little mistress. And your nanny's name is not Ayah, it's her *job*,' Sahib roars.

Alice's dream-memory ends here and she's quite pleased that she cannot picture/recall what happened next…

Memsahib's cheeks are thin, papery. She is pale as the skin on the milk Ayah makes Alice drink every morning 'so you grow tall and strong'. She smells of sleep, sweat and roses. Her eyes are the broody blue of the sky at dusk, huge and watery in a narrow face.

Alice prefers Ayah's substantial arms, smelling of onions and comfort. Her hands, brown and gnarled and yet so soft and gentle with her.

She likes it best when it is just herself with Ayah and Raju – her favourite people.

Memsahib's room is always dark, the curtains pulled shut to keep out the day.

'The mosquitoes, the bugs, the sticky, unrelenting heat, the incessant spices added to *everything*, even pudding,' Memsahib complains, her eyes hard, flashing fire – a startling contrast to her milky face. 'No moderation. Everything done to extremes in this horrid country.'

Alice and Raju have overheard Ayah gossiping with Cook: 'The memsahib is an English flower, unsuited to and wilting in this heat. She's wanted to go home since she set foot here.'

Home? Alice wondered. *Isn't* this *home? How can Memsahib not like it here? How can she be unsuited to the golden sunshine that makes things grow, thrive?*

Alice loves the heat, the food, the people. She even tolerates the bugs.

For Alice *is* at home.

*

'Memsahib's always been a sickly one,' Alice and Raju heard Ayah whispering to Cook.

They were meant to be having their naps but had sneaked out to eavesdrop – Alice the instigator, Raju as ever following her lead.

Alice's face was pressed against the wood of the door, with its scent of sawdust and secrets, one eye positioned perfectly in the gap at the hinges so that she had a view of the kitchen, one hand tucked into Raju's hand, sticky with perspiration and friendship.

Ayah paused, taking a big sip of ginger-and-cardamom-infused tea.

'Here, have a samosa to go with it. New recipe. I've added peas to the potato mixture,' Cook said, the oil sizzling and sputtering as she took a freshly cooked samosa out of the frying pan.

Alice's stomach rumbled and Raju stifled a giggle, his teeth glowing yellow against chocolate skin.

'This is delicious,' Ayah said and Cook beamed, sitting herself down opposite Ayah, setting a plate of samosas and another of – was it *rasgullas?* – between them.

Alice's stomach rumbled again and Raju suppressed another chuckle.

'We'll have them when we "wake up". Not long now,' he whispered in her ear, his breath hot and sweet, flavoured with the tartness of the fresh mango he was always munching.

'Memsahib's pregnancy was difficult and the birth itself an ordeal. That is why, as soon as Missy Baba was born, she was handed to me,' Ayah said. 'Memsahib is to have no more children, doctor's orders. Apparently, her constitution will not be able to survive childbirth again. One seems to have destroyed Memsahib as it is.' Ayah sighed deeply. 'My Raju barely a year old when Missy Baba came along. I'd feed Raju from one breast and her from the other. I worried he'd be jealous.'

'Never,' Raju mouthed, squeezing Alice's hand.

Cook agreed, snorting. 'Far from it.'

A line of ants marched up the fraying wood of the door beside Alice, small, black, purposeful.

Ayah chuckled. 'I was worrying for nothing. He was enamoured with her from the start. So protective of her, even when barely a toddler. And she following him round, bossing him. The little madam.' Ayah cackled, affection in her voice. 'She started calling me Ma; she heard Raju, see. Had my work cut out getting her to call me Ayah. She refers to her mother as Memsahib even though I've corrected her a hundred times. I worry she'll say it to Memsahib's face one day and then where will we be?'

Cook clucked, shaking her head. 'Take another bite of the samosa. You've hardly eaten a thing.'

Ayah finished off the samosa in two huge bites. 'They are really good. Missy Baba and Raju will devour these.'

In the shadowy darkness wedged behind the door, Raju nodded vigorously, grinning at Alice.

'I think they'll like the *rasgullas* better. Finally got the texture right. Here, try one.'

Alice watched Ayah take a bite of the syrupy sweetness, her mouth watering, wondering if she and Raju should reveal themselves. The scents of roasting spices and stewed tea mingling with honeyed milk made her stomach rumble so loudly, to Raju's continuing mirth, it was a wonder the women didn't hear.

'Your best yet.'

Alice could wait no longer.

'Come,' she whispered to Raju, tugging at his hand, and they ran into the kitchen as one, the ants startling and dispersing as the door banged behind them, Alice announcing, 'I'm *starving*.'

The women exchanged smiles and Ayah opened her arms. Raju and Alice perched one on each knee, Alice on the right and Raju on the left, their favoured positions; Ayah's substantial lap comfortably accommodated them both.

Ayah's voice started as a rumble in her chest. 'Up already? Smelt the feast Cook has been preparing for you monkeys in your dreams, did you?'

And Alice leant against her beloved Ayah, her friend beside her, Cook's *rasgullas* stuffed whole in her mouth, nectary perfection, thinking, *I'm glad Memsahib has left me with Ayah. There's nowhere else I'd rather be.*

*

'Come in,' Memsahib calls and Alice enters her room in Ayah's wake, taking refuge in the folds of Ayah's sari.

The windows are shut with curtains drawn in Memsahib's room so it takes Alice a few minutes to adjust to the gloom after the bright morning outside.

They've been catching butterflies in the garden to distract Alice from missing Raju and to pass the time until Memsahib was up and could see them. The elusive creatures, with their custard-yellow wings blending into the gilded sunshine, flit between the fruit trees – guava and banana, mango and jamun – alighting on the fat, prickly pineapples, which are budding moons within their womb of starburst leaves. They are as colourful as the vivid dreams Alice has every night, fading in the glare of morning, leaving only an impression of happy, vibrant colour.

Memsahib is always in her room during the day, and she is 'not to be disturbed'.

'But why?' Alice once asked.

'She's resting.'

'But why? She's missing out on the day. There's so much to see and do.'

'For you there definitely is, curious soul that you are,' Ayah had laughed, patting Alice's cheek fondly.

'Memsahib is not tired when she has to go out or when there's a party here.'

When Memsahib dressed for a party, or a dance, or went to the clubhouse, she transformed into an unearthly being. A goddess.

Like the peacocks, so ordinary with their plumes dragging in the dust, and their plaintive squawks, except when they opened their tails into fans of glorious, kaleidoscopic colour.

Out of bed, Memsahib was a different person, almost as tall as Sahib, draped in flowing fabric that shimmered and glittered when it caught the light, her lips shiny red, cheeks pink, face glowing, eyes sparkling with secrets.

Sahib – 'Father to you,' Ayah repeatedly admonished – was transformed too, and not as forbidding, his gaze soft and bright when he looked at his wife, as if some of her colour had reflected onto him, putting a rainbow twinkle in his eye. 'You look beautiful, darling,' he said to Memsahib and she glowed, looking even more resplendent if possible.

Ayah nudged Alice, and Alice closed her mouth, wide-eyed with awe at this otherworldly sprite that had taken the place of the memsahib she usually encountered dwarfed in bed.

How would it feel to touch this goddess? Would some of her glamour transfer to her? Alice wondered as she moved forward to kiss her. She smelled just as glorious as she looked, fruity and fragrant as a summer meadow basking in sunshine.

Memsahib said, her breath vinegary sweet like fermented fruit, 'Ah, careful now. I wouldn't like my rouge to be smudged.'

Alice stepped back.

Memsahib directed Alice to kiss the air near her cheek.

Alice understood.

Like goddesses, she could only be adored from afar. Paid homage from a distance.

'Will I transform into a goddess when I have to go out when I'm older?' Alice asked Ayah afterwards, and Ayah laughed as if she had cracked a very funny joke, wiping the tears from her eyes as she shared it with Cook and Mali, although Alice was perfectly serious. 'Memsahib looks so different when she has to go out. Why is she tired when I want to show her the caterpillar or the flower with the different coloured petals that I found, and you tell me no, she's resting?' Alice persisted.

'You're full of questions, aren't you?' Ayah sighed, plying her with syrupy *jalebis* and melt-in-the-mouth *gulab jamuns* sticky with sugar, the heavenly sweetness distracting her so it quite slipped her mind that Ayah had not actually answered her question.

*

Alice loves the parties her parents host at home, although she's always sent to bed before they are due to start. From her room, with the window open, she can hear the tinkle of laughter, the gurgle of conversation, the clink of glasses; she can smell the tobacco of the men and the perfume of the women. She can see them in the courtyard, the women all goddesses (though none as beautiful as Memsahib) in their sweeping gowns, jewels glinting on slender necks glowing white and gold in the enchanted darkness, the familiar garden transformed to a secretive paradise in the flickering saffron glow of tea lights. The house – chandeliers lit and sparkling, flowing bodies, silvery light – is alien to Alice, who peers down between the gaps in the banisters.

She can see Sahib changing too, as the fog of cigar smoke descends over everything, cloaking the pulsing lights within its navy embrace. Alice looks forward to these evenings, hearing Sahib's rare but welcome laughter, watching Memsahib's exuberance; the musical lilt of camaraderie.

Drifts of conversations lift up to Alice on a breeze scented with unfamiliar perfume: 'The Indian Councils Act has been passed by Parliament. What is Viscount Morley *thinking*, introducing these reforms, increasing the involvement of natives in the governance of India?'

In the morning when she wakes to Ayah and Raju, there's not a sign that the house, whose every nook she knows intimately, having explored even its most elusive crevices with Raju, had revealed a different, decidedly mysterious and novel side the night before. That it had swelled with chat, rocked with laughter, that it was heady with smoke, perfume and secrets. That it had become a palace filled with beautiful people, twinkling with intrigue, absorbing spilled confidences and shining with gilded light.

Alice loves the mornings after a party almost as much as the night before.

'Come,' she'll command and together, she and Raju will comb every inch of the house and grounds until they find evidence that something different, magical, had happened the previous night. A streamer in a forgotten corner. The back of an earring glinting in the shadows. A sequin, starburst silver, wedged into the sliver of space between two dull red bricks.

Memsahib's transformations, which Alice so looks forward to, are rare.

Much of the time, she is to be found in bed, not to be disturbed.

On those mornings when Sahib is home, she gets up for breakfast and so, instead of wishing her a good day in her room, Ayah takes Alice to the dining room to greet both her parents. Her mother, picking at her fruit, will post a wan look her way, cringing, it seems, from the light. Her father will look up from his newspaper, fix Alice in his stern gaze. 'And how are you this morning, young lady?'

Although her father's perusal causes Alice's stomach to flutter with nerves, she has learnt to meet his gaze steadily. 'I'd like you to look me in the eye when I'm talking to you, Alice,' he's stated severely, more than once.

'I'm quite alright, S—' Then at a discreet nudge from Ayah: 'Father.'

'Good day to you, Alice,' her father nods, with a hint of a smile on his face.

This relaxing of her father's face makes Alice very happy and so, like he wished for her, she *does* have a good day.

In the evenings, Sahib returns only after Alice is in bed, so she says good night to Memsahib in her room.

When Sahib returns home from work, he and Memsahib have dinner in the dining room downstairs, their steps outside her room, the tinkle of cutlery, the muted murmur of their conversation peppering her humid, sweaty dreams.

But Sahib is often away.

'Why does Sahib have to go away?'

'Your father is the Deputy Commissioner. A very important man.' Ayah announces the unfamiliar English title carefully, weighting each syllable with import, sounding suitably grave.

'But where does he go?'

'He has to oversee many villages and towns, some so remote that he can't get there and back in a day, so he stays overnight.'

'Ah.'

'Your father is a great man, Missy Baba.'

Alice thinks of Sahib, his quivering ginger moustache. His sharp eyes the silvery blue of a knife blade glinting in the sun. 'He's a little bit scary too.'

'He *has* to be, for all those people to listen to him,' Ayah laughs.

*

Memsahib's room smells of boredom and gloom.

The small form hunched in the big bed draped in mosquito nets is lost among a tangle of sheets, a far cry from the goddess who appears every once in a while, smelling exotic and looking divine.

Alice edges closer to Ayah, trying to disappear within her bright, soft sari with its scent of sweat and spices and comfort.

Ayah nudges Alice.

'Good day, Mother.' Alice's throat is dry – it always is when she is here, as if the closed, musty room sucks the moisture out of her throat. Perhaps it's the air inside, bereft of sunshine, dark and broody, sapped of joy and colour, infused by the dank aura of despair.

There's no movement from the bed, no indication her mother has heard Alice's greeting.

'Memsahib,' Ayah says, 'Alice has been tearful this morning. My Raju is ill so I left him with my sister. Alice won't settle. She misses him. Can I take her to visit him? I'll make sure she doesn't get too close to him so she doesn't contract his fever.'

Memsahib stirs, pulling a pillow down over her eyes. Her voice when it comes is high and nasal, the whine of a trapped fly. 'Do what you think best. And please shut the door on your way out.'

Ayah squeezes her hand and Alice grins as she blinks in the blinding sunshine outside the room, coming in through the window of the corridor, making dancing shadows at her feet.

She will be seeing Raju soon. Hopefully then she will feel whole again.

All this long morning, she's only felt half herself, incomplete without him.

Chapter 4

Janaki

1944

Outside

'Children line up with your partners: boys in one line, girls in another,' Sister Nandita calls.

Janaki does as she's told – she likes rules: the comfort of knowing that if you follow them, your life runs smoothly. Otherwise you're told off and depending on the nun and the severity of your misdemeanour, taken to Mother Superior to face punishment. Janaki has only had to face Mother Superior a couple of times (and that was enough for her to learn her lesson). Both times it meant kneeling on the rough floor of Mother Superior's room and praying rather than – worse – being hit on the knuckles with the dreaded wooden cane.

Janaki shivers when one of the orphans has to face the cane. She shuts her eyes, unable to bear the charged thrum as the cane slices through the air, the ominous crack as it connects with tender knuckles. The boys (and it is usually the boys whose misdemeanours call for the cane) pride themselves on not crying out when they are hit, but Janaki cries out for them, a wounded whine, Arthy jolting her arm to shut her up so she doesn't draw the nuns' attention.

Afterwards the boys display their bruises for the girls to *ooh* and *aah* over, teasing Janaki for her tears on their behalf, the horror writ large upon her face.

'Cheer up, Janaki, it's not that bad,' they joke, but she notes how they wince, involuntarily, if someone accidentally brushes against their knuckles, how they mask it immediately with a nonchalant smile.

'I can't understand how some of the boys *still* won't do as they're asked, despite having endured punishment countless times,' Janaki marvels to Arthy.

'I know!' Arthy shudders her agreement. 'And they show off their knees, bruised from kneeling, and their knuckles, bloody from the canings they've received, so very proudly!'

There are no boys over nine at the orphanage.

'Why?' Janaki asked Sister Nandita, when the boys she had grown up with – and quite liked although they were cheeky – were sent to the missionary orphanage at the other end of the city once they turned nine.

'We wouldn't be able to provide older boys with the nurture they need here. As it is, you girls are a handful,' Sister Nandita said, sighing. 'In any case, the priests at the missionary orphanage will make sure the boys grow into responsible young men, be good role models for them.'

Janaki managed not to crinkle her nose as she wondered how priests like old Father Mahesh, who visited their orphanage every Sunday to conduct Mass, with his lips set permanently in a grimace and his drone of a voice, which always put Janaki to sleep, could be an example for the boisterous orphan boys.

There aren't as many boys as girls at the orphanage; only two or three as opposed to fifteen to twenty girls in each year.

'Why do you think that is?' Janaki had pondered out loud to Arthy.

An older girl had heard her in passing and deigned to reply, exhilarating both Janaki and Arthy, who were used to being completely ignored by the older girls, unless they were asked to run errands.

'It's because boys bring a dowry,' the older girl said. 'They are an asset to any family so they are rarely given up. The only boys to come here are those born out of scandal, to unwed mothers and the like, or those with missing limbs, like Chandru, or disfigurements, like Somu.'

Janaki and Arthy had spent the rest of the afternoon pondering what it meant to be born in scandal – they hadn't dared to ask the older girl and betray their ignorance. They were thrillingly shocked by the fact of unwed mothers.

'Imagine!' they kept saying to each other, Janaki knowing that Arthy was wondering, just as she was, if *they* had the notoriety of being born out of scandal, whatever that was, or to unwed mothers.

*

'Good girl, Janaki.' Sister Nandita is smiling at her.

The others are dawdling, pushing each other, continuing conversations.

Sister Nandita claps her hands to bring them to order.

'If you don't line up, you're not coming on the walk outside the gate.'

Outside.

The word spreads through the children, a treat to be savoured, an anticipatory hush descending as they quickly fall into line.

'Stay with me, hold your partner's hand and cross only when I say so, understood?'

The children nod. Leaving the orphanage is a great event and they're excited.

Sister Nandita is the only one who takes them, and only when Mother Superior is away on one of her retreats.

'Too dangerous,' the other nuns sniff. 'It's an effort, keeping you all in order and out of mischief – it's hard enough to control you *inside* the grounds. Don't know why Sister Nandita risks taking you out there!'

'You need to see the world. We can't shelter you from it forever,' Sister Nandita insists, in her calm, rational way.

Mother Superior has banned it, of course. 'We have a large compound in which you can play. There's no need or cause to leave the orphanage until you're old enough to.'

'Right,' Sister Nandita says now, 'if you don't follow the rules, you'll get lost. You'll be one of those children begging on the streets, sleeping on the train tracks.'

They shudder. They've seen *those* children.

'Feral,' Sister Malli calls them, out of the other nuns' earshot, sniffing with disapproval.

The 'feral' children rattle the gate, begging to be allowed inside.

'We can't take everyone, although of course we wish we could. We don't have the space, or the resources,' Sister Nandita says, sighing.

'As it is, we don't have enough to eat ourselves,' Arthy grumbles, her stomach rumbling loudly to underline her point.

'That's because you give all your porridge to me if you see a worm in it, which is nearly every day,' Janaki says.

*

They are not allowed to waste food; if anyone dares try, they are subjected to a lecture – 'children on the streets would give anything to have what you take for granted' – and a caning, before having to finish the congealing, cold mess under the watchful eye of the nuns, no matter how long it takes and how much the little ones, who don't know better, protest.

Watching the little ones being forced to eat induces physical pain in Janaki's stomach.

'You cannot go hurting for everyone, Janu,' Arthy says gently, rubbing her friend's back, even as Janaki doubles over, clutching her tummy, tears squeezing out of her eyes. 'We were little too, not so long ago, and were made to do the same. It's how we've learnt.'

'*You* haven't,' Janaki recovers enough to say. 'All you do is offload your food to me.'

'Well, that's because you're fool enough to accept it.' Arthy shrugs and Janaki forgets her angst enough to smile.

This is how their friendship works, how they get through the days, each sustaining the other when life becomes overwhelming, a little too much to bear.

*

Days at the orphanage follow a strict routine, which Janaki likes.

They are punished if they don't adhere to the routine, or try to depart from it, which she doesn't like.

They are woken by a bell at 6.30 a.m. They all have to get up when it sounds, even the little ones.

'I don't think it's fair,' Arthy complains. She struggles to fall asleep each night at the allotted time, keeping Janaki awake with gossip, if there is any, telling wild tales if not, and is then loath to wake in the morning.

'Those are the rules,' Janaki says, for the hundredth time. 'If we don't stick to them, how will the nuns look after *all* of us?' She dutifully parrots the reason given by the nuns, which she has taken to heart.

Truth be told, Janaki secretly wishes they could sleep in at least one day a week. Sundays would be ideal as there were no lessons on that day, if it weren't for the fact that they have to wake even earlier than usual for Mass.

'You always see the bright side,' Arthy grumbles.

'If we don't, we'll be miserable. And we *are* better off than most.'

'So you say,' Arthy sniffs grumpily.

Once they wake – or in Arthy's case, sleep standing up – they wash and brush their teeth with neem leaves by the well under the pepper trees in the courtyard at the back of the compound. Morning air, still scented with the night and its secrets, stroking their cheeks, the new dawn tinting the sky with pink and gold.

Then, prayers and breakfast: sludge masquerading as porridge, mischievous Arthy shifting most of her portion onto Janaki's plate.

After this, lessons, with liberal smacks from wooden rulers if homework has not been done to the nuns' satisfaction; if they think you're not paying attention; or if you don't answer the questions lobbed at you.

Mid-morning snack of chapatis.

Break time, when they play hide-and-seek in the trees behind the orphanage.

More lessons, then lunch – chapatis and stony red rice.

Playtime again in the compound behind the orphanage building.

Afternoon nap, during which Janaki sits under the mango trees by the jasmine bushes, threading the fragrant cream flowers into garlands with Sister Shanthi and listening to her stories. She enjoys Bible stories, especially the one of the man eaten by the whale, then vomited out whole after three days.

But best of all she loves Sister Shanthi's tales of gods and demons and the epic wars between them.

'What are these stories?' Janaki queried once.

'They're from Hindu epics, the Ramayana and the Mahabharata.'

'How do you know them?' The orphanage cat, Bittu, rubbed its straggly fur against their legs.

'I used to be Hindu before I was called by Jesus, found my vocation and became a nun. But I haven't forgotten these stories. Let's keep them a secret between the two of us.' A pause, then, '*I* named you Janaki, you know. It was the name for Sita, wife of Lord Rama from the Ramayana.'

Janaki beamed. The sun angled through the canopy of mango leaves, green-gold, dappling criss-cross patterns on the red mud beneath her bare feet.

'With your glowing skin and unusual blue eyes, you're blessed by the gods... But, Janaki—'

'Yes, Sister, vanity is a sin.'

'Quite so.'

During the mellow twilight evenings, the children play in the compound and, sometimes, they hear answering cries from outside the walls.

The orphanage children are afraid of their urchin counterparts, who have had to fend for themselves and who beg on the streets, living on scraps.

*

Now, outside the gate: 'You could be those children but for the grace of God,' Sister Nandita says, nodding at the street kids with their hungry, desperate eyes, hands angled for alms, as the orphans step into the busy, vast community outside the sheltered compound that is their home, their world.

They blink, awed and a tad disorientated.

Although Janaki tries to appear collected, she is cowed by the noise, the carriages with neighing horses, the carts piled high with hay pulled by bullocks with devilish horns and sleepy eyes, the sheer number of people with their tired faces and darting gazes.

Sister Nandita is calm and unruffled despite being hounded by vendors.

'Sister, buy some *churmuri.*'

'Sister, beads for the girls, balls for the boys.'

'Sister, good-quality skipping ropes, good rates, only for you.'

Arthy's hand in Janaki's is sweaty and slick. Her hot, neem-scented breath fills Janaki's ear as she whispers, 'Do you think our mothers are here somewhere?'

Janaki looks around, at the bustling, heaving humanity: vendors hawking colourful wares in baskets slung across their necks; glass bangles glimmering gold in the sun; cloth puppets with lurid skirts and sneering smiles; kaleidoscopic spices, potent enough to induce sneezing fits; wilting vegetables attracting legions of flies. Will she find her mother here if she looks hard and carefully enough? The women with their sunken eyes peer through their veils, followed by their hordes of children; the men munch *paan*, their lips stained red.

'No, I don't think our mothers are here,' she tells Arthy.

'*Your* parents must have been rich.' Arthy's voice has the dark green of envy. 'You were left wrapped in a beautiful cardigan.'

'Perhaps it was given to my mother, a precious gift, the best thing she owned. Perhaps she hoped that by wrapping me in it, I'd be guaranteed preferential treatment by the nuns.' Janaki lists all the reasons she has concocted. She likes making up stories, especially regarding the mystery surrounding her birth and origins.

'Ha! You don't need a cardigan to get preferential treatment, you're the favourite of all the nuns.'

'It's because I'm sensible and do as I'm told, unlike you.' Janaki playfully nudges Arthy's arm. 'But, seriously, Arthy, I think we're lucky to be at the orphanage.' She says out loud what she tells herself over and over, when she has to pick out worms from her food, when Mother Superior raises her voice, a prelude to punishment, when one of the children is hit with the dreaded wooden ruler and they all flinch, experiencing the pain as keenly as the smacked child. 'If we were with our parents we'd be working like those girls over there. They're younger than us, carrying pails of water on their heads, lighting fires, cooking. Look, some of them are even begging, with their siblings in their arms. Who knows what their lives are like, what they have to face every day.'

Janaki shudders as she catches a girl's eye. She looks young and she's bedraggled, lying down by the ditch, a stone for a pillow. Janaki has to look away from the suffering in the girl's countenance; her expression is defeated, disconsolate, infinitely weary. Her heart feels heavy as she says, 'I think we're much better off – at least we're well looked after.'

'Even if our clothes are hand-me-downs from do-gooders,' Arthy says, sighing and smoothing down her slightly short, ill-fitting dress with the hole in the sleeve.

'At least we *have* clothes,' Janaki says, echoing Sister Shanthi's oft-repeated words. 'We have three meals a day. We get an education and, who knows, one day we might even have jobs.'

'Jobs? Are you serious? We're *girls*.'

A bullock cart careens very close to them, almost pushing them into the rubbish-infested ditch and the beggar sprawled atop it, snoring away, exuding the fetid reek of body odour.

'Watch out!' Sister Nandita's calm demeanour has taken a beating; she sounds flustered.

'Us being girls shouldn't make a difference,' Janaki says, once they're safely out of harm's way. 'Sister Shanthi is of the opinion that it shouldn't hold us back, that we should work if we so wish.'

'*I'm* never going to work. I'll be adopted by a rich family and marry a millionaire,' Arthy says, her voice thrumming with wistfulness and hope.

Janaki smiles fondly at her starry-eyed friend.

Across the road, a mother smooths her son's hair, the expression on her face tender. The boy smiles up at her and she beams at him, her face glowing with love.

'It would be nice to be part of a family.' Janaki can't quite keep the longing from her voice.

Arthy tucks her hand in Janaki's. 'It *will* happen, but until then, we're each other's family, my friend.'

*

Once in a rare while, there's excitement in the orphanage, the hum of anticipation.

All of them are dressed in their best clothes and seated orderly in the hall for inspection by prospective parents, who will choose one of them for their very own.

'They're very rich but desperate, these prospective parents, so once adopted, we'll have a charmed life,' Arthy declares confidently.

Janaki agrees with Arthy – the women who come to the orphanage are musical, the jewels round their necks, the bangles on their arms and the anklets on their feet singing a merry tune each time they take a step. Janaki's heart sings with hope when she sees them. They wear saris that glitter and twinkle, shimmer and dazzle, in a way Janaki has not seen before on the women they encounter in their rare excursions outside the grounds. But their eyes, as they peruse the orphanage children from within the confines of the veils covering their faces, are the same as their poorer counterparts: radiating sorrow, ringed by pain.

Janaki knows they're rich, she can see they're desperate if they must come to the orphanage to adopt a child, but she wants to know how Arthy has come by this knowledge that she spouts with such authority.

'I overheard Sister Malli talking.'

'Eavesdropped on purpose, you mean?'

'Do you want to know what I heard or not?'

'Sorry, go on.'

And Arthy, too eager to impart what she knows to withhold it further, continues: 'She said these women have tried all means possible to have children and our orphanage is the last resort – for everyone knows ours is the best orphanage around here. The husbands are modern enough to agree to adoption, which means those of us lucky to be chosen will have a good life.'

'Did you learn Sister Malli's words by heart?' Janaki teases.

'I happen to have a very good memory; another of my many and varied talents,' Arthy says smugly.

'You haven't mentioned your beautiful hair,' Janaki quips, grinning. Arthy is quite vain about her hair, painstakingly combing it free of knots and tangles every evening without fail.

'That goes without saying,' Arthy says primly. Then, sighing, 'If only one of these prospective parents would *look* at us, Janu – but all of them only seem to want the little ones, especially the boys.'

*

On the few occasions when prospective parents do visit, Janaki and Arthy wait along with the others, tentative hope arching fragile in their hearts, despite experience dictating, most likely it will be cruelly dashed.

It is an excruciating process. Each time they're a little older and their chances of getting picked are that bit slimmer – it's always the younger children who are chosen, and as Arthy has pointed out, most often it's the boys. And yet, when an imminent visit from couples looking to adopt is announced, hope buds, treacherously bright, stubbornly refusing to listen to sense.

This time it will be me.

And it is this hope against all the odds that has Janaki making an effort, smiling sweetly and demurely, answering the choosing couple's questions, although their gazes skim over her, settling instead on the angelic faces of the little ones.

After the last couple had left, having chosen a younger boy, Janaki and Arthy took turns imparting comfort.

'We have each other,' Arthy said, but her voice lacked conviction.

'We'll be picked next time,' Janaki stated fervently, a promise and a prayer. 'The couple, not able to choose between the two of us, will decide to take us both.' It was their much-rehearsed and worked-upon happy fantasy.

Smarting from the most recent rejection, Arthy could not bring herself to believe it. 'It will never happen, Janaki. You always look on the bright side and foolishly, I go along with you.' Arthy's eyes shone, her lower lip wobbling dangerously.

Janaki took her friend's hand in hers. 'Arthy, we have to believe we'll be chosen some day, otherwise we…'

Two fat tears glistened on her friend's cheeks.

'Arthy…' In desperation, Janaki mimicked Mother Superior's stern voice: 'Smile or else...'

'Pah, even the littlies can imitate Mother Superior better,' Arthy grumbled and there it was, a ghost of a smile, like the impression of sun through rain clouds.

*

'Now, children,' Sister Nandita says, coming to a stop in front of a cart, where the sweet vendor is using a perforated spoon to fish golden *gulab jamuns* from sizzling oil and dropping them into a vast bowl of nectary sugar syrup. 'Since you've been so good, you're entitled to a sweet each.'

'Hooray!' the children cheer and Sister Nandita smiles, fumbling in her habit for her purse.

The street kids watch, wide-eyed, as one by one the children from the orphanage are handed a *gulab jamun* each, sticky with syrup.

'Come on then, line up,' Sister Nandita says to the street kids, sighing, and they grin widely, displaying yellow stumps of teeth in decaying gums.

The vendor's syrup bowl seems to have an endless supply of *gulab jamuns* and Janaki watches in awe as the line of street kids gets longer by the second, more and more children appearing as if from nowhere.

'This is all I have,' Sister Nandita says, turning her purse upside down and emptying the coins into the sweet vendor's hand.

'You're kind, Sister. The gods will bless you and your charges,' the man says, as he resumes doling out *gulab jamuns* to the street kids, who keep on coming.

*

'Where do you get the money to look after us?' Janaki asked when the question occurred to her, in the midst of a maths lesson on profit and loss, wondering why she hadn't thought of it before.

Sister Nandita, who taught the subject, had smiled happily at Janaki. 'Good question, Janaki. Very relevant indeed. This orphanage was founded by missionary nuns from England, who have left it in our charge but still send the funds to keep it going.'

'And the worm-ridden flour too, I bet,' Arthy whisper-grumbled under her breath to Janaki.

'I suppose it's fresh when it leaves England. But by the time it gets here…' Janaki whispered back.

'It's seething with worms,' Arthy finished for her. 'I wish they'd send more money instead.'

*

Janaki thinks of this conversation as Sister Nandita tucks her empty purse back into the skirt of her habit, the vendors who had been crowding her sighing sadly and dispersing, knowing they're out of luck, but not before directing mean looks at the sweet vendor, who is packing up now that all his sweets have sold.

The children walk back savouring the heavenly, melt-in-the-mouth nectar of freshly cooked *gulab jamuns*, sighing with relief when they are inside the gates of the compound, the busy restlessness of the city replaced by calm order, the comfort of routine: wash, homework, chores, playtime, supper, prayers, bed.

Janaki drifts off to sleep beside her best friend Arthy in the girls' dormitory of the only home she's known.

Chapter 5

Alice

1909

Constant

Alice skips out of the grounds beside Ayah, the servants they encounter along the way pinching her cheeks, patting her head. 'Going to see your friend?'

She grins with excitement and anticipation, nodding vigorously. She cannot wait.

Missing Raju is a great big emptiness within her, throbbing with hurt. He's usually always there, constant as the sun and just as taken for granted, from the time she wakes to when she goes to bed.

Raju features in her earliest memories, both of them side by side on Ayah's lap, warmth and love. He is the one who soothes her when she's hurt; with him beside her she is at ease.

'That's why you're so happy, eh?' the maids chuckle, stuffing *peda* and *laddoo* in her mouth, milky warm, honey rich.

When Mali makes to pat her cheek, Alice flinches from his dirty fingers, the mud embedded in his fingernails, and he laughs. 'Don't catch your friend's fever, mind,' he says, giving her a sliver of ripe yellow jackfruit.

'I'm tired,' she says, tugging at Ayah's hand. 'My legs hurt.'

'Missy Baba, we've only just left the grounds! And you're four now, not a toddler any more and almost too big to be carried.' Nevertheless, Ayah bends down and gathers Alice in her arms.

*

It is comforting being carried in the sari pouch Ayah has fash-ioned, able to hear Ayah's heart pounding with exertion and breathe in her scent of sweat and spices. Her wide, soft body is like a cushion.

Alice is excited about this adventure. This is the first time she has been outside the compound. The grounds are too big for her feet to cover and even though Raju usually offers her piggyback when she's tired, he too cannot reach the end before tiring.

'Good thing too as we're not allowed outside,' he said the last time they tried, being a stickler for rules. He was panting with the exertion of carrying her as he set her down gently.

'But we can't even see the gates from here.' Her lips trembled, a preamble to tears.

Raju immediately hefted her onto his back again, taking her to the kitchen so Cook and her posse could spoil her.

He hated to see her cry, like that time she fell and her knee cracked open and he could see that she was terrified at the sight of the blood. She kept on crying even after Ayah had wrapped it in a cloth bandage and it had stopped hurting. When all his attempts to make her stop crying failed, Raju had started to cry himself. It had taken Ayah an age to comfort them both, each child crying at the sight of the other's tears, the other's sorrow.

The rhythmic motion of being tucked in Ayah's sari pouch must have rocked Alice to sleep, because the next thing she's aware of is being jolted, bombarded by noise: a cacophony of joyful sound, an explosion of colour and chaos.

She blinks as she takes in the surroundings, as different to the sedate grounds of her home as it is possible to be. People, talking all at once, it seems, some standing, others squatting right there in the mud, appearing blind to, careless of, the dust staining their clothes. Suddenly there are animals: cows, dogs, cats, horse carriages, bullock carts topped with hay and even a pig or two weaving between the laughing, chattering, eating, shouting, fighting, crying crowd. Mounds of multi-hued spices are spread out on newspaper beside baskets of fruit and vegetables baking in the sun.

A woman gutting fish is attracting flies. She flings the blood and entrails beside her and a clowder of cats fight over them. Dirt and worse fester beside people drinking tea and munching on snacks. A woman stirs a pot on a hearth right by the mud road, a cloth tent propped up on sticks behind her. Spiced steam is rising, a gaggle of scrawny kids are watching with hungry eyes, clothed in nothing but dust; even their matted hair and eyelashes are stained red with it.

Alice takes the mayhem in, breathless with concentration so as not to miss a thing. It is hypnotic and she is mesmerised, her heart for a brief while forgetting to ache.

People stop what they're doing to stare at Alice. They fire questions at Ayah, who says, 'Can't stop now. Must get this little one back home, just taking her for a walk.' Alice loves how she can hear the words start in Ayah's chest and rumble up her throat, bursting out of her mouth in a breathy exhale.

They slip into a dark alley, huts on either side crowding the strip of pebble-littered mud that passes for a path. Dogs and beggar children follow them, a motley procession. The children's curious gazes drink Alice in, and they comment on her eyes: 'bright blue like the sea, the sky'; and her hair: 'spun gold, look how it shines in the sun'; and her fair skin: 'pink and white like pomegranate seeds'.

Ayah is sure-footed, even though her feet are bare, adeptly navigating the muddy strip of path between huts so small that

Alice wonders how people live within them. Entire families gather outside as they pass, crowding the narrow path so that there's barely space for Ayah to walk by. All of them gawking, saying how beautiful Alice is and offering advice to Ayah: 'Mind she doesn't catch the evil eye.'

The sun beats down but Alice is nice and cosy, if slightly sweaty, in Ayah's arms. She looks inside the little huts, which are merely tents held together with poles, the cloth torn, some with tin sheets for roofs. They are all dark inside, some with old folk lying on mats, calling to the kids, who jump in and out. The huts are interspersed with shops selling all manner of knick-knacks: glass bangles that glint and shimmer tantalisingly, kaleidoscopic ribbons, betel leaves and piles of coconuts.

Eventually, Ayah comes to a panting stop in front of a hut.

'Sarla?' she calls.

Alice blinks as Ayah ducks into the hut, her eyes adjusting to the gloom.

'Mayuri, what're you doing back so early?' A woman emerges from the shadows in the recesses of the small space, wiping her hands on the skirt of her sari.

'This little one won't settle without seeing her friend,' Ayah tells her sister, laughing.

The woman, a thinner, taller version of Ayah, smiles at Alice, pinching her cheek. 'You're a pretty one, aren't you?'

'How's he been?' Ayah asks.

'Not good.' Ayah's sister sighs. 'He didn't eat, no appetite.'

'Raju?' Ayah calls.

At the name, Alice cannot contain her excitement and happiness, realising that the 'he' Ayah had been talking about is her friend.

'Raju!' she yells. 'Raju!'

From the corner of the room: 'Missy Baba.' The voice is weak, but definitely that of her friend.

Alice blinks in the direction of the sound. She can just make out the mat and the silhouette huddled there.

She tugs at Ayah, wanting to be let down.

'No, Missy Baba. You can't go near him, you'll catch his fever.'

All the hurt Alice has been feeling since she woke rises to the fore. She has *missed* her friend and now she is here, where she can see him, hear him, she cannot get close.

She opens her mouth to cry, but she hears Raju say, 'Missy Baba.'

And although he sounds different, sapped of energy, there's a smile in his voice, that special smile, that tone of voice he reserves for her, and it settles her heart.

'How do you do that, Raju?' Ayah marvels. 'You knew she was about to cry and so you comforted her. It's as if you two can read each other's minds.' And to her sister, 'They have a special connection.' Ayah's voice is fond, proud.

'Yes, well, mind they don't get *too* close,' Ayah's sister says.

But Alice is not paying heed, for Ayah is bending down to sit and there's just enough give between the sari pouch and floor for Alice to jump down and run to the mat that houses her friend.

'No! Come back, Missy Baba!' Ayah cries, but Alice has one thought only: *Get to Raju.*

She reaches the mat and climbs onto it, throwing her arms around her friend. She is shocked into tears by how hot he feels, his burning breath, his flushed face, so unlike the Raju she knows, his fresh-mango smell now distorted with scarlet heat.

She cries and cries, distressed by this boiling-hot, floppy version of her friend. Raju tries to comfort her but he doesn't appear to have the strength to even move and she sees reciprocal tears bloom in his reddened eyes.

She sobs as Ayah prises her off Raju's mat, shaking her head and sighing. 'This was a bad idea.'

Ayah's sister's voice echoes louder than Alice's wails. 'You need to keep them apart. It doesn't do for a servant and the daughter of the house to be so close.'

'*You* try keeping them apart.' Ayah's voice is a thundering growl, causing Alice's wails to briefly sputter, as she says, 'Look how distressed she is.'

'That's just my point.'

'Oh, what harm can it do? They're like brother and sister.'

'But they're *not* brother and sister.'

'As they grow older, they'll grow apart.'

This registers with Alice and she thinks, *We will never.*

'Let's hope so.'

Alice sobs all the way home, the beggar children, a few adults, cows and dogs following in procession all the way up to the gates of Alice's home, the adults offering advice and admonishment.

'What have you done to upset the pretty little girl?'

'It's her fair skin and light hair, makes her more prone to upset.'

'Look how red her skin is when she cries.'

Ayah finally yells at them, 'Shush! I can't hear myself think!' Her voice possesses an agitated screech so unlike her usual voice that Alice momentarily swallows her sobs and quietens, only to remember again the burning-hot, fragile imposter who was lying on a mat in the hut, in place of her friend, and starts wailing all over again.

The next day Alice wakes up hot all over, her limbs aching and heavy, unwieldy. She is inconsolable until Raju is carried into the sickroom by Ayah's sister, Sarla.

'Since you're both ill, you might as well be together,' Ayah grumbles, feeding them spoonfuls of ginger tea and milk laced with medicinal spices. She applies cold compresses to their foreheads and sings gentle, soothing lullabies.

Alice drifts in and out of consciousness, her hot, moist hand tucked tight within her friend's, Ayah's voice a lullaby in the background. 'It's a blessing she doesn't have it as bad as Raju. My boy is hardy, he'll come through, but Missy Baba wouldn't be able to bear it.'

'They feed off each other. What one gets, they both do, but *she* doesn't suffer as much. What does this tell you?' Sarla's voice is sharp, hurting Alice's achy head.

'Stop it, Sarla! Don't go looking for things that aren't there.'

'It's just not right.' Sarla's voice is as bitter as the bright yellow fruit Alice had bit into once, thinking it would be as sweet as it looked inviting. 'An omen, I tell you. If you don't do something about their bond now, there will be nothing but trouble, and more so for our Raju.'

Sarla's voice fades as clammy sleep claims Alice.

All she cares about, all she's aware of as the fever claims her, is that her friend, her Raju, is beside her, and although she doesn't feel right in herself, she doesn't suffer that hollow ache of missing him any more.

Chapter 6

Janaki

1945

Fantasy

'Children, don't fidget,' Mother Superior chastises. They're in their best clothes – the ones with no obvious holes – and the older girls, having plaited each other's hair, are making sure the younger ones are clean.

Janaki, Arthy and their friends have been entrusted with the task of washing the little ones under the pepper and neem trees in the back compound by the well – at nine years old they are considered responsible enough.

It is great fun, the sweetly potent scent of neem and ripening peppercorns, the children shuddering as the first pail of cold water hits their grubby heads, then dancing as the silvery cascades, glittering jewels in the sunshine, wash the grime from their bodies.

Now they are all gathered in the hall where they usually have their meals, sitting in rows on the floor. The room smells of the porridge they had for breakfast.

'They're here,' Sister Nandita announces.

There's a rustle of clothing as they all stand up, having waited not so patiently, whispering and nudging and pinching each other, their clothes and plaits unravelling. As the prospective adoptive parents enter, the children raise their voices in song, as they've been taught.

Janaki, from her place near the back of the hall, looks the couple over. The woman is in a resplendent sari the colour of summer, dazzling gold, her husband behind her, their eyes bright as they take in the children.

They both clap when the song is finished, the woman gushing, 'How lovely.'

The couple mingle with the smaller kids at the front, chatting to them all. Shali, one of the littlies who loves stories and pesters the older girls to read to her, hands the woman one of the tattered books she lugs around with her, her huge eyes pleading.

The woman obliges, sitting down right there on the floor, not caring about her beautiful sari acquiring a layer of dust. And it is this that instantly endears the couple to Janaki, and judging from the wistful sigh from Arthy next to her, she knows her friend feels the same.

Traitorous hope is rising in Janaki's chest, singing, *Please let it be me*. Despite having schooled her heart against expectation, a picture blooms in her mind of herself with this couple, the woman holding her with love sparkling in her eyes, the man smiling proudly down at her. Her *parents*.

Her glowing fantasy dissipates as she watches the little ones, both boys and girls, climbing all over the woman, a few, Shali among them, are ensconced on her lap. The woman's voice is gentle as she reads to them, her husband gazing at the children surrounding his wife, transfixed, his expression tender.

Arthy nudges Janaki, looking defeated, her voice a resigned sigh. 'It'll be one of them who's adopted, won't it?' Her friend has a knack of voicing just what Janaki is thinking.

She quashes the last lingering remnants of her fantasy and, although her throat is bitter with swallowed-down disappointment and crushed hope, assumes her familiar role of optimist, putting her arm around her friend and whispering, 'Arthy, it's not so bad here, is it?'

'Oh, Janu, I just want someone to love me.' Yearning colours her friend's voice soft blue. 'I want to be the centre of someone's world.'

I do too. Just then something snags at the corner of Janaki's eye.

One of the little ones congregated around the couple, shy Bina, has been pushed to the back of the circle and is chewing her thumb, distressed, tears falling down her cheeks unchecked. The woman is busy reading, the man is looking at his wife and the children on her lap. The nuns are smiling indulgently at the children being read to, but all of them seem to have missed Bina's anguish; easy to do as Bina is hidden away behind the other kids.

Bina is directly in Janaki's line of sight; Janaki has chosen this place at the back for this very reason. She always keeps an eye on Bina; she has a soft spot for the little girl, who is so quiet and undemanding, as a result of which she tends to be ignored.

Before she has properly thought things through, Janaki is standing up, pushing past the other children and making her way to Bina.

'Janu, where're you going? You're not supposed to… You'll be told off,' Arthy says, shocked out of her misery at Janaki's uncharacteristic rule-breaking.

But Janaki has already reached Bina and is asking her why she's upset. Bina throws her arms around Janaki and sobs into her chest. 'I wanted to hear the story too,' she whispers. 'But I was pushed away and…' She can't complete the sentence for hurt and upset.

'I'll read to you, okay?' Janaki promises, undone by the little girl's anguish and almost near to tears herself. Bina nods, her sobs easing into hiccups.

It is only then that Janaki is aware that the lady has stopped reading and that she is smiling at Janaki. 'What a kind girl you are! What is your name?'

'I'm Janaki…' But before she can say anything else, Mother Superior is beside Janaki, her eyes glinting stones, cold and hard.

'Janaki, who gave you permission to leave your place and come here?'

'I saw Bina was upset and I…'

'She knows to go to Sister Malli, don't you, Bina?'

Bina goes rigid in Janaki's arms and nods silently.

'Mother Superior' – Janaki finds her voice, knowing Bina's sobs, only just stilled, are about to start up again – 'she was going to, but I got to her first. It's my fault, I'm sorry.'

'I think what you did is very kind indeed,' the woman interjects before Mother Superior can release the full extent of her wrath and name Janaki's punishment.

With a glance at her husband, who nods, she says to Mother Superior, 'We've made up our minds.' Then, smiling gently at Janaki – a look Janaki has dreamed of in her fantasies a million times – this woman says the words Janaki had hoped against hope to hear, but did not dare believe she ever would: 'We'd like to adopt Janaki here, please.' And, to Janaki, 'That is, if you're happy to come home with us, my dear?'

Janaki, still holding Bina, can only nod, disbelieving.

The woman – *her soon-to-be mother!* – reaches across and gently cups her face with one hand, her touch as tender as all Janaki has imagined love to be.

Chapter 7

Alice

1914

Centre Stage

Alice sprawls among the reeds by the lake, watching the frogs squatting on lily pads and trying to trap flies, Raju beside her.

Ayah is asleep on the kitchen veranda, her thundering snores chasing away the mosquitoes and flies that dare hover anywhere near her. Raju and Alice had been lying on mats on either side of her, pretending to be asleep until she nodded off, when they'd escaped to the lake.

The air is sluggish, tasting of burnt heat. The dust-stained foliage bordering the lake droops in the humidity beneath relentless sunshine. The algae-and-weed-infested water glints silver and ripples gold, fish swarm and water snakes glide among water lilies dotting the surface.

Alice turns over, lies on her back and closes her eyes and bubbly figures dance gold before her shut lids, the secret world behind her eyes taking centre stage. All of a sudden, she becomes aware of something, the barest flutter, a glancing kiss, a tender tickle, on her palm. She opens her eyes. Blinks.

Translucent wings, the gilded gossamer of a rosy dream, are fluttering open and close. The most beautiful butterfly she has ever seen, for all the world at home on her palm!

'Look.' Barely able to speak for awe, she nudges Raju.

'Wow!' Raju beams.

And right at that magical moment, the somnolent silence is broken by the rumble of carriage wheels clattering up the drive and stopping at the house. Alice sees her father alighting from it, joined by another man, presumably his second-in-command.

Alice is surprised. Her father, the Deputy Commissioner, is *always* busy and usually only home after she's in bed, even though, now that she's nine – *'I'm almost ten, almost grown-up,' she declares grandly to the servants and they laugh delightedly, pinching her cheeks: 'You'll always be cute little Missy Baba to us!'* – she's allowed to stay up later. Her father is talking, the man with him nodding intently.

'Come,' Alice says to Raju, getting to her feet very carefully, so as not to disturb the butterfly. They start towards the house, Alice walking gingerly, hand stretched out, mindful of her extraordinary visitor. But the butterfly sits like a dream, a wish, comfortable upon her palm.

Alice, almost without thinking, is walking towards her father.

Raju hangs back, and as Alice's intent becomes clear, whispers urgently, 'Missy Baba, what are you *doing*?'

But Alice, caught up in the unprecedented magic of the afternoon (the butterfly claiming her palm as if it is its natural habitat, her father arriving home early, surely to see her?) ignores her friend.

'I knew war was looming, imminent, but to hear it announced is still a shock,' her father is saying to his companion.

'Father,' Alice calls, 'look.'

The miracle of the butterfly on her palm makes her forget herself for a moment, wanting to bring him, her father, inside her happiness. But in reality, her father is a stranger. She wishes him good day every morning and his reply is to nod, with a hint of a smile, before turning his attention back to his kedgeree and toast, sausages and eggs, her mother beside him, always looking tired.

After Father leaves for work in the carriage that awaits him in the creamy glow of jasmine-scented morning, Mother goes back to bed. Alice sometimes sees her father on those evenings when he and Mother leave for parties or to go to the club, or host parties at home. When she says good night, her scrubbed-clean-of-dirt cheek is tickled by her father's bristle.

Now, close beside him, Alice extends her hand to show him her miracle, eager to see his face light up like Raju's had, sharing in this awe and wonder.

But Father's face darkens. 'What are you doing, wandering about the grounds?'

'I… I wanted to show you this butterfly…'

The butterfly, as if picking up on her fear, her distress at her father's anger, flutters on her hand. From the corner of her eye, Alice sees Raju slip into the bushes behind them, hoping to hide. Alice's lower lip trembles with the effort of holding back tears at her father's booming, brusque voice.

'Where's your nanny?'

The butterfly flexes its spun-gold wings.

Don't go, Alice pleads silently.

'She's supposed to look after you, not let you run willy-nilly about the grounds. Damn coolie! You!' – her father turns to the groom, who's rubbing down the horses – 'Find Mayuri and bring her here. She's meant to be taking care of my daughter, that's what I pay her handsomely for.'

With a final ripple of its dreamy wings, the butterfly flies away. The tears Alice is holding back start to fall.

Ayah comes rushing on the groom's heels, looking flustered, her hair escaping her bun.

'I've a good mind to send you away for your negligence,' Father roars.

Alice's heart stops. *Send Ayah away?*

'I… Missy Baba was asleep beside me, Sahib.'

'Your job is to look after my daughter. If you can't do it, what's the use in you being here?'

It is only then, her heart beating so loud she thinks it will explode out of her body, that Alice understands that she can lose Ayah. That Ayah is with her only because her father says so. Some part of Alice has always known that Ayah is a servant, but because she is so important to her, she has assumed that Ayah could never leave. Now she remembers that other servants are frequently replaced when Father is annoyed, or decides they are not up to the mark.

'I want Ayah,' Alice cries, cursing the impulse that made her run to this cold-eyed, grim man and throwing her arms around Ayah, who smells odd, musty, a scent that Alice will come to recognise as terror when she is older. Now, Alice wants nothing more than to disappear within the folds of Ayah's sari. She wishes she was younger so Ayah could carry her in her sari pouch close to her heart.

'S… So sorry, S... Sa... Sahib, it won't happen again.'

Ayah's stuttering makes Alice even more afraid, if that were possible.

She cries, 'Please, Father, I will never roam the grounds again.'

After what feels like an age, Father nods curtly, then turns to Ayah: 'Alice's attached to you so you can stay. But you'll lose two weeks' pay. And take this as your last warning. Be sure to mind her at all times. If I see her wandering around again...' A muscle in Father's cheek is working furiously. His eyes, when they brush over Alice and Ayah, are charged with disdain.

'It will not happen, Sahib,' Ayah says, in an unrecognisable, cowed voice.

*

Later, Ayah, returned to her usual self, comforts Alice and, once Alice's tears have dried, she admonishes both Alice and Raju, though mostly Raju, 'You're older, you should be responsible, mature!'

Raju meekly takes it for Alice's sake, although running off to the lake was Alice's idea, as such daring adventures always have been. After Alice and Raju have promised not to go wandering when they are meant to be asleep, they retire to the kitchen.

Cook and Ayah are friends, so they say. 'How can you be friends when you argue more than you play with each other?' Alice once observed, causing both Cook and Ayah to guffaw loud and long, Cook spitting out her tea, Ayah gathering Alice to her soft bosom, which smelt of onions and love, and kissing her cheeks.

Cook plies them with spicy samosas and sweet *lassi*. Once Alice and Raju have had their fill, Ayah says, 'Go and play, but stay where I can see you.'

Alice, her stomach full and life returned to normal, her father's admonishment, the fear it aroused and the sadness of losing the butterfly fading, eavesdrops on Ayah saying to Cook, 'When he said he had a good mind to sack me, I thought that was it. If it hadn't been for Missy Baba…' Ayah shudders and Cook gently pats her hand.

That night, as Ayah is tucking Alice into bed, she asks, 'Ayah, if it is your job to look after me, does this mean you don't love me?'

'I do, of course,' Ayah says smoothly.

'But if you weren't paid, you wouldn't look after me?'

'It's not like that…' Ayah colours and Alice reads the truth on her face.

'Raju? Are you paid to play with me?'

'No!'

'But if Ayah was sent away, you'd go too.' She realises then how precarious it all is.

Ayah and Raju are the two constants in her life but they could disappear if her father so decided. They are the centre of Alice's life but for Ayah, it's a job.

I am just a job.

As if intuiting her fear, Ayah pats Alice's forehead, her hand gnarled yet soft, her gaze glazed caramel, her scent of fried onions, chilli, coconut oil, washing soap and sweat. As familiar as Alice's own. Beloved.

I love you. But do you love me for me? *Do you love me at all? Do you look after me because you have to, not because you want to? If you had the choice not to look after me, if you were not paid, would you? I'm scared to ask because I'm afraid of the answer.*

'Who loves me? Without it being their job to do so?'

Ayah, gentle, stroking Alice's hair ('Like honey, spun gold, blessed by the gods,' she's remarked often) in place, 'Your parents, of course.'

Alice thinks of Father as he was that afternoon: his hard, flashing eyes, anger rampant as he looked at her. Mother always in bed, barely glancing at Alice when she bids her good day and good night. 'I… I don't know if they love me,' she whispers.

Ayah cups Alice's face in her hand. 'Of course they do.' She laughs gently, chidingly.

Why does Alice not have Ayah's certainty with regards to her parents?

Ayah continues, conviction colouring her voice the bright yellow of sunshine, 'You're their only child. You're their *life*, like Raju is mine.'

A shaft of jealousy stabs Alice at the fondness in Ayah's voice, which is pulsing with love and pride *for Raju*.

Does Ayah love Alice that way?

Before now, Alice would have thought she did. Now she is not so sure… And that hurts her. She is suddenly deeply envious of Raju. She wants Ayah to be her mother and at the same time is scornful of that needy part of herself. For how can Ayah be her mother? Alice is British, Ayah is Indian.

'Damn coolie!' Father had barked this afternoon, disparagingly. Raju and Ayah, like every other servant, look up to her parents and to Alice herself. What Alice commands, what she wants, they go to great lengths to procure for her. For she is Missy Baba. The little memsahib.

'How much do you love Raju?' Alice asks.

Ayah laughs. 'Oh, Missy Baba, what's got into you today?'

'I want to know, Ayah.'

'Raju is my child, I love him unconditionally,' Ayah says.

'What does that mean?'

'It means, I will love him no matter what.' Ayah bends down to kiss her. 'Your parents love you unconditionally too, I promise. It is what parents *do*. Sleep tight, Missy Baba.'

But Alice cannot sleep. She thinks of Father's remote disinterest, Mother's bored indifference with regards to her. As her parents, loving her is not a job they're paid to do, but what they are *meant* to do. According to Ayah, they should love her unconditionally. *Do they?*

Alice would swear that Raju loves her, and that Ayah does, even though looking after her is only Ayah's job. She would even add Cook and, at a stretch, Mali to this list.

But her parents?

That night, which follows the day when England declared war on Germany, something fierce rages in Alice's heart. Her last thought before she falls asleep is: *I'll make them love me. I will be what they want, what they expect me to be. They* will *love me, I'll make sure of it.*

The irony of it, that they are supposed to love her *unconditionally*, no matter what she does, will only hit her later, when she is older. She dreams of butterflies alighting on her body, with brilliant heart-shaped wings the colour of unconditional love.

PART 2

....

India

Visitor

Chapter 8

Alice

1986

Ordinary

Alice's life changes on a perfectly ordinary afternoon in the midst of a perfectly ordinary week.

She is in the little room off the nursery, which passes for her office, catching up on paperwork, while the children have their afternoon siesta, when there is a knock on her door.

'Come in,' Alice calls, her joints creaking audibly as she stretches.

When did I get so old?

Outside the open window, a lazy breeze, hot and humid, caresses the tamarind trees, their knotted brown fruit contrasting with the bright, dust-tinted green of the leaves. Crows natter among the branches and spots of bright colour among the bed of mulch and leaves at the base of the trees tantalise the eye: cloth dolls, lying where the children have arranged them for a tea party at playtime, clad in colourful pieces of sari and the occasional sequin. The dolls glint like a kaleidoscope when they catch the gilded sunrays spilling through the tree canopies.

Kali pops her head round Alice's door, smiling as always, bright-eyed and eager. One of the first children Alice took on, Kali is now a mother to three of her own, but still helping out here when she can.

'There's someone asking for you.'

Must be another of the desperate mothers Alice often sees; someone who has heard of Alice from the women she has helped before.

'Please take my kids,' they all plead. 'They'll have a better life here than I can ever give them. He comes home drunk, having spent all he's earned, hits us senseless, then has his way with me. Now, with another one on the way…'

They pat their burgeoning stomachs, tears pooling in their fraught eyes.

Alice listens. She says, 'I understand.' And they can see that she does. She says, 'Giving your children away is not the answer.'

'But…'

'You're all they have. Leave him.'

'It's not so eas—'

'I'll help you.'

And she does, escorting them to the refuge, assisting in any way she can, being there for them until they find their feet.

Afterwards, they come to thank her.

It will be one of them.

'This one's different,' Kali says, having read Alice's mind.

'Oh?'

Alice stands, intrigued, her joints once again putting up an audible protest.

She closes the office door and makes her way to the visitor, along the corridor of the house she had opened to street kids when anguished and grieving, lonely and desperate, broken and hopeless herself, all those years ago.

She walks towards her visitor, unaware that everything is about to change. That nothing will ever be the same again.

PART 3

India

Upset

Chapter 9

Alice

1915

Anticipation

'Good night, Mother.'

'Ah, Alice...'

Alice, her hand on the doorknob, swivels around to look at her mother, shocked into stillness.

When Father is not around, which is most of the time, Mother takes all her meals in her room. Usually, when Alice pops in to say good night, her mother does not reply, merely nodding her head, barely sparing a glance at Alice, her face stamped by sleep, eyes drowsy and swollen, smelling of roses and boredom.

Ayah is not with Alice. The day Alice resolved to make her parents love her, she decided that she would say good morning and good night to them on her own. Perhaps they *did* love her already, very much so, but showed it in a different way to Ayah, who was all open affection; after all, they were British, they did things differently. Hadn't her father allowed Ayah to stay on when Alice asked, even though he wanted to sack her, that day when Alice had tried to share with him the miracle of the butterfly landing on her palm?

'I'm almost ten and quite old enough to greet my parents by myself,' she'd declared, and Ayah had smiled affectionately at her.

'Yes, you're growing into a young lady all right,' she'd said, beaming.

*

This evening, as always, Alice waited until after Ayah and Raju left for the night, before knocking on Mother's door. Father is visiting one of the remote villages in the district that he oversees. He will be away for a couple of days and so Mother is taking supper in her room.

'Do you go to sleep immediately?' Mother asks now.

Alice *does*, drifting off the moment her head hits the pillow. But her mother does not usually speak to her – in fact, Alice can't recall the last time she did – and from the inflection in her voice, Alice instinctively understands what Mother would like her to say.

'No,' she replies.

Mother smiles. It is perfunctory, but a smile nonetheless, directed at *her*.

'Your father's away and I think you're old enough now to keep me company.'

Alice cannot keep the grin from taking over her face, her heart scudding with excitement. Her plan is working although she has barely done anything! She wanted to make her parents love her and now Mother is reaching out to her.

'The evenings drag without your father and I'm wide awake. Habit. I rest during the day to escape the heat, so I am bright and ready in the evenings. But Robert's away almost every other day now with the war riling the natives into violence. I'm often alone in the evenings, so you'll keep me company.'

Alice beams, unable to speak for happiness.

Mother nods at her untouched supper tray resting on the occasional table beside her bed. 'I'll have supper now. Please come back and knock in half an hour.'

*

In her room, anticipation makes Alice restless, unable to keep still. She kneels upon her bed, leaning out of the window, looking down into the courtyard around which the house is built. All the windows open either onto the courtyard or onto the land attached to the house, which stretches into the distance on all sides.

The courtyard appears mysterious in the darkness. Shadows seem to dance across the grass. The fruit trees, waving in the banana-scented night breeze, are giant people beckoning with skeletal hands. Crickets chatter, frogs croak, a lone owl calls, and the wind whispers and sighs. In the darkness, everything looks sinister; what should be familiar is distorted, unrecognisable. The well, with its pulley and rope, is a hangman's noose; the elusive glimpse of water within its depths, rippling dark and heady with secrets. Only flashing orange eyes pierce the dark; nocturnal animals lurking. A dog howls, low and mournful. A sudden harsh caw splinters the silence. Alice rears back, startled, heart thudding.

Stop being silly. You're old enough to keep Mother company now, so you shouldn't be afraid of a crow!

She checks the bedside clock: ten minutes to go. She cannot stay in her bedroom any longer. She ambles up and down the corridor, and although she has walked along here often, this too, with the shadows angling along it from the window shutters, appears unfamiliar in the pressing, suspenseful dark. Every so often she peers into her room, watching the minute hand move, very slowly, it seems, counting down time until she can go to Mother's room, the taste of anticipation, syrupy sweet, in her mouth.

Chapter 10

Janaki

1945

Lucky

'Goodbye, Arthy. I'll write every day, I promise.' Janaki holds her friend close and Arthy clings to her, smelling of neem and love.

'How will I sleep without whispering all my secrets and hopes to you?'

'You'll be adopted soon too, I know.'

'Janu,' Arthy says, smiling, even as her voice cracks, 'you break rules for once in your life and you get rewarded for it. The rest of us are not so lucky.'

'*You* will be.'

'Be happy. You deserve it.'

Tears fall unchecked down her friend's cheeks as Janaki's new parents lead her gently to the waiting motor car.

Arthy stands on the steps of the orphanage, by the nook where Janaki was left as a baby, waving with all her might, Bina, Shali and others beside her, until the motor car turns the corner and Janaki travels towards her new life.

The motor car, like the mother and father in Janaki's new life, is sleek, elegant, luxurious, as it moves smoothly through the crush of people, the street kids watching, envious at Janaki being comforted by her new mother, like Janaki used to do when *she* was the one snatching hallowed glimpses of that seemingly unattainable, longed-for treasure: family.

Janaki marvels, even through her tears and anguish at leaving Arthy behind, that *she* is the lucky one, with parents who love her, have chosen her, to whom she is the world.

'Please can you adopt my best friend Arthy too?' was one of the first things Janaki had asked her new mother, once the fact that she was actually being adopted, that the dream she'd thought impossible was coming true, had sunk in.

She had asked this even though she was scared it might make them decide against her, when she was at the stage – she *still* is – of being awed and feeling completely overwhelmed by it all, worrying that if she did not agree with everything they said, if she cried, or looked unhappy, they might decide they didn't want her after all.

But Arthy was so important to her that she had to try. Janaki had to risk being rejected for the sake of her friend and the dreams they had woven together in the dark hours of night. When the other girls were sleeping, they had spun fantasies as bright as the stars they couldn't see, but which they knew twinkled above the roof of the orphanage.

'If we were adopted together, we'd be sisters, that's even better than best friends,' Arthy had enthused.

'My darling,' Janaki's new mother – *her mother!* – replied, eyes shining, 'I wish we could, believe me. If it was up to me, we'd have a house full of children: you, of course. Little Bina, who you so kindly comforted, Shali, the girl who loves stories and Arthy, your friend.'

Her eyes were soft and warm, her gaze was shiny with love. Janaki had to pinch herself because that gaze, the love, was for *her*. For a brief, wild moment she pictured how wonderful it would be to have Arthy and Shali and Bina living with her as part of her family, sisters all. But then she noted the regret in the warm eyes looking at her, the sorrow evident there, and she was sorry she had subjected this kind, wonderful, loving woman to pain.

'I didn't mean to…' she began, her own eyes shining.

Her new mother gathered Janaki in her arms, surrounding her with the scent of roses and comfort. 'It's fine, my love. You can ask us anything you want to.'

My love. Janaki revelled in the feeling those words evoked. It warmed her heart, which was anxious and flitting between disbelief, exultation and worry that even now, it could all go wrong. 'Is it just you and Baba and now myself at our house?' she queried, to change the topic, even as she luxuriated in saying '*Baba*' and '*our house*', as her new mother had urged she should.

But her question had the opposite effect. 'Oh.' Was that troubled unease Janaki sensed emanating from her new mother? 'There are the servants of course and also your daada.'

'Daada?' Janaki looked to her new mother, hoping for explanation about this person she had heard nothing about – *why?* A hard ball of worry was choking her, so the word shook as it finally left her suddenly dry mouth.

Her mother would not meet her eye, patting Janaki's head very gently instead. 'Your father's father. The head of the household.'

'What if he doesn't want me? Will you send me back?' Janaki squeezed the words out over the terror seizing her chest.

'Of course he'll want you, you're our child now,' her mother laughed.

Was it Janaki's imagination or was there a false note in her laughter, a tendril of fear?

Chapter 11

Alice

1915

Light

Golden light spools in the minuscule gap between the door to Mother's room and the floor. *Light!* It surprises Alice so much that she stops short, never mind the sinister silhouettes edging into the corridor through the windows with their mesh screens to keep out mosquitoes and bugs.

Her mother is such a contradiction: lying all day in her darkened room, curtains shut to keep out the sun, flinching even from the mellow mauve-and-rose evening light, saying, 'Shut the door on your way out, please,' when Alice comes in to say good night.

And now, when it's properly dark, there's light in her room! Tentatively, timidly, Alice knocks on the door. No sound comes from within. Has her mother forgotten her invitation? Or has she changed her mind and does not want her daughter to keep her company any longer? Perhaps Alice misunderstood what she said?

Her mother – a distant entity barely featuring in Alice's colourful world – usually sighs from her bed when Ayah calls upon her for direction regarding Alice's care. 'Whatever's easiest,' she will murmur, waving her fingers tiredly, leaving Ayah to make decisions on Alice's behalf – which suits Alice just fine for she knows how to manipulate Ayah into doing what she wants.

Did Mother really want to see me? Once again, as she has done countless times in the past few minutes, Alice replays her mother's unusual invitation – was it issued or has she imagined it? No, her mother *definitely* invited her. And it has been exactly half an hour, like she said. The excitement Alice has been unable to tamp down is replaced by sick unease.

Standing in front of her mother's door, wondering if she will be invited in or ignored, she thinks of her father, another absentee figure in her life. The impression she has of her father is of busyness, distance, preoccupation. Alice is scared of him at the same time as admiring him, wanting to please him. She wants him to notice her, love her. But the only time he has paid any attention to her that she can recall – she discounts the dream/ memory where her father laughed and lifted her skywards as she can't quite give it credence – was that miraculous, magical day when the butterfly alighted on her palm as if it was the most natural thing in the world to do, as if her palm was the most comfortable place to be. She had tried to share the magic with her father and still remembers the look on his face: irritation and annoyance, ire at her intrusion igniting amber flames in his icy, opal eyes.

Does he love her?

He must.

A sound from within. Her mother's voice: 'Come in.'

Alice lets out the breath she has been holding, and relief, honey sweet, floods through her.

Mother is sitting by the window in a pool of lamplight, knitting. Her fingers are flying as the needles click and twist, loop and thread. Alice watches, mesmerised.

Her mother, in her nightdress, is framed by the open window, which is showing a slice of night: a sliver of silver moon, twinkling stars, lustrous as happy thoughts; her golden hair hangs loose around her shoulders, her hands are busy with a spool of beautiful cloth, the colour of the summer sky at dusk.

In the lamplight, her mother glows, looking younger and brighter than Alice has ever seen her. Her hands seem to knit of their own accord, independent from the rest of her. Alice is quite fascinated. She feels charmed, seeing this side to her mother. 'How do you do that? It's magic,' Alice says, quite forgetting to be cowed as she has often been in the presence of her mother, until recently taking refuge in Ayah's skirts and peering out from behind them.

Her mother looks up at Alice and her face is sharp, all angles, her eyes spitting fire. 'Alice, you'd do well to remember you're not a *junglee*. I'd very much appreciate it if you spoke in English with me.' Her voice, like sun-sizzled stones, sharp and blazing, is flung at Alice.

Upset overcomes Alice, dousing her awe, as she realises that she spoke in Hindi, the language of her heart, undone by excitement at this unusual audience with her distant mother, this glimpse into her secret world.

'Y... yes, Mem...' She bites her tongue hard, until she tastes blood, brine and iron. In her nervousness, and confronted with this harsh-tongued woman, with her flashing blue-sabre eyes, whose fingers click a forbidding rhythm, she wishes for the safety of Ayah's wide skirts to hide in. Alice has regressed to her childhood self, almost compounding her blunder by calling her mother Memsahib.

She swallows down the Hindi words, starts again, desperate not to squander this longed-for chance to spend time with her stranger of a mother. Her salty voice now hoarse, the English words are unfamiliar and elusive on her tongue: 'I... I'm so sorry, Mother.'

Her mother waits, her silence forbidding, and Alice stumbles on, trying to rectify her mistake. 'I... I'm honoured to be here.'

She scrambles for the right words, even as she sends up a little prayer. *Please.* 'It's… it's such a privilege that I got carried away.'

She notices her mother unbend a little, her lips relaxing slightly. 'You will not speak in *junglee* tongue again in my presence.'

'Yes, Mother.' And her mother's slight unstiffening giving her the courage to say, 'I… what I meant to say was… I think what you do is sheer magic, taking yarn and creating something so intricate from it.'

At this her mother smiles.

And with that smile, the acrid fear of rejection that had taken Alice's heart hostage disperses into the darkness, sifting and sighing in the window behind her mother. It is as if Alice is *seen* for the first time by her mother. 'You can't sleep, Mother?' Alice asks, making sure that she does not slip into Hindi again.

Her mother sighs. 'It's cooler at night, the heat is bearable.' The windowpanes are wide open, even though the mesh screens are shut to keep out bugs and flies. The breeze angling in is redolent with the haunting scent of night jasmine and a whisper of rain.

'I'd like to spend the summers in Shimla. It's cooler there, almost like England, Mrs Jesmond says. Everyone who's anyone is there, so I've heard. It's a social whirlpool: card parties, tennis, masquerades, balls…' Mother's voice is wistful. 'Although you've got to take what Mrs Jesmond says with a pinch of salt.'

Alice listens, amazed that Mother is talking to her almost as if she is her friend.

She loves me after all.

Mother falls silent, her gaze becoming distant, while her fingers knit away busily. Alice is loath to stem her mother's flow of confidences, but since her mother has stopped talking, she gathers up the courage to ask, 'Why won't you go?'

Her mother blinks, the faraway look leaving her eyes, her gaze focusing on Alice. 'I'm sorry?'

'Why won't you go to Shimla?'

And if you went, would you take me along?

'Your father wants me to stay here with him.' Her voice is melancholy.

Alice stands there, thrilled and overwhelmed by her mother's sharing with *her*. This is the most her mother has ever spoken to her, and she is stunned and grateful to be here in this strange, lamplit haven, with night framed in the window and the jasmine-and-intrigue-scented breeze eavesdropping on spilt secrets.

'Would Father go to Shimla with you?'

Her mother sighs. 'His work is here and you know how much he loves it.'

I didn't. But now I do. 'What about England?'

'Well…' Her mother's eyes acquire a melancholy cast. 'Your father was born here, like you, and cannot countenance living anywhere else. For him, this is home.'

Father is like me. Alice feels a thrill of wonder, imagining the stern, remote man loving this country as she does, its very essence pulsing through his skin, stamped upon his heart.

Revelling in her joy, Alice barely pays heed to her mother's next words.

'Anyway, I couldn't go now on account of this blasted war dragging on far longer than anyone expected it to. Your Aunt Edwina writes that England is being bombed by German flying machines called Zeppelins and that it is nothing at all like the country of our childhood. All ruins and rubble, she says.' Mother sighs, long and drawn-out. 'I've been bored. More so recently because Robert has been away more often than not, trying to stem the increased unrest across the region. When you came in to say good night just then, I realised you could keep me company.'

Mother smiles at Alice – *again!*

'Sit down.' She nods at the armchair beside hers, her fingers dancing in practised rhythm, the spool of yarn transforming before Alice's eyes. Alice tastes relief, sweet as Cook's ginger *halva* studded with pistachios in her mouth, even as she sinks gratefully into the chair. She will not be sent away; she is forgiven her mistake of speaking in Hindi.

Just to make very sure, having surmised that the best way into her mother's favour is by complimenting her, Alice says, 'You're very good.' And her mother *is*, the click of the knitting needles hypnotic, the bright colours festive.

Her mother laughs. It is the first time Alice has heard her mother's laughter. It's a joyous sound, like the taste of a ripe mango, or the wonder of discovering a perfectly arched rainbow after a storm.

'There's something soothing and satisfying to knitting that I like.'

And just like that, Alice knows how to further her plan of making her parents love her. She'll start with her mother: 'Can you teach me?'

Her mother looks surprised. Then she smiles. 'Why not?' She nods at a chest of drawers next to an occasional table. 'Open the top drawer, please.'

Alice does as she's told, gasping as the drawer reveals spools of yarn in every colour imaginable.

'Choose one.'

And Alice, awed and mesmerised, chooses thread the sapphire of her mother's eyes, glowing in the lamplight.

As they begin knitting lessons, Alice's mother describes avidly the lush green vistas of her childhood home, the England she remembers and longs for: honeysuckle and lavender, afternoon tea in the conservatory, cucumber sandwiches and Victoria sponge, gingerbread and scones with clotted cream, riding and deportment lessons, debutante balls and card parties.

Alice tries to picture snow and ice falling from the sky, and being so cold you can see your breath leaving your mouth and your tears freezing on your cheeks. She loses herself in her mother's world, even as her mother shows her how to wield the knitting needles. She enjoys the feel of the soft brush of yarn, the sight of her mother's eyes, radiant, and the sound of her voice, wistful and melodious, as she describes in vivid detail the land of her youth.

It becomes a habit; their thing to do.

The nights when Father is away, Mother summons Alice to her room, where Alice makes an effort to be the child her mother expects, sitting up straight and stiff, a young lady with not even a trace of *junglee*. She is careful always to speak in English, imitating her mother's polished cadences, shiny as the pearls Mother wears always – a gift from Father – glinting at her slender neck, the soft, burnished cream of dreamy moonlight.

They knit together in the susurrating dark, populated by night jasmine and a zesty breeze spiced with secrets, with owls calling and nocturnal animals rustling. The sweet taste of shared confidences and her mother's memories: women in beautiful gowns swishing in a land where tendrils of mist and screens of fog mask a land barren in winter, but green and lush in summer. A place strange, yet coming alive through her mother's stories; just as her mother is to Alice during their time together.

Chapter 12

Janaki

1945

Ogre

Janaki dreams she's in heaven, floating on a warm cloud of exquisite comfort, enveloped by honey-sweet, golden waves of love. She wakes in a soft, rose-and-incense embrace, a gentle voice whispering in her ear, 'We're home.'

Home. Janaki sits up, anchored by her mother's arms, and blinks, thinking, *It is my dream come to life.*

The motor car is winding up a drive lit by twinkling lamps, keeping night at bay. Immaculate lawns stretch out on either side, bordered by regimented rows of flowers, which must be colourful during the day but are now rendered, like the lawns, a shadowy, night-breeze-swayed monochrome. At the end of the drive, looming large and wide and endless – a palace.

The car comes to a stop. Janaki's father helps her out.

Janaki smells sweet grass and mysterious night, shimmering with possibility, where dreams come true and the syrupy taste of amazement explodes, exotic, tantalising, in her mouth, yet carrying a tart, biting aftertaste of fear.

What if it's too good to be true?

There are so many rooms, each one bigger, more opulent than the last, plush with furniture and ornaments, divans and occasional tables, elaborate screens and intricate tapestry, paintings and sculptures, carved cornices and mirrored wardrobes. Carpeted corridors hint at other sections and winding staircases lead to other floors.

This could house everyone in the orphanage and the street kids as well! I wish Arthy was here with me, sharing this.

'You must be hungry and tired, my dear, and I promise we'll eat soon, but first, let's introduce you to your daada.' Her mother tries to sound upbeat but there's that something in her voice that Janaki had sensed earlier when she mentioned Daada, a pulse of… fear? Worry? It lodges in Janaki's heart, the unease that was nudging at the corners of her awe now taking over.

What am I doing here? I do not belong. They'll see that now and send me away, send me back.

The walk to her grandfather's rooms – 'He occupies the west wing of the house' – seems endless, especially since the anxiety that she senses in her parents is making her legs sluggish, uncooperative.

The room he receives them in, like all the others in this mansion, is huge, but her grandfather himself is a shrivelled, bald, question mark of a man, dwarfed by his armchair.

'Ah, you're home. And have you…?' He leans forward in his chair, squinting at them, even though the room is blindingly bright, the glare of a multitude of lamps scaring even the smallest hint of shadow into retreat.

'Yes, Baba,' Janaki's father says, and he is firm, smiling reassuringly at Janaki, taking her hand and leading her to his father. 'Here she is. Her name is…'

'What is this?' The old man roars so loudly that Janaki flinches, stumbling blindly backwards into her mother's waiting arms, hiding her face in her comforting embrace, fear throbbing through her in time with his hurled words, sour with rage. 'You said you'd adopt a *little boy*. A son and heir.'

'Baba, we went to adopt a boy but we fell in love with Janaki. She is our daughter.' Her father's voice, soft and assured, is in direct contrast to his father's raging.

We fell in love with Janaki.

Her heart is warmed by these words, even as she shakes with fear as the old man explodes with: 'I gave permission for you to sully our bloodline by adopting an heir, given your failure to provide me with a grandchild of my own, and you come home with a *girl…*' The final word is a snarl.

Janaki's father's voice stays even and unyielding as he says, 'Baba, we have chosen Janaki and if you give her a chance, you'll see why we love her so. She is kind, big-hearted, perfect. We are so proud to have her as our daughter and…'

'Get out! Go away! You've disgraced me, you've…'

He's still ranting when they leave, his voice carrying all the way down the corridor, hounding them through the endless rooms of this gigantic house.

Janaki dreams of an ogre, stalking her, yelling, 'What are you doing here? You're not welcome, you don't belong.'

She wakes in a strange bed, big enough to be lost in, not a mat on the floor beside sleeping girls, their familiar scent of sweat and dreams. Shadows populate the huge room she finds herself in, with darkly menacing nooks and corners where ogres could easily hide. She whimpers and is immediately enveloped by soft arms, soothing assurances.

The scent of rose water and love.

'Janaki, shhh, it's okay, you're alright.'

She remembers then, her fantasy come true. As her eyes adjust to the dark, she sees her mother: gentle face, eyes soft with care, shining with love. For *her*.

'I'm here,' her mother whispers.

And the question that had loomed sour in her mouth the previous evening but refused to leave her lips for fear the answer was yes is suddenly loosened by terror and this strange, half-dreamy light: 'If Daada doesn't warm to me, if he continues to be angry, will you send me away?'

Her mother holding her close, rocking her, is crying even as she smiles and says, 'Of course not. We love *you*. You are our daughter now and for always.'

But Janaki is not convinced, remembering the old man's contorted face, the vehement loathing in his voice, the disgust in his eyes when they briefly connected with hers.

'You're so kind and full of heart, Janaki. Your father and I both saw it at once, fell in love with you instantly...' her mother is saying. *Fell in love with you instantly.* Janaki savours each word, hugging it to her. '...and this is why we had to have you, even though your daada, the head of the family... He... You see, he's very old-fashioned. When he realised I couldn't have children, he wanted his son to marry again...'

A note of pain is throbbing through her new mother's voice. Janaki instinctively nestles closer to her, offering comfort. 'When your father stood his ground, your daada wanted us to adopt from within the family. But there were no children among the relatives, even distant ones, that we could adopt.'

Thank God, thinks Janaki.

'Finally, your daada gave permission for us to look elsewhere on one condition. He wanted a boy, an heir...' Her mother pauses, stroking Janaki's hair gently. 'You asked if we could adopt

Arthy too. I would love to, but you see now why we cannot, my dear…'

Somewhere in her too-dry mouth, Janaki locates her voice. It is hoarse, breathless. 'But… He's the head of the family, can he send me away?'

'No, my beautiful, darling child. He might be the head of the family, but he cannot control our hearts. We've picked *you*. And you're here to stay.'

Her mother's eyes are shining with conviction, and, anchored in her arms, secure and comforting, finally Janaki's heart eases and she slips, gently, into nightmare-free sleep.

Chapter 13

Alice

1915

Adventure

Alice presses her ear to the dining-room door, smelling the syrupy scent of woody resin. The corridor is seething with shadows, the night air cool and redolent with jasmine, roses and anticipation, as she eavesdrops avidly on her parents talking about *her*.

Father is home this evening and so Alice was not wanted by Mother. But she is now used to staying up past her bedtime and spending the nights knitting with Mother when Father is away.

In those secret lamplit hours, her mother's nostalgia-burnished voice has regaled Alice with tales of the country she calls home, which Alice can only picture through the gauze of her mother's sun-dappled, honeysuckle-scented, marmalade-sweet memories. A country blanketed in snow in the winter, carpeted in buttery-gold fallen leaves in autumn, budding to life in spring and riotously, gloriously colourful in summer, its lush greenery unmarred by dust. A place painted vividly bright by her mother's words, coming alive through the music of her voice.

Nights given to the England of her mother's dreams, pristine and remote, and days stickily humid, spiced with friendship, heady with the sweetness of guava and adventure. Alice is happy but tonight, she could not sleep. The perfumed breeze swayed the curtains. In the well, the water rippled and danced with silvery shadows. Night animals scurried and owls hooted. The moon shone down on a garden that was dark and mysterious, bushes swaying as they listened to secrets whispered by the wind.

She heard Father come upstairs, then both Mother and Father going down after Father had changed his clothes. The scent of cologne, spiced ginger, and Mother's floral perfume. The sound of Father's deep rumbling voice and the lilting jingle of Mother's laughter.

Their steps receding… And then, one word floating up to her, clear and sharp, in Mother's musical voice: *Alice.* That was it. She couldn't stay in bed any more. She couldn't *not* know what they were saying.

She had tiptoed to the dining room, her white nightgown billowing about her in the breeze entering through the open panes of the windows, although the mosquito mesh was secured shut.

'She's running wild, spending too much time in the company of that woman Mayuri and her son,' Father is saying. His voice is clipped, disdain colouring it the acrid navy of ash as he speaks of Ayah and Raju.

Is that worry for Alice making it so? Alice is gratified even though part of her is outraged: *I'm not running wild. We have adventures. Fun.*

'I have her in hand. I'm spending time with her most evenings, teaching her how to be a lady.'

All Mother does is spin stories of her childhood in England while teaching Alice to knit. But Alice will not debate the point. And she does try to be more ladylike in Mother's company, emulating Mother's speech and manner, so she is never in danger of being accused of behaving like a *junglee* again. Now her heart is warm with joy to find her parents are talking about her, worried for her welfare. *They care,* she thinks, her ear pressed against the cool wood of the door, the scent of sawdust and happiness.

'Nevertheless, she needs some structure to her days,' Father says now.

The clink of cutlery. The song of liquid dancing in glasses.

'We can't send her to board in England.' Father sounds thoughtful. 'Not with the war…'

England. She pictures rolling hills swathed in white, conjured by her mother's imagination and vivid in Alice's mind. Weather the opposite of here: so cold you can see it, the air frozen into stones and creamy, powdered ice.

'Here, the weather rages in furious monsoons, in punishing droughts, ranting in humidity, manifesting in sweat. It is loud and obvious, melodramatic like the Indians. Everything is over the top. In England, the weather is understated, like us. In winter, the cold is a blue chill that seeps under the skin and haunts your very being, freezing your breath, cutting you with pebbles fashioned from ice, stinging you with stabbing icicles,' Mother had said the previous night, while they knitted together.

Now she says, 'I could accompany Alice to England. We could stay with my sister. Edwina is lonely now that Bertie has signed up. She'd be—'

'It's *unsafe*, my dear. England is being bombed and battered.' Father is firm. 'There's a girls' school in Nainital—'

'Oh, Robert, you can't send her away! I enjoy her company of an evening when you're not home. If she goes to the hills too, I'll positively die of boredom.' Her mother's voice is girly and high-pitched, a tone Alice hasn't heard before. Nevertheless, Alice is thrilled, joy seeping into her every pore.

Mother enjoys my company! She wants me here with her.

A small part of her demurs: *All she wants is someone who will listen to her stories of home.* Alice shushes it. *Mother enjoys my company!* She repeats this firmly to herself, silencing the annoying voice of dissent.

From the garden, through the mosquito-net panels, a burst of moist, guava-scented air wafts into the corridor, caressing Alice's sweaty face.

'Can't you employ a governess to teach her here? Please?'

Again, that girlish cadence to her mother's voice.

A pause... Then, Father: 'Make sure she doesn't run wild around the estate. She's growing up and must behave with decorum. I'll see about a governess.'

Alice stands there, breathing in the honeyed, intrigue-spiked aroma of eavesdropped confidences, listening to her mother thanking her father, the sound of kisses being exchanged. Then she climbs the stairs to her room, thinking, *Mother wants me here, she enjoys my company. She said so.*

She firmly suppresses the errant voice that pipes up: *She only wants you because her friends are in Shimla and she is bored. She enjoys your company because you listen to her, allowing her to talk about what she wants. She doesn't want to know about your day, what you like, how you are.*

She shuts up the voice that is trying in vain to douse her joy, thinking, *Father cares for me, worries about me.* As for the small matter of not running wild, *Well, who's to keep watch? Father is away and Mother is asleep during the day.* The servants won't tell on their Missy Baba, so her parents will never know!

Alice has absolutely no intention of curbing her adventures. She enjoys her time with Raju, it's *fun*. With Raju, she is the boss, devising games, deciding what they will do; he goes along with what she says, only hesitating if it involves breaking the rules.

When she's with her parents she feels small, never knowing for sure if they care for or love her, whereas she knows without a shadow of a doubt that Raju would do anything for her. Even the games he thinks are too risky, he will try, just to make her happy.

Raju dutifully accompanies Alice on capers in the afternoons while Ayah naps. They'd kept their promise to Ayah, of not wandering off when they were meant to be napping, for a week after the incident with Father and the butterfly, after which Alice had talked Raju out of it.

'Please, Raju?'

'But we promised, Missy Baba.'

Alice made to cry.

'Don't be sad, Missy Baba. I suppose if we're very careful, nobody will know.'

And so their afternoon frolics under the golden sun, while Ayah is asleep, continue, the air thick with heat and redolent of spices and fruit; Alice the intrepid explorer, Raju her trusty aide.

As soon as Ayah starts snoring, they escape: climbing the mango trees and spying on Mali from amid the tart green foliage; rescuing millipedes entangled in the velvet moss of the well rim; hunting for snakes; mimicking the monkeys mimicking them; watching the frogs in the lake trapping flies; carefully observing ant armies; and tickling Ayah's nose so her snores stutter and sputter before resuming their loud serenades.

Raju completes Alice. With him, she feels important, looked up to, adored, simply for being herself. With him, all her insecurities and her worries regarding her parents disappear, because with him, she can bask in the simple but heady conviction that she is loved for who she is.

Alice goes into her room in the jasmine-scented dark, pleased that she will not be sent away to school, that her days will follow their usual, comforting rhythm. She is thrilled that her parents care enough to be discussing her, worrying about her.

She enjoys a deep, happy sleep, dreaming of a rainbow-hued blanket woven of her parents' love, Alice wrapped plush and secure in it. Her parents are not overtly affectionate but they care.

They *care*.

Chapter 14

Alice

1915

Presentable

'Missy Baba, you need to get changed. Your lessons start today,'
Ayah says.

Alice ignores her, content to lie in the grass, munching on the
ripe cashews Raju has fetched for her, her face now splattered
with juice. The sweet air is aromatic with the chrysanthemums
that Mali has planted, bordering the lake, and musty with the
mildew and weed odour of the stagnant water.

'You know you're not supposed to be here,' Ayah says, tutting.

At this, Alice is indignant. 'Raju is looking after me. He'll
make sure I don't come to harm.'

Ayah laughs and sighs simultaneously, something only she
can do, displaying *paan*-stained gums in the process. The peepal
trees wave gently in the tepid breeze, already thick with humidity,
although it's merely a few hours since sunrise. A frog jumps into
the water with a loud splash, rupturing the skin of dirt, dead
leaves and broken twigs formed on top of the lake.

'Come on,' Ayah sighs, 'you can't possibly greet your governess
in those clothes. Look at you, filthy already and it's barely nine
in the morning! She will be here at half past ten.'

'Do I *have* to?'

'Yes,' Ayah says sternly.

'Can Raju sit in with me?'

'Missy Baba, these lessons are for you…'

'Please?' She looks up at Ayah in that way she knows Ayah won't be able to resist.

'Oh, alright then, what harm can it do? He'll sit in the corner and sift through the rice for Cook, checking for stones.'

'No, let him sit beside me. He'll mind Miss Kitty for me…'

On one of their afternoon jaunts, Alice had heard a mewling.

'Listen!' She nudged Raju.

'What?'

'I think it's a kitten needing rescue, help me look.'

And indeed, trapped within a fragrant mimosa bush by the lake, a kitten!

'Now where did you come from?' Alice asked, gently.

After having coaxed the frightened kitten into her arms, feeling its little heart beating through scraggly fur, so soft and warm and defenceless, she turned to Raju: 'We've got to get it to the kitchen, feed it some milk. We'll call it… Hmmm… What *shall* we call it, Raju?'

'You decide, Missy Baba.' His adoring honey-chocolate gaze a reflection of the look in the green eyes of the kitten now purring and burrowing into her arms.

'Can you tell if it's a girl or boy?'

Raju examined it, his nose scrunched up in concentration. 'I think it's a girl.'

'What about Miss Kitty?'

'Miss Kitty it is,' said Raju, beaming.

In the kitchen, perfumed with cinnamon and roasting spices, Cook looks up from where she is frying cashew nuts in *ghee*, her tone indulgent: 'Aren't you two meant to be having your nap?' And, taking a closer look, 'What've you got there?' Her tone changes, resigned, 'Oh, this one survived? There must have been a hole in that gunny sack.'

'What do you mean?' Alice's eyes are wide, her heart contracting as a shiver shudders through her. The kitten, sensing her change of mood, mewls plaintively.

'It's one of the litter of the tabby that hangs about by the well. A nuisance, no one knows where it came from, it just turned up one day and now it thinks this is home and it can help itself to food from my kitchen as it pleases…' Cook takes a breath. 'Assuming it belongs here is one thing, reproducing quite another. I asked Mali to drow—'

Raju interrupts: 'Can we have some milk for the kitten?'

'What was Cook going to say?' Alice is upset, even as she strokes the downy, black and grey fur of the kitten, who looks at her with trusting emerald eyes.

'Nothing.' Raju is cagey.

Gunny sack… Mali… Miss Kitty found in the bush by the lake…

All of a sudden the significance dawns, accompanied by a disbelieving chill: 'Mali *drowned* the other kittens? How could he? Why?' Alice bursts into tears, the kitten mewling plaintively and Raju almost in tears himself, trying in vain to comfort her.

Cook plies her with *gulab jamun* – 'Soft and syrupy, my best yet.' Alice refuses, distraught at the plight of the other kittens. Cook thrusts *kheer* at her, the milky pudding studded with plump honeyed raisins and nuts roasted in *ghee*.

'I don't want it.' Alice pushes the plate away, sobs shuddering through her. Cook apologises, Mali is summoned and told off. He promises solemnly never to drown another living thing again.

Raju says tenderly, 'Missy Baba, you can't be sad. The kitten needs you, it's finished all the milk and is looking for more.' And finally, Alice's tears wane as she tends to the kitten, even as she resolves never to talk to Mali or Cook again, a promise that lasts all of two days.

'I don't think it's a good idea for either Raju or the kitten to attend lessons with you, Missy Baba. Let's ask Memsahib what she thinks,' Ayah says, sighing now.

'No,' Alice says, a little too quickly, but Ayah does not seem to notice. 'Raju can sit in the corner sifting rice, Miss Kitty beside him. There's no need to disturb Mother.'

She doesn't think Mother would even register Ayah's request if Ayah were to ask, just mumbling, 'Do what you think best,' and pulling the pillow over her head, like she usually does on matters concerning Alice. Nevertheless, safest not to draw attention to the fact that Alice wants a 'coolie' to sit in on her lessons.

Since that evening when she had eavesdropped on Father and Mother discussing her education, Alice has taken care to play with Raju out of sight of her parents, which has been easy considering Father has rarely been home and Mother is always in bed.

A few weeks after she overheard her parents' plans for her, Alice was summoned in to see Father. This unexpected audience with her father had sent both Ayah and Alice into a tizzy; Ayah smoothing Alice's clothes, patting her hair in place, all the while tutting, 'How you manage to get so much dust on your clothes and in your hair in the space of an hour I don't for the life of me know!' Alice not paying heed to Ayah's grumbles, as she mentally catalogued her transgressions, wondering which of them had come to Father's notice.

Was it the afternoon she had challenged Raju to jump off the guava tree branches and Alice had landed on Mali's vegetable patch, destroying quite a few of his beans, tomatoes and *brinjals*, much to his chagrin? Or the one when she'd dared Raju to a race up to the gates and back, only stopping when they'd seen Father's carriage approaching? She'd been sure Father hadn't seen her…

Father looked up when Alice knocked on the door to his study, then opened it a little, releasing the musk-and-navy aroma of ink and paper and tobacco. And then, setting down his pen, he *smiled*.

'Ah, Alice, come in.'

Alice's heart, which had been skipping with fear, now began somersaulting with pleasure, even as she beamed widely at her father.

'You're ten now, young lady, aren't you?'

'Yes, Father.'

'Your mother and I think you'd benefit from some discipline and structure to your days. To that end, I've employed a governess, the best in all of Jamjadpur, so I'm told. You will be starting lessons with Miss Simmons in two weeks.'

'Thank you, Father.'

'You will apply yourself, make your mother and myself proud, won't you?'

'I will.'

'Good girl!' Her father nodded. Then, his voice changing, 'I heard about the kitten you rescued.'

'Um…' *Was he angry with her?* Alice couldn't quite make out his tone of voice. Nevertheless, she stood up straight and looking right at him, said, 'She's called Miss Kitty.'

And again, her father smiled. This smile even wider than before! 'I've met her. Affectionate, isn't she?'

Alice's heart was lifting, singing, glowing. 'She is.'

'I don't hold with the coolie habit of drowning the poor animals.' Father is grim, his smile replaced by a scowl. 'Rest assured, they've been told.'

Alice stood up even straighter, her voice fierce, 'I've told them as well that it is *not* to happen again.'

Her father made a strange sound and it took her a moment to realise that he was chuckling! This was a day of surprises.

'Well done, Alice,' Father said, when he stopped chuckling, his face creased into a bright smile directed at her. Then, 'I had a pet cat while I was growing up. She was called Cuddles.'

The words were out of Alice's mouth before she had thought them through, Father's mellow mood loosening her tongue: 'Cuddles is a nice name and I'm sure your cat was lovely but I think Miss Kitty is just perfect.'

As soon as she heard herself, Alice wondered if she had made a mistake. But then...

A rumbling, tumbling roar of a sound. Her father was *laughing,* great big chortles, and it was... so familiar. How? Then, realisation dawning: it was the soundtrack to her dream/memory involving Father, where he carried her high up in his arms.

And now, she knew, without a doubt that it was not a dream but a memory. It *had* taken place. For here was Father, laughing again because of something Alice had said, a brilliant, joyful celebration.

'Now, remember to converse in English with your governess,' Ayah says, as they walk back to the house through the grounds.

'Yes.'

'And you'll be on your best behaviour?'

Something in Ayah's voice – an uncharacteristic tentative note – causes Alice to sneak a glance at her. Ayah looks preoccupied as she contemplates her charge. It strikes Alice then that Ayah wants her to make a good impression on the governess for it will reflect well on her; she has been solely in charge of Alice up until now.

A burst of affection for Ayah pulses through Alice. She pats Ayah's hand. 'Don't worry, Ayah, I won't let you down.'

The worry lines creasing Ayah's forehead relax and she smiles. It's like a rainbow in an overcast sky. 'You're a smart one, aren't you?' She swoops down to plant a kiss on Alice's cheek, warm affection, coconut oil and spiced cardamom. 'I know you won't, Missy Baba. Now, come, let's make you presentable.'

Ayah washes Alice in the central courtyard, around which the house is built, underneath the tamarind tree beside the well. This is where the linen is hung to dry 'to get an airing', the maids state officiously, and this is where the servants congregate during their breaks. It is directly below Alice's room and she loves to listen to their chatter, their high-pitched giggles, their bangles and anklets tinkling as they gossip away. They are louder and more musical than the noisy, bright-green parakeets clustering in the fruit trees, or the crows, pigeons and mynah birds, which also like to gather in the inner courtyard, pecking at the soft, muddy mulch beside the well, hunting for worms. Peacocks find their way here too, from the grounds, and some mornings, Alice is treated to their wide-arced welcome, multihued, kaleidoscopic, when she wakes.

Ayah draws water from the well, and Alice and Raju stand side by side, holding hands, eyes closed in anticipation.

'Here it comes,' Ayah calls and the next moment a cascade of tumbling water, icy-cool, douses them as Ayah tips the pail of shimmering silver upon their heads. They screech and dance on the cement surround beside the well, with the tabby – Miss Kitty's mother – who loves to sun herself on the rim, screeching in disgust at their disturbing her peace and splashing her nicely dry coat.

'Again!' Alice cries. She loves being washed here with glittering sheets of fresh well water, flavoured with sunshine, tasting sparkly, of silken secrets, rather than in the bathroom inside.

'You're a growing girl, Missy Baba, and about to start lessons with your governess.' Ayah's voice is fond as she wraps Alice in a towel. 'This is the last time I'm washing you outside.'

Alice pays no heed, confident she can talk Ayah round.

Chapter 15

Janaki

1946

Wrath

'Janaki, my love, your father and I have to attend a wedding...'

'Can't I come too?'

'It's two towns away – a tedious journey. And it will go on until late into the night. You'll be bored, tired. You're better off staying here. Devi and the other maids will look after you. You can say good night to Daada with us, before we leave, and you don't have to see him again until we get back. We'll visit him together then.'

Janaki's parents are fiercely protective of her, especially when it comes to Daada. They insist she pay her respects to him every morning and night, but they also make sure to be present when she does so.

Her first morning, when she went to touch his feet, like her mother had, her grandfather had pointedly tucked his feet under his body, turning away as she approached, so her mother had instructed her to greet him verbally and that was it.

Daada does not scare Janaki, not now she knows that whatever his opinion, her parents will not send her back to the orphanage; that they love her. Moreover, his blustery rages seem contrived and over the top; Mother Superior's cold wrath had been much worse. But it hurts her parents that he will not accept Janaki, she can see, and so, for their sake, she makes an effort.

Apart from scary Daada – who doesn't bother her *that* much as she can forget about him for the most part, confined as he is to his rooms in this palatial house – it has been an idyllic life, family being everything she'd hoped for and more. Slowly, she has come to believe that she is loved. That she *belongs*.

One day, as she and her mother were reading from the Mahabharata – Janaki had told her about enjoying Sister Shanthi's stories from the epics and they were going through them together – Janaki had experienced an epiphany.

She'd smiled widely at her mother as they read about the Pandavas, the five brothers, and the fights they had with their cousins, the Kauravas.

'Why are you smiling at such a gruesome story?' her mother asked fondly, ruffling Janaki's hair.

'I was thinking that I truly am part of a family now. A family is made up of all sorts. Dhritarashtra made his adopted son the ruler and this upset his own sons. In our house, Daada is none too happy with you adopting me. This is how it is in every family.'

'You're a wise one, you are.' Her mother kissed her cheek. 'We're so lucky to have you.'

Janaki misses Arthy but writes to her every day, as she had promised.

When she receives Arthy's replies and reads about the orphanage antics, she feels a pang of missing, but that's all it is – a small tug of ache for her childhood companions.

'Oh, Janu, I just want someone to love me,' Arthy used to say when they dreamed of being adopted. 'I want to be the centre of someone's world.'

I do too, Janaki would concur, full of prayer and longing. Now, here, she *is*.

She wakes to wailing.

When she leaves her room, she sees the servants collected in little clumps, sobbing. Terror settles in her chest, robbing her voice so that when it does finally leave her throat, it is in a cowed whisper: 'What's happened?'

The servants stop crying to look at her, and she is speared by their sorrowful gazes in the sodden, dreadful silence. Finally, one of them, Devi, speaks, 'Your daada wants to see you.'

'But Ma said I was to wait for her and Baba…' She shrinks from the pity in Devi's eyes.

Her heart is screaming, *No. It is not what I think. It cannot be. Please.*

The walk to her daada's rooms has never felt longer – and she has only ever done it with one or both of her parents beside her – but she wants it to go on forever. She doesn't want to arrive, face him, hear what he has to say. This is the first time he has summoned her to him. Why? Where are her parents?

They had kissed her good night. Her father was unfamiliar in his suit, smelling of peppermint and musk. Her mother was in a glittering sari, jewels shining from her neck, glinting in her ears, bangles winking gold on her wrists.

'You look so grand and glamorous,' Janaki had said, awed, and they'd laughed, pleased, even as they'd swooped down to hug her one more time.

Now, she closes her eyes, trying to imagine her mother's arms, roses and comfort. How secure she felt in them. How loved.

*

Her grandfather is on his feet and roaring even before she has stepped foot in the room.

'They're dead!'

It can't be. He's lying, isn't he?

'Caught in the crossfire between Hindus and Muslims. Killed in the riots, both of them.'

Riots.

As if from a distance she hears Sister Shanthi's voice: *Oh, your arrival was dramatic. It was right in the middle of the riots.*

She was abandoned by her birth parents at the orphanage during riots between Hindus and Muslims. And now… Riots have snatched the parents who chose her…

It cannot be.

She saw them a few hours ago. Surely they'll come back? They *promised* and they've always kept their promises. She blinks, trying to focus.

'It's your fault.' Her grandfather is spitting the words at her. 'Nothing but bad luck since you came into our lives. The business failing. The British cancelling their contracts with us and moving back to England ahead of independence. My son and daughter-in-law dead.'

'Ma, Baba are—'

'Don't call them that! They took you on and you brought about their deaths. You do not belong here, you never did. You will leave immediately, go back to where you came from, taking your bad luck with you!'

Chapter 16

Alice

1916

Approval

'I've heard there've been uprisings in some of the villages you oversee, Robert?' Alice hears.

She is kneeling on her bed, her face pressed against the mosquito screen, eavesdropping on her father's conversation with his friends through the open window.

'Yes,' Father is saying, languidly, his voice spiced with tobacco. 'Easily quashed though. What the natives need is a good smacking. They only understand the language of violence.' Then a steely undertone lends his voice a harsh cadence: 'They want independence, self-rule, but without us they would not manage at all. They need us to run the country.' Now disdain pulses through: 'Incompetent fools, fighting among themselves! Good for nothing!'

Rosy air spiked with the vinegary tang of alcohol, burnished gold with the low rumble of conversation, is wafting up to Alice's room. 'The Germans have turned for home at Jutland. This is the beginning of the end, surely?'

Talk has turned to the war, which is *still* ongoing and which, for Alice, is as distant and dreamy as England itself: 'I heard from the powers that be that they're preparing to launch an offensive at Somme. That should gain us a decisive victory.'

Alice used to long to be included in these gatherings, which transformed her remote parents into glamorous strangers. She would listen, awed, to their rare laughter and wish they'd laugh with her, or, if not, allow her to join in these parties where they let their guard down.

One night she sneaked downstairs and hid under the table, staring at legs encased in flowing silk and pressed trousers, some of them entwined. The heady excitement of having got away with it; the music of liquid flowing into clinking glasses; the chatter of cutlery conversing with china; the zesty tang of spices and the sweet pungency of fermented fruit had eventually lulled her to sleep.

The lady whose leg had connected with Alice – waking her up so she yelped in pain – had screamed in shock and fainted right away. That was when Alice discovered just how fearsome Father could be. She had been sent to bed, a muscle twitching in Father's cheek, his eyes glinting dangerously, his breath smoky vinegar, hissing in her ear, 'I'll see you tomorrow in the dining room.' She would never forget the smacks she received, the stinging shock, the throbbing hurt, the resulting welts. The telling-off afterwards: Father's voice soft but menacing; his eyes hard and flinty, sharp blue stones fit to draw blood.

She's never ventured from her room during a party since; instead, listening to and absorbing the myriad, exciting vibes from her room, her face pressed to the mesh screen.

When she goes in to say good morning to her parents the following day, there's a strange man sitting beside Father at the table in Mother's stead.

'Alice, this is Major Goodwin. He was at the party yesterday.'

'How do you do, Major Goodwin?' Alice says politely.

'What a courteous young lady you are.' Major Goodwin smiles widely. He is quite bald, his head oily and shining.

Alice is about to ask to be excused when he says, 'Will you join us for breakfast?' Alice looks at Father. This is quite unprecedented, but then this morning is turning out to be unusual. This is the first time Mother has not been present when Father is at breakfast.

As if reading her mind, Father says, 'Mother has a headache and will not be joining us. Do sit down, Alice.' He nods at Mother's place.

Alice is thrilled. She feels quite grown-up, taking Mother's place, listening in on the conversation of the two men. Major Goodwin talks to her as if to an equal. 'I'll be accompanying your father to one of the villages in his district where there has been an uprising,' he says.

A piece of sausage is stuck between his teeth and his tie is stained with egg, but Alice likes him anyway for treating her like an adult. Sharing this with her. She nods, and remembering the overheard conversation from the previous night says, 'The coolies need to be kept in their place. The only language they understand is violence.'

'Hear, hear,' Major Goodwin says, raising his teacup to her. 'You have a very intelligent daughter, Robert. Beauty and brains. But then I wouldn't expect anything less.'

Her father smiles and later, as Alice bids goodbye, he pats her shoulder: 'Good girl, Alice.'

Alice beams, her heart glowing, feeling warmed, floating on a cloud of well-being for the entire day.

That afternoon, she looks at her white hand against Raju's brown one, mulling over the conversation she overheard the previous night and the chat with her father and Major Goodwin that morning, her heart still suffused with joy at her father's smile and approval.

She and Raju are sitting side by side in the kitchen, sipping milky, spiced tea, eating *bondas* dipped in coconut chutney, and *jalebi*. Cook and Ayah are busy discussing a recipe for *methi* chicken, each shouting louder than the other, both convinced their version is better. Miss Kitty stands at the door to the kitchen, inside which she's not allowed, looking mournfully at Alice with glowing eyes, the emerald of the lake at dawn, and mewling piteously.

'Nice try, but you're still not allowed inside.' Cook takes a breather from arguing with Ayah to talk to the cat.

'Just this once?' Alice asks.

'No.'

Once Cook goes back to debating frenziedly with Ayah, Alice tugs at Raju's hand, sticky with syrup from the *jalebis*.

'You know,' she says, 'you need us to run this country.'

Raju turns to look at her. 'What do you mean?'

'You coolies need us, Sahibs and Memsahibs, to manage you,' she says confidently.

Raju is staring at her, a strange as yet unencountered expression on his face. 'My da says we managed quite well before you came along and we'll manage again when you leave…'

'When we leave?' Alice is shocked. 'I was born here! This is my *home*.' Her voice is a screech.

Ayah and Cook stop talking to stare at Alice.

'What's the matter, Missy Baba? Not *arguing*, are you?' Amused surprise in Ayah's voice as her gaze spins between Alice and Raju.

Alice makes her voice suitably indignant while Raju colours. 'We *never* argue.'

Cook and Ayah smile indulgently.

'Well, *we* do,' Cook says, turning back to Ayah, firm. 'No, you don't crush the *methi*, you add it whole, it cooks down in the sauce.'

'Crushing the *methi* releases flavour, I tell you,' Ayah shouts.

Cook and Ayah seem to enjoy this verbal sparring, each louder than the other. They go on and on until one of them says, 'I don't know about you but my mouth is dry. *Paan*?' After which they will sit on the kitchen stoop leading to the vegetable-and-herb garden, watching Raju and Alice play while they set the world to rights.

'Raju, you're being mean,' Alice says, when Cook and Ayah have gone back to arguing. She wishes Miss Kitty was allowed in the kitchen so she could have her warm body to hug for comfort.

'So are you. You started it,' Raju says and now she sees that the strange, flushed expression is anger. Raju is angry. *With her!*

All the happiness she had felt, the warmth and pleasure at her father's approval is dissipated by Raju's anger. And this makes her annoyed. Upset.

'I was happy. And you... you've ruined it.'

'You did it first.'

'I only told the truth.'

'It's *not* the truth.'

'How can you say that?' She's appalled. Her throat is hot with salt and betrayal. Eyes stinging. She's always taken Raju's regard for granted. She's believed him to be, if she gave it any thought at all, an extension of herself, always agreeing with her, doing what she says, going along with her schemes.

Raju, seeing she's about to cry, loses his hard expression, his face dissolving into concern. 'Missy Baba...' Taking her hand.

She shrugs him off, runs to Ayah.

'What's the matter, eh? Overtired, are you?' Ayah, argument with Cook pushed aside, gathers Alice onto her lap, even though she's getting too big for it, planting kisses flavoured with cardamom and sugar syrup upon her cheeks. 'You're hot.' She feels Alice's forehead. 'Early bed for you, I think.'

For once Alice doesn't protest, so Ayah takes this as further proof that Alice is coming down with something.

Hurt churns in Alice's stomach even as Raju, when he says good night, squeezes her hand and looks into her eyes, earnestly whispering (out of his mother's earshot), 'I'm sorry for upsetting you. Friends again, Missy Baba?'

And she, looking at Raju, feels an avalanche of emotions engulf her. He's a coolie, to be disdained, if she is to believe Father. But Raju is also her friend; her best friend; her *only* friend. She cannot bear to be angry with him. It is too upsetting.

'Friends,' she says, squeezing his hand back and when he beams, all is well in her world again.

PART 4

India

Curious

Chapter 17

Alice

1986

Lifeline

The visitor is a teenage girl.

Alice is surprised. She waits a moment, watching her through the window. The girl is young but poised, sitting primly at the edge of her seat, hands crossed on her knees. Her face is set in an expression of determination as she looks about the room, taking it in. Her right knee jiggles and it is that which gives her away: she is nervous.

As if aware she is being watched, the girl turns. Her gaze meets Alice's through the window. Alice smiles, instinctively, immediately. The girl's gaze is frank, curious. Assessing. Familiar.

What is it about her that is so... so *known*? Her open gaze? Those eyes, wide and inquisitive, missing nothing?

Alice flips through the list she keeps in her head of the children she has looked after over the years in this place she started when she was at her lowest point, offering the comforts and love of home to street kids.

It has been as much her lifeline as theirs, which is why, when they come to thank her, she is discomfited, for she has gained as much as they have, if not more. She remembers them all, can picture each one in her mind's eye. She might be getting on in years, but her mind is as sharp as ever. This young visitor is not one of *her* children.

Perhaps it is the daughter of one of them who has come to see her?

The girl stands as Alice enters the room. Her smile is tentative.

'Hello, I'm Alice. You wanted to see me?' Alice smiles gently. 'Please sit. Would you like some tea?' She is overcome by an urge to reassure the girl.

Close up, she is even younger than Alice thought. Barely sixteen, if that. Clear skin, lovely face. The girl doesn't sit. Instead she clasps her hands together as if praying and says, her voice awe and wonder, 'You're not at all how I imagined you to be.'

PART 5

India

Dreams

Chapter 18

Alice

1918

Help

'Miss Harris, did you do the sums I set you?' the governess, Miss Simmons, asks of Alice. Alice, who has been observing a bee trapped inside the room, looking for a way out, flying towards the window but not realising it needs to fly *through*, looks blankly at her.

'Miss Harris, what is the answer to the first question?' Miss Simmons' face is a raging storm, her words uttered through gritted teeth, as though she is holding herself together with difficulty.

Alice has, as usual, blithely ignored her homework. 'Um…'

From behind her, Raju whispers, 'Three hundred and seventy-seven.'

Raju has a prodigious memory and although he sits in a corner, doing odd jobs for Cook – today, he's topping and tailing green beans – he absorbs and assimilates the lessons and remembers the homework. He has helped Alice out of many a tight spot before now by discreetly whispering the answers to her when Miss Simmons' back is turned and they are always right. Alice forgets the lessons and the homework she is meant to do the moment she is out of the classroom, revelling in the joy of release, concentrating on the much more interesting task of planning adventures instead. But this time, her luck has run out as Miss Simmons picks up on Raju's prompting.

'Mr Kumar, do you have something to say?' Miss Simmons asks, her voice as icy as Alice imagines an English winter from Mother's childhood to be.

*

'Who are you?' Miss Simmons had asked at the start of their very first lesson, staring pointedly down her long nose at Raju, who was sitting in the corner (far enough away so as to appear non-intrusive, yet still within whispering distance of Alice), sorting through a bag of rice, putting the stones in a cane basket by his side, with Miss Kitty snug in his lap.

'He's my ayah's son, Raju Kumar, Miss Simmons,' Alice had said smoothly. 'He's here to look after my pet, Miss Kitty. She's nervous and will not settle anywhere without me, but she'll stay with Raju if I'm in the room.'

Miss Simmons' lips had disappeared, her mouth puckering like the seed of a mango chewed clean of juice. 'I do not like animals or coolies in my classroom,' she announced coldly.

Alice had watched Raju blanch before gathering the bag of rice he had been sifting with one hand and Miss Kitty with the other. As he'd stood up to leave, Miss Kitty had started mewling plaintively in protest; she had been quite comfortable on his lap and hadn't wanted to be disturbed.

'Miss Simmons, my parents do not care for those cruel to animals. They'd be quite appalled by Miss Kitty's distress,' Alice had said, thinking fast and recalling her most cherished interaction with Father, when they'd bonded over their pet cats.

Miss Simmons' eyes had been flinty as she'd said, not looking at Raju, 'You can stay.'

*

Now, Raju stammers, 'I…'

A burst of laughter from the maids outside wafts on the sugared breeze angling into the room. Sunlight, bright gold, shines like suspended nuggets of treasure, holding the dust motes to ransom.

'What did you say, Mr Kumar?'

'Three hundred and seventy-seven,' Raju mumbles.

Miss Simmons' demeanour unbends a little as she checks her notebook.

'And the answer to the second question in the homework I set Miss Harris yesterday?'

'Five thousand four hundred and twenty-one,' Raju replies without hesitation, not looking at either Alice or Miss Simmons, but stroking Miss Kitty, who purrs contentedly on his lap.

'The third?'

'Four thousand five hundred and fifty-two.'

'Impressive. Well done.' Miss Simmons nods at Raju, her narrow face quite transformed by her smile.

Then, to Alice, the smile disappearing, 'Miss Harris, you could do well to follow Mr Kumar's example.'

Alice feels something bitter flood her chest. A sharp, hot and biting pang.

Afterwards, they sit by the well while Miss Kitty plays in the swampy mud left behind by water spilt from pails.

Alice tastes sunshine, warm caramel on her lips, but it will not ease the fiery churning in her chest. She says to Raju, 'You don't have to be in the classroom with me any more.'

'Oh.' Raju's liquid almond eyes sparkle with dawning knowledge. 'Not jealous are you, Missy Baba?'

'Of course not.' She is aware of colour rushing to her cheeks. 'I just thought you could help Mali or something. What use is book knowledge to you when you're only going to work in the fields?' Her voice is sharper than she intended.

Raju jumps off the well rim, stands facing her, his eyes bright, flashing amber sparks. 'You *are* jealous. I was only trying to help you, Missy Baba.'

'I did not ask for it.' Her voice is red, pulsing with a sudden burst of fury.

Miss Kitty, picking up on the tension, mewls, rubbing her wet and muddy fur first against Alice's legs, then Raju's.

'It was not my intention to undermine or outshine you.' Raju's voice is tight, short. 'And there's no need to speak to me so.'

'Why not?' she asks, coolly. 'I'll speak to you how I like. I'm Missy Baba and you're just a coolie.'

Raju's face closes up and he nods shortly. 'Right then, Missy Baba. Of course.'

Alice sits on the well rim, stroking the velvet moss sprouting there, the humid air fragranced with ripe mango caressing her face, fighting tears as she watches her best friend walk away from her.

Chapter 19

Janaki

1946

If

All the way back to the orphanage Janaki wonders, *If I had tried harder with Daada... If I had asked Ma and Baba to stay back, not go to the wedding... If I had gone along... If I had been a better child... If... Could I have prevented this happening?*

The nuns are kind, gentle with her. Arthy throws her arms around her, whispering, 'I'm so sorry.'

But Janaki is numb. She cannot feel, cannot think, even as Shali, Bina and the others try to comfort her in their own little ways: Shali by sharing her book with Janaki, Bina by clumsily plaiting Janaki's hair.

It is as though she had never left the orphanage; as though the interlude with her adoptive parents had never happened. But she had tasted love, she had been loved. It had been glorious. She had been the centre of their world, as they had been of hers. And now...

Here she is, orphaned *again*, back with all the others, who are looking at her with such pity. These same children who had been so envious when she was adopted. Who had wished that it had been one of them instead of her going to a family.

That night Janaki tries to cry quietly on her mat by the door, the place that the others have saved for her, ambushed by the blue-black darkness of dashed dreams, crushed hopes and the bleak reality she thought she'd left behind. Arthy puts her arms around Janaki but she shrugs them off. She wants other arms: her parents who had loved her, with whom she had felt complete. For such a devastatingly short time.

She knows Arthy is hurt but she cannot find the words to say: 'I'm sorry, it's not you. I just... I... I can't.'

So, she says nothing at all.

I cannot care. I cannot love. It hurts too much. From now on, I will be independent. I will not rely on anyone.

Chapter 20

Alice

1918

Surprise

'Missy Baba, are you awake?' Alice blinks as Ayah draws open the curtains in her room and brilliant sunshine angles inside.

She hadn't been able to sleep well the previous night after her argument with Raju. She had tossed and turned, wishing for Miss Kitty, who usually kept her company; her soft body, warmth and comfort nuzzling into Alice. But she had escaped into the night. Ayah believes she has an admirer.

Alice looks to the doorway outside which Raju usually waits, singing, 'Good morning, Missy Baba.'

It is empty. Her stomach dips.

Is he still angry with me?

'Where's Raju?'

Ayah ignores her question, saying instead, 'There's a surprise waiting for you outside. Wash and change, quick.'

'Ah.' Alice rubs her palms together, anticipation and excitement building in her stomach. 'I *love* surprises! That's where Raju is then, with the surprise?'

Ayah does not answer.

The surprise is a dancing monkey; a scrawny little thing, thin and malnourished, attached to a rope, which its handler pulls to make it dance. Its coat is straggly and sore-infested. It looks like a sorry cousin of the monkeys that sneak into the orchard to steal fruit, who Mali chases away, yelling, 'Thieving nuisances!' while muttering much worse insults under his breath.

The mothers with babies clinging to them run, but some of the bigger monkeys stand and stare at Mali, as if daring him to catch them. Alice roots for them even as Mali charges with a thick stick until, finally, just as Mali advances upon them, they sprint to join their chattering fellows, speeding up the trees at the edge of the orchard and away, out of the compound, the babies holding tight to their mothers' tummies.

As Alice approaches the scrawny monkey, the handler pulls at the rope, urging it to 'Dance for little memsahib', pulling harder when the monkey hesitates.

Alice is incensed, the taste of rage like a mouthful of chillies, hot red pounding in her ears: 'How dare you?'

The man blinks. 'I… I thought…'

'It looks ill. You're abusing it.'

'But…'

'Set it free now.'

'I… It's my livelihood. I can't work, you see…' Holding out his hands to her, swollen and misshapen.

'So, you ill-treat a defenceless animal, you…'

'Missy Baba…' Ayah intervenes.

But Alice cannot hear. Blinded by anger, she marches up to her mother's room and knocks.

If Father were home, she would have turned to him, knowing he does not abide cruelty to animals, recalling when he commended her for rescuing Miss Kitty. She knows her mother will be asleep, having been up even after she sent Alice to bed, when Alice was drooping over her knitting, but this is an emergency.

Ayah has followed her. 'Missy Baba, your mother doesn't like to be disturbed this early in the morning.'

But Alice continues to pound on the door until she hears the soft, sleepy tones of her mother's voice: 'Who is it? What is it?'

Alice runs straight up to her mother, who is sitting up in bed, groggy and dishevelled. She flings herself into her mother's arms – the first time she has done so despite their evenings knitting together.

Her mother pushes her away, none too gently. 'What is the meaning of this?' Her voice is sharp. 'Barging in like this when I'm…'

'I'm sorry, Mother, but there's a man with a monkey—'

'Do what you think best,' her mother cuts in. 'And please do *not* disturb me again.' She sinks back into bed, drawing a pillow over her head.

The monkey is freed and given to Mali to introduce to the colony that terrorises his fruit trees; its handler is generously recompensed and offered a position at the house doing odd jobs. Mali, his face a study in disgust that this job should fall to him, eventually warms as the monkey, which is a cowed, frail thing, sticks close to him, so he finally feeds it one of his precious fruits, cajoling it out of its fear and hesitation.

It is only then that Alice realises that Raju is not there.

'Where's Raju?' she asks Ayah, as they watch Mali coaxing the monkey into joining its boisterous cousins, who are chattering among themselves and staring disdainfully at this scrawny excuse for a relative. Some are sitting on the mud road outside the gate, which has been left wide open to entice the monkey to join the freedom of the jabbering horde in the peepal trees outside the compound.

But the newly freed monkey is having none of it and is stubbornly sticking close to Mali instead.

Mali approaches the biggest of the peepal-tree monkeys sitting boldly in the middle of the mud road. As he takes one step forward, rescued monkey at his side, the big monkey takes one step back, dust rising off the road as it drags its bottom along it, while its companions squeal support and encouragement from the trees.

'Ayah…' Alice begins again, more urgently now that her angst is soothed. The laughter at Mali's frustration with his loyal monkey, which has been bubbling in her throat, is choked out of her as she watches Ayah's face.

'He's in the fields with his father. He said you didn't need him in the classroom any more.'

The pain is a spear lancing her heart.

'No! I didn't mean… I *need* him to be there.'

All the monkeys, including the newly rescued one, turn to look at Alice, their natter stilling at her raised voice. It hurts more than she can put into words, even to herself, that Raju took their argument seriously, that he is happy to work in the fields rather than spend time with her. She misses him when he's not around. Doesn't he miss her?

She's always basked in his uncomplicated adoration of her. She's taken it for granted. But now… Yes, perhaps she was harsh the previous day and shouldn't have said what she did, but… They've never argued like they did the previous day – in fact, they hardly argue at all, and if they *do* have a minor disagreement, Raju always gives in. Which is why she was sure he would forgive her, certain he would be here this morning as usual, his face lighting up upon seeing her.

'*You* have lessons, Missy Baba. He just accompanies you, but they are of no use to him,' Ayah is saying.

'He enjoys them.'

'Perhaps, but his destiny is—'

'This is why you arranged the "surprise"? Did you think a dancing monkey could replace my friend?' The lack of Raju, the missing, rising in her throat, manifesting in a shrill scream, 'I want Raju. I'm Missy Baba and you will do as I say.'

Ayah raises her eyebrows, hands on hips, an expression of surprise mixed with disappointment upon her face. She opens her mouth to speak but the monkeys begin screeching all at once, imitating Alice.

And into this din comes Miss Simmons. 'Shoo!' she snaps at the monkeys sitting in the road in her no-nonsense tone. 'Get away, you beasts!'

But they ignore her, their attention focused on Alice, who is sobbing. Scorching hurt is spilling out of her as liquid heat. Alice knows she's behaving like a spoilt child much younger than thirteen, but the hurt is a gaping wound in her chest, chafing from the stabbing ache of Raju's absence. He was angry with her, but she never believed he would carry the anger on to today, take her at her word and not turn up...

The only way she can bear the pain is by voicing it, but it feels too huge and involved to put into words, so instead she calls for her friend as loud as she can to drown out the voice in her head, which is whispering: *Raju doesn't care for you as much as you think he does. He doesn't need you as much as you need him.*

'Stop making such a racket, Miss Harris. It is unbecoming and entirely unnecessary,' Miss Simmons snaps, walking gingerly around the monkeys and inside the gate. A thrum of fear pierces Alice's upset – what if Miss Simmons complains to Father?

So far, Raju sitting in on lessons has not been mentioned – Father has been very busy and Mother self-absorbed, the evenings when she knits with Alice given over to her glorious past in England. She's not at all interested in the present, in Alice's activities during the day, and Alice is glad of it. Alice had prepared an excuse in case she was ever asked to account for Raju's presence in the classroom – the same one she gave Miss Simmons, about Miss Kitty being nervous and needing to be with her, Raju looking after the pet while also doing odd jobs for Cook.

But what if Miss Simmons brings to Father's attention Alice's childish behaviour today? She has threatened to involve him every so often when Alice has persistently failed to do her homework, but so far, she hasn't carried out those threats.

Alice has lived in constant fear of being summoned by Father and of being told how disappointed he is. 'You will apply yourself, make your mother and myself proud, won't you?' Father had asked and Alice had solemnly replied, 'I will.' At the time she had meant it, but that was before she knew how *boring* the lessons would be. She wants to please Father, she has the best of intentions, but applying herself to her studies is another matter altogether. Thankfully, he is rarely home; he must be paying Miss Simmons' fees no questions asked, preferring to believe that since there haven't been any complaints, his daughter is not running wild.

Even though Alice knows she must stop crying, she cannot. It's as if her pain has an agenda of its own, it will not be silenced.

'You should be celebrating, not sobbing in this unseemly manner.' Miss Simmons' thin lips curve upwards a fraction.

Is that a… a *smile*? Although on her governess's pinched face it resembles a strained grimace more than anything. Nevertheless, the unprecedented smile, as well as her words, give Alice pause, her sobs catching in her throat.

'The war's ended,' Miss Simmons declares, her lips moving more fully upward.

The war has hovered over every conversation, colouring and clouding everything, and appears to have been going on *forever*. Alice understands, from eavesdropping on conversations between her parents and at the parties they host, that there have been severe losses, deaths of relatives and friends. She is pleased the war has ended, she *is*, but right now hurt takes precedence again, rising in sobs that will not be stilled.

Miss Simmons, meanwhile, the rare smile tucked away and her face wearing its customary frown, is shooting disdainful glances at Mali, finally saying to him, while nodding at his weedy primate companion, 'You really shouldn't make a habit of consorting with these pests.'

Mali gives her an ignorant look and scratches his head, although Alice knows he understands much more English than he lets on. If she wasn't so upset, she would find this funny but now all she is aware of is the Raju-sized laceration in her heart.

'Shut the gate,' Miss Simmons commands Mali and when once again he pretends not to understand her, she repeats the instruction to Ayah, who relays it in Hindi to Mali.

The rescued monkey stays close to Mali, who sighs dramatically and says, 'You might as well come with me, then.' Seemingly understanding Hindi, the monkey happily follows Mali back into the compound, not sparing a second glance at the other monkeys who, once the gate is closed, hold onto the bars and jump on each other's shoulders to try and scale it, and when this fails, chatter indignantly while peering inside.

'Miss Harris, your lesson starts in fifteen minutes. I want you ready and in my classroom by then. You're not a child any more but growing into a lady. That wailing is unseemly, you'd do well to stop it at once. The war ending is a cause for joy – England is celebrating, rightly so, and we will do some suitably victorious activities in our lesson today.' Miss Simmons smiles again, while sweeping up the drive towards the house.

The rescued monkey squats beside Mali as he starts digging in the vegetable patch and Alice, even in her distress, clocks the look on its face, which can only be described as smug, while Mali's is resigned.

'Missy Baba, you heard your governess...' Ayah's voice is gentle.

And now the words come in an anguished gush. 'This is why you arranged the surprise, isn't it? To distract me?'

Mali sighs, turning to Ayah, 'All your surprise achieved is me being stuck with this little thing.' But his voice is affectionate as he looks at the monkey: 'What shall we call you, eh? My little shadow. Saaya. Yes, that'll do.'

'Missy Baba, it's almost time for your lesson...'

'I'll not attend without Raju,' Alice cries.

Ayah concedes defeat. 'I'll send for him.'

Alice has got her way. But why, she thinks, as she waits by the gate for her friend, does she not feel comforted, even when she sees him arriving, up the mud road, past the nattering monkeys? For he is red-faced and sullen, a scowl on his usually beaming face. He will not meet her eyes. She swallows as he approaches, says around the boulder in her throat, 'Hello, Raju.'

He looks up at her, unsmiling. His familiar, dear features are distorted by the unfamiliar grave expression in which they've arranged themselves. 'Here I am, Missy Baba, a coolie doing your bidding.' Every word hard and hot, like a sharp-edged, sun-grilled pebble piercing soft skin.

Raju is almost like an extension of herself. He reads her mind, knows her thoughts, he's her playmate, her friend. Yet right now, he's unrecognisable. Alice feels a thrill shudder through her. A mixture of fear and hurt and anger and pain and joy that he is here despite everything. She wants to throw her arms round him but is strangely shy, nonplussed by this version of the boy she thought she knew inside out. She doesn't know how to behave with this new version of Raju and so she hesitates.

He pushes past her. 'I'm going to see Cook, find out what she wants me to do while I sit in on your lessons. But rest assured, I won't be giving any answers. In fact, I—'

'Raju,' she says, taking his hand.

She has held his hand so many times before but now she is aware of the thrill intensifying, electric, convulsing through her body. He stops, looks at her. It is as if he has experienced it too, for his hard eyes soften, the unforgiving chocolate tempered with a molten dash of honey. But then he turns away, rudely shrugging off her hand.

'Don't be angry with me,' she says. 'I can't bear it.'

Her voice trembles and it is that which returns the Raju she knows to her. He has never been able to bear seeing her hurt, distressed. The last of the hardness leaves his expression and his eyes shine caramel gold.

'Shall we go in? You're very late, Miss Simmons will be furious.'

Even the niggle of worry that this will be the last straw, propelling Miss Simmons to make good her threat of complaining to Father, cannot dampen her joy at *her* Raju returned to her.

'As if I care,' she says, beaming.

Chapter 21

Janaki

1951

Optimistic

'Janaki, my dear, do you have any idea why I've summoned you here?' Mother Superior asks. Seated behind her desk, the nun looks old. Tired.

Janaki muses on how she used to be terrified to be in this room, with its scent of incense and penance, sandalwood blue, frantically going over her actions, wondering what she had done wrong. How innocent she was then! How naive!

'Janaki, dear, it's a terrible tragedy, what happened, but I rather hoped by now you would have moved past it.'

Resentment and anger flares within Janaki. *I lost the only family I have ever known. How can I move past that?*

'It's been five years.'

As if I haven't counted every single minute of every day.

'You used to be such a happy girl, so full of life.' Mother Superior sighs. 'So... *optimistic*. Always looking on the bright side.'

That girl died with her adoptive parents.

'Anyway...' Mother Superior clears her throat. When she speaks again, she is brisk, the earlier nostalgic tone quite gone. 'You're fifteen now and it's time you started thinking about your future. Sister Shanthi tells me you mentioned wanting to work?'

Janaki thinks of the girl she once was, sitting with Sister Shanthi, weaving jasmine garlands and spinning dreams on somnolent afternoons perfumed with brewing tea, rising dough and baking dust. That happy, positive girl seems a world removed from who she is now. Although she's angry with Mother Superior for suggesting she should move on, Janaki knows she's right. And she *has* tried – for Arthy's sake as much as for her own.

Janaki had come upon Arthy in tears one afternoon, some weeks after she returned, bereft, to the orphanage. Arthy was sniffling into her mat when they were meant to be napping. At first, Janaki had ignored her friend, angry at her. *Why are* you *crying, what have you got to cry about?* she'd thought sourly. But she couldn't ignore her sadness for long. 'What's the matter?' she'd asked.

'I…' Arthy couldn't seem to find the words at first and then they arrived in a gushing burst. 'I know you're hurting, Janu, and I don't know how to help. I cannot bear to see you like this. I want my friend back, not this automaton who has taken her place.'

Somehow her friend's sorrow on her behalf had finally triggered her own, jolting her out of her numbness. She had sobbed unrestrainedly for the first time since she'd heard of her adoptive parents' deaths, Arthy holding her and crying right along with her.

Afterwards, she had promised Arthy that she would attempt to recover the girl she had once been. She had started by acknowledging her friends' little gestures of love and commiseration, instead of rebuffing them and retreating inside the protective shell she had encased around herself. She found that feeling and sharing *hurt*. Numbness was so much better.

But Arthy looked at her with love and worry, as did the little ones, and so she had tried. Whatever she did, she couldn't quite retrieve the cheerful self she had once been, always looking for the positive.

That girl was gone forever.

Five years on, she is still grieving for her parents. She is still dreaming every night, in glorious colour, of being encased in the warm arms of love; still musing about what might have been, and waking every morning to a world that, when compared with the loving, bright, kaleidoscopic world of her dreams, is drab and wanting.

For a too-brief time she had known what it was like to be loved, to be the centre of someone's world, and although she has attempted to move past what happened, and to accept her life as it is now, she cannot quite recapture the spark that had glowed bright within her; the conviction that she was worthy, that she was wanted, that she mattered.

'Janaki, you're extremely bright and I see you've applied yourself diligently to your studies,' Mother Superior is saying.

They've been a distraction. When Janaki studies, does her homework, she is able, for a brief while, to forget. Concentrating on historic battles, tussling with grammar, writing essays, solving maths problems engages her mind, takes her beyond herself.

'You're far ahead of your classmates in *all* of your subjects. You can choose any profession you want to and achieve success in it. Have you thought of what you might do, in which field you'd like to work?'

'No.' She has not given any thought to her future at all.

Mother Superior smiles kindly. 'Well, *I* have.'

Janaki looks at this woman and wonders how she could have been so afraid of her when she was younger. She's discovered this since she lost her adoptive parents. Seen through the lens of her tragedy *everything* is muted: fear, anger, all emotion.

With the air of someone bestowing a great honour, delivering a fabulous surprise, Mother Superior says, 'I've arranged for you, Arthy and some of the other girls who show promise in their studies to visit a very special lady. It will be an inspiring visit and I believe you'll come away changed.'

Chapter 22

Alice

1918

Falling

Alice is falling and there is no one to catch her.

'Raju?' she calls. 'Ayah?'

'Raju's in the fields with his father,' Ayah says, briskly. 'And I'm busy.'

Alice is dizzy, breathless with fear. Her eyes are shut tight so she can't look down, only aware of weightlessness as the air buffets her, her clothes puffing out around her.

'Mother?' she cries.

But Mother pulls her pillow over her head, annoyed. 'I have a headache. Sort it out yourself.'

'I need your help, Mother. *Please.*'

'And shut the door on your way out.'

'Father?'

'He's away,' Ayah says shortly.

'Mali?'

'He's tending to his plants aided by his little monkey shadow, Saaya.'

She opens her eyes and, suspended in the air, she can just see Father on his way to one of the towns within his jurisdiction.

'Father?' she calls.

He does not respond.

She cries louder, but he does not give any indication of having heard her, although she can hear *him* well enough, muttering to his companion: 'The war is ended in Europe but here, it's escalating. These coolies have upped their demand for self-rule, goaded by Bal Gangadhar Tilak, that traitorous Annie Besant and now Gandhi. The coolies look up to the man, revere him, call him *Gandhiji*. He can do no wrong in their eyes. It's a damned nuisance…'

In desperation, Alice looks around, sees Mali with Saaya, crouched in the vegetable patch, planting seedlings. 'Mali!' But Mali too is not to be disturbed as he gently, efficiently, works the soil.

And then, in the distance, she sees Raju toiling in a rectangle of green beside his father. '*Raju!*' she shrieks.

He looks up. Her heart beats out a rhythm of hope. *He's heard me. He'll save me.*

'*Raju…*'

He shades his eyes with his hands and squints into the horizon. '*I'm here! I need you!*'

Raju looks in her direction and for one tantalising moment she is seen. *He'll save me.*

Then he too turns away.

'I'm here…' Her throat is sore, her voice a whisper, 'I'm here, Raju.'

But he's dropped his hands and is turning to his father. She shuts her eyes. Her mouth tastes of salt and disappointment, briny blue. The wind batters her body.

Her heart breaks. She falls.

*

'Missy Baba, wake up!'

The throbbing, panic-flavoured taste of hurt and betrayal is in her mouth. Her heart is thudding, wounded… Beating. It hasn't stopped.

Her body is not battered and broken but whole. *It was a dream. Just a dream.* And yet… Her heart beats too fast, making as if to burst out of her ribcage. *The sense of something missing, awry. Not quite right.* Not just the dream rendering everything skewed...

Raju.

For the second day in a row, Raju is not waiting by her door. She is instantly awake, instead of being eased into wakefulness by his sing-song voice. Anxiety, sharp and cutting, is pushing away any lingering remnants of slumber, even as the fear and panic from the dreadful dream rises sharply to the fore.

'Where's Raju?' *Please don't say fields again.*

Ayah sits beside her on the bed, taking her hand. 'Missy Baba, you're getting older, growing into a young lady. It's not seemly for Raju to wait outside your room any more.'

'Why not? He doesn't come in. Where is he?' she asks again.

'He's waiting for you in the courtyard. Now, which dress shall I set out for you to wear today?'

But Alice is not listening. She is looking out of her window and down into the courtyard.

Raju is sitting on the washing stone by the well, talking to Mali while petting Saaya, the rescued monkey, who Mali is feeding with fruit. There's a girl sitting beside Raju, dressed in a sari the colour of dew-speckled fields, her face covered by one end of the sari draped over her head. She is stroking the velvety-emerald moss growing on the rim of the well, and her face, although hidden, is turned towards Raju. While Raju watches the monkey, grinning as it eats guava and bananas from Mali's hand, the girl is watching Raju.

Bile is rising in Alice's mouth. She wants to be sick, to disgorge the bitter remnants of the dream that pulses through her. *Everything is changing. Raju should be here with* me *instead of having another playmate watching him frolic with the animal that* I *saved.*

'Missy Baba,' Ayah is saying, 'you need to get ready or you won't have time for breakfast. Your governess is coming early today to make up for—'

'Who is she?' Alice asks, her voice vomit green.

Ayah comes to stand by her, looking down at the girl and her son, an indulgent smile upon her face. 'Jyoti, my cousin's daughter.'

'What's she doing here?'

'I thought it would be a good idea for her to spend time with Raju, seeing as they are betrothed and will be married when she comes of age.'

The sensation of weightlessness, of falling, with nothing to support her, no one to help… *Her dream.* Not really a dream, but an omen warning of what is to come. A premonition.

Chapter 23

Janaki

1951

Promise

'Mother Superior has arranged for us to go to the *slums*?' Arthy is aghast.

'It's an incredible opportunity. You'll be meeting Mother Teresa, who has started her own religious order, helping the poorest of the poor.' Sister Nandita's voice is thrumming with awe. 'I am to take you. It's an honour to meet such a pioneering nun.' Sister's eagerness and enthusiasm is palpable as she continues, 'She lives among the most underprivileged, saving lives that are deemed cheap, worthless by most.'

They arrive at the slums: tin, cardboard, mud and cloth huts crowded around reeking, overflowing sewers, packed with the destitute living in desperate conditions. Mothers with emaciated babies and sunken, pleading visages. The injured with open sores attracting flies, their helpless expressions scored with pain. Children, their skeletal bodies encrusted with dirt, faces hungry, snot dripping down noses and into open mouths.

Janaki is floored by shame. She has been wallowing in self-pity when there are people so much worse off.

They come upon a hive of bustling activity taking place in a makeshift cloth tent. A group of white-and-blue-sari-clad nuns are busily tending to the afflicted, who jostle and crowd as they wait to be seen, spilling out of the tent and onto the strip of mud that passes for a path beside a foul-smelling drain.

Sister Nandita comes to a halt, nodding at a small nun with a gentle face, who is deftly cleaning a stomach injury of a prone child.

'There she is,' she whispers, her voice thick with admiration, 'Mother Teresa.'

Mother Teresa is serene, her face calming. Her voice, when she addresses Janaki and her friends, is soft, and yet everyone around them falls silent. Kindness radiates from her.

'You are not alone, you have each other. You are loved by the nuns who care for you and most of all by God, who has created you. He's put you in this orphanage for a reason, to inspire, to grow in love and caring, and to set an example for everyone. It is our duty as God's children to look out for and help those who are struggling, in trouble, in need.'

Janaki listens, spellbound. She watches Mother Teresa and her aides tending to the sick, feeding and comforting the destitute. Mother Teresa is tender, empathic, unfazed by the worst afflicted, the very ill, her patience never failing as she provides solace, ministers, listens and soothes.

'She's amazing,' Janaki is moved to confide in Sister Nandita.

'She *is*.' Sister Nandita is effusive. 'She says it's her calling, to live among and help the poorest of the poor.'

Later, as Janaki attempts to bandage a wound, Mother Teresa comes up to her. 'You're a natural.' Goosebumps erupt on Janaki's skin at being praised by this nun.

'What would you like to be when you grow up?' Mother Teresa asks.

'I… I'm not sure.'

Mother Teresa smiles. 'You have soothing hands, a healer's aura. You are calm and don't flinch from wounds. I think you'd make an excellent doctor. As it happens, we need more women doctors, there're hardly any. It's hard to become one, and it's almost exclusively a man's world, but I see something in you. I think you'll make it.' Mother Teresa pats Janaki's head, her eyes bright. 'I'll pray for you, my child.'

On the way back after their visit to Mother Teresa the girls are quiet, reflective, absorbing all they saw and experienced.

Arthy slips into place beside Janaki, her face shiny with perspiration, eyes glowing with emotion.

'You know,' she says, 'when I saw all those people, suffering, desperate, crying out for help, I understood what you meant when you used to remind us how lucky we were to be at the orphanage—' She stops then, but Janaki knows what she wants to add: *Before…*

Before you were adopted. Before you experienced a different life and came back changed.

The air that wraps itself around them is soupy, flavoured with humid heat, the reek of stale vegetables, rotting fish and drains mingling with sizzling oil and roasting chillies.

'Do you think you'll take up Mother Teresa's suggestion and become a doctor?' Arthy asks.

Janaki looks at the blinding sun, the hot white sky, yawning, endless. 'I… I don't know. When she said it, I believed I could.'

Arthy slips her hand inside Janaki's, sweaty and slick. Her voice in Janaki's ear is firm, coloured with bright, hot conviction. 'You will. You can.'

'How can you be so sure?' Janaki is curious.

'Janu, I was inspired today by Mother Teresa, just like Mother Superior hoped we'd be. I know you were too. Mother Teresa said there aren't enough women doctors. Shall we make a promise to each other? We'll both try our hardest to be doctors, spur each other on. What do you say?'

Janaki thinks of Mother Teresa, her gentle eyes passionate with promise and zeal. Her kindness, her ability to soothe. Her words: '*He's put you in this orphanage for a reason, to inspire, to grow in love and caring, and to set an example for everyone.*'

She looks at her friend who has stood by her, enduring her moods and her upset, loving her through it all. 'Yes, let's,' she says.

Chapter 24

Alice

1918

Truth

'Missy Baba, where are you going in such a hurry?' Ayah calls.

'Missy Baba? Aren't you having breakfast? What about lessons?' Raju cries when he sees her.

As she did with Ayah, Alice ignores Raju, his urgent voice only just piercing the drumming in her ears, the whoosh of hot blood flooding her veins, ringing in her heart. She had persisted in thinking – despite understanding that Ayah is at Father's mercy, despite knowing that being such close friends with a coolie wasn't the 'done' thing – that she and Raju would continue always, just as they were.

She had chosen to believe that Raju, too, couldn't countenance any alternative; that he too felt as though a vital part of himself was missing when she wasn't there, each incomplete without the other. How foolish she had been.

Despite being aware of their differences, she'd been lulled by their continuing friendship into disregarding them. She had only seen what had always connected them: their closeness; how Raju read her thoughts as they entered her mind, sometimes even before she'd made sense of them herself; how he had always been there, her friend and companion, featuring in her earliest memory and almost every one after that.

'Come back, Missy Baba, where are you off to?'

She ignores the servants' cries, trying to outrun the knowledge splintering her heart.

The monkeys, emboldened by Mali's adopting one of their kind, have colonised the fruit trees *inside* the compound. Crows cackle and peacocks dance. All around, there's the scent of ripening fruit and crisp morning.

Maids are shelling tamarind – tart, tangy, knobbly brown – and setting chillies, bright, fiery red, in neat rows on cane mats to dry. The voices calling for her fade away, all except Raju's, because he is still behind her. She cannot, will not, stop, needing to outrun her pain and the turmoil rabid in her chest.

If she'd thought of the future at all, she'd pictured it as a continuation of the present. With her and Raju doing everything together. She had not allowed reality to intrude into this fantasy: the fact that her parents wouldn't approve; that they might get wind of her closeness with a coolie and put a stop to it. That Raju would, one day, marry. That she would, too. That people would come between them.

That girl, whose face she still hasn't seen, small and wearing a sari... Right for Raju, she knows. He will look after her like he has looked after Alice. *She will come first.*

It is that thought that sparks a fiery blaze.

I am never *first, not for anyone. Especially not for my parents. For Father, it's work. For Mother, herself. For Ayah, Raju comes first. I thought that at least with Raju...*

It is all too much. Alice is at the lake but she doesn't stop, she cannot. She wants this roiling, scalding upset to be extinguished. She runs right in.

'No, Missy Baba! It's deeper than you think! Dangerous!'

It is a relief when the water takes over, swilling currents pulling her down. There's a sensation of being weightless, suspended. Like in her dream. Cool green water is enveloping her, tasting of weeds and slime, smelling of mildew and algae, filling her ears, a rushing whoosh, drowning out her anguish, taking away her ability to breathe.

Water, enveloping, gushing, obliterating… A moment's fraught peace from her thoughts as her body fights for breath. This fight is physical and nothing to do with her. Then hands are jerking her, pulling at her. 'No!' She opens her mouth to scream, 'leave me!'

But water rushes in, swallowing words, leaving only sensation. Hands are on hers, strong, familiar. *Raju.* Gasping. Panting. Struggling for breath as he treads water, pulling her to the shore.

She is sick again and again, bringing up earth and bile. Spent, she lies there, among the reeds, her wet clothes clinging to her, shivering in the soft morning breeze, which smells of swamp and sun. Frogs croak, water lilies float serene. The sun, warm gold, beneath her closed eyelids.

'What were you thinking, Missy Baba?'

Her eyes fly open at the uncharacteristic, barely controlled rage in Raju's voice.

'Good job I'm taller than you, eh?' Relief throbs through the fury. He has shot up in recent months, now towering over Alice, his shoulders broader.

'I was able to tread water a little further than you, pull you to safety. Thank the gods! You know I can't swim, you could have drowned.' His voice breaks. 'What would I have done then?' His eyes are wide and shining with hurt in his dripping face.

She manages a hoarse, 'You would have coped.' Her mouth is still slimy with the taste of stagnant lake water. 'You have your betrothed.' Her voice is small, beaten, choked with bile and tears.

He squats down beside her, takes her hand in his. 'Missy Baba, she is not *you*.' His voice is soft, thick with emotion. 'Nobody can take your place. No one.'

She looks into his eyes and sees all they have shared, all they have been to each other. No one can take it away from them. She realises now that it won't always be like it has been, even between the two of them, but in this moment, she is comforted.

Having seen into his eyes, she knows that even though everything might change in future, what she has believed about what they have is shared by him too. It is truth, *their* truth. And for now, regardless of what is to come, it is enough.

From the house Ayah calls, 'Missy Baba! Raju!'

Raju smiles at her, gently. 'You gave me a fright, Missy Baba.'

She nods, emotion taking over, robbing her of words.

He says, his voice wobbling, 'I thought I'd lost you.'

It is just how she had felt when she saw his betrothed sitting beside him in her place.

'Here…'

He wades into the water and returns with a water lily squatting on entwined leaves the burnished emerald of a promise. Tenderly, he hands her the lily, its petals the buttercream of dawn's first kiss, enclosing a golden heart smiling at Alice from two heart-shaped leaves.

'That's you,' Raju says, pointing to one of the leaves. 'And that's me,' nodding at the other. 'And this is what we have together.' He smiles, pointing at the lily: 'A beautiful, pure friendship.'

Chapter 25

Alice

1918

Taint

That evening, when Alice is summoned to Mother's room (Father is away, sorting out a skirmish in one of the border towns), she takes along Raju's gift: the gold-tinted water lily nestling on its cushion of entwined leaves.

Mother is sitting by the window as always, framed by jasmine-scented shadows that sway and swell with the tantalising promise of secrets. Sweet, perfumed breeze, cool with the portent of night, thrums soothing lullabies. Mother's hands fly, knitting needles clacking, even as she nods at her daughter.

'Mother,' Alice says, 'would it be possible for me to knit a scarf in this pattern?'

Her mother frowns at the entwined leaves holding the water lily within. 'I think I have yarn in those colours. Look in the drawer for me, will you, please?'

As she guides Alice's fingers, their two golden heads bent side by side, Mother says, 'My mother could knit any pattern, however intricate.'

'You're good too,' Alice says, knowing by now what will elicit a smile from Mother.

'I try.' Her mother beams. 'Mother wanted to teach both my sister and myself, but Edwina wasn't interested; she wanted to travel, to see the world. Yet she's in England, with Bertie home safe from the war, thank goodness, while here I am. Unlike Edwina's dreams, mine were simple. A dashing husband. A great big mansion in town. Soirées and masquerades. Tennis and card parties.' Mother sighs deeply. 'I did get the dashing husband. As for everything else...' Another sigh. 'During the daytime when the harsh heat crawls under my skin and I cannot be comfortable, I dream of the cool green vistas of home and imagine a different life.'

Do I feature in this different life? Alice wonders, as she looks at her mother's pensive face and starry eyes, with their longing and their faraway dreams; hears her voice, full of aching and yearning peppered with nostalgia. But of course, deep down she knows the answer.

Everybody but Alice knows where they belong. Mother thinks she belongs in England, she longs for it, a vivid pulsing wound of craving. Father belongs with his job. Raju's life has been decided for him. He will marry his betrothed. He will be a farmer.

Where do I belong? What is my destiny 'Ow!' Lost in musing, she's poked herself with one of the needles, reopening a cut on her finger that had just begun to heal.

Blood, bright scarlet, is blooming on blanched, creamy skin and staining the pattern that is taking shape on the scarf: a minuscule crimson taint on the white lily petals.

She will finish the scarf, bemoaning the tiny, ruby smear marring the pure perfection of the lily, and give it to Raju. He will beam, his whole being alight, fingering the scarf. 'You *made* this for me?' he will say, his voice awed.

She will blush, embarrassed. To deflect his attention away from her flaming cheeks, she'll point to the rust-red of dried blood blotting the edge of the lily. 'Sorry about that, I pricked myself.'

His eyes will open wide, upset shining in their caramel depths. 'Where, show me?' Taking her hand.

'It's nothing. I've done so a hundred times. You get used to it when learning to knit. I should have been paying more attention really, I should know better by now than to...' She will waffle on to hide the heat spreading through her as he very gently runs his finger over every one of the welts and calluses on her hand.

Then he will look up at her, his gaze earnest. 'Thank you, Missy Baba. I will treasure this scarf always.'

And Alice will feel tears sting her eyes, a jumble of emotions taking her body hostage. She will be glad of Miss Kitty, who will choose that moment to wrap herself around Alice's legs, purring. She will bend to pick the cat up, bury her confusion in its warm fur, while also bereft at having to reclaim her hand, wanting to leave it in her friend's tender clasp forever.

Chapter 26

Janaki

1951

The Centre of Someone's World

'Wake up, Arthy, the bell has gone and Sister Nandita has no patience with dawdling older girls,' Janaki mutters.

'You know better than to break the rules,' Sister Nandita admonishes sharply, if they are even a minute later than she expects.

Arthy has never been one to wake up on her own, she always needs a nudge. But usually once Janaki whispers urgently in her ear, she startles awake. Not so today.

'We don't want to be punished,' Janaki says, sighing.

Punishment for the older girls is sweeping and mopping the floors of the entire orphanage, cleaning and polishing the holy statues in the chapel, of which there are many (Arthy swears they multiply every night; evidence of the miracles the nuns keep going on about), and doing the most difficult and unpleasant jobs in the kitchen; all this in addition to their mountain of homework and their other chores.

Janaki will not countenance leaving Arthy to get up when she wants, to face punishment on her own. She bends to shake her friend and that is when she realises that Arthy's face is flushed, her body hot to the touch. 'Arthy?' Janaki's voice is a frightened, cowed sliver of a thing.

Her friend does not stir. How could Janaki have lain beside Arthy and not known her friend was ill? She thinks back to the previous evening. Arthy had complained of feeling tired but Janaki had not paid heed. They were always complaining to each other. It is what they *did*.

Arthy, Janaki realises now, thinking back frantically, has been complaining of being tired more often recently. Always thin – they all are at the orphanage – she has recently got even thinner, her skin darker, almost scaly.

Janaki had commented on it, two evenings ago, when she put her arm around her friend and noted just how bony she was getting. 'You really should eat your porridge and chapatis instead of shifting them onto my plate, never mind the worms, Arthy. You're getting positively skeletal and your skin is dry and flaky. If you don't watch out, you'll wake up as a lizard one day and then you'll have to eat flies!'

Arthy, instead of laughing or hamming it up, as she usually did, had sighed irritably. 'I'm *fine*.'

The previous night, she had slipped into sleep almost as soon as they had lain down on their mats. Now, Janaki wonders why she hadn't questioned this; it was a first for Arthy, who usually needed to unwind by talking about her day, whispering all her observations to Janaki, analysing and dissecting what she had seen and done. Then she would speak of her dreams.

She'd stopped talking of wanting to be adopted after Janaki had come back in deference to Janaki's hurt, but Janaki knew she still hoped for it, although gradually that hope must have dwindled. Not many prospective parents have come to the orphanage looking to adopt in the time since Janaki has been back.

Since their visit to Mother Teresa, Arthy has focused on their dreams for the future. 'We'll be women doctors in a man's world. We'll have our pick of boys.'

'Is that why you want to be a doctor?' Janaki had teased. 'I thought it was because you were impressed by Mother Teresa.'

'That too. We'll rise to the top of the profession, of course. And having all those men looking up to us won't hurt.'

Arthy had squeezed Janaki's hand, her own soft and sweaty in the humid darkness, pulsing with wistful, fantastic dreams. Her voice, fired with conviction for a dazzling future, had chased away their sadnesses and day-to-day upsets with starry-eyed hopes.

'Arthy,' Janaki cries now, panic knotting her stomach.

Her friend stirs just slightly but she doesn't wake. Her body is too hot, her dark face flushed.

Janaki runs all the way to Sister Nandita, who scolds, 'Why are you not…?' And then, taking in the expression on Janaki's face, the annoyance leaves her. 'What's the matter?'

'It's Arthy. She's ill.'

Sister Nandita immediately accompanies Janaki to where Arthy lies unresponsive on her mat. The nun rests her hand on Arthy's forehead, her face grim. She shakes Arthy gently, 'Arthy? Child?'

Arthy mumbles something incoherent without really waking up.

'I'll take it from here, Janaki,' Sister Nandita says firmly.

'But, Sister—' Janaki protests.

'Arthy will be fine, it's just a fever. It will heal, we'll make sure of it. Go, attend to your chores.'

And, with one last glance at her ailing friend, Janaki, momentarily soothed by the conviction in Sister Nandita's voice, does as she's told.

All that day, whenever she gets a moment, Janaki checks up on her friend, who has been moved to the sickroom.

Arthy is delirious, mumbling incoherently, her fever not coming down despite the nuns' ministrations.

That night Janaki cannot sleep, the empty mat beside her bereft of Arthy and her sweet voice pouring out plans for the future she has envisioned for the both of them, colouring the darkness with a vivid rainbow of wishes.

Over the next few days, Janaki spends all her free time in the sickroom keeping vigil by her friend, alternating between fear and torment, prayer and pleading.

Please, Arthy, get better.

The nuns make potions, feeding them to Arthy, but she immediately vomits them back. They wrap her in saris to bring the fever down. They put cold compresses on her forehead. But the fever shows no sign of abating: Arthy is getting thinner and thinner until she's just flimsy skin encasing jutting bones.

When her glorious fall of hair – 'My best feature,' she's always maintained – litters the rolled-up sari standing in for a pillow in long, brittle strands, the panic that has been Janaki's companion since she woke to find Arthy ill escalates into full-blown terror. 'Why isn't she getting better?' she asks the nuns, begging for reassurance.

'She will,' they say, as they busy themselves changing Arthy's cold compress and pounding herbs for yet another poultice: the green, spicy, fennel-and-cumin scent of evasion. 'These fevers take time to break.'

Their voices lack the credibility Janaki is seeking, leaving her even more anxious and agonised rather than less. She is unable to settle, worrying despairingly about her bright, vivacious friend wasting away in the sickroom, her weight and her beautiful hair falling off in spades, when she should, by rights, be going about her day, trying her best to make her dreams a reality.

As the days go by, with Arthy showing no sign of improving, Janaki becomes more and more anguished. She cannot sleep and during the dragging moments of night, unalleviated by her friend's presence beside her and Arthy's breathless voice spinning happy fantasies, Janaki's fears populate and multiply, flaring into demons that taunt and terrorise her.

When one week becomes two and Arthy is *still* ill, Janaki begins negotiations with the gods.

I haven't prayed to you properly since my parents died. But now I come to you, humbled. Make Arthy better and I will do anything you want. I will sing your praises. I will devote an hour to prayer each day – more. Please.

She's all I have.

'Come on, Arthy,' she implores, sitting by her friend's bedside, taking her scorching hand in hers, a measly collection of fragile bones, so scarily flimsy. 'Remember our dreams? We'll be pioneering women doctors. We'll fend off the men who come flocking…' She pauses to wipe away a tear as her friend lies, immobile, her face gaunt, eyes closed. 'Arthy, where has your determination gone? Please get better for me. You have so many things to do, a life to live.'

Fear now replaces Arthy as Janaki's constant companion.

Every day, as she sits by Arthy's mat in the sickroom, noting, without meaning to, the signs of her friend's gradual fading away – how she takes up less than half the mat now, how the strands of hair that remain barely cover her scalp – Janaki tells her friend, 'You *will* get better. The nuns have tended innumerable sick children over the years, some of them much worse than you,

Arthy. Munnu, for example. We all thought he would die, but that was just the fever having its way, like it is doing with you. Munnu was up to his usual cheeky mischief a few weeks later. You will be too.'

There is no question of sending for a doctor. It is an outrageous expense that cannot be justified unless it's something like a broken bone protruding through skin, which cannot be fixed through the nuns' ministrations. 'We have more experience than any doctor,' the nuns have reiterated often, 'especially when it comes to children and their illnesses.'

'Have there been any children you haven't been able to cure?' Janaki garners the courage to ask now.

'Yes,' the nuns agree, their eyes dimming, their gazes haunted by those they couldn't save. 'But very few and far between.' And, seeing Janaki's expression, 'Child, it's two or three over the many decades this orphanage has been running. Although we're devastated to have lost those children, it's a very small percentage. Doctors lose more in a year than we have all this while. There, that should set your worried little heart to rest.'

So, Janaki spends her days in constant terror juggling with hope.

Praying, bargaining with the gods, and wishing.

Her steps quicken with the hope, each time she nears the sickroom, that she will find her friend awake and protesting in her melodious voice, reminiscent of birdsong: 'I go to sleep and wake to find myself bald. What sort of trick is this?' Her friend, who is able to conjure a smile even when there is none to be had, who finds something to joke about even in the most horrific of circumstances, and who in these and other ways makes life bearable.

Janaki's fantasy propels her along the last few paces to Arthy's sickroom. At the doorway, courage suddenly leaves her, hope dwindling more quickly than it has arisen.

She pauses, sending up a prayer. *Please.*

Walking to Arthy's mattress, feet dragging, hope dissipated, despair descending, even as she finds her friend unconscious, as always. Boiling hot. Unresponsive.

None of the nuns' remedies appear to have made any difference to Arthy's condition, Janaki notes with rising panic. It has, in actual fact, been getting worse. *It's just the fever having its way,* Janaki tells herself. But with every passing day, she is finding this harder to believe. Arthy's skin, brittle and flaky, starts discolouring in patches. She smells of heat and illness, vomit and bile.

One morning, when Janaki visits, she notices her friend's stomach jutting out. Arthy hasn't been eating a thing, yet her belly is protruding; soft, insistent, obscene, when compared to the rest of her emaciated body.

Janaki watches with a heart crushed by a boulder of panic as the nuns lose their cool, one by one, their faces grim, eyes anguished. Even Mother Superior, usually unflappable, is looking flustered as she says, 'Send for the doctor.'

At this, Janaki's fear moves to a whole new level. Mutely, she holds her friend's scalding hand, praying, *Please. Save my friend. Please.*

The orphanage cannot afford the expense of doctors. In all her time here, the doctor was called only once that Janaki recalls, when Maya broke her arm falling off the mango tree where she was not supposed to climb.

For all other ailments the nuns are there with their potions and a big bag of medicines which they've sifted through and tried feeding Arthy to no avail.

All that long day, Janaki keeps vigil, refusing to move from beside her friend.

'Where's the doctor?' she cries as Arthy's fever rises higher and higher.

'He's coming.'

As the sun dips behind the horizon, her friend goes very still. 'Arthy?'

Janaki watches her friend's chest. *Please.*

After a beat, two, it rises. Janaki lets out the breath she herself is holding.

Although Arthy is breathing, each breath is laboured. So very slow.

'Arthy,' Janaki tries, the taste of desperation and terror blue-black and hopeless in her mouth, 'remember our dreams? The promise we made to each other of being doctors together?'

She tries to keep the panic that swamps her from her voice, aiming for upbeat. It requires immense effort: 'You need to get better. Please.' Here, Janaki's voice shakes despite her best efforts. 'We're going to be roommates while studying, we agreed. And after we become doctors, we're going to live together. Remember? We're going to make a difference, change lives, like Mother Teresa, your idol. But for that, you have to get better.'

Her friend's breathing is getting more uneven. Slower. One breath to three of Janaki's. '*Please,* Arthy.' And then, shakily, 'I can't lose you too.'

When Sister Malli returns with the doctor, it's far too late. Janaki's friend is unnaturally still, her body rapidly cooling.

'Black fever,' the doctor says, sighing. 'You should have called me sooner, she could have been saved.' Shaking his head. 'I see this all the time. What a waste!' But he charges for his visit, of course. An exorbitant sum.

The doctor's words go round and round in Janaki's head, a horrific chant: *You should have called me sooner, she could have been saved.*

Her friend's life has been lost just because doctors are expensive.

Arthy.

Bright. Vivacious. So full of life. Happy-go-lucky, mischievous and cheeky, but kind. Loving and wanting to be loved. 'I want to be the centre of someone's world,' she'd say, with wistfulness and yearning.

You were, of mine, especially after I lost my adoptive parents.

'I want to make a difference,' she declared.

I will make a difference on your behalf. I will become a doctor, do what we promised each other, make the dreams you spun for both of us a reality, live for both of us. I won't charge exorbitant fees and I will make sure I am always available to those who need a doctor, regardless of whether they can pay or not.

You will not have died in vain, my friend. I promise.

But no more loving for me. No more caring for or depending on anyone. I cannot, will not, risk it again, Arthy. Everyone I care for dies. Leaves me.

My heart cannot take it. It can't.

Chapter 27

Alice

1920

Prophecy

'Stop peeking! You'll get us caught before we've even started.' Raju pulls Alice back down into the nest of dirty linen, settling it over both of them, the pungent odour of stale sweat assaulting Alice's nostrils.

At Raju's touch, Alice experiences a thrill that rocks her being. *Does he feel it too?* she wonders, looking at him.

'What?' he asks, and she blushes, looking down at the white top she's fingering, yellow at the collar with sweat.

Alice has been shy on and off around Raju lately. It flares without warning, every so often when Raju grabs her hand without thinking; when she realises just how much taller than her he is now, although, at sixteen, only a year older than her; when she registers his new, deep voice, the hair sprouting on his face.

It is a hot, indolent afternoon, suffused with the scent of roasting earth, with drowsy bees sated on nectar and flies clustered around ripening fruit. Raju and Alice are hiding in Dhobi's linen cart.

If Ayah was to see Alice now, she'd be scandalised. 'You're growing into a young lady, Missy Baba. You're not meant to be swanning off on adventures with a boy, even if it is only my Raju!' she'd say. But Ayah is soundly asleep; she thinks Alice is having her afternoon siesta beside her – a tradition she insists on continuing. Alice doesn't mind, because that is the time she escapes on jaunts of her own, away from Ayah's eagle eye.

Ayah is snoozing as she does after her heavy lunch – rice and chapatis, fried okra and *dum aloo* – in a room off the kitchen. There's no more sleeping on the veranda: 'You're a growing girl, it's unseemly.' Raju is shooed off after lunch to help Mali; he is not to stay with them as before, for the same reason.

Ayah still hasn't cottoned on to the fact that Alice does not stay napping alongside her. Alice knows, through years of observation, that Ayah never wakes for at least two hours after she's fallen asleep, and, just before she does, Alice slips beside her, her breath tasting of the adventures she's had with Raju; sweet, stolen moments, hidden escapades all the more wonderful and exciting for having got away with it. She lies there, eyes shut tight, stirring only when Ayah yawns.

'You always protest about this nap but you wouldn't be disturbed even if the sky fell down around you,' Ayah says fondly, when Alice stretches as preamble to waking, yawning long and loud. 'I had a little shut-eye but kept checking on you. You were in such deep sleep; you need it, growing girl!'

Today, Ayah has not been well and knowing she'll rest long into the evening, Alice snuck outdoors as soon as she fell asleep, meeting Raju at their pre-arranged place among the tamarind trees in the orchard, which are right by the gates.

Seeing Dhobi arrive at the gates with clean linen in his bullock cart, Alice had been struck by sudden inspiration and had come up with this plan to escape in the cart. Raju, always rule-abiding, had tried to dissuade her.

'Just outside the gates, Raju. Just this once. We'll be back before Ayah wakes.'

'What if we're caught?' His eyes were wide, worried.

'We won't be, if we stick to my plan.' Alice was confident. 'Please?'

And Raju had given in, just as she knew he would.

Alice and Raju had discreetly followed Dhobi's bullock cart on foot. It had come to a stop at the servants' entrance into the kitchen. While Dhobi handed the washed linen over, Alice and Raju had climbed into the cart, taking care not to disturb the neat piles of clean clothes still waiting to be delivered to Dhobi's various customers. They hid under the piles of dirty laundry tossed haphazardly at the back, which Dhobi had collected from other houses along the way.

Dhobi is engaged in intense discussion with Mali, while the maids go through every item of clean and pressed clothing he's handed over to check that it's all in place.

'I'm taking part in the Satyagraha March on Sunday,' Dhobi is saying. 'You should come too, show your support for Gandhiji's non-cooperation movement. The more of us, the better. It's time we showed them that atrocities like that massacre at Amritsar last year, when their troops killed several hundred of us, cannot be allowed. We need India to be governed by Indians, not this lot.' Dhobi waves his hand in the direction of the house while spitting vehemently into the rose bushes.

'Shhh,' Mali says as he works the soil, Saaya beside him, looking surreptitiously around, before wiping the perspiration off his face with the back of his muddy arm, 'The walls have ears, you know.'

'Dhobi,' one of the maids checking the pile calls officiously, 'there were five trousers to be pressed and three dresses. I can see only two dresses.'

Dhobi spits even more vigorously onto the rose bed before turning, all smiles, to the maid. 'I'm sure you're...' he's saying, but Alice does not hear the rest of his sentence as Raju pulls her back down.

Hidden among soiled linen, dried sweat, trapped dust, faint perfume, the taste of adventure displaced by the hot fiery burst of ire at Dhobi's words, Alice queries, 'Are Mali and Dhobi planning to usurp us, take our place?'

'O... of course not!' Raju's gaze is flustered, shifting away from hers. 'They're upset that so many people were killed at...'

Alice knows what happened at Amritsar: how General Dyer opened fire on a gathering of Indians. It has dominated Father's conversations during his rare evenings at home. Alice has shamelessly eavesdropped upon him, this being her only means of getting to know the father she rarely sees. 'There was rioting. Englishmen were murdered, a missionary whipped,' Alice whispers heatedly, repeating Father's overheard words.

'That was *before*. But in retaliation, General Dyer killed hundreds of unarmed Indians, women and children among them.' Raju's breath is hot and pungent.

'Are you in cahoots with Mali and Dhobi, Raju?' Alice hisses.

'No!' he says, but his reply is weak, unconvincing.

Alice is overcome by an impulse to pinch him, hard, to vent her fury. She wraps her hands around her waist instead, saying, 'Well, they, and you, if you join them, will have to reckon with Father.'

But Raju is cocking his ear. 'Shhh, he's coming!'

They squat down low as a bundle of clothes is unceremoniously flung onto the interior of the cart. Her mother's scent wafts from the clothes: vanilla and boredom, sour sweet. The cart judders as Dhobi climbs on, he mutters at the bullocks and they're off.

Adrenaline replaces the anger caused by Dhobi's words. Alice pokes her head out of her disguise of other people's soiled clothes. She nudges Raju, dutifully ensconced within the foul-smelling fabric.

'We've done it!' Smiling, she watches his cautious head poke out, overcome by sudden affection, bright and blinding as her anger of earlier, for her friend with his tousled head, his worried expression, who does most things she asks, even if he is not completely comfortable with them.

Outside the gates, the cart stumbles on the unpaved road – no Mali to remove the stones here, to keep the path clean and smooth. Alice and Raju are jostled up and down on the cushion of soiled linen.

After a bit, the cart shudders to a stop. It sways as Dhobi presumably jumps off the front.

Alice and Raju, as one, duck down, pulling dirty laundry atop them as Dhobi comes round and roots among the clean linen. He grumbles to himself as he digs through it and when he has found the bundle he wants, he lets out a low whistle of relief.

When Dhobi's footsteps fade out of hearing, Alice whispers, 'Now!' and she and Raju shove off the linen and jump down the back of the cart

Alice and Raju blink in the sunshine, watching Dhobi disappear into the house across the road in a haze of dust. Monkeys are sitting on the branches of mango trees beside the road, heavy with unripe mangoes, tart green. The monkeys bite into the fruit, their keen and curious gazes switching from the bullocks to these humans who have suddenly appeared out of nowhere.

Alice and Raju run down the mud road.

It feels so freeing to be out of the stale fug of old linen, but the sun is hot and they are sweating in no time.

'What's that?' Alice asks.

Pairs of slippers are lined neatly on the mud beside steps that lead up to an awning with a bell attached to it. Although Alice stands on tiptoe, she cannot see beyond.

The monkeys, who have been following them at a discreet distance, eye the slippers too.

'The temple,' Raju says, nodding up the steps, 'you're not supposed to wear slippers in there.'

Alice looks at Raju's bare feet, inured to the scalding earth, clad only in dust.

'The temple is visited by everyone, you know, even those not rich enough to afford slippers.' Raju grins, his teeth glowing in his golden face.

Alice swats affectionately at him, the monkeys mimicking the gesture. Raju laughs, the air perfumed with flowers and incense, thick with dust swirling in the afternoon haze, seasoned by his waterfall of a giggle.

Women carrying baskets of flowers, fruit and a pail of milk between them approach. 'Shoo,' they say to the monkeys, who skirt up the peepal trees by the side of the road, chattering indignantly and, once safely ensconced among the branches, warily watching the women and their bounty.

The women, in their turn, eye Raju and especially Alice, curiously. 'What are you doing here, little memsahib?' they ask, smiling indulgently.

It is Raju who speaks up. 'I've brought her to see the guru.'

'World-renowned, he is.' The women nod. 'Come with us, we're going to see him ourselves.'

Alice leaves her shoes beside the rows of slippers. Once up the steps, she tugs at the rope to ring the bell, sound pealing, sombre gold from hammered bronze. The women lead them to the shrine directly ahead, of a deity smothered in garlands, the bright-orange scent of marigolds clashing with the more sedate, creamy tones of jasmine. When she is close enough to get a good look, Alice recoils from the deity's lurid blue face and bright red tongue.

A priest emerges, reeking of rose incense. He smiles at Alice and Raju, and as with the women they're following, he adorns their foreheads with vermilion and deposits *laddoos* into their palms.

'These *laddoos* represent Prasadam, a sacred offering blessed by the gods,' Raju says as they sit on the steps leading down to the temple pool, which is located in the centre of the vast temple courtyard, beside the women.

'Just to take the weight off our feet a minute,' one of the women had said, smiling. 'We're not young like you, you see.'

'This *laddoo* is tastier even than Cook's,' Alice says, marvelling, her legs dangling in the water lapping at their sweaty feet, washing away the dust. 'That god must be powerful to make this *laddoo* taste this good, although he doesn't look like much.' She scrunches up her nose as an image of the blue face and red tongue appears in front of her eyes.

'It's *she*,' Raju chuckles, starburst magic, 'the goddess Kali.'

Alice can't help but grin, Raju's laughter is infectious. 'Ah, that explains the *bindi*, the dot on her forehead,' she says.

There's a crowd of at least twenty gathered around the guru, but the people smile admiringly at Alice, patting her hair: 'A golden cloud' and pinching her cheeks: 'Look at you, so fair', and allow her to go to the front, with Raju tagging along.

The guru squats under the sprawling banyan tree in the temple grounds adjacent to the pool, a cobra – more menacing in appearance than the rat snakes that routinely invade Mali's territory in search of frogs – straddling him, hissing and flicking its tongue as they approach.

The guru opens his eyes. He is wearing a *dhoti*, a loincloth, his torso bare except for the snake that bisects it. 'You, girl with the golden hair,' he calls, his voice deep and cutting as a knife, slicing through the chattering crowd, 'come.'

Alice takes a few steps forward, staring at the man whose black eyes are bright and solemn as the sky heralding a storm, refusing to appear cowed although her heart is thudding so loud, she is sure all the assembled people can hear. 'You will suffer,' he says to her after a bit, his brooding gaze never leaving hers, 'in love and in life.'

A demurring sigh sifts through the crowd like wind soughing through fields. Even as Alice tries to absorb what the guru has told her, those all-seeing eyes shift to Raju: 'Oh.' The guru's eyes narrow, his pupils are pinpricks beneath the harsh heat of the sun beating down. The scent of fear and prophesy permeates the heat as the snake undulates across the man's body.

'Send someone else. Come!' The guru points at a woman in the crowd.

Alice is incensed, her fear forgotten in the face of injustice: 'What about my friend?'

The snake hisses, hood poised to strike, forked tongue darting wide at Alice's insubordination. A whisper rumbles through the collected crowd. She can sense Raju's fear, like an echo of her own.

'Some things are best left unsaid, child.' The guru's voice melancholy, seasoned with foreboding, causes Alice's heart to throb with apprehension. Every instinct cautions her to stop asking questions, to leave well alone. Raju tugs at her hand, wanting the same.

But she persists, stubborn, 'What do you mean?'

The guru closes his eyes.

Alice turns to the crowd, 'What does he mean?'

Raju whispers in her ear. 'I think it means my future isn't good.'

'Mine isn't either, he said I'll suffer. Why didn't he say anything about you?'

'Perhaps,' Raju says softly, carefully, 'because I have no future.'

'What rubbish!' Alice says, too loud to hide her panic at her friend's calm declaration. It cannot be, it cannot. She simply cannot picture a future without Raju in it.

'If you follow the path you're meant to tread, my son, you might be free of harm.' The guru has spoken. He has opened his eyes, which are grave and depthless as endless pools of glittery, swirling dark. He is looking right at Raju, who seems to shrink before Alice's eyes.

'First, you declare that some things are best left unsaid, then you say he might be free of harm. Make up your mind!' Alice's voice is harsh.

The crowd sucks in a collective breath. The snake has raised its hood and is hissing at her.

The guru ignores her, his gaze focused on Raju: 'Do what you're supposed to and you may just be able to avert the fate that is your destiny.'

As if that explains it, the guru closes his eyes again. Beads of sweat tremble above his lips. He looks spent, his complexion wan, as if looking into their future has cost him.

Alice, more afraid and angry than ever before, says sharply, to mask the fear and fury ricocheting through her, 'Let's go, this guru is useless.'

In a flash the snake is slithering down the guru and coming towards her, fangs bared, hissing. Alice stands where she is, stunned, sweaty fingers clinging to Raju's as behind them shocked whispers scud through the crowd.

'Come back,' the guru calls. His eyes are still closed, his voice calm yet compelling, hypnotic as the shadowy spell that is cast when night falls. The snake stares at Alice for a heart-stopping minute, its onyx eyes glinting with a thousand threats. Then it glides back up the guru's body, gently resting its head in the crook of the guru's neck.

Alice is shaking as she and Raju leave, still holding hands, the crowd silently parting for them. As soon as they have walked away from the temple, she feels lighter, the fear gone, but her anger is growing.

'He calls himself a guru, he's nothing but a trickster,' she rails all the way back home in the sunshine, the monkeys following at a safe distance, crows watching them from the trees.

Raju is silent, his lips set in a grim line so unlike his usual smiling countenance. His sombre expression reminds Alice of the hopelessness in his voice when he whispered in her ear: *Perhaps I have no future*, and some of her earlier fear returns. Can it be true? How can he have no future? What does it even *mean*? How dare the guru scare them so?

Only as they near the gates to her parents' home, when Alice declares, 'He's completely and utterly wrong,' does Raju speak.

'He's not.' So softly that she has to strain to hear above her panting breath, her pulsing anger. 'There was another sadhu Ma took me to.'

'When? Why didn't I come? Where was I?'

'It was that time you were ill. We went to pray for you. The sadhu said I would die young.'

The air tastes hot and metallic, of spilled secrets and fear. 'Wh— what do you mean? How young?' Alice cries.

'I… I didn't ask. I couldn't,' Raju says.

'They're all lying,' she whispers fiercely as they slip into the grounds.

The gatekeeper is, as always at this time of the afternoon, fast asleep, the gate left slightly open as they'd hoped it would be.

'It swells in the heat and sticks so it's easier to leave it slightly open than shut it all the way,' they'd overheard him telling Mali one afternoon and now Alice is glad for the eavesdropping that has served them well today.

Once safely inside, she squeezes Raju's hand. 'We shouldn't set such store by these gurus. Nobody can see into the future and if they claim to, they're nothing but tricksters.'

He nods, tries a smile, but he's not fooling either of them.

'That man is a scaremonger, a liar, a fake,' she tells Raju firmly, to convince herself as much as her friend, resolutely dumbing down the niggle of doubt, fear and worry. She is overcome, again, by bitter anger at the guru for causing this upset, for ruining their exciting, adventurous afternoon. Raju *does* have a future and it *will* include her. For she needs Raju in her life to validate who she is, make her feel better about herself.

She needs Raju in her life.

PART 6

India

Talisman

Chapter 28

Alice

1986

A Photograph

'You're not at all how I imagined you to be,' her visitor says.

'I'm sorry, do I know you?' Alice is wrong-footed by this girl, her exclamation, wonder and awe.

'No,' the girl says. 'No, you don't.' She takes a deep breath. 'But I was hoping you could help me.'

'Yes?' Help she can do.

'I…' The girl seems to be floundering, her confidence suddenly draining away, so that she appears even younger.

Why does she seem so familiar? Who does she remind Alice of?

'What did you expect?' she says, smiling encouragingly to try to make the girl feel comfortable.

'I'm sorry?'

'You said I'm not like you expected me to be.'

'I… I thought you'd be Indian.'

'Oh.' Alice smiles. 'I might not look it, but I *am* Indian. I was born here and have lived here almost all my life. For me, this is home.'

'I'm sorry, I… I didn't mean to offend…'

'No offence taken. I know just what you meant,' Alice reassures her.

She likes this girl. She is charmingly naive, she clutches her bag close to her as if it is a talisman.

'Tell me, what do you need help with?' Alice nudges kindly, for the girl appears more than a little lost.

'Oh! I do hope you can help and I haven't come all this way for nothing,' she says, all in a rush. 'I was convinced, you see, that I'd got it right. If you can't help, I'll have to start all over again and I have no leads other than you.' She seems close to tears and once again it strikes Alice just how young this girl is.

'My dear,' she says gently, 'tell me what the matter is and I'll try my very best to help you.'

Very carefully, the girl opens her bag and takes something out. She clutches it to her chest, briefly, fiercely, before handing it to Alice.

A photograph.

PART 7

India

Meaning

Chapter 29

Alice

1921

Blessings

Alice sits on the low-slung branches of the mango tree, breathing in the tart green scent of fresh mango, her dress ruched around her thighs. Raju is beside her, digging in his pocket for the rock salt he has stuffed in there, applying it to a mango and handing it to her first, before doing the same to his and taking a bite.

The sharp sweetness of the mango, mixed with the brine of salt, tingles Alice's taste buds, making them sing. Sunlight, like dappled butter, filters in through the canopy of leaves and pastes golden blessings warm upon her head.

Raju has taken the guru's prophecy to heart – although it's been months since their encounter with that man (charlatan, in Alice's opinion). He is often pensive, lapsing into a thoughtful moodiness, a sadness etched into his face, which Alice cannot dispel no matter what she says to try and convince her friend.

'He was just trying to create drama. First, he said he wouldn't tell your future and then all of a sudden, he changed his mind,' she's lectured. While Raju is still mulling over the prophecy, to Alice their encounter with the guru has acquired a dreamy quality, as if it didn't quite happen. 'And did you see how he called me first? Because I was different, standing out from the crowd? He was creating a sensation using me.'

'You don't understand,' Raju has countered. 'This guru showed me a way out. He told me how I could escape my fate, although I wish he'd been less vague.' Then, leaning closer to Alice, his breath, mango and mint, 'I'll work it out, it'll come to me. Anyway, he was certain about one thing; he said as long as I do what I'm supposed to, I'll be alright.' Then, looking at her, eyes wide and concerned, 'Do you think it means I shouldn't be meeting you here when I'm meant to be helping Mali?'

'Of course not! He meant the *big* things. Do what you're meant to do, don't try to be someone you're not.' Alice is improvising wildly.

To her surprise, Raju nods ponderingly. 'Yes, I think you're right.' Smiling, so that the worry lines creasing his forehead disappear, Raju of old, pre-prophecy, returns to Alice.

Alice and Raju lounge among the branches of the mango tree while Ayah naps, thinking Alice is doing the same beside her.

In the kitchen, the servants wash up the lunch dishes and start concocting tea-time snacks – frying *puris* and straining curd, chopping coriander to sprinkle over the spicy fried aubergine, roasting cashew nuts in *ghee* for *kheer*.

A burst of hot air ruffles the mango leaves and caresses Alice's face, carrying the cardamom, caramel and nectar aroma of a feast. Voices waft on the gritty breeze, approaching towards them. Alice exchanges a glance with Raju, pulls her legs up and squats cross-legged among the branches, Raju doing the same, their backs flat against the mango trunk.

It is Mali and Dhobi, with Saaya, the monkey, dancing alongside Mali, chattering away, its squeaking echoing the men's voices. 'Gandhiji is visiting the city centre on Sunday to talk about how we can all get involved in his non-cooperation movement against the British. It will be a chance to meet the leader of the Indian National Congress – you've no excuse.'

'But, I…' Mali hesitates.

'It's your duty as an Indian. Gandhiji needs every one of us to step up to the cause. It's the only way we can obtain independence. Already, thanks to his tireless efforts, the government is taking notice. Just imagine how much more effective it would be if we all presented a united front.' Dhobi is emphatic.

'I'll try my best to be there,' Mali says.

'That's the spirit, my friend.' Dhobi claps Mali on the back.

'India should be run by Indians.' Mali sounds determined now, as if Dhobi's endorsement has fired him up.

The monkey, as if picking up on the enthusiasm of the two men, is chittering faster, louder.

'The British have robbed us, drained us,' Dhobi says.

Alice gasps, quickly stifling the sound. The monkey, Mali's pet, stops walking, looking around it, puzzled, trying to place the sound.

'They take and take,' Dhobi is saying.

The breeze flings dust and grit into Alice's hot throat. The sun is harsh and bright, angling white-gold through speckled leaves, making her eyes smart. She plucks a mango from the tree and chucks it down. It glances off Dhobi's ear.

'What're you doing?' Raju mouths, even as he folds himself further into the branches.

Dhobi lets out a little 'ow' of pain and looks up, clutching his ear. 'Someone up in that tree threw a mango at me,' he says, indignantly.

Mali looks up too.

Alice pushes her back against the trunk, pulling her knees up to her chest, trying to disappear among the foliage, grateful she's wearing her green dress.

Mali blinks, the sun in his eyes, so he cannot see Raju and Alice, who are in shadow. 'Must be the monkeys. They're a nuisance,' Mali spits. Then, in a softer voice, patting his pet, 'Not *you*.'

But the monkey ignores him, looking right at Alice, pointing and chittering, beady eyes accusing.

After the voices have drifted away – the monkey remains standing resolutely beneath the mango tree until Mali calls, 'Come on, Saaya,' – then, with one last, angry glance up at them, it goes running to catch up with its master, tail sweeping the air – Raju says, 'You shouldn't have hit Dhobi, Missy Baba.'

'I *wanted* to.' She can still taste anger and hurt, fiery red, completely masking the taste of mango.

'They don't mean—'

'Don't.' She stares at Raju until he looks away, the sun painting shadows on his face.

'Anyhow, I got away with it.' She tries sounding nonchalant, so he cannot see how shaken she is by the extent of Dhobi's anger, his vehemence against British rule and Mali agreeing with him.

'The monkey wasn't fooled,' Raju says, trying for a lighter tone.

But Alice doesn't feel like smiling. She climbs down from the tree and runs away into the orchard, in the opposite direction to Mali and Dhobi. She runs until her panting breaths sound out the clamour in her heart. She runs to the lake and looks at it, stagnant and besieged by flies. She picks up a stick and throws it in the water with all her might, watching a cloud of flies swarm into the air.

When Raju catches up with her, she asks, without looking at him, 'Will you come with me on Sunday?'

'Where to?' Raju is alarmed.

'The city centre.'

'But, Missy Baba, no good can come of…'

'I just want to see…'

'We won't belong…'

'You mean *I* won't belong?'

'No, I…'

'I'm going. With or without you.'

'You can't go alone.'

'Why not?'

'Oh, alright then! I can see your mind's made up!' Raju sounding vexed.

'I thought you didn't belong.'

'Do you want me to come or not?'

'As long as you don't sulk.'

'I *never* sulk. So, what's the plan? How do we do this?'

She smiles, feeling her heart bloom open like a water lily, some of the joy of earlier on redeemed.

Chapter 30

Alice

1921

Freedom

Jamjadpur city centre is buzzing.

There's an energy here, a pulsing, raw thrill. '*Azadi through Satyagraha!*' shout people wielding placards. 'We will achieve freedom from British Rule through civil disobedience, non-violence!'

Alice watches, agog. She is wearing a sari – Raju's suggestion – the veil covers her face and she's glad that it does, for there are no white faces here. As it is she stands out; there are very few women.

'I'll get you one of Ma's saris to wear,' Raju had said.

She'd stared at him. 'Are you crazy?'

'Your hair, Missy Baba. It's beautiful, like spun gold, but honey-coloured hair will stand out.'

'Why should I hide?' she had asked.

'*Please.*' Raju had sounded desperate. 'We don't know what the mood will be like. Just wear it until we get there and then, if everything is okay, you can take it off.'

Although she gave in to Raju reluctantly and only because he very rarely pleaded with her to do something his way – more often than not he went along with her wishes – now, she is glad that she did.

The strength of nationalism, the hatred directed at people like her, frightens her. She pulls the end of Ayah's sari that she's using as a veil closer round her face. It smells of Ayah, sweat and coconut oil, ginger and onions. The soft, worn cotton imparts comfort.

'We want them out! They've raped our country, molested it, stolen from it long enough! We want control! We need freedom!' People keep arriving, spilling into the streets, barefoot and dusty, carrying cloth parcels on their backs; they must have walked all morning from their villages to be here. Those who live in the city gather at their doorways, children agog, women hiding behind veils, their eyes shy yet curious.

These people must be like Mali and Dhobi, working for sahibs such as her father, tending to their children. *But they hate us.* The thought makes Alice's heart beat faster, a shudder rocking through her, the bile-green taste of fear in her mouth.

Vendors taking advantage of the crowd circulate with *bhelpuri* baskets slung across their chest, the scent of raw onion, the tang of lime and spices. They sell groundnuts in paper cones and tea and coffee in small kettles, dispensing them in stainless-steel tumblers, then washing them under the trees using jugs of water, which they also carry.

The enthusiasm, the energy, radiating through the crowd brings to mind a great big party, but in honour of getting rid of people like Alice, whom they've decided don't belong.

But I belong, I do. This is my home.

A sudden hush descends on the crowd. Alice nudges Raju, 'What's going on?'

He nods towards the makeshift stage constructed of planks of wood piled atop each other. All heads are turned towards a man wearing a dhoti, who appears to have just arrived. He is small, unassuming. Bald head, bare torso, except for a white string bisecting it, a kind face, glasses.

Beside her, Raju goes very still. 'Gandhiji,' he whispers, his voice soft with awe.

'*This* is Gandhi?' The man everyone here speaks of with such regard and her father with great contempt?

And then, into the pulsing, anticipatory stillness, Gandhi speaks.

His voice is low but carrying. Every word is imbued with earnest, sincere passion and throbbing with urgency. 'We must set our differences aside and unite, Hindus and Muslims alike,' he says. 'We want India to be ruled by Indians and we will achieve freedom from British rule through *satyagraha* and non-violence.'

When he's finished speaking, there's a moment of pure silence then a rousing cheer. Alice finds herself cheering along, completely, thoroughly taken in. For a minute there, she has forgotten that *she* was the one they want freedom from. When Gandhi leaves, there's fierce discussion and a growing restlessness as the crowd digests and regurgitates what it has heard.

Caught up as they are in the patriotic passion instilled by Gandhi's words, it takes the crowd a while to register the shouting. A man has climbed onto the stage where Gandhi was just a few minutes before.

'Gandhi is mad to ask Hindus to join forces with the cow-eating Muslims. It's an insult to us Hindus!' he yells. 'It's sacrilege! Who is this Gandhi and what ulterior motives does he harbour? Why is he for Muslims at the expense of his own caste?'

The crowd erupts. Chaos. Rage. Clamour. Calls of: 'How dare you?' 'Who are you to defy/defile Gandhiji?'

Someone throws a stone at the man on the podium. In minutes, Gandhi's words are forgotten, his call for non-violence ignored, as people turn on each other.

'Down with Muslims!'

'Kill Hindus!'

Insults are exchanged. More stones are flung. Arms and fists are flying.

Raju grabs Alice's hand. 'Missy Baba, we need to get you away.'

They try to slip through the crowd, so docile while Gandhi was speaking, but now wild. Rabid with violent hatred.

As they run, Alice's sari veil slips.

'What is *she* doing here? Have the British sent a woman to spy on us?'

And suddenly people are turning on Alice. Surrounding her and Raju.

Alice cannot breathe. She wants to scream but is rooted to the spot, her mouth dry, sound swallowed up by fear. The mob is advancing, surrounding, entrapping… sour breath… thrumming… barely controlled rage, raised fists, fiery eyes.

Someone is pulling at her sari.

'*No!*' Raju, who is so quiet and kind, has suddenly become a tiger. He stands in front of Alice, her personal guard, and yells at the crowd, 'Is this what Gandhiji urged you to do just now? Torment innocent people? She is here, just like all of you, to support Indian independence. She's brave enough to turn her back on her own people to support us in our struggle for freedom for India and you want to pick on her? You should celebrate her! Don't you see how brave it is of her to come here? Instead of making a hero of her, using her as an example, you are turning on her. Shame on you!'

The crowd falls silent, considering.

Into the taut stillness, Raju says, 'Come, Missy Baba.' He takes her hand, leads her boldly forward. Alice's eyes are shut tightly as she stumbles in Raju's wake, her hand clammy in his, waiting for the heat of a slap, the pungent potency of saliva, the sting of mud, the wound of stones being flung at her.

But there is nothing. She opens her eyes a fraction: the crowd is parting for them, gazes averted with shame. Alice, her heart pounding with fear before, now full of admiration for her friend and rescuer. Raju, whom she has known from childhood and yet who has managed to surprise her.

They round a corner, then another, and stop, surprised. This section of the city is completely deserted. Shops, businesses, houses are empty. Baskets of spices, fruit and vegetable carts, kaleidoscopic cloth, utensils and multihued bangles are all glinting and wilting in the sun. Even the dogs and cows have gone to the city centre along with every single person it appears, so as not to miss the action.

They stand in the empty street trying to catch their breath. From the direction they've left come sounds of discord. The mob has resumed fighting: yells, screams, thuds, cries reverberate.

Alice throws her arms around Raju: 'You're my hero.'

His face is next to hers, his burnished caramel eyes are shining. She leans into him, bridging the gap between them, charged by impulse, relief and sudden, blinding desire.

She kisses him.

There is just the two of them, everything else – the sounds of rioting, people who were only a few moments previously united by Gandhi's words, their yearning for freedom, now divided, turning on each other – fading.

The taste of a thousand moments, a thousand lives. Her future, present, past, her everything given meaning. Here. Now.

'What do you think you're doing?'

The sound jars. The voice, familiar yet strange in this setting, is pulsing with fury, intruding into bliss. And then they're being pulled apart.

'I come here to quieten a mob and I find my daughter...' Father's voice is jerky with rage. '*My* daughter *canoodling* with a servant. Have you no sense? Have you gone mad?'

Alice, woozy from the kiss, upset at being separated from Raju, is terrified that Father has found her like this and unprepared for what happens next. Just as she becomes aware of the charged air, electric with rage, a hot throbbing is stinging her cheek, a ringing as her father's hand connects violently with her skin.

The shock of the slap propels her from loved-up dreaminess into the present.

'No!' Raju cries, hurting for her.

She had expected violence from the crowd, not from her own flesh and blood. Raju had saved her from the mob's anger but he cannot rescue her from her father's wrath, because he is being dragged away by her father's men.

In just a few seconds she goes from heaven to hell. From happiness and completeness, to upset, shock and hurt. As the events and the emotion of the afternoon catch up with her, she faints, his name, the taste of him in her mouth.

Raju.

Chapter 31

Janaki

1954

News

Dearest Arthy,

As always, it was wonderful to receive your letter, hear all your news.

I'm so happy you've applied to Cambridge University to study Medicine and are waiting to hear from them. You'll get a place, I'm sure; you've such talent, they'd be crazy not to take you. Thank you for the sketch you sent with your letter, it's such a perfect likeness of the orphanage! It has a wistful, nostalgic feel, it's almost as if you miss being here with us, ha ha!

Janaki sets down her notebook, her eyes filling up. It's three years since her friend died, but the pain is as fresh as ever.

She has constructed an elaborate new life for Arthy. It is the only way she can cope with her friend's loss; her constant, pulsing, throbbing absence.

After Arthy's death, Janaki had floundered. She had taken to her bed, hoping Arthy's fever would consume her too. She had forgotten the promise she'd made at Arthy's deathbed, that she'd live for both of them: she had just wanted to die.

She couldn't go on, not after the loss of the friend who had helped her cope with her other devastating loss; the friend who had been so vibrant, finding joy where often there was none, always making light of things that others found hard to endure, thus rendering them bearable. Always laughing, living life to the full.

How could she be gone?

Janaki wouldn't get up from her mat, wouldn't eat, wouldn't study. She ignored Bina, Shali and the others. The nuns used threats and when that failed, pleas.

It was Sister Shanthi who had got to Janaki in the end. She had sat beside her and said, gently, 'Arthy would hate to see you like this. She was in tears when you were apathetic on returning here after your adoptive parents passed, now she'd go to pieces.'

'Well, she's not here,' Janaki had been moved to reply.

'She'd want you to live for her, do all the things she didn't get to do,' Sister Shanthi had continued, unfazed.

And this, stated in Sister Shanthi's mild, matter-of-fact voice, had pierced the despair barricading Janaki's mind. Because it was exactly what she had promised Arthy at her deathbed; exactly what Arthy *would* want her to do. Now, Janaki could see that she was breaking her vow to her dearest friend.

'She'd want you to become a doctor, to realise your ambition and hers,' Sister Shanthi had pressed on. 'She'd be shuddering at your wasting of time, of your *life*, the squandering of the opportunities available to you, especially when she's been robbed of them.'

Janaki had pressed her face into the pillow, scented with her grief, trying to shut her ears to Sister Shanthi's voice stating truths it hurt to hear.

'I have to go now, the younger ones have a lesson with me,' Sister Shanthi had said after a bit, 'but I'm leaving this notebook behind.' Then, 'Write to her, Janaki. Imagine she's here, in this world, only far away. Create a life for her. Perhaps it will help.'

After Sister Shanthi had left, Janaki had sat up for the first time in days and, although light-headed, she'd picked up the notebook, leafed through the empty pages waiting to be filled, and had begun to write…

In Janaki's fantasy, Arthy is living the life she had always yearned for. She has been adopted by a kind and modern English couple (for, to Janaki, England is a world away while not being *too* inaccessible). They've taken Arthy to England with them and although she had found it a bit of a culture shock at first, cold and different, she loves it there now. She is the centre of her adoptive parents' world, loved to bits, just as she had always wished to be. She is happy and thriving.

If Arthy were here, she'd have adored this life Janaki has imagined for her:

> *Arthy, I missed you terribly when you first left, and to be perfectly honest, I miss you still.*
>
> *I did not fully comprehend how much I relied on you, how you lit up my life, from whispering secrets in the clammy darkness when we were supposed to be asleep to making me laugh with your wry observations. I even miss your grumbling and complaining. While I am happy you got what you wanted, adoptive parents who chose you – I'll never forget the look of awe and disbelief on your face when Mother Superior said the Langdons had picked you and*

that they wanted to take you with them to England – I did not realise how vital a part of my life you'd become.

Missing you hurt so much that I've decided not to get too close to anyone ever again. I can imagine your raised eyebrows, that way you shake your head, the fond exasperation as you say, 'But, Janu, you need to rely on someone.'

'Emotions are messy, caring for people renders you vulnerable. Best to rely on myself only,' I'd reply, if you were here in front of me.

'You care for me, *don't you?'*

I do, Arthy, but I wish I hadn't got too attached; I wish I'd kept my emotional distance from you too.

Although I wouldn't say this out loud, you'd read my mind, squeeze my hand. You'd be gentle as you chided, 'You cannot live your life without love, Janu.'

I can *and I will.*

Arthy, thank you for your congratulations, your happiness on my behalf.

Isn't it wonderful that we've both done what we promised each other we'd do? It's such a shame that we're not studying to be doctors together, but that's life, isn't it?

I cannot believe Sister Shanthi sent you the newspaper clippings! I'm quite embarrassed by it all and nervous as well. After all the build-up I have to succeed.

I can see you rolling your eyes, hear your voice, 'Of course you will, Janu.'

I hope so. I know it's going to be tough. I'm the only woman on the medical course and the only student on a full scholarship. The nuns are even more excited than I am!

It was Mother Superior who agreed for the newspapers to print my story. She said it will inspire the younger kids. They've asked me to stay on at the orphanage, thus saving on accommodation costs, which are not included in the scholarship. The medical college is just two buses away and I can commute every day.

In return for lodging at the orphanage, I'll help out with the children, teach them when I am able and tend to their illnesses. Be the doctor in residence (and part-time teacher). Sounds grand, doesn't it?

'You know how expensive doctors are; we only get medical care when it is for something we cannot attend to ourselves. But with you here, we'll be able to divert the medical costs to other things,' Mother Superior said.

Janaki pauses, her tears soaking the page. *If only there had been a doctor in residence when you were ill, Arthy! If you'd received medical help in time, you'd have been saved. But if I think like that, that you died in vain, I feel like giving up. And I cannot.*

As a doctor, I'll make it my mission to prevent other children from becoming casualties of not receiving medical help in time.

With effort, a final sniff, Janaki stops crying, turns her attention back to the letter and the imaginary world she has created for her friend:

Anyway, enough from me. Waiting to hear from you and to celebrate the news that you've been accepted into Cambridge, the best university in the world! We've both come a long way, eh?

Much love,
Janaki

Chapter 32

Alice

1921

Wanting

One perfect moment when their lips had met, their mouths and hearts had fused and Alice had felt complete, that hankering part of her stilling, her soul filling.

And then. Shouting. Accusations.

Her father's slap. Dragged home in disgrace.

Her heart yearning after Raju, worrying for him.

Wanting him. Wanting.

Mother woken up, blinking in stunned shock. 'He's a *coolie*.'

'Mother, I love him.'

'Love?' She blanches, disbelieving.

'Like you love Father.'

Her mother flinches as if slapped.

Alice's own cheek is pulsing with heat and torment.

'Don't cheapen my relationship with your father by comparing it with… with your disgraceful actions,' her mother says, hand on her heart, voice cold.

'I love him,' Alice reiterates stubbornly.

Her mother's gaze is frozen blue, stony, as, Alice imagines, the hailstones she's described to her daughter in great detail. 'What you feel for the coolie is not *love*.'

'You've run wild here, had your own way for too long.' Her father's voice is soft but carrying, hard and deadly. 'You need structure. You'll go to boarding school in England now the war is over.' His face is set in unforgiving lines with not even the slightest edge of softness. Impenetrable.

'*No!* Please. I want to stay here. This is my home. Mother?'

Her mother's face is bleached pale as fish bones at the mention of England. Longing and envy briefly flash across her face before she turns away from her daughter. And Alice knows then that she has lost any – minuscule – chance there might have been of her mother interceding with Father on her behalf. For Alice's punishment is what Mother yearns for, more than anything. And yet, Alice tries.

'Mother, I love India like you do England. I love Raju like—'

'That's enough!' Father's voice carries, sharp and final as a whip slicing skin. 'You *will* go to boarding school in England.'

No. No. No.

Her heart is more inflamed than her face, where her father slapped her.

Please. No.

PART 8

England

Exile

Chapter 33

Alice

1921–5

Symbol

Her mother's sister is waiting for Alice when the ship arrives at City of London docks. Alice, aged sixteen and heartbroken, prepares to finally meet the aunt she has come to know through her mother's stories.

The docks are busy and bustling but nowhere near as haphazardly chaotic as in India. Alice steps off the ship and into a freezing world as frigidly blue as her broken soul, the wintry air pummelling her with icy slaps.

Edwina is a taller, bonier version of Mother. She wears a long coat that accentuates her height, fur gloves, and a hat set at a jaunty angle. She smiles at her niece: 'You're the image of Caro! Come on then.' She leads Alice to a horse-drawn carriage, nodding elegantly at the porter who, along with the groom, loads Alice's cases into the back.

Alice's first impression of England is that it is not at all like she has come to expect from her mother's stories. It is tired, grey, rubble and dust, with yawning holes where buildings should be. From the window of her aunt's carriage, she sees a man huddled in a doorway, hat pulled down low over his face, scruffy coat sitting oddly on his body.

It is only when their carriage has gone past that Alice realises, with startled comprehension, what was odd: the man had no hands, the arms of his coat had been flapping emptily in the frosty breeze.

A way ahead, there's a man on a bike, holding a trowel and wearing a cardboard placard that states: 'Wanted. Work. Gardening. Odd Jobs'.

Aunt Edwina notes Alice's befuddlement: 'There are not enough jobs for all the men who returned home from war.'

Alice's eyes connect with those of a woman carrying a covered basket, battling the gusty wind, which stabs with knives of pure ice. Her eyes are fathomless caves of pain. She nods at Alice – who is shivering despite the greatcoat Edwina had brought along and handed to her – perhaps recognising a kindred soul, flattened by loss, undone by missing.

Aunt Edwina and Uncle Bertie live in a sprawling house amid beautiful grounds on a hill overlooking the River Thames. 'We're right beside Richmond Park. We can go for walks in there when you've recovered from the journey, my dear,' Aunt Edwina declares brightly as the carriage draws to a stop.

Alice looks up at the house and hears her mother's voice, soft with longing, spinning tales of her past in England during those evenings when they would knit together. This, the life Aunt Edwina is living, she understands finally, is what her mother wanted, what she yearns for.

Uncle Bertie is a short, blustery man with a bald head and kind eyes.

As he sets down his newspaper to greet his wife's niece, Alice's eyes skim over the headlines:

Unemployment reaches
a post-war high of 2.5 million

Adolf Hitler becomes leader of the National Socialist
German Workers' Party

Uncle Bertie follows her gaze. 'It's all doom and gloom nowadays. The nation has still a way to go to recover from the losses of war.' He sighs and cocks his head to one side. 'Is India faring any better?'

India… Alice feels the longing rise up in waves.

'Excuse me,' she says, and it takes all of her willpower not to run but to go sedately from the room, bothering with manners even now she's been banished to England, *still* trying to please her parents through her aunt and uncle.

Her parents, who are meant to love her no matter what, but will only do so if she meets certain conditions that she has now come to understand: love the right person (*not* a coolie); behave a certain way, as befits your status, your class.

* *

She had not believed it *would* happen, that her parents would really exile her to England. She had tried to run away, to find Raju, the very evening she was brought home in disgrace. But one of the maids had stopped her. 'You're not to leave your room, Missy Baba.'

She'd tried to push the maid aside. There'd been a flash of sympathy on the girl's face; she was scarcely older than Alice. But…

'Sorry, Missy Baba.'

And she had looked sorry.

'Where's Ayah?' Alice had asked.

The maid would not meet her eyes. 'She's been let go.'

Alice had swayed on her feet, her eyes streaming. She could not believe it was possible to feel worse than she had been feeling. Her voice had been barely a whisper, her courage failing, but she'd *had* to ask.

'And Raju?'

The maid had sighed. 'He also.'

'Where are they? Are they with Ayah's sister in the village?'

She noticed the maid flinch from the naked hope in her voice. 'She's been asked to leave too. *And* Raju's father.'

'But his land…'

'It wasn't *his* land, he was merely working it. And what's more, none of them have been given a reference.'

'But where will they go?'

'Who knows?' The maid shuddered. 'I wouldn't want to be in their position. It's a hard enough life but without references, it's much worse.' The maid's voice had become bitter. Now she met Alice's gaze steadily, her eyes flashing. Alice read the message in them: *All your fault.*

She had ached for the comfort of Ayah's warm, familiar embrace. She had yearned for Raju. She was terrified for them both. Where would they go? What would they do?

She'd paced her room, worried, anxious, missing, wanting.

She'd tried leaving again and again the maid had stopped her.

'I'd like to see my mother.'

She would appeal to Mother; they had a rapport from their nights knitting together, didn't they?

'I'm sorry, the memsahib asked not to be disturbed.'

It had taken two maids to wrestle Alice back into her room, screaming, 'I'm her *daughter*, for Christ's sake! Her only child…'

And so it had remained: Alice had been imprisoned in her room, all her attempts at escape foiled. She had been unable to go outside, or talk to her parents even, and had been watched at all times by several maids.

Then one day a maid had come in, bearing two large trunks, and had started to pack Alice's things.

'What are you doing?' Alice had raged.

'You're going to England.'

No amount of outrage, hurt, tears, and when it was inevitable that she was really leaving, desperate pleading on her part had helped. She was denied an audience with her parents and had been bundled into the ship as unceremoniously as the trunks containing her possessions.

She never even got to say goodbye.

All through that endless voyage to England, Alice had drawn the symbol of her friendship with Raju: two entwined, heart-shaped leaves holding a water lily within.

'This is what we have together. A beautiful, pure friendship,' he had said, eyes aglow.

She had known then, as she had known always, although it took their kiss for her to admit it to herself, that this boy was her destiny, that she was only home when she was with him.

*

England.

Despite being torn by war, there are occasional glimpses of her mother's homeland and then it is like living her mother's words.

Alice is devastated, heartsick and homesick, but despite this, she can appreciate the irony of it all. She is in England but longs for India, while her mother, who yearns for England, is exiled in India.

But at least Mother is with her love.

*

During Alice's first few days in England, when she is disorientated and confused, Aunt Edwina takes her in hand. In her brisk, no-nonsense way, she cajoles her niece into action, not letting her wallow in self-pity.

'You don't have anything suitable for an English winter,' Aunt Edwina tuts and takes Alice shopping for a new wardrobe. Afterwards, they lunch at the Regent Palace Hotel and take tea at Lyons Corner House, Aunt Edwina smiling at Alice over the menu. 'It *is* nice having a companion, my dear. Bertie has become an awful bore since being demobbed, not wanting to go out, preferring to stay home.'

Aunt Edwina introduces Alice to her acquaintances and friends, of which she has many: 'This is Caro's girl, isn't she quite something?', with a twinkle in her eyes and warmth in her voice.

Alice thinks of her mother then, for whom her daughter was a sewing companion and soundboard for memories of home. A mother who turned away from Alice when she found out about her romance with Raju, exiling her to England without a goodbye.

Aunt Edwina must know what Alice has done, and the circumstances which have brought her here, yet she is happy, even *proud*, to be seen with her niece and to present her to her friends.

When Alice looks melancholy, Aunt Edwina says, 'Why the long face? We can't have a young thing like you getting bored. Come, let's go for a walk. The fresh air will do you good.' She is content, during their ambles around the lush grounds, and in nearby Richmond Park, to leave Alice alone with her thoughts, simply providing quiet company, reassuring her that she is not alone.

Again, like Alice had done when she first learned of unconditional love from Ayah, she cannot help but contrast Aunt Edwina's quiet caring of a niece she did not know until now with her parents' benign indifference, morphing into angry exclusion when she did something that went against what they believed was right. It hurts so very much, even more so now she is experiencing something approaching love from her near-stranger of an aunt. Why is it so hard for her parents to love her without conditions, boundaries, love her simply for who she is?

After two weeks with her aunt and uncle, Alice is packed off to boarding school. The school is in a grand old house furnished with antiques. Dark passageways connect endless rooms smelling of chalk and ink and scholarship, populated with grim-faced teachers and nattering girls. The grounds are beautiful, untouched by war. These surroundings do reflect the England that her mother so often described to her, but for Alice, boarding school is just a prison. Another place to be endured until she is reunited with Raju.

And we will *be together, Raju. I promise you that. I'll come and find you as soon as I'm old enough to be independent, free of my parents' guardianship, not obliged to heed their decisions on my behalf.*

If she were an adult, she wouldn't be here, pining in a land halfway across the world from her love, her home, and all that is familiar.

*

Boarding school.

Pierced by scores of eyes: curious, imperious, dispassionate, scornful; judged and found wanting.

Smirks hidden behind cupped palms at her accent; although she is careful to emulate her mother's polished cadences, she stresses the wrong syllables, emphasises consonants that don't need it, drags out vowels meant to be crisply succinct. 'Why don't you go back where you came from?' This from those who deign to talk to her. Most ignore her: their jaded gazes the blind blue of indifference, the icy green of disdain.

Alice, lost in this country that she cannot warm to, that is not home, grieving for her friend and all she knows, feels invisible, hovering on the periphery of others' lives. Never a participant, always an onlooker.

In the dormitory she is spurned, her attempts at conversation rejected, her friendly advances snubbed. The other girls' chatter dries up every time she approaches, so she learns to stay away, keep to herself, pretend she doesn't care.

While shutting Alice out, the others whisper among themselves: the hot, pulsing flavour of gossip, shimmery with intrigue. They share treats drawn from hiding places under pillows and beneath mattresses, exuding the inviting aroma of vanilla and chocolate, creamy velvet.

Alice huddles under her blankets, shivering. She can never get warm in this cold country; is it the weather mirroring the frosty demeanour of its people or the other way round? The taste of loneliness swills biliously in her mouth; the warm hug of companionship just a tantalising glimpse into someone else's happy dream, elusive and out of reach.

The other girls appear carefree and gay, discussing boys and balls, coming-out dances and dance cards, lacrosse and ponies. Yet for all their light-hearted capers, their eyes are haunted by their experiences of war. Their faces are grave, expressions resigned as one of them says: 'I overheard Matron say that the recent census found there were so many surplus women that only one in ten of us will marry. There aren't enough men to go around. The blasted war has seen to that.'

One night, Alice is woken by sniffles. The girl in the bed next to her – Lily – is smothering her sobs in her pillow. From everywhere else in the dormitory come the sounds of gentle snores and soft, sighing, dreamy breath.

Alice knows that Lily might not want anyone – least of all Alice, whom she has steadfastly ignored, rebuffing all attempts at conversation, her back to Alice when she's tried making small talk – to be party to her grief. So, although every instinct in her wants to comfort this desolate girl, she pulls the pillow over her head in a bid to block out the sound. But, try as she might, she cannot ignore Lily's sorrow, and so she asks, tentatively, 'Lily, what's the matter?'

Lily flinches, but does not reply.

'Is it your brother?' Alice queries softly.

Lily has woken Alice up many a night with her night-time mumblings, her plaintive cries, her dream-addled pleading: 'Don't sign up, James. Please.' And another time, 'I'd rather you were a coward but alive, James. I want my brother back, not a corpse. Mother is a shadow of her former self. She coped, just, with losing Father, but to lose you too…'

All those times, Alice had sat up in a bid to comfort Lily, only to realise that the girl was crying out in her sleep. In the morning, ignoring Alice as usual, her eyes swollen with the memory of the vivid dream in which she lost her brother all over again to the war. But this time it is different. Now Lily is very much awake. 'Go away,' she is muttering, fiercely, wetly, which somehow wakes Dot, who occupies the bed on the other side of Lily and has slept through every one of Lily's tormented dreams so far.

In the next instant, the other girls in the dormitory are all awake. They crowd round Lily, offering comfort, shutting Alice out.

'I understand, you know,' Alice whispers softly.

They turn on her, as one, hissing, 'You don't know *anything*. You weren't here.'

But I know loss, she wants to say. *I know how it feels to have your heart wrenched, to lose everything familiar and beloved, to ache for what was.*

But they've turned away from her, their linked arms, pointed shoulders forming a sharp white wall, blank and closed, barring her entry. And as she tries but fails to sleep, frigid loneliness her only companion, she muses as she has over and over since she arrived: *I don't belong here in England.*

During school lessons, Alice discovers that she doesn't know any of the right things, as it appears the governess hasn't taught her anything of import. Her own insistence in doing very little homework has also played a part in this, leaving her woefully unprepared. She does excel at needlework, thanks, perhaps, to all the knitting that she did with her mother.

Do I belong in India? I *think so but the Indians don't.* She remembers at the non-cooperation rally, at the end of which she'd realised that what she felt for Raju was love, Hindus and Muslims alike had glared at her: 'What is *she* doing here? We want freedom from the likes of her.' Raju had bravely, single-handedly, protected her from their fury…

I only felt I belonged somewhere when Raju kissed me. Only then.

So, Alice endures the four long years at boarding school and finishing school, ever the outsider, all her attempts to try and fit in rebuffed, her overtures shunned. She inks the symbol of her friendship with Raju – the entwined leaves with the enclosed water lily – on her body and knits it onto scarves, wondering what happened to the scarf she'd gifted Raju with their symbol knitted onto it, the white of the water lily blemished by a droplet of her blood. Does he wear it and think of her, miss her, as she does him? Where is he now? *We are meant to be together and we will be, one day.* It is this hope that keeps her going.

She writes letters to Raju, care of Sarla, Ayah's sister in the village, but they are returned to her, still sealed. Although she was told he was no longer in the village, that they were all asked to leave, she has never stopped hoping…

In letters home, she asks her mother about him. Mother, who had refused to see Alice again after that day she was brought home in disgrace for kissing Raju, has written to Alice since she has been in England. And Alice, desperately homesick and yearning for news from someone who might know something about Raju – even if that someone was involved in keeping them apart – had pounced on the letters, scouring them, reading between the lines. But Mother's letters were empty of any information and mundane, and told her nothing at all. She didn't know why she had expected or hoped for more from the parent who had so completely let her down.

The days fade into each other. Alice feels cauterised, as if her self, her better self, has been amputated, removed rudely from her body.

Alice's dreams are of India, of the home she knew and loved every inch of, the compound that was her playground. Of a boy with a cheeky grin and a dust-stained face. Ayah, bangles tinkling, the music of anklets, her scent of onions, coconut oil and comfort, her gentle voice, her formidable snores when she took her afternoon naps. Knitting with Mother, as jasmine-scented breezes spiced with night and intrigue whispered gossip to the curtains flapping at the open window through the mosquito mesh; Mother's hands working and her mouth telling stories thick with longing, coloured with nostalgia. Raju, his caramel eyes sparkling, his lips meeting hers, her heart settling for the first time ever, replete for a brief but perfect moment with that elusive, longed-for feeling of completeness.

Chapter 34

Alice

1925–6

Divine

The telegram is waiting when Alice returns to her aunt's home from a tea party at Lady Odell's stately mansion.

'You must attend,' Aunt Edwina had urged. 'I would, too, if it were not for this ghastly summer cold. Lady Odell's dos are divine!'

Since she finished school and returned to her aunt's home, Alice has been living the life her mother has always yearned for: card parties and musicals, theatre and tennis, masquerades and balls, the scent of gossip and coquetry, perfume and intrigue, roses and scandal.

It is as if she is living in her mother's stories, which were spun alongside the knitting of sweaters and scarves in all colours of the rainbow, on tropical evenings heady with jasmine, while night pressed against the window and the perfumed wind murmured secrets to the waxing moon, many thousands of miles away in another life.

Alice is at ease with her uncle and aunt in a way she has never been with her parents; she knows they care about her and that she is welcome in their home.

'I always thought I'd have children, but somehow it never happened so it's wonderful, my dear, to have you staying with us,' Aunt Edwina confided during one of their strolls in the grounds.

And another time: 'I was very close to Caro, but then Robert came along...' Aunt Edwina had sniffed and said no more. But that disdainful sniff and the lengthy pause following her words said it all. Later, as she had clipped roses for the arrangement in the drawing room, the brisk evening air perfumed with their lilting scent, Aunt Edwina had asked, her voice too casual, 'Is she happy, your mother?'

Taken aback, Alice had only been able to stutter, 'U... Um...'

'I thought as much.' Aunt Edwina had sighed, tossing the roses, a profusion of red and yellow, haphazardly into her basket with none of her usual care. 'Caro never wanted to travel, she was a home body. She wanted this...' She had waved a hand around the grounds, vast and colourful, where flowers, orderly in their beds, flanked neatly manicured emerald lawns and the air was flavoured with roses, honeysuckle and wistfulness. 'But Robert turned her head, promised her the world.' Another sigh. 'Her letters are bland, telling me nothing at all.' Aunt Edwina had blinked, her faraway gaze coming into focus, mortified, as it had settled on Alice. 'I'm sorry, my dear. I got carried away in my recollections and quite forgot you. Forgive me, please. It was...'

Alice had not been able to bear seeing her usually composed aunt so flustered. 'Mother's letters to me are bland too. I want to know more, know *everything*, but she only ever talks about her knitting.'

Aunt Edwina had smiled, her furrowed brows relaxing. 'She's quite something with the knitting needles, isn't she?' And the awkward moment had passed as, once again, they had ambled companionably together, as the fragrant evening settled gently around them until the breeze picked up, with a definite nip to it.

*

Alice understands with certainty that Aunt Edwina loves her. She cannot pinpoint when she arrived at this realisation, but it is there and it is the truth. Uncle Bertie is benevolent towards Alice. Her relationship with her aunt and uncle, with whom she's only stayed during holidays these past few years, is effortless and uncomplicated. Yet with her own parents there's a barrier that she cannot seem to cross.

She likes being with her aunt and uncle but she is homesick for India.

She had hoped to return home after she finished school when she turned twenty a few months ago. 'When am I to return to India?' she'd asked at supper on her first evening back with her aunt and uncle.

Her uncle had paused in his chewing, glancing at her aunt, who set her cutlery down, giving up all pretence of eating. 'Aren't you comfortable here?' her aunt asked.

'I am,' Alice said. 'But I'd like to go home.'

Aunt Edwina had flinched at the word 'home' and Alice knew she was hurt because her niece didn't regard this house as her home even after all these years. She did not answer Alice's question and Alice, not wanting to upset her aunt further, did not push.

'When can I come home?' she had written to her mother. But as she was adept at doing with subjects she did not want to talk about, Mother completely ignored the question, her letters as usual monotone, colourless, giving no information about India, about Raju, about anything at all.

Frustrated, Alice had tried to find work, to obtain the means by which she could travel to India. She'd kept this secret from her aunt and uncle, knowing they'd be scandalised and perhaps even forbid her to do so. But she'd found that unemployment was rife and there were no jobs, especially not for women, with men returning from war having reclaimed those that were available. Now, with the general strike on, services were grinding to a halt, with bus, rail and dock workers striking in solidarity with the miners, and there is no hope of her finding work at all.

Her uncle had thrown down his newspaper that morning, announcing in disgust: 'The country is going to the dogs! Is this what we fought for, what so many of our men gave their lives for?' His voice wavered for a brief, alarming moment, so that both Alice and Aunt Edwina had looked up from their breakfast.

And so Alice had been waiting to come of age. When she turned twenty-one in a few months, she would come into money left to her by her maternal grandparents. Then she would book a passage home, find Raju, her love; the one person who loves her for who she is. Until then, there was nothing to be done but live her mother's dream, waiting out her days in England by attending social events that seem vapid and pointless; a haze of courting and flirting.

Her aunt had been trying to nudge Alice into marriage, no doubt urged by Alice's mother in her letters to her sister. Several young men had proposed to Alice, declaring undying love, some of them very eligible indeed. She'd been flattered by the attention, but…

She could see the shadow of the war in their eyes, in what they were not saying, in their pensive, faraway expressions when they thought no one was watching them. And she recalled the other girls at boarding school ganging up on her, their linked arms and spikes of bony shoulders turned away from her: 'You don't know *anything*. You weren't here.'

If she married one of these men, she'd have to stay in England and she cannot countenance becoming like her mother, forever pining for a country she loves, imprisoned in one she cannot take to.

And Alice's suitors – handsome, suave and charming though they might be – do not *know* her, just as she doesn't know them. They do not understand her and likewise she will never fully understand them, or what they've been through and endured. They do not love her like Raju does – with their all – they cannot, whether because they've left some of who they are in the battlefield – the war shaping them, changing them – or because they do not know what has shaped her, made her who she is; cannot picture the land where she grew up.

India is where her heart is. She *will* return, find Raju, finish what was started with that kiss. She is convinced only then will the emptiness within her, the loneliness that dogs her even while surrounded by people, the feeling of being incomplete, be assuaged.

'Get married,' Mother nudged in her letters now, wanting her daughter to be safely attached to a suitable man from the right social class so as to negate the effects of scandal Alice once caused by kissing a coolie. 'I hear there are suitors interested in you. Your aunt says Baron Norton was paying court to you.'

'Your aunt says you're rejecting *all* of your suitors.' Her mother's letters were becoming increasingly desperate. 'This is madness, Alice…'

Then: 'Your father has a new assistant, Edward Deercroft. I quite like the young man; he's well-mannered and genial, and although he doesn't come from quite the same class, he more than makes up for it with his genteel ways. Your father's taken to him as well.' Her mother had written in the most recent letter.

It had annoyed Alice, her mother's far from subtle attempts to try and push this man at her when she was rejecting all her suitors in England. But it had also given her hope. Did this mean Mother and Father were considering allowing her to return home? Father never wrote to her, Mother merely added a sentence at the bottom of every letter: 'Your father sends his love.'

And now, a telegram from Father. The first time in all these years that he's written to Alice. 'Your mother is ill. She's asking for you. Please return home immediately.' Holding the telegram in her shaking hands, Alice realises, as she counts back, sensing guilt and anxiety bitter in her throat, that it's been a long time since Mother's last letter. Why hasn't she noticed?

Alice has always pictured her mother in her room at twilight, the windows open, the evening breeze rattling the mesh screen, the scents of ripening fruit and dying day, writing to her daughter before picking up her knitting. Had she missed Alice, even a little bit, and how they had knitted together, while she had regaled her daughter with stories of England?

'She's been ill for a while?' Alice asks her aunt, fear viscous in her mouth.

'Yes.'

'You knew?'

'When she didn't write, I was worried. I sent a telegram.'

Why didn't I think to do so? Why wasn't I worried?

'We… we didn't want to worry you. We hoped she'd get better, but she's suddenly taken a turn for the worse…' Aunt Edwina is saying.

Alice is ambushed by a rush of anger, directed at her aunt for not telling her about her mother's illness, but it is as mercurial as it is sudden, swiftly squashed by guilt and remorse. Alice is racked by recrimination, too busy chastising herself to pay heed to the rest of Aunt Edwina's sentence.

She might be angry with her mother for not loving her unconditionally, for being self-absorbed, for not acknowledging her love for Raju, but Alice does love her. And yet, Alice has proved as selfish as her mother; she didn't think to wonder why her mother had not written, or query the reason for it. In fact, she didn't even *notice* that her mother's letters had not arrived at their usual time.

Every moment Alice has spent in England she has wished her mother could be here. Her father loved her mother so why couldn't he see how much she pined for her childhood home? Why make her stay in India, where she wasn't happy?

And now she was so ill that her father had sent his exiled daughter a telegram asking her to return home to her mother. Did this mean Mother would die in the country she hated?

Mother, who had taught her to knit. Mother, the memory of whose voice describing scenes of England visits Alice's dreams alongside Ayah and Raju.

And then, as the implication of the telegram sets in, a sliver of excitement, bright pulsing red, is nudging for space alongside purple guilt. *Please return home immediately…*

Home. Raju. She is angry with herself at the anticipation she feels; the sudden, instinctive overwhelming relief and, yes, joy at being invited home at last.

How can I be happy when Mother is so ill that it has prompted a telegram from Father, who has ignored me all these years?

'Alice?' Her aunt sounded worried. 'Child?'

'I…' Alice tastes the words on her tongue before she says them. They are sweet and bitter, weighted with anxiety, tart with pain, bright with longing, slick with prayer. 'I'm going home.'

PART 9

India

Unwise

Chapter 35

Alice

1926

Prayer

When the ship docks at Bombay port, Alice takes a deep breath of the air of home.

This land that has haunted her all the time she's been away, sparking longing, inciting ache, the scent of spices, the scorched stamp of baking earth, the taste of sunshine and sweetness, honey cream, dirt and incense seasoned with yearning.

She looks at the muddy yellow water lapping against the ship, at the men in white gathered along the banks praying, at the people waiting eagerly for their loved ones, and offers a little prayer: *Please let Mother be alright. Please let me find Raju and be reunited with him.*

Her father isn't among the hordes of people scouring the faces of disembarking passengers. Instead, she spots a man she has never seen before holding aloft a placard with her name printed upon it.

Disappointment is bitter in her mouth. *You should know not to expect him,* her conscience chides. *When has he ever been there? You should be happy. You were worried as to what you would say to him, what conversation you would make.* Her lasting memory of Father: the ringing slap when he discovered her kissing Raju. Her cheek tingling even now with remembered hurt.

*

The man holding the placard grins widely at Alice, even as he rushes to relieve the steward Uncle Bertie engaged to help her during her journey of Alice's cases.

'Memsahib, I'm Nadim, the chauffeur, come to collect you.'

She opens her mouth and the requisite Hindi words – the language of her heart, which she learnt on Ayah's lap, alongside Raju, the tongue in which Ayah would hum lullabies and regale Raju and Alice with stories – arrives effortlessly, although she hasn't used the vernacular in years.

'Where's Sajiv?' The chauffeur and groom throughout Alice's childhood up until she left India.

The man looks troubled. 'He was let go, Memsahib.'

'When was this?'

'All the staff were replaced some years ago, Memsahib.'

'Oh.'

They must have been replaced after what happened with me and Raju. There was no way of knowing who was complicit, so Father must have replaced everyone.

She closes her eyes and throws her head to the sky. She has changed into a simple summer dress, but even that is soaked through with perspiration and her hair, under her wide-brimmed hat, sticks wetly to her head. Indian sun, potent; the port with its myriad voices: vendors hawking everything from spices to snacks; live chickens to glass bangles, sparkling and glimmering gold in the sun; cloth puppets; garish toys; bright saris. Everything is so colourful and infinitely familiar, and yet after Alice's sojourn in England seeming just that little bit too bright and loud and over the top, an assault to the senses.

A vendor thrusts roasted groundnuts at her, their sharp, spicy scent infusing her nose. She realises how much she's missed this even as it overwhelms her: the chaos and colour, the welter of languages, the amalgam of scents, spicy sweet mingling with festering sewers and rotting garbage.

A young woman Alice's age throws her arms around an older woman, 'Mother!'

The worry niggling at Alice's heart balloons. 'Has Mother taken a turn for the worse? Is that why Father couldn't come to collect me?'

'Oh no, Memsahib, that's not the reason Sahib isn't here.' His brow creasing, 'There have been widespread communal riots, in Sahib's jurisdiction also. Sahib is trying to control that, bring some order. He prepared the placard with your name, for I can't write in English, and sent me in his stead.'

'I see.' She takes a breath, transported to another riot, the taste of Raju's kiss, the heat of her father's hand connecting forcefully with her cheek.

*

When they arrive in Jamjadpur, she experiences the rioting first hand. Marching men, blazing eyes, hands and voices raised in passion, aiming to block traffic.

Alice's eyes scan them for a glimpse of a familiar face. Raju feels so very near here. And again, her thoughts return to another riot, in this very city, when she and Raju had snuck into a quiet alley. Cries from the angry crowd had drifted up to them but failed to puncture their bubble, lost as they were in each other until they were violently prised apart.

The car jerks to a halt, surrounded on all sides by angry men with raging brown eyes, wielding sticks. None of them look familiar and yet… she searches.

Crash! One of them brings his baton down hard on the metal of the car, sending it swinging like a pendulum. Alice bites her lower lip, tasting blood: salt, metal and rust. The chauffeur's caramel eyes in the mirror are shiny with fear.

Then men on horseback come charging through the mob, whipping the rioters as though they were animals.

Hating herself for her cowardice, Alice cowers in her seat and shuts her eyes, wishing she could shut her ears as well to the cries of pain and outrage. When the yells finally die down, she opens her eyes tentatively.

The road is clear except for some men sprawled by the side of the road, half in and half out of the rubbish-infested ditch. She tries not to look at them, even as every instinct in her shouts silently: *Are they dead?*

But then her eyes are dragged of their own accord to each of the men draped by the sides of the road. One of them moans, another hauls his body forward. She tastes relief – *No, they are not* – mixed in with fear, salt black in her mouth.

They aren't dead but their bodies are broken, their spirit destroyed. Guilt is sprouting at her relief that Raju isn't among them. And then, in her next breath: *This might have happened to him elsewhere.*

No, please.

The chauffeur inches the car slowly forward.

Men arrive, the same men who had been surrounding their car, now ignoring them, helping their comrades up and off the road. Has she lost Raju to something like this? *No, it can't be. I'd know if anything had happened to him – I'd feel it in my heart.*

*

The car speeds up and the city is left behind, and with it, the rioting and unrest. Soon, they are driving into a landscape as familiar as her own body. They are approaching the temple where she and Raju once encountered the supposedly wise guru spouting his unwise prophecies. Monkeys, bold as ever, run nimbly away from the road and up the trees as their motor car approaches.

The gates to her childhood home loom up ahead. People might be killing each other in the city, but here, it is as if nothing has changed. Her home seems untouched by time, peaceful. The house and grounds are slumbering in the sunshine. It is so very familiar and beloved.

She feels tears gather in anticipation and love. Raju will be waiting for her here, surely? This house cannot be without Ayah and Raju. But the gatekeeper opening the gates is not the man she knows. Nor is the *mali* who looks up from the patch he has been digging, wiping the sweat off his forehead with the back of his arm. There's no monkey by his side. Old Mali has gone.

The sweeper is different, too, although the fruit trees, the flowers, the house all look the same. The maid servant who greets her isn't one she recognises. 'Memsahib, welcome,' she says, smiling. 'Shall I take you to your room? Your cases will be brought there shortly.'

'I'd like to see Mother first.'

The maid servant nods, turns.

Alice stands at the threshold of the house, so familiar to her and yet at the same time alien, without the people who made it *home*.

She breathes in the scent of fruit and dusty air, her eyes pricking with tears and tiredness, and, weirdly, with homesickness for a time long gone; for home as it was once; for what she had taken for granted and will never be the same.

Chapter 36

Janaki

1959

Fine

'I love you,' Rajesh, her fellow resident, says as they do their rounds.

'You don't know me,' Janaki replies, without breaking stride.

'I do. I've been observing you for ages. I love the way you twirl your hair when you're thinking about something.'

Janaki snorts.

'I've been in love with you for months,' Rajesh continues, sounding slightly desperate. 'Will you—?'

It is a quiet night in the hospital for a change, no emergencies yet. Janaki is looking forward to sitting in the medics' common room with her textbook and a cup of coffee. Her mind is on preparations for her post-graduation exam, which is looming. She is abrupt with Rajesh: 'Sorry, I'm not interested.'

His dark eyes harden and he says, sneering: 'You're really as cold as they say.'

'Colder, actually,' she says, pleasantly. 'Now, if you'll excuse me…'

And she swans into the common room and sits at the table by the window – the city busy and bustling below – that she's appropriated for herself, burying her head in her notes, which are straightforward, easy to understand and not at all irritating, unlike the unwanted attention from the men – fellow medics and professors, married and single alike – that she has been warding off, like so many persistent flies, since she started her course.

The downside to studying medicine is being the only woman on the course. Even the teachers, established doctors, have been horribly forward, propositioning her when they have wives at home; assuming because she's unmarried – and showing no signs of looking to become so – she's loose, available, game.

Janaki has loved the course itself, easily coming top in the exams. She puts her book learning into practice at the orphanage, where she is staying while she completes her course, earning her bed and board in this way.

It is bittersweet and emotional for each ailing child she helps to heal brings regret with regards to Arthy; if only Arthy had had this help – a doctor at the orphanage tending to her – her friend would still be here.

At the weekends, Janaki volunteers at the refuge/hospital for the destitute, which Mother Teresa has recently established among Jamjadpur's slums. It is a rewarding, illuminating and intensely humbling experience. She sees the worst of humanity – children dying from snake bites and other curable ailments because they've been brought to a doctor too late, their parents and relatives having previously relied on village gurus and their quack cures instead – and the best: the poorest of the poor, ill and desperate themselves, helping each other.

Working at the refuge puts the setbacks Janaki has experienced – the grief she still battles every day – into perspective, making her realise how lucky and blessed she is.

'We need more women doctors like you.' The nuns at Mother Teresa's refuge/hospital are effusive in their gratitude. 'Women die, pointlessly, first because they don't go to a doctor, suspicious of what they call "English" medicine. Then, when they finally do, their husbands don't want them seen by a man, so you're a godsend, Janaki. But you'd be even more of a help if you specialised in women's problems.'

This is why Janaki has made up her mind to do her Masters in obstetrics and gynaecology. She is more determined than ever to make a difference, which was something she and Arthy had planned to do together, and to save as many lives as she can, in order to make up for not being able to save her dear friend.

*

'Isn't it time you considered marriage, Janu?' Sister Shanthi asks, as they sit in the courtyard weaving jasmine flowers like they used to.

The nuns have been nudging her to get married, but to all of them, Janaki replies, as she does now: 'Wanting to get rid of me?'

'We want the best for you, child.' Sister Shanthi smiles gently at her. 'You need companionship of the kind we cannot provide.'

'Not me.'

'Janu, you cannot go through life as an island, you need love.'

It's the last thing I need. Loving renders you vulnerable. It hurts.

'I don't have time right now. All my spare time is spent studying; I want to win a postgraduate gynaecology placement.'

'Gyna… what?'

'A branch of medicine that deals with diseases affecting women and girls.'

'That's all well and good, child, but you're *not* a nun. By the time you specialise all the eligible men—'

A crow flies off the mango tree above them, startling Sister Shanthi so that she loses her train of thought. The bird swoops low enough for the air displaced by its wings, tart and fresh with the scent of rain and the honeyed sweetness of ripening fruit, to brush Janaki's cheeks, a fragrant caress.

'Sister Shanthi, I'm fine,' Janaki says firmly, hoping her tone will deter the nun, but in vain.

'Men don't like women who are better educated than they are; they feel threatened by clever women.'

'I wouldn't want such a man anyway.'

'We don't want you to be lonely. You're so kind and caring, you've got so much love to give.'

'I'm not lonely, I have you all.'

'You won't have us forever.'

'I'm *fine*.'

Even Mother Superior, who would drop subtle hints that Janaki expertly deflected, has taken to asking openly: 'Don't you think you should find a man?'

'Is this your way of asking me to move out of the orphanage?'

'Of course not!' she bristles. 'You're integral to us now, you know that.'

'Well, then...'

'We're very proud of you, but as your guardian I feel responsible.'

'Mother Superior, I'm *fine*.'

Janaki passes her postgraduate exam with flying colours, then tells the nuns: 'I've been offered a free place to study gynaecology in return for working part-time at the hospital.'

'That's wonderful, we're very proud of you.' And, in the next breath, 'Now that's settled, you've time to look for a man. In the absence of parents, it is our duty to—'

'I want to finish my Masters before I—'

'Don't you want children? You might be too old for them when you finish your course. Are you sure you want to wait?'

'I'm sure.'

Yet they persist.

'You'll be delivering other women's babies, don't you want one of your own?'

'No,' said through gritted teeth. *They mean well. Calm down, Janaki.* 'I. Am. Fine.'

Chapter 37

Alice

1926

Wish

Alice walks down the corridor of her childhood home after a sojourn of five long years. The windows looking out onto the central courtyard, with its well and the washing stone – repositories of innumerable nostalgia-seeped childhood memories – are wide open, and although the mesh screens to keep out bugs are in place, the bustling chatter of maids at work drifts in on a mango-and-marigold-scented, dusty breeze.

Sun angling through the mesh creates a cross-hatched pattern of gold and grime on the corridor tiles. There's the zest of frying spices, sizzling onions, boiling potatoes, caramelising sugar inside. Outside, washing is flapping in the afternoon breeze; a maid pesters the *mali* to dig up vegetables for dinner. There is a cat sunning itself on the well rim, but this is not the cat she rescued. Is it her kitten? Perhaps. Everything is the same and yet different, now tinted bruised purple by wistfulness and ache.

'Missy Baba!' she expects Raju to say, jumping from round the corner, arms open. 'Surprise! Fooled you, didn't I?'

She closes her eyes to shut out the pain, the yearning; her shattered heart bruising all over again.

*

Alice knocks on Mother's door, recalling the evenings when she would run down the corridor and wait there eagerly to be let in – all those nights Father was away – and they would knit while Mother regaled her with stories of England.

England. What will she tell Mother when she asks? That her beloved homeland, sundered by war, is slowly rebuilding itself? That rubble is everywhere, instead of greenery? That war brought fire and ruination. And loss.

As she waits, she remembers her mother the last time she saw her: Mother's sapphire eyes hard and cold as frozen water. 'Don't cheapen my relationship with your father by comparing it with… with your disgraceful actions.'

She knocks again.

No answer.

'Mother?' she calls.

And when, again, there's no response, she turns the knob.

Mother's room is in darkness, as it always was. The curtains are pulled shut. But today, the musky fug of illness, hot and moist, haunts the room.

Mother is in bed, as per usual. Alice feels as though she has travelled back in time and is a child again. Only, there's no Ayah this time, with sari skirts to hide behind; skirts that were fragranced with a familiar scent of onions and coconut oil and comfort.

A pang hits her. It is the memory of Ayah's face when Father brought Alice home in disgrace after kissing Raju. She can see the utter devastation on it…

Mother is a wraith, barely making an impression upon the sheets. Was she this small, this insubstantial before? A woman dozes beside her bed in the chair Alice used to inhabit during their nightly knitting sessions.

'Mother?' Alice says.

Her mother doesn't stir but the woman beside her startles.

Her eyes are puzzled at first, then she smiles in welcome as she takes Alice in. 'You're the image of your mother. I thought it was her standing there, all better.' Extending her hand. 'I'm Margaret, your mother's nurse.'

Alice takes her hand. 'Alice.' Then, inclining her head towards Mother, 'How is she?'

'Not good.'

'Oh.'

'She's not responding to treatment. The doctor comes every day, but…'

Her mother stirs. Alice pulls up a chair close to her, takes her hand and nearly drops it. It is shockingly hot. Now that she's up close, she sees that Mother is distressingly thin. Her skin stretches over her bones. She feels brittle, as if about to break. And she is so very hot.

This small, broken bird of a woman is her mother?

Alice had worried, over the course of her journey here, what, if anything, she would say to her parents; how their reunion would be after the awkwardness of parting on such bad terms. She had feared the bile which rose in her throat whenever she thought of her mother's words to her that dreadful day, and the revulsion on her mother's face when Alice had said that she loved Raju, would still come between them. She had wondered how she would equate the mother of the bland letters they've exchanged with the mother she would return to…

Now she sees all those worries were insignificant, petty. *Please*, she prays to a God she only turns to when she's out of her depth. Just the one word: *Please.*

Her mother's eyes open, her gaze confused, agitated, as it falls on Alice. One moment. Two…

Then her mother's whole body relaxes as recognition dawns, chasing away the incomprehension. She smiles, her gaunt face aglow. The smile fills Alice's heart. Her mother has *never* looked at her like this. This openness so visibly on display is uncharacteristic of her mother. But illness seems to have stripped her reserve, taken away her defences.

'Look at you. Quite the beauty!'

'Mother, I—' Alice is overwhelmed.

'Alice, I don't have much time.'

'Mother...'

'I can't go on.'

Every word is a struggle for her mother. She is raw, all her feelings and emotions out in the open. For the reserved mother Alice remembers, this is akin to being naked.

'I have one wish: I'd like to see you married. Life is not easy for a woman on her own and you can't persist in foolishly…'

Alice bites back the fury that consumes her, as sudden and overpowering as the upset on seeing her mother like this, as overwhelming as her joy at the warm welcome from Mother, all the better for being so unexpected. That she cannot vent her anger on this pale sprite her mother has become frustrates her. 'Mother, I—' she begins, her voice deliberately mild.

'Edward Deercroft, your father's assistant,' her mother interrupts, 'he's been very good to me.' Her voice a whisper. 'I mentioned him in my letters.'

Alice's heart dips even as rising ire scalds.

'Please meet him, give him a chance. For me.'

'Mother…'

Her mother's face is skeletal yet hope colours it bright.

Alice is in turmoil. *Is this why you wanted me to come? To use your illness to manipulate me? You know you're going to die and you want to go with people commending you on making a respectable match for the daughter who caused scandal by her dalliance with a coolie; although you tried your hardest to hush it up, I expect the news got out anyway.*

Even now you care for status more than you do for me. When I was a child, you used me for company when Father was away. Now once again, you're using me.

But… Alice looks at her mother, reduced by illness. What harm would it do to agree to her request? She is looking at her with such hope, her ravaged face alight. *I'll search for Raju in secret but I will give her this.*

'Alright,' Alice says, even as a voice within her chides: *There you go again, bending over backwards to please your parents. Making good the promise you made your younger self to make them love you by giving in to them. How much of yourself will you give?*

Mother smiles and in that moment she looks like the woman who would go dancing with Father, bending down to kiss the air around Alice's cheek, smelling of exotic escapades and effortless glamour. Then the colour leaves her face as quickly as it came so that she is as pallid as fog on a winter's morning in England.

'I'm tired, I'll rest now. I'll see you in the morning. Edward usually breakfasts with your father, you can meet him then.'

Her mother closes her eyes.

With a heavy heart, Alice leaves her mother and walks down the corridor to her childhood room, looking out of the window at the moss-encrusted well, the view as reassuring as her heartbeat.

I'll find you, Raju. I'll meet this Edward for my mother's sake, but I will find you.

Then she sinks down on the bed, which she has outgrown, a child again, hoping, praying with all her heart that she is woken, as she was nearly every day of her childhood, by Raju calling from the doorway, 'Missy Baba, wakey, wakey!'

Chapter 38

Janaki

1966

Alone

'With all due respect, Doctor, I think it's toxaemia.'

Janaki swivels to stare at the speaker, Prasad, who has recently joined the hospital, fresh from completing his MD at King's College London.

They are at a patient review meeting; something Janaki has introduced since she was appointed head of gynaecology the previous year; at twenty-nine, the youngest doctor and only woman to have been afforded the post.

'Wonder Woman!' newspaper headlines had screamed. 'Saviour of Women', 'A Beacon of Hope'; a photo of Janaki taken at Mother Teresa's hospital for the destitute accompanying the glowing (and extremely embarrassing) write-ups.

'You're a trailblazer,' Mother Superior said, beaming, as she plastered the articles all around the orphanage. 'An inspiration to the children. It gives us great pleasure to see you making headlines for all the right reasons.' Then, gently, 'But your personal life…' The nuns' litany is the same these past years.

'I'm happy. Fulfilled. I don't have the time for romantic entanglements.'

'You must make time,' Sister Shanthi said.

Sister Shanthi has been gradually going blind, refusing treatment despite Janaki referring her to her ophthalmologist colleagues at the hospital. 'They're the best in the country, they'll make you see again.'

'I'm old. Losing one's faculties is a natural part of aging. And this way, I get to see the auras surrounding people rather than people themselves and I think that's infinitely better.'

When Janaki visits, Sister Shanthi traces her features with her gnarled hands. 'My child, I'm so proud of you, but I can sense the loneliness radiating from you.'

'I'm fine.'

Janaki has finally moved out of the orphanage.

'You can stay as long as you like,' Mother Superior had said.

But Janaki knew it was time to move out when she finished her Masters and was offered a position at the hospital, her salary allowing her to rent a small flat near to it.

Moving in had been an emotional experience.

She had walked in and recalled promises made and plans finalised: hot, assurance-filled whispers in the thick, fruity darkness, Arthy's hand, trusting and slick in Janaki's, her friend's breathy voice, sweet with hope, 'We'll both become doctors and move in together, that's a promise.'

And while Janaki revelled in having her own space, she also missed the noise and bustle of the orphanage: never a dull moment, the nuns' mentoring, their gentle mothering. She had craved silence and the space to think, to be, but sometimes she found the flat *too* silent. However, this was only very rarely. Most of the time she was too busy to notice, merely using the place to catch up on a few hours of sleep between shifts.

In time, as she climbed up the ranks at the hospital, she managed to save up enough money to buy the flat. *Independence, at last.* And again, her happiness was mingled with sorrow as she realised, on her own, the dream she and Arthy had conjured together.

Janaki visits the orphanage a couple of times during the week, depending on her shifts, to tend to the children who need medical care. At the weekends she divides her time between the Mother Teresa refuge and the orphanage.

'Thanks to you,' Mother Superior often repeats, a proud grin on her face, 'more women are studying medicine; more of our children have hope, ambition, drive.'

Janaki had interviewed Prasad when he applied to work in her department at the hospital. He was smart. Better still, unlike the other male doctors, he was neither cowed nor threatened by her. Articulate and intelligent, he kept up with the latest trends in gynaecology. So now she's unsurprised when he's the only one who disagrees with her. She peruses the patient's chart again. 'It can't be toxaemia. She doesn't have protein in her urine,' Janaki says, feeling a niggle of irritation at his interruption, wondering if she has made a mistake in hiring him. Perhaps what she took to be confidence was just a colossal ego and arrogance. Perhaps he's one of those men who think they're right and will go to any lengths to stick to their opinion even when they're blatantly wrong.

'When I was interning at King's there was a woman – with toxaemia – displaying the same symptoms.'

'I've never come across a case of toxaemia where there's no protein—' Janaki begins.

But Prasad cuts in, 'That doesn't mean it doesn't happen.'

'I have years of experience.'

'That's as may be, but I've *seen* a case like this. We need to operate, prepare her for delivery or else…'

The other doctors' eyes are wide with horrified awe directed at Prasad for daring to contradict their formidable boss.

Janaki takes a deep breath. It's been a long day. She goes over the patient's chart again. 'The patient's only thirty-four weeks. Are you sure about this?' she asks, glaring at Prasad.

'Positive.'

'Well, then, I entrust the care of this patient to you. If anything happens, either to her or her child, I will hold you personally responsible and you'll not be working at this hospital again.'

He nods, standing up. The other doctors release their held breath.

'That's it for today,' Janaki says.

She goes home but her flat, with its wonderful, cool welcome, does not relax her in the way that it usually does.

That man with his new-fangled ideas, his cool stare. The way he had held her gaze, his eyes the chocolate gold of a twilight sky, has got under her skin. She dreams of a woman crying out in desperate pain, giving birth to a child with abnormalities. She wakes, heart thudding, in the flat that is her haven; this space she has carved for herself, and she feels lonely. Alone.

When she arrives at the hospital, she is told that Prasad operated on the patient during the night and that mother and baby are doing well. She visits the woman in the ward, and her child in the neonatal unit; she studies their charts. She summons Prasad to her office.

He looks tired, his eyes hollow, craters under them. His expression when he meets her gaze is wary. 'I have looked at the stats of the patient you suspected of toxaemia,' she says.

He raises an eyebrow.

She takes a deep breath. 'You were right.'

She has not had an occasion to say these words before, she realises. They stick in her throat and come out sounding grudging, bitter. *She* is the one who is always right.

He beams, the hollows in his eyes disappearing, looking like a little boy who has won a big trophy. His grin is infectious, making her want to return it.

She bites her lower lip to hold in the impulse. 'I'm sorry for doubting you. Well done for spotting the toxaemia and taking quick action. You saved the patient and her child. Good work.'

He nods, still grinning widely. 'I'm pleased I won't be leaving this hospital. I do love working with you, even though you're an extremely scary woman to cross.'

Shock incites a surprised chuckle from her throat. *Nobody* dares talk to her like this. They give in to her, subdued and sullen or meek and subservient. Her reputation precedes her and no one dares to proposition her in the way that used to happen when she was studying.

'So,' Prasad says, 'friends?'

He holds out a hand.

She eyes it.

'I don't bite. Besides, you owe me.'

'Do I?'

But she is smiling now, unable to resist his boyish charm. It is innocent, perfectly friendly and open, nothing more. He treats her as an equal. There is no leering undertone, none of the flirting or the knowing glances she has come to expect from other men, who assume that, since she is unmarried, if she smiles at them or is in any way friendly, she is coming on to them.

When she finally shakes his hand, he says, 'Will you come out for a meal with me this evening? We can discuss this case and the similar one I saw in London.'

She is surprised to find herself considering it. It is the first time she has entertained such a thought, despite receiving several such offers since she started studying medicine.

'I'm sorry, I'm busy tonight.' She's visiting Mother Teresa's refuge, where one of the inmates is desperately ill.

'Tomorrow, then?'

'You don't give up, do you?'

'I can be very persistent.'

She looks at him, his tired eyes shining, his open face eager and enthusiastic.

Why not?

'Alright,' she says.

He beams and she finds herself beaming back.

Chapter 39

Alice

1926

Known

Alice wakes to sunshine inveigling under closed lids. It is bright, persistent. *Known.*

Her heart jumps – making the connection before her mind does – and a rush of joy takes her hostage as she opens her eyes to see the sun streaming in through the mesh screen, making the dust motes dance like golden wisps of happy memories.

The morning breeze, gentle and soft, is scented with promise and fruit as it jives in through the open window. She realises that she must have forgotten to shut it the previous night, after she'd watched night descending upon the courtyard, so familiar and beautiful; a view she'd taken for granted every single day of her childhood. She's home!

The moss on the well rim glows velvet-emerald. The dew on the plants glistens, hibiscus and bougainvillea carolling in riotous colour. The cat stretches lazily, a grey and white, thin little thing, unlike the fat, overfed pet of her childhood. Alice sits up in bed and looks towards the doorway, half-expecting Raju to be there, waiting while Ayah comes in to nag her into getting dressed for the day.

I will find him, she tells herself, remembering, even as she does, her promise to her mother the previous evening.

Her mother.

Guilt settles heavy in her heart, her mouth bitter with it. She is pleased to be home and ashamed to be happy when her mother is so unwell. She is upset that it needed her mother's illness for her exile to finally end. How frail Mother is, how reduced!

Alice thinks with bitterness of her mother's wish that she should marry well, all the while choosing to forget, ignore, discount Alice's love for Raju; utterly convinced that Alice won't fare well without a man.

Where has a man got you, Mother? Here you are, dying in a country you don't love, which you have endured for him.

Alice wanders downstairs, determined to talk to the maids and find out about Raju. Someone must know *something*.

Every room she passes is familiar, dense with a thousand memories, all involving Raju. The room where she had her lessons, Raju sitting in, Miss Kitty ensconced on his lap; the one where they hid from Ayah; the one where they – Alice – decided to pull down the curtains and cut them up, Raju going along with her despite being terrified of the trouble they'd be in. Ayah was livid, but after much pleading had managed to hide the deed from Father, using the housekeeping money to get new curtains.

Alice turns the corner and—

'Ah, there you are! Welcome home, Alice.'

Father, looking just the same as ever, stern and preoccupied. *It's not fair,* she thinks, *that he remains unchanged while Mother…*

As if on cue, he says, 'Have you been up to see your mother?' His lips press together, the muscle in his jaw works, while a brief melancholy flickers in his eyes, quickly controlled.

This small, unprecedented glimpse into the workings of her remote father's heart and mind warms Alice, softens her towards him. 'Yes, she's…' She stops, not knowing what to say.

Again she sees the raw ache in her father's gaze, urgently masked, but not before Alice is afforded another rare, surreptitious glimpse.

'Your mother's always been sickly, as you know; she's never quite taken to the weather here.' Father's voice is abrupt, perhaps to mask his upset. 'But this… She can't seem to shake it.'

His words douse the sympathy Alice had been feeling towards him, anger flaring bright red in her chest. If he *knows* that this weather does not agree with Mother, why hasn't he done something about it? But, just as quickly as it arose, guilt now pushes her fury away. *Who am I to judge? I did not even notice when Mother's letters failed to arrive. I didn't think to question what the reason behind it was. And when I received Father's telegram, I was upset about Mother, yes, but I also couldn't contain my relief and joy that I was finally coming home.*

'Sorry I couldn't meet you yesterday,' Father is saying, having apparently said all there is to say on the topic of Mother's illness. 'It's…' His jaw is working. He rubs his hand on his chin and smiles at her. 'It's nice to have you home. It was quiet here without you.'

His unexpected words make her heart glow. He *cares*. But another, cynical part of her is asking: *Why didn't you ask me to come home then? Why didn't you write?*

'I was busy trying to contain the communal riots these feckless coolies are engaged in. I heard you were affected by them in the city…'

'Yes, we—'

'They're still going on,' her father cuts in. 'It won't do at all. We'll stop them, of course.'

Alice pictures the men lying beaten in the ditches beside the road. How she had feared one of them might be Raju. She gathers saliva into her suddenly dry mouth.

*You're not a child any more. Speak up, say what's on your mind.
But it will destroy this warm moment between us.*

'I saw your men use unwarranted force on the protesters.
Surely that's…'

Just as she'd feared, any trace of softness leaves Father's countenance. He laughs, a harsh, mirthless bark. 'Surely *you* do not
presume to tell me how to do *my* job?' His eyes are small and
sharp now, glittering, boring into hers.

'I just think—'

'I've neither the time nor the inclination to discuss this with
you. We'll be leaving directly after breakfast. Come and join us.'

'Who's *we*?' Alice asks, although she has a fair idea.

Father ignores her, marching off to the dining room – where
Alice only ever went to wish her parents good day and good
night, having all her meals in the kitchen with Ayah and Raju –
expecting Alice to follow.

A very big part of her is tempted to walk right on, ignoring
his summons. But…

Alice discovers that, although she is now a young woman as
opposed to a child, she hasn't changed much. She has ever been
in Father's sway, admiring him at the same time as being afraid
of him, and always wanting to please him.

Although she doesn't want to do as Father says, and although
she's tempted to thwart him, it's just a thought, barely entertained
before it is rejected. Taking a deep breath, Alice, hating herself for
it but drawn by her inherent desire for parental approval, follows
Father into the dining room.

A tall man stands to attention when they come in, beside
the dining table heaving with fruit and kedgeree, sausages and
bacon, toast and eggs.

'Alice, meet my assistant, Edward Deercroft. Edward, my
daughter Alice.'

Never in all these years has any of Father's assistants been invited to join the family for breakfast or any other meal for that matter. This man must be someone her father respects, even cherishes.

Edward smiles, taking her hand, kissing it.

'It's a pleasure to meet you.'

He is pleasant, charming, attractive.

He is in both Mother's and Father's good books – a place where Alice has longed to be and has yet to achieve. But...

He is not Raju.

Chapter 40

Janaki

1966

Awry

'Are you ready to go?' Prasad asks. He's arrived in her office just as Janaki is finishing for the day, his wide smile in place, looking dapper, as if they haven't both had a long day, adrenaline-filled emergencies taking precedence over their usual lists, sending their schedules awry.

She's tired and wants nothing more than to go home and lie in bed with a book, a mug of cardamom-and-ginger-infused tea and some chilli *pakoras* stuffed with spiced potato, which she will pick up from the cart doing brisk business outside the gate to her apartment complex. Will it do to pretend she's forgotten?

She widens her eyes as if in surprise and opens her mouth to lie, but he intercepts: 'I know you're tired and want me to go away, but believe me, this place I'm planning on taking you to is worth the small detour before you go home.'

He's read her mind and is being gracious. How can she refuse without looking churlish, especially when she'd agreed to this the previous day?

Janaki is surprised when Prasad leads her down the thriving alley-way behind the hospital, where the smells of roasting cinnamon, stewed tea and rancid rubbish hang over bustling stalls hawking all manner of goods from luggage to carpets, toys to bangles and even catheters, which she's pretty sure are pilfered from the hospital.

'The restaurant's here?' she asks, fully expecting him to say no.

But he grins widely at her, with that open, friendly smile that she likes very much, and says, 'Wait and see.'

When they'd set off, Janaki had looked at her salwar – a suit crumpled from long working hours, carrying the faint whiff of anaesthetic – and wondered if it would do, before deciding that it would have to. She didn't have a change of clothes and in any case, she wasn't going to go out of her way for a meal with a colleague. Prasad didn't seem like those other men, lecherous and inappropriately flirty, but she wasn't taking any chances and she didn't want him getting the wrong idea.

He stops so suddenly that she almost bumps into him. They're outside a little shack, with no sign to advertise it as an eatery, but the aromas of hot seasoned rice, onions sizzling in *ghee*, caramelising sugar and roasting spices are tantalising.

Janaki had expected some high-end place considering he's just returned from England and seems well off, with his impeccable clothes and his confident demeanour. She laughs. He's put her in her place, she understands. She shouldn't have judged him on his appearance and the front he presents – she would have hated it if someone had done that to her.

'You were expecting a five-star hotel, weren't you?' Prasad says, still smiling but a tad shakily. 'We can go to one, if you like, but I promise you, the food there will be nothing like it is here.'

'I'll be the judge of that,' she says, smiling.

The anxiety disappears from his eyes and he grins expansively, bowing gallantly, 'After you, Ma'am,' indicating the stooped entrance to the shack, a beaded curtain serving as a door.

The interior is dark – it is like entering a fragrant cave, replete with delicious aromas, spicy sweet, warm and comforting, sensuous and satisfying. The proprietor welcomes Prasad like an old friend. 'The best table for you and your guest,' he says, beaming and bowing to Janaki.

The men – all the other patrons are men – look curiously at her. It doesn't faze her; she's used to all manner of stares and glares after years of being the only woman in an all-male environment. The proprietor leads them to a table at the back of the small room, tucked into the wall, and once they sit down, the men's eyes return to their food.

Even before she tastes the food – just from the smell and the heaped plates of the other patrons she knows it's going to be heavenly – Janaki has to agree that Prasad has chosen well. If they had gone to a hotel, there would have been gossip. Even more gossip than there already is about her – unmarried at the ripe old age of thirty, working with and bossing men around – all started by the men, most of them married, whose advances she has turned down.

'This is unusual,' she says, once the proprietor leaves.

'Isn't it just?' In the dim interior, Prasad glows.

She cannot resist asking, 'Have you brought me here to this tucked-away secret of a place because you're ashamed to be seen with me?'

He blanches and, watching the colour leave his face as his smile disappears, she regrets asking the question.

'It's an honour to be seen with you. You're a legend.'

He is so earnest. She feels herself flushing with embarrassment and receives a sudden bright stab of pleasure, but bites her lower lip to keep her expression on an even keel.

'You see, I want you to come out with me again,' he says.

Now she's on steadier ground. *This* she knows how to deal with. 'The evening hasn't even started yet,' she says briskly.

'I know, but I also know that I'd like to spend more time with you.'

The man is not shy to court her and express his interest in her, yet it doesn't irritate her. For it is different from the proposals and attention she has received until now, all of which were an unfortunate and pesky by-product of her position. Prasad is sincere. He is looking right at her. He is honest and matter-of-fact. Not leering.

'You're an enigma. I want to know all about you,' he says now.

'Well, don't hold your breath. I haven't decided if I want to come out with you again and…'

'Ah, but that is why I brought you here. There's no menu, they only do *thalis*, but they're the best, believe me. Once you eat this food, you'll be spoilt for any other. I discovered it quite by accident on the day of my interview. I hadn't eaten anything that morning for nerves.'

'You were nervous? I didn't notice.'

'I was terrified. They told me you'd be thorough and vigilant in your questioning but I didn't realise quite how much.'

'I rather think "they" used much harsher words than "thorough" and "vigilant".'

He colours, not meeting her eye, a little boy caught out in a lie.

It makes her warm to him and so she says, smiling, 'So when you survived the interview you discovered you were ravenous?'

'Not quite. I was awed by your knowledge, bowled over by your expertise. I wanted to work with you, but was convinced I'd messed up and wouldn't get the chance.'

Once again, she has to bite her lip to hold in the blush trying to take over her face at his effusive but apparently sincere compliment, delivered in such a heartfelt manner.

'Dejected, I wandered the streets beside the hospital and ended up in the alleyway outside, the scents from this place drawing me in. Somu – that's the proprietor who met us just now – brought me my *thali* and said, "Everything feels better after you've eaten." There never was a truer word spoken. When I heard I'd got the job, the chance to work with you, I came here to celebrate and now I come as often as I can. This is the first time I've brought a friend.'

He smiles, guilelessly, warmly at her.

Friend.

Touched by his words, despite her mind cautioning her to be wary, she smiles back.

Their food arrives: fluffy rice, golden pickles, steaming naan, creamy curries, and Janaki realises just how hungry she is, her stomach rumbling loud assent. There is silence as they both tuck in.

It's been a while since she's eaten such wholesome food. She thinks briefly of the worms in the porridge at the orphanage. There's better food there now, she's made sure of it by donating some of her salary so that the wheat is germ-free.

Only when she has cleaned her plate, realising she hasn't felt so satisfied in a very long time, does she look up to find him watching her, an indulgent smile on his face. 'You eat like you do everything else, from delivering a baby to sewing up a woman's belly: elegantly.'

What is it about this man that his compliments – the same compliments that from other men seem vulgar and which she cuts down sharply and with no regrets – sound heartfelt, real? She distracts herself from her confusion and embarrassment by going to wash her hands.

When she comes back, he says, 'What did I tell you? Isn't the food here the best?'

'Well…'

'Come on, lying doesn't suit you.'

She smiles then, even as the proprietor brings a plate heaped with golden yellow *jalebis.*

She is full, but cannot resist taking a bite; the *jalebi* is still hot from the frying pan, sticky with nectar-sweet syrup, melt-in-the mouth with just the right amount of crunch.

'Okay. I agree, it's brilliant,' she concedes, her taste buds dazzled by the wonderful sugariness of the *jalebi.*

'So, shall *we* come again?' he asks, stressing the 'we'.

And she surprises herself by saying yes.

Chapter 41

Alice

1926

Tired

As Alice takes Mother's place at breakfast, she recalls the first time she was invited to do so, when Major someone-or-other had stayed the night after a party. How important she'd felt then, how grown-up, how *thrilled* to be sharing the table with her remote, distant father!

Now, she savours the tropical fruit platter – mango and pineapple, papaya and guava, cashew and coconut, all juicy and fresh – the taste of her childhood; sweet, sun-kissed ripe perfection; while Edward and Father discuss the riots.

'They want us out of the country but there'll be no one left to govern it if they insist on killing each other,' Father is saying.

'We should just leave them to it,' Edward says and Father guffaws, pleased.

'My daughter thinks we should go easy on the coolies.'

That time Alice had breakfasted with Father and the Major, she'd said something derogatory about coolies that had pleased Father, she recalls. He'd patted her head and she had preened, a warm glow pervading her heart.

'I'm sure she didn't mean it like that. *Your* daughter wouldn't sympathise with coolies.' Edward's voice is hard, steely, providing a glimpse of why Father likes him, of why he is here, sharing Father's table when none of his other assistants have in all these years.

Alice is reminded, sharply, of the time Father had come across herself and Raju fashioning a castle from dirt and twigs in the churned gooey swamp by the well, beneath the shade of the guava and mango trees.

'Get away from the mud!' Father had roared. 'No child of mine scrabbles around in the earth like a coolie, *with* a coolie.' He had directed a punishing glance at Raju, who had shrivelled visibly in front of Alice's eyes.

'I was not playing with him, Father. I was instructing him as to what to do,' Alice had said, standing up straight, Raju squatting in the mud at her feet, beside the castle they'd spent most of the afternoon lovingly building and embellishing with sticks and pebbles.

Father had smiled then and she had beamed. 'I know how to keep coolies in their place.'

'That's my girl.'

His praise had made up for the hurt Alice had seen in Raju's eyes, the crushed look on his face, and how he did not speak to her, not properly, for two whole days.

After breakfast, Edward smiles at Alice. 'I'll go up to see your mother. She expects me to visit – it's become a habit.'

'I'll be along in a few moments,' Father says.

Edward is waiting and so is Father.

Alice, recalling her promise to Mother and desiring to please Father by doing what is expected of her, at the same time as hating herself for it, says, 'I'll come with you.'

Now that she's home, it feels as if there are two of her: one wanting to be the Alice her parents expect, the other not. It's exhausting being pulled in two directions at once. Perhaps this is why she felt complete when she was with Raju, for with him she could just *be*.

Mother's room is thick with the angst of illness and the musty odour of fever and heat, with the curtains shut to the day. She is sitting up in bed, propped up by pillows, but she looks smaller and frailer even than on the previous night.

Her face lights up when she sees Edward and even more so when Alice follows him into the room. 'Hello, Edward, what do you think of my daughter? Isn't she lovely?'

Mother has lost all inhibitions. It is frustrating and embarrassing to see. Alice wants to run away, out of that room, down the stairs to the courtyard. She wants to sit by the well, stroking the cat and eavesdropping on the maids, whose laughter and chatter had drifted up to her, along with the scent of fresh linen, as she had walked along the corridor in Edward's wake to Mother's room.

'Even lovelier in person than I was led to believe from your description of her,' Edward says gallantly.

The two of them chat away, seemingly at ease with each other, but her mother tires quickly, taking deep breaths between words.

Edward, to give him credit, acts as though nothing is amiss, continuing to converse with her when she is able, filling in gaps with great tact to make it appear as if it is a normal conversation. Alice wonders why he is doing this; why he is spending time with an ailing woman not long for this world? Is it ambition? Does he hope to further Father's regard for him?

Whatever the reason, this man has inveigled himself into her family and achieved what Alice hasn't been able to all these years: the respect and attention of both Father and Mother. So much so that they consider him a suitable match for their only daughter, despite the fact that he is not of the same class. But, Alice supposes, in her parents' eyes, Edward is a great improvement on Raju, despite his lowlier birth.

As if thinking about him has conjured him up, Father arrives at the door to Mother's room. He sits by Mother's side, taking her hand in his and kissing it gently. Seeing them together hurts: Father is vibrant and vital, Mother pale and wraithlike, shrunk by illness.

And yet, Father is looking at Mother as if she is the most beautiful woman in the world. That look of love and heartfelt adoration, encompassing a lifetime's worth of memories and shared moments, excludes everything and everyone else, so that the nurse and Edward and Alice herself feel superfluous and awkward, as if they are intruding on the intensely private moment they are party to.

In that one moment, the fact that her mother is almost on her deathbed and her father is not does not matter. In that moment Alice understands why Mother gave up everything she loved – her country, her way of life – to live in a land she hates. In that moment, seeing her parents through newly adult eyes, realisation dawns as to why she always felt uncomfortable, as if she was intruding, when with them. Her parents were a universe unto themselves and she was extra, unnecessary, never to be part of the inner circle.

Now she understands why she gravitated towards Ayah and, especially, towards Raju. In the moment when that look passes between her parents, Alice misses Raju more than she has ever before. For he used to look at her like that, with adoration and devotion, love and respect.

Gradually, Alice becomes aware of another gaze upon her. She tears her own away from her parents and finds Edward looking ruefully at her. Alice blushes, embarrassed and weirdly apologetic on behalf of her parents. She does not want to be here, longing instead to be in the kitchen with the maids; to find out if Cook has also been replaced (which she very much suspects is the case) and to start asking after Raju.

After what feels an eternity, Father kisses Mother's papery cheek, lays her hand down gently on the bed, saying, 'I'll look in on you in the evening.' And, purposeful now, his face sets into its customary, preoccupied frown: 'We'd better get going, Edward.'

'Pleasure meeting you, Miss Harris,' Edward says.

'You can call her Alice,' Mother prompts, a smile in her voice.

Once the men are gone, a lingering hint of lime and musk all that's left of their presence, Mother pats the seat beside her bed. 'Come, Alice.' And to the nurse, 'Please give us a minute, Margaret.'

The nurse leaves, closing the door behind her, and then it's just the two of them in the dark room heavy with illness and all that's unsaid.

Alice sits where her mother indicated. It is the chair Mother used when she was teaching Alice to knit. The morning air is soft and cool, containing only a hint of the heat to come. It tastes of mango and jackfruit and caresses her cheek as it wafts through the mesh screen and the minuscule gap in the curtains.

Mother is feverish, heat emanating from her in waves. 'What do you think of Edward?'

Alice shrugs, sighing inwardly. She knew her mother would ask this. 'He's alright.'

'Just alright?'

Her mother will not let this go.

'He seems nice.'

Her mother's smile is wider now. 'He is.' A beat. Then, 'Will he do?'

Alice shifts uncomfortably in her chair, knowing just what her mother is asking. The room is stifling suddenly. 'I… it's too soon, Mother. I need' – *to escape… to find Raju* – 'more time.'

Her mother nods. Then, softly, 'I'm tired, Alice.'

'You should rest,' Alice says, making to stand. She can't leave fast enough.

'No, sit, please.'

Defeated, she slumps back in her chair.

'I meant,' Mother says, 'I'm tired of living.'

'Oh.'

'It requires such effort.' Her mother's voice a whisper. 'But I won't go yet. I'll wait until you're... settled.' It's an effort for her to speak and yet she does.

'Mother...' Alice colours, feeling upset and angry. She did not come all this way to be emotionally blackmailed, she does not need this.

'I'm sorry we didn't send for you sooner. I'm sorry we had to send you away at all.'

'Why did you then?' Alice can't help growling, furious. Part of her is angry at herself for raging at this barely-there woman who, despite everything, she loves.

'I've missed you. I enjoyed our knitting sessions when your father was away.'

Alice blinks back the tears that sting her eyes, anger dissipating in a wave of emotion. She's yearned to hear these words from her mother, an admission of love, of care. 'I did too.'

'I... I'm sorry I wasn't a better mother to you. If I had been then perhaps you wouldn't have formed your unfortunate attachment to that boy...'

So *now*, her mother decides to discuss Raju. Fury consumes her, white-hot, at her mother blithely, callously, dismissing her love... 'Mother, it wasn't—'

Mother holds up a hand, palm facing outward. It is shaking, the skin taut, brittle, and Alice swallows down her rage, reminding herself, once again, that her mother is an invalid.

'I feel so guilty. I left you to your own devices, relinquished all control to your ayah, and I was' – her mother pauses, takes a breath – 'I was grateful she had a son your age, a playmate for you. I refused to see what should have been obvious.'

'Mother—'

'You didn't get affection from me or your father. I was too tired during the day to care for you and your father was too busy. It stands to reason that…'

Now Alice cannot stop herself. 'I love Raju.'

Her mother blanches, her head sinking into the pillows. 'You *thought* you did.'

'Mother, don't—'

'Alice, please. It's over, they're long gone.'

From outside a peacock calls, long and loud for its mate. A tinkle of a laugh carries on the sugary breeze. 'You thought you loved him because you didn't get love from us. It was a child's transference of affection.'

'Mother…'

Her mother lays a hand on her chest, looking spent.

Alice bites on her lower lip, hard, until she tastes blood.

'Alice, you're young, you've your whole life ahead of you. You cannot waste it pining for an unsuitable, married coolie.'

'*Married?*'

'The moment you left.'

Alice swallows and speaks around the lump that is sitting squarely in her throat. 'Where is he?'

'They left the village. I don't know where he is now. Must be the proud father of several kids.'

An image of the girl Raju had been supposed to marry, her veil covering her face, rises in front of Alice's eyes.

Raju, holding out a water lily resting on entwined heart-shaped leaves to Alice: 'This is what we have together. A beautiful, pure friendship.'

Oh, Raju.

Her mother stretches a hand towards Alice, a plea. Alice regards its blurring contours and after a moment, takes it.

'Please. Don't squander your life on a pipe dream. He doesn't belong to you, he never did. Edward is a good man. He spends time with me, an invalid. He is kind.'

Is he? Or does he have his own reasons for spending time with you? Alice feels worn out all of a sudden. *When did I get so cynical?*

'I can tell he likes you. He'll look after you.'

How can you tell? How can he like me on the strength of a single meeting? Will he look after me as Father has you, keeping you imprisoned in a country you detest? But her mother's hand in hers is fragile, vulnerable as a hopeful heart, so Alice keeps her musings to herself.

'Alice? At least allow him to pay court to you. Give him a chance, will you, my dear?'

And looking into her mother's dim eyes, already more part of the next world than this one, the plea in them, the hope, Alice wonders: What does it matter? What does any of it matter?

Her love is married. He is lost to her. He is the father of children with another woman.

All they shared was one kiss, stolen from fate, in the midst of a riot. They are not meant to be. She will never have the love shared by her parents so why not settle for second best, do what her mother wants, please a dying woman? What has she got to lose when all that matters to her is lost?

'Will you consider Edward?'

All her life Alice has tried to please her parents. And this man, Edward, seems to have both parents' apparently unconditional approval. Very slowly, her heart, her soul aching, she nods.

That evening, while Mother rests, Alice wanders the grounds. It is a bittersweet experience for everywhere she is faced with memories of adventures with Raju, surrounded by the perfume of mango, tamarind and reminiscence; the taste of guava and nostalgia. Salty loss clogs her throat, choking her.

'Miss Harris… Alice. Your father invited me to supper and as we turned into the drive, I spotted you among the fruit trees. May I join you?'

It is Edward.

It is an effort to collect her thoughts, to smile, to say, 'Yes, of course.' A part of her is annoyed at his intrusion into her private contemplation, but another, bigger part is grateful for the company. It will, hopefully, take her mind off all she has lost and stop her dwelling on what Mother told her about Raju being married.

'Feels odd, doesn't it, being back home after time away? Familiar and yet different,' Edward says, gently.

'Yes.' Alice is amazed. She looks up at this man, who truly understands what she is feeling. 'How…?'

'I've felt displaced too, Miss… er… Alice.'

This is a man favoured by her father and mother, something Alice has yearned to be all her life, yet he is hesitant to take the liberty of using Alice's name. Alice likes that. It renders him human, approachable, as do his next few words: 'I lost my parents to consumption when I was thirteen.'

'I… I'm sorry.'

'I moved from England to Shimla when my Uncle Reg and Aunt Lucy took me in. But then the war…' He swallows. 'Uncle Reg and I joined up. I came back, Uncle Reg didn't.'

'Oh, Edward…'

'Forgive me. My intention was to cheer you up, not get you down. You're a good listener, Alice.' He smiles, a little wan. 'I… What I meant to say was… It's just the first couple of days when you feel out of sorts. You'll soon be settled back here again and it will be as if you'd never left.'

A breeze flavoured with mango, gritty with dust brushes her cheek, teasing her hair onto her face. She looks at this man, in his earnest way trying to make her feel better – he must have observed her melancholy mien when lost in musing – and she thinks she understands why her parents like him.

'Edward is a good man. He spends time with me, an invalid. He is kind. Give him a chance, will you, my dear?' Mother had asked that morning.

I will try, Mother.

Chapter 42

Janaki

1966–7

Enigma

Dining at the restaurant in the alleyway behind the hospital has become a regular weekly affair and, despite herself, Janaki looks forward to these evenings with Prasad; she savours the scent of stewed tea, cinnamon rice, roasting chillies, the taste of caramelised sugar and companionship.

'Admit it, you were getting too big for your boots until I joined the team. You need me to keep you in check,' Prasad teases.

'Oh shush!' Janaki is too busy tucking into her delicious, perfectly spiced meal to think of a cutting response.

If her other colleagues were to see her now, hear this junior doctor's cheeky banter and, especially, witness her mild reaction, they'd be shocked. What is it about Prasad, she wonders for the umpteenth time, which stops her from getting riled when he says such things? If it were one of the other men, she'd have sacked him by now.

Prasad is younger than her yet wildly irreverent. He does not hesitate to stand up to her and put her in her place every so often. Sharp, bright, witty, he treats her like a friend. Not a woman, not a boss. *A friend.* He's her first friend since Arthy.

Arthy. She did not want to allow her heart to soften, she is wary of emotion. But her friendship with Prasad seems to have happened without her realising. *Beware,* the cautious part of her warns when she cannot fall asleep unless she pictures his soft gold eyes, and when she greets a new day with a smile, having dreamt of him.

'What're you doing at the weekend?' he asks now. He is perpetually, unashamedly curious about her life outside of the hospital.

'Are you sure you don't want to go somewhere more upmarket, more befitting your celebrity?' he'd asked the second time they came to this humble eatery.

'I like it here.' She did. The atmosphere, cosy and discreet, populated with warm, tantalising aromas, the proprietor welcoming them with lemon sherbet, poppadums and a beaming smile. 'And I'm not a celebrity.'

He'd grinned then, that infectious smile she found hard to resist. 'Of course you are, you're in all the newspapers: "Trailblazer", "Wonder woman".'

Blood had gone rushing to her face.

'Oh my, I never thought I'd see the day! I didn't know you could be *coy*, I thought you were impenetrable.'

She'd blushed deeper. 'I hate those headlines,' she'd mumbled.

'It's true what they say.' His voice was awed as he'd added, 'To get where you are despite the odds stacked against you…'

'It's not that—'

'Don't make light of it, you're amazing,' he'd said earnestly, looking right at her, his eyes sparkling with pride and another emotion she couldn't quite place, but which stirred something within her, almost overwhelmed her.

'You're an orphan,' he'd said, softly. 'I am too now.' His voice had been yellow with melancholy. 'I lost my parents in an accident a couple of years ago when I was in England.'

'I'm so very sorry.' *I understand,* she'd wanted to say, tasting the loss of her adoptive parents, nauseous purple in her mouth. She'd been surprised by the impulse to reach across the table, touch him, wipe the sadness from his eyes. *I know how it feels.*

'They left me very well off; my father comes from a long line of landowners, but I'd rather they were here instead.' He'd swallowed and then, visibly pushing away his sorrow, smiled at her. 'I'm sorry, I didn't mean to put a dampener…'

'It's fine…'

'Ah, here's Somu with our *thalis*. Food for the soul, thanks, Somu.'

Prasad's appetite to know about Janaki is insatiable. 'You're an enigma. You're so clever and yet so aloof, so kind and yet so sharp.'

He had a way of drawing her out so that she ended up saying much more than she wanted to, revealing more of herself than she meant to. She told him about meeting Mother Teresa as an impressionable youth: 'It's what made me decide to become a doctor.'

Ever perceptive, he picked up on what she was not saying: 'There's something else, isn't there?'

She couldn't mention Arthy, she was unwilling to go there. She hadn't shared the extent of her grief at losing her friend, her frustration and helplessness at watching her die, because a doctor couldn't get to her in time, with anyone, and she would not start now. So, instead she said, 'Mother Teresa has since opened a refuge and hospital for the destitute among the slums. I help out there when I can.'

'I'd like to help too.'

And this was another thing that she liked about him. How he would not press her about things she didn't want to talk about, but was happy to go along with her deflection instead.

'Well, if you're sure. They're under-staffed and grateful for help.'

Since then, Prasad has been helping out regularly and earnestly at Mother Teresa's refuge – so much so that Janaki expects him to be there when she turns up and, to give him credit, he always is.

Now, as he eats his *matar paneer*, he waits patiently for her reply to his question about her weekend plans.

'I'm visiting the orphanage.'

'Where you grew up?'

'Yes.'

'May I come?'

And looking into his bright, eager eyes, she finds herself saying the opposite of what she should. 'Why not?' she says, and he beams.

Chapter 43

Alice

1926

Late

Alice dreams of Raju. He stands in front of her, shielding her from an angry crowd. 'Missy Baba,' he urges, 'run!'

The crowd advances towards him. 'Go, I'll manage them. Please, Missy Baba, be safe.'

The crowd rounds on Raju, begins to hit him. She wakes sobbing, her pillow wet with tears. His scent of raw mango and rock salt and love; his features are stamped upon her eyelids. All these are so vivid in her mind and feel so tantalisingly within reach.

I cannot give you up so easily. I will not take Mother's word that you're married and a father, I will find out for myself.

She corners each servant, asking them in turn, 'Do you know Mayuri, she was my ayah? Her son, Raju? No? Well, what about the *mali* before this one? The cook, then?'

They blush when she mentions Raju, as if embarrassed on her behalf. It would seem they've all heard colourful accounts of what happened between Alice and Raju.

She goes into the village. It is just the same, sleepy and quiet. The ditches are piled high with rubbish, the vendors are selling groundnuts and spices. There's the sweetly pungent scent of cardamom, dust, stewed milk and humid heat infusing the air.

Communal riots, and the Indian struggle for independence from British rule, do not appear to have touched the village. But the people wage their own war here. It is the war to exist, day to day, on whatever pittance they can earn. The battle here is also waged with the weather; everyone praying to the gods for the monsoons to arrive on time so that the crops will yield enough for them to survive through another season.

Relying on memory, Alice winds her way between huts and after taking a couple of wrong turns, comes to the one where Raju's aunt lived. The place where Ayah had brought her as a child to visit a sick Raju. When she enquires after Raju, nobody seems to know him, or, if they do, they clam up when she asks.

Her presence in these alleyways – strips of mud with ditches either side, piled high with festering garbage – garners curious stares. Bedraggled, hungry-eyed children follow her. She hands out sweetmeats and asks if they know of Raju, of her ayah, Mayuri. They swallow the sweetmeats whole and shake their heads.

Disheartened, she is about to go back when a little boy tugs at her hand. 'My grandpa might know,' he says and leads her to a hut by a ditch overflowing with rancid water, where a cloud of gnats feast on fish scales and decomposing vegetable skins.

The other children and even a few adults follow, full of curiosity. A wrinkled old man lies on a mat by the open doorway of the hut; the monkey beside him, keeping watch, squeals as she approaches.

There's a sudden welcome glimmer of recognition. 'Mali!' Alice cries.

The old man blinks blindly in her direction. 'Come closer, so I can see you.' His voice quivers with age but is recognisable all the same.

She squats next to him and he peers intently at her while she takes him in. Like her mother, he too is reduced by illness. He's lost all his hair, his face is gaunt, his skin fragile, but it is, definitely, Mali.

She feels light-headed, overcome with affection for this man, her one link to the past, to her love. Mali, flashing her a toothless grin, says, 'Missy Baba?'

'You recognise me!'

'I'd know that bright yellow hair, those lively eyes the colour of sky anywhere! You look even more lovely all grown-up, Missy Baba.'

The monkey chatters non-stop, picking up on the excitement. 'This is Saaya?'

'Yes.' Mali smiles. 'Faithful as ever, never leaves my side.'

'How are you, Mali?'

'I'm no longer Mali. Haven't been for… let's see, almost six years now. Sahib sacked everyone, replaced all the staff. Most of us, myself included, did not get another job.' His voice is a spiky cocktail of anger and resignation.

The mob of villagers collected behind her whisper among themselves. Alice ignores them, her entire focus on Mali. 'I'm so sorry.'

Into the tension comes the sound of the monkey chittering, a cow mooing.

'Mali, do you know where Raju is?' Her voice carries the bright orange tang of desperation.

'It's nice to see you, Missy Baba. I've nothing against you but you need to let it go. What you did… It was a children's game with horrible consequences.'

Horrible consequences…

'What do you mean?' Her heart feels leaden.

'He died.'

No.

Alice feels faint, dizzy.

Behind her the crowd is abuzz with rumour, gossip flitting around like a butterfly in a flower bush. The pungent scent of drains hovers, smothering the soupy air. She touches her heart; there's the pulse of life. *Her dream… with the crowd hitting Raju while she escaped. Was that a premonition of what Mali would tell her today?*

But I would have known, surely? I would have felt his loss in that secret part of me that misses him, aches for him, is incomplete without him.

A dog barks, a crow cackles. A vendor comes by, yelling his wares. Children, bored with the drama the adults watch agog, throw pebbles into the foul stream, watching the cloud of gnats rise startled into the muggy sky.

He can't be dead.

The prophecy when they went to the temple, that she disregarded and Raju believed. A shudder as she recalls the guru's solemn gaze, the forked tongue of the snake adorning his neck, slimy and venomous, Raju's hot whisper in her ear, smacking of fear and hopelessness, 'Perhaps I have no future.'

'Raju is gone,' Mali is saying.

He loved me, the only one who did.

'You need to look forward, lead your life.'

A half-life, at best, without him.

Alice locates her voice in her dry, parched throat. 'Ayah?'

'She was heartbroken, losing her only son. She went too, soon after.'

No.

'We were all ordered to leave this village. But now I'm dying, I'm not afraid of the consequences. After all, what can your father do to a man at the end of his life? I mean to die here, in this village where I was born. But you…' Mali pauses to cough, a long-drawn-out hacking that rips through his frail body. 'You shouldn't be here,' he whispers when he can talk. 'If your father finds out…'

*What does it matter? What does any of it matter when Raju…
My Raju…*

'Leave, Missy Baba, before he gets word.'

She kneels down, takes Mali's hand, presses money into it. 'This is for medicines.'

'It's too late, but thank you all the same, Missy Baba.'

The crowd parts for her, their curious and scandalised gazes following her. A sudden, capricious gust of wind flings grit at her while claiming her hat and tipping it into the ditch. The children run after it, rescue it, hold it out to her.

She shakes her head – she doesn't want it – and watches dispassionately as several of them fight over the soggy, soiled thing as if it is the greatest treasure.

The sun brands her bare head. *Too late,* her heart laments.

How could Alice have been living her life when Raju was no longer in this world and not have known it? How could her heart have kept on beating when his heart stopped? Raju and Ayah are gone, Mother is dying and Mali too, with the monkey sitting vigil by his side.

Too late, her heart cries. She stares into the wide white sky, her eyes throbbing and stinging, her soul shattered, devastated by loss.

Chapter 44

Janaki

1967

Blind

The moment Janaki agrees to take Prasad to the orphanage, she decides against it. 'I actually meant—'

'Ah, no changing your mind! You don't do it at the hospital, unless of course *I'm* in the right and you're in the wrong…'

'That happened *once*.' But she is smiling, he has a way of getting round her.

'How do you do it?'

'What?' He's all raised eyebrows, innocent eyes. 'I didn't do anything.' He stretches both hands, palms outward, shrugging innocently. Then, 'I'll meet you there, shall I?'

'Do you *have* to come? It's boring! Nuns and sick children.'

'Just my kind of weekend.'

She sighs. He's determined and she's resigned.

He charms them all, of course, from the infants to Mother Superior. Mother Superior shows him all the cuttings she's saved from the various newspaper articles about Janaki, from the time of Janaki's outstanding matriculation results to now.

'You're boring him, Mothe—'

'No, I'm loving this. Our girl has a habit of making headlines wherever she goes, eh?' His eyes twinkle as he beams at Janaki.

And instead of bristling at his use of 'our girl', Janaki finds she quite likes it.

'That she does.' Mother Superior's gaze is fond as she brings more newspaper articles for Prasad to peruse. 'Take this one, for instance…'

Prasad sits patiently while Sister Shanthi traces his features with her gnarled, wise palms. There are tears in his eyes when she's done. Sister Shanthi, ever perceptive, picks up on it: 'Why're you crying, my son?'

'How did you—?'

'Just because my eyesight is gone doesn't mean I cannot see. In fact, it makes me see things others miss,' Sister Shanthi says gently. She smells of jasmine and comfort, prayer and peace, the nostalgia-tinted scents of Janaki's early childhood.

'Your touch reminded me of my mother, brought her back to me,' he says.

'Ah, my son. Tell me about her.'

And sitting there in the sunshine by the jasmine arbour under the mango trees, weaving jasmine garlands, just as she had as a child, while watching Sister Shanthi, with her blind eyes closed but ears cocked, listening intently to Prasad's memories of his mother, Janaki is immensely moved.

I'm glad I listened to my heart and not my head. I'm glad I brought him here, she thinks as she watches Prasad sniff, wipe his nose with the back of his arm – a curiously boyish gesture – and say, 'Thank you for listening, Sister.' And, nodding at Janaki, 'I had one mother, she has many.'

Sister Shanthi smiles and cups his face gently in the palm of her hand. 'I expect you to visit again, my son, to recount more stories of your childhood.'

'I surely will,' he says. And to Janaki, 'If you don't mind?' She is flustered by his gaze, those eyes caramel gold, carrying the recent shine of his tears, intense, upon hers.

'Of course she doesn't,' Sister Shanthi speaks for Janaki, her hand patting Janaki's knee. 'She'll be only too happy, won't you, Janu?'

Janaki is staying at the orphanage. She does so on those weekends when there's been a spate of ill children and the nuns need a break from tending to them. Later, when Prasad has left, and after supper and prayers, Sister Shanthi beckons to her: 'Come.'

They sit in the arbour listening to the cricket chorus, enveloped by the scent of night jasmine and prayer, cooling earth and fermenting fruit. 'He's a wonderful boy. And completely besotted with you, Janu. He was worth waiting for, you've chosen well,' Sister Shanthi says.

'Sister, I… He's just a friend.' *I've been silly bringing Prasad here,* she chastises herself in her mind. *Of course they'd think this.*

'Oh, Janu.' Sister Shanthi is gently chiding even as she takes Janaki's hand in hers, stroking it. 'Open your eyes, child. You've no reason to be blind.'

'He's younger than me,' she says, for some reason their difference in age the only objection she can come up with.

Sister Shanthi laughs softly. 'When your minds and hearts are perfectly matched, what do mere numbers matter?'

That night Janaki tosses and turns in her room at the orphanage, fitful sleep tormented by soft gold eyes adorned by the icing of tears. Looking at her with affection, pride and, yes, *love*, saying, 'our girl'.

Chapter 45

Alice

1927

Pronouncement

'Good evening, Alice.'

Alice is under the mango tree among the branches where she used to hide, remembering how she would while away the somnolent afternoons, with Raju beside her, enjoying friendship and happiness… when Edward catches up with her. He has taken to joining her on her ambles in the grounds every evening – reminding her of her walks with Aunt Edwina in England – and she has grown to quite like his company. They talk about Gandhi's *swaraj* – self-rule – movement and the economic situation in England. Unlike Father, who does not listen, expecting everyone to fall in line with his opinions, Edward *does* listen, and he and Alice engage in some quite lively discussions. It takes her mind off her sorrow; the festering wound of missing Raju.

Edward tells her of his childhood in England, before his parents' death and, afterwards, when he went to live with his Aunt Lucy and Uncle Reg in Shimla: 'I loved it there. It is a beautiful place.'

'Mother has always wanted to visit. She's heard it's like England.'

'It's better,' Edward says, his eyes glowing. 'I think it's the most beautiful place in the world. But after Uncle Reg's death, it lost its allure. Both Aunt Lucy and I were grieving, and for me the place was too full of memories of Uncle Reg.'

I understand, Alice thinks, *more than you know.*

'I *had* to leave. Aunt Lucy understood and gave her blessing. I came here and started working for your father. You know the rest.' He pauses underneath the tamarind tree and smiles at her. 'What about you, Alice? Have you settled back home yet, or are you still feeling displaced?'

The tart tang of the knobbly brown tamarind is flavoured with loss sharp in Alice's mouth and Mali's shocking words reverberate in her ears: *Raju died.*

It has been a few weeks since Mali's pronouncement and Alice has yet to allow the words to sink in. When night presses, insistent, shadows reign and doubts multiply, owls call and nocturnal animals tussle; when the dark is busy and alive with intrigue and the moon shines into her room through the open windows, even then, she cannot believe it.

She has walked to the lake from which Raju once rescued her after she had found out about the girl he had been promised to in marriage. He had handed her his gift of entwined heart-shaped leaves enclosing a gold-tinted water lily, its petals coloured the buttercream of hope. His eyes had been bright with promise and his voice fervent when he'd said: 'This is what we have together. A beautiful, pure friendship.'

I would rather you were married, Raju, a father. I would rather that than you were dead.

She was in India, the home she had longed for, where the warm air tasted of baked earth, the scent of ripening guava, dusky pink, the tart tang of tamarind and the lush vegetation. It was all as familiar as her heartbeat; it was welcome and yet... she had never felt more alone.

The earth, the trees, the lake, the mud road, the monkeys as daring as ever, the food, *everything* reminded her of Raju. *It was hard to comprehend that he was gone.*

She had walked into the lake, ignoring the reeds brushing her legs, the swampy ground squelching beneath her feet. She had walked until her head was submerged and in the stillness below water, the muffled watery grave, she had opened her eyes, taking in the wavering blue world. Reeds were brushing her body and water snakes glided past. But even there, struggling for breath, she had not felt it, his death. *She could not believe it.*

She had stayed like that, her lungs desperate, until she'd heard him, distinctly: 'Get out from under there, Missy Baba, are you mad?'

She had emerged, breathing in great panting gasps of slime and brine air. She had walked back to the bank and sat down on it, allowing the sun to dry her wet clothes, hair and body; grateful that nobody was around.

I heard your voice, Raju. Does that mean you are dead? But I cannot believe it. I do not feel it, Raju. I do not.

She went to the village again, where bedraggled children followed her, as did many stares, hostile and curious, along with a procession of vendors haranguing: 'Try this, Memsahib?'

As before, the tang of poverty, rancid rubbish and desperation mingled with spices. She followed the ditch, fetid and stinking, the rank water thick with faeces and grime, until she came to Mali's hut.

It was empty. 'He died a few days ago,' some villagers said.

'Oh.' She choked back the tears that threatened to spill from her eyes.

'The monkey?'

'His pet? It's over there, look.'

And sure enough, Saaya was sitting beside a man hawking coconuts, shaking each one and grinning at the water clunking inside.

'It's a nuisance. We all feed it otherwise it steals food. It will not go and join its fellows in the trees.'

She thought of Mali, his gentleness with plants and with his pet monkey. How tender he was with seedlings, talking and singing to them, coaxing them to grow.

'How exactly did Raju die? What happened?' she had wanted to ask Mali. The questions she had not thought of on that first and, she now realises, only time she would see Mali since her return to India, so stunned was she to hear of Raju's death.

She asked around the village again, but no one else admitted to knowing Raju. She tried bribing some of them with money. They didn't talk. She wondered how much her father had paid them to keep quiet or if he was using threats instead. It was as if Raju, together with his mother and his family, had been wiped out of the collective conscience. Whatever hold her father had on the village, it was very effective.

She sat with her mother, knitting.

Her mother watched her avidly, and although too frail to knit herself, kept admonishing Alice: 'You're not doing it right. You dropped a stitch there.'

While Alice undid the stitches, she accidentally pricked herself. Looking at her blood tinting the thread reminded her of the scarf she had made for Raju; the pattern she'd knitted, with *their* symbol, stained with her blood. She wondered where it was now.

Her mother rudely nudged aside her reverie: 'How is it going with Edward?'

'Alright.' She didn't tell her about their walks every evening, not wanting to encourage her hopes. Alice liked talking to Edward, she enjoyed his company, but she wasn't attracted to him. She didn't ache for him when he wasn't there or miss him with the throbbing, heart-flailing intensity with which she missed Raju, his loss always keenly *there*.

Why was Edward visiting Mother every day? Why was he paying court to Alice? Was it because he liked her, or because she was a means to an end? If so, to what end? *What did Edward really want?*

'Alice, things are so unsettled, both here and in England. Just because I'm shut in this room doesn't mean I don't know what's going on. England is still recovering from war. And here in India, there are communal riots for one thing. And, well, the simple truth is that the natives don't want us here. They want us to leave, go back home. But your father doesn't want to go; he will not. "*This* is my home," he insists and I know you agree. But with things as they are... volatile...' Mother paused. Then, softly, 'I... I had a fiancé who died."

'You did?' Alice looked up at her, surprised. 'I thought Father was your one true love.'

'He *is*. But Freddie, my fiancé, was the one who *taught* me to love, to give of myself.'

'Oh.' Another layer had just been peeled back from the enigma that was her mother.

'What I'm trying to say, Alice,' her mother's every word was an effort, 'is that you can love more than one person in your lifetime. Every love is different, but not exclusive. You *will* forget that boy, the coolie. Even if it was love you harboured for him and not childhood infatuation...'

'Mother—'

'I thought Freddie was my one true love. And at the time he *was*. But he died and I married your father. You will grow to love Edward.'

Will I? 'Why do you want me to marry Edward, Mother, really?' Alice wanted to ask. 'Is it for my sake or yours? After years of putting yourself first, before me, your daughter, I cannot help but wonder if it isn't still the same now. Are you thinking of yourself and Father? Of how much this match will suit you both, wiping away the last, lingering whiff of scandal associated with my abrupt departure to England, rather than of my future happiness?'

But she was afraid of what she might see in her mother's eyes, now that the mask of inhibition and reserve was pulled back to show the raw, pulsing emotions underneath.

'I know I keep repeating this,' her mother's words were farther apart, with each subsequent sentence followed by a wheezing breath, 'but I don't have much time left and if I know you're to be with Edward, I'll die happy.'

Why? Why with Edward?

'You see, I failed you in your childhood.'

'You—'

'And now, with everything so uncertain – this country rebelling, wanting us out, England undone by war – it would be best to have someone by your side, my dear. Someone to love and look after you.'

Is that the only reason?

But Mother was in no position to talk further, falling back against the pillows, spent, her eyes closing, as if the conversation had taken everything out of her.

*

In the afternoons, while her mother rested and before Father and Edward returned, Alice went to the village to continue her questioning of the villagers, trying to jog their memories, hoping that by her sheer persistence (or if not that then with money and bribes), someone would tell her *something*.

Raju and Ayah are dead. Mali's words reverberated in her head when, every day, she came back disappointed. *Then why does my heart not believe it?*

Later, in the evening, she would walk in the grounds with Edward. Edward would have supper with them before returning to his house – 'When I first started working for your father, your parents insisted I take breakfast and supper with them instead of dining alone, and now it's become a ritual!' The sky would be kaleidoscopic with sunset and birds crooned soft lullabies until the light became the soft pink of the inside of a ripe guava, and the evening air was filled with the scents and sounds of waning day, goodbyes, fruit and dust.

Now, on this day, Edward finds her under the tree where Raju and Alice used to sit together, munching on mangoes, their bare, dirty legs dangling from under the branches. Raju would produce salt from his pocket to make the tart fresh mangoes palatable.

If she looks up, will Alice see the ghosts of their younger selves? Will she experience Raju's wide-eyed, beautiful grin that lit up his whole face?

He is dead. I am alive.

Alice shivers.

'What's the matter, Alice? Are you cold?'

'I'm alright.'

'Are you sure?'

'I would have said that it was cold if I hadn't spent the last few years in England,' she tries on a smile.

Edward smiles back. But there's something in his eyes…

Before she can decipher his expression, he takes one of her hands in both of his; something he has not done before.

And now she knows.

'Alice,' he says, 'in the time I've known you, I… I've come to care for you. I believe I love you. I dare to hope that you feel the same. If so, will you do me the honour of becoming my wife?'

She has known this would come. It is what Father and Mother want for her, but does *she* want it?

She likes Edward. But love? She is grieving for Raju. At present, there is no room in her mourning heart for a new love.

'You will grow to love Edward,' Mother has promised.

How do you know this, Mother?

She looks into eyes that are the colour of the moist green of English meadows and is haunted by bright eyes that are the deep toffee of shimmering pools of rainwater on a mud road at sunset.

He is dead.

Do you really love me or am I just the next rung in your ambitious step up the career ladder?

Do you love me or are you doing what is expected of you by your employer and his wife?

Does it matter?

In her mind's eye, Raju appears, holding the water lily in its cradle of heart-shaped leaves out to her.

Alice blinks, and he disappears. In his place, her mother looms, frail and earnest: 'You will grow to love Edward.'

Why do you want me to marry this man, Mother? For my sake or for yours and Father's? To cancel out the disgrace I wrought upon you by kissing a coolie?

Again, she thinks, *Does it matter?*

Mali's words echo in her head: 'He died.'

Edward shifts from foot to foot.

Above her, among the branches of the mango tree, her ghost self laughs with childhood abandon, revelling in Raju's company.

Stop this whimsy now.

'Alice, will you marry me?' Edward's voice trembles just a tiny bit as it is raised in questioning. And it is this hint of vulnerability that decides her.

'Yes,' she says and he smiles, drawing her into his arms.

In her mind's eye, the lily flower crumples, its cushion of bright emerald leaves igniting into ash.

Missy Baba, a chocolate voice calls, *what have you done?*

PART 10

India

Precious

Chapter 46

Alice

1932

Spark

Bang! Alice wakes to the sound, which reverberates in her skull. She breathes in the acrid odour of smoke, which is harsh and out of place, completely obscuring the clean, bright scents of morning. She runs down the stairs of her marital home, which still feels unfamiliar to her despite the fact that she has lived here since her marriage to Edward five years ago.

When she first moved here with Edward, she was relieved. It was new, different. It did not have its cache of memories of Raju everywhere. She could finally mourn him without her heart telling her that he couldn't be dead. She could start to fall in love with her husband.

But married life has not grown on Alice as she had expected it would; as her mother had promised. Mother, who had died soon after Alice and Edward were married, just after Alice's twenty-second birthday, with her wish for her daughter fulfilled. Satisfied, a cynical part of Alice thought that her daughter was prevented from causing further scandal now that she was wed to a respectable man.

Alice had hoped that by marrying Edward, and so doing what her parents wanted, she would, finally, win their love. And for a few glorious months this *was* the case and she had basked in the glow of parental approval.

On her wedding day, Father had said, heartily, 'Good on you, Alice! I can vouch for Edward. You have chosen a capital man.' His declaration had warmed her heart and she had wondered what, if anything, he had said about her to Edward.

Father mellowed after Alice was wed; he was easier to talk to, not as grim or forbidding, smiling more, including Alice in conversation and taking her opinion seriously, instead of disregarding or mocking it. But once Mother was gone, Father became more distant than ever, burying himself in work. She tried reaching out but he rebuffed her, all her attempts spurned, reminding her of the way that the girls at her boarding school had treated her. His withdrawal wounded Alice and she was left to grieve for Raju and Mother and adjust to married life alone. She sometimes thought that it would have been easier if Father had ignored her completely always, rather than opening up to her and then abruptly stopping again; treating her as if a stranger, looking through her rather than at her. She tried to rationalise his remoteness: *I remind him of Mother and it is painful for him*. Nevertheless, whatever his reasons, his renewed aloofness *hurt*.

Father visits Alice and Edward almost every day – their house being just across the village from his, only a ten-minute drive away – and has dinner with them more often than not.

Alice has tried to bring Mother into their conversations, thinking this would help Father by showing him that he was not alone in his grief. But Father has always changed the topic immediately, shying away from anything personal, his talk focusing upon ways to stop the growing mutiny of the Indians, led by Gandhi.

'That man is never out of the news despite being imprisoned for orchestrating his third civil disobedience movement,' Father had muttered the previous night, setting down his tumbler of whisky at Alice and Edward's table.

'What's he done now?' Alice had asked.

Her father had not bothered to answer her question, but Edward had replied, 'He is conducting a hunger strike from prison in protest at the government's decision to separate India's electoral system by caste.'

'But surely dividing Indians by caste is not the best—'

Now Father had acknowledged Alice's presence, cutting her off rudely: 'You don't presume to know more about governing this country than the Viceroy, do you, Alice?'

Alice had looked to her husband but he was looking at her father with an expression of rapt attention, nodding along to his words. And so she had picked up her glass and left the room, ignoring Edward calling after her, bemused, 'Alice, my dear, what's the matter?'

Afterwards, Edward had found her on the veranda, lulled by the gathering darkness, the monotonous whirr of crickets, the buzz and drone of mosquitoes and flies, and the soothing rose scents of dusk.

'Alice.'

She waited.

'I understand you were upset, my dear, but your father is of a generation where they do not entertain opinions from—'

'A woman? A daughter?' Alice had cut in, her voice bitter black, bristling with hurt and anger, the darkening world around her blurry and distorted.

'I was going to say from anyone at all, if it differs from their own opinions.' There'd been a smile in Edward's voice.

'I'm glad one of us finds this funny.'

'Alice, your father doesn't show it but he's finding it very hard to cope without your mother.'

'I know. And I've tried to speak to him about her…'

'That's not his way. He'd rather carry on as if nothing has changed,' Edward had said mildly. 'Be patient with him, my dear.'

'It is hard when he ignores me or talks over me.'

Edward laid a hand on hers. 'He will come round, give him time.'

They'd sat like that, hands linked, watching night steal the glow from evening, until Alice's anger had dissipated, soothed by her husband's gentleness.

Edward was kind. He was patient. She liked him. Why couldn't she love him?

*

Alice had hoped that the physical side to married life would, if not fill the hollow emptiness within her left by the loss of Raju, then at the very least assuage it. But it is nothing like she had expected. It is mechanical, methodical, precise, like everything Edward does. There is no *passion*.

Materially, she doesn't want for anything. Every evening after Father has left, she and Edward sit together on the veranda in quiet companionship, nursing their drinks and their thoughts, the silence not stifling but calming.

She can envision them getting old together. And yet…

He does not look at her in the way that Raju used to: a mixture of adoration and awe, love and affection. There's no spark. There *is* amity, but no *love*, at least not of the kind Father must have shared with Mother; the kind that charges and fizzes; that excludes everyone else, even their offspring.

Alice had thought that love would come. But as the long days have bled into one another, she has come to the gradual realisation that it might not. That this is it. Her life.

She paces the vast compound of the grand house, lush and riotous with creamy jasmine and starry bougainvillea, rose and marigold, cashews and lime, peppercorns and pineapples, and hankers for something *more*, her traitorous soul yearning for Raju.

She knows that Edward likes her. But does he love her? Did he marry her because he had to, because it was what was expected of him from his employer and his wife? What was he after when he asked her to be his wife? Power? Ambition? The advancing of his career through her? Was he doing it out of duty? Love? All of these things?

Is he happy with her? Or does he also sense the lack of something essential, like she does?

Alice longs for heart-stopping, heart-breaking, fantastic, over-the-top love. A love where she knows without doubt, without question, that she is necessary, indispensable. She yearns for someone to look at her as though she is their world; for someone to need her to complete their world.

Some nights she wonders if perhaps it would have been different if she had married one of her suitors in England. She had refused them because she wanted to return to India, to live in the country she considered home. But now she thinks that perhaps precisely because she *is* in India, the country she loves, but without her love in it, she is feeling claustrophobic. Restless. It's as if she is waiting for something to happen; for something to change. Waiting for love. Longing for it. As she has been all her life, her soul constantly yearning for its missing half to complete it, except for that one glorious, too-brief moment when Raju had kissed her.

*

Now, Alice follows the harsh reek of charred smoke to the garden.

Among the pineapple bushes, underneath an awning of bougainvillea singing in kaleidoscopic colour, she finds carnage.

The remains of a watermelon, seeping into mud, the tainted crimson of sin.

Edward is handing his rifle to his groom, a muscle jumping in his cheek. 'I'm sorry, my dear. Did the noise wake you?' He looks up at Alice, his green eyes black with glittering upset, rife with shadows.

She rests a hand on his arm, saying, softly, 'What happened?'

'I was cleaning my rifle. We use rifles to scare the coolies, you see, when they are gathering in groups, protesting for self-rule. We fire into the air and they scatter like ants under a stamping foot.' He shoots a glance that Alice can't quite read at the gardener and his helper, who are cowering beside the bleeding mess of the watermelon. 'The rifle went off accidentally.'

Before she can make sense of what is really going on, Edward takes her hand, folds it under his arm, 'Shall we go into breakfast?'

As Edward spoons kedgeree onto his plate, Alice prompts, 'Edward, you can handle that rifle with your eyes closed. Will you tell me what really happened just now?'

His gaze when it meets hers is hard: 'They were talking about us, the gardener and his boy.'

And Alice knows instantly, a shaft of hurt flooring her, what Edward is *not* saying. She can read it in the ring of pain crusting the hardness in his eyes. The servants must have been discussing – as surely everyone is, given that Edward and Alice have been married for five years now – why Alice isn't yet with child.

Alice has wished and prayed for offspring, fancying children will inject that vital something that is missing in her relationship with her husband. Her bleeding has never been regular – she has been to multiple doctors who have assured her that nothing is wrong, that her womb *will* quicken with child – but month after month, she is disappointed.

Edward himself has not pressured her, although Father has had no such qualms. He has been hinting about how he'd like to be a grandfather for a while now and has recently taken to asking outright.

Now, Edward is saying, 'The servants are careful not to gossip in your presence, my dear, for you know Hindi. They think that I don't, but I understand more than I let on.'

Alice cannot eat. She is pushing fruit around her plate, seeing in her mind's eye the watermelon's insides spattered messily on the mud beside the spiky yellow pineapples, and the fearful gazes of the gardener and his boy.

What had they been saying?

'I've sacked them.'

'Oh.'

'They'll not be getting a reference from me.'

Guilt harpoons Alice as she recalls Mali's voice: 'Sahib sacked everyone, replaced all the staff. Most of us, myself included, did not get another job.'

How many servants will hold me responsible for their loss of jobs and livelihoods? But it isn't my fault this time. They were talking about us. It's their fault. But isn't it human nature to gossip?

She shudders, trying to push away the warring voices of her conscience; thoughts of Mali bringing back the words that had shattered her heart: *He died.*

'My dear, I'm sorry if this has upset you.' Edward is sounding apologetic.

Mali's words are echoing in her head, reviving the hopelessness that they engendered, which has never really left her: *He died.*

Alice cannot prevent the tremor that rocks her.

'Excuse me, please, Edward.' She leaves the table, walking carefully, her head held high, until she's outside the room, at which point she lifts her skirts and runs, pushing aside servants who stare, shocked at her unladylike behaviour.

I'm igniting fresh gossip, she thinks, as salty sobs tinged with bile and hysteria threaten. She makes it to the nearest bathroom where she is sick, over and over, trying to disgorge her guilt, her hurt, her pain, the emptiness that stalks her, a small part of her stubbornly hopeful that she might be pregnant, while her mind, frantically doing calculations, knows she cannot be.

Chapter 47

Janaki

1967

Havoc

Janaki wakes in her room at the orphanage, her vivid dream about Prasad playing havoc with her mind.

She seeks Sister Shanthi out. 'What you said yesterday about Prasad…'

Sister Shanthi smiles knowingly.

'I…' The question she wants to ask sticks in her throat, so she settles for, 'Emotions are messy.'

'Too late now.' Sister Shanthi laughs. 'You love him.'

You love him. The realisation she has woken up with. *I do. But I cannot. I lose those I love and it* hurts.

'You've given him your heart.'

I have.

'I'm frightened,' Janaki whispers.

Sister Shanthi cups her cheek. 'Nothing to be frightened of, my child. Love is beautiful, glorious.'

'Everyone I love dies.' Janaki confesses her deepest fear in a panicked gush.

'*I* haven't. Neither has Sister Nandita, Sister Malli, Bina, Shali, nor Mother Superior.'

'I…'

'I know what you mean, and why you are fearful, but it's too late now, Janu. You've already given your heart to Prasad. And, my child, you cannot live your life being afraid, shying away from love. What happened to you was terrible, but that doesn't mean it is the norm, that it will happen again.'

Sister Shanthi's words, said with complete conviction, calm Janaki's agitated heart somewhat. Since she is confessing everything anyway, she blurts out, 'He hasn't said anything.'

'He will.'

'What if he doesn't love me?' There. She's said it now, acknowledged the doubt rampant in her heart alongside the knowledge that she loves him.

This is another reason she was afraid to love, to give of herself; loving someone renders you vulnerable. It is terrifying, like jumping off a mountain without a parachute.

'He does.' Sister Shanthi is matter-of-fact.

The jasmine-perfumed air tastes of relief, the confidence in Sister Shanthi's voice affording Janaki the comfort she seeks.

'Janu,' Sister Shanthi's voice is gentle. 'Why wait? You've done everything differently. You've been a trailblazer. Why don't you ask him if he loves you and when he says he does, ask him to marry you?'

*

Prasad is already at Mother Teresa's refuge, assisting a woman who is giving birth, when Janaki arrives. Her heart fills when she looks at him; he is deft, focused, confident. He beams when the baby is delivered.

I love him. Why didn't I see it before? What if he doesn't love me? Sister Shanthi is not right all *of the time.*

This, she thinks as fear engulfs her, leaving her breathless, *is why I have shied away from emotion.*

I'm the lone woman in a man's world, she reassures her doubting, flailing self. *I've delivered countless babies against all odds; I've saved them and their mothers from certain death. I can do this. I can accept rejection if he doesn't like me in quite the way I like him.*

But her mind shrinks, cringing, from the thought.

The object of her furious internal debate looks up at her and smiles that beautiful, infectious grin, which makes her heart flip, blissfully oblivious to her raging turmoil.

That evening, as Janaki and Prasad say goodbye before returning to their respective homes, Janaki, who has spent the day alternating between fear that Prasad doesn't love her and certainty that he does – while savouring the realisation of how comfortable she feels in his company, how right – knows that she *has* to find out if he feels the same way. Deciding that she cannot wait any longer, she blurts, 'Can we go for a *thali*?'

Prasad is surprised. 'Today? But you allow only one day a week for our *thali* dinners and we already went on Thursday.'

She's been regimental in sticking to routine in case he reads too much into their weekly outings and now it's working against her.

'I...' Her mouth is dry. *Please say yes.*

'Are you okay? You've not been yourself all day.'

'I'm fine. But I'll be better after a *thali*.'

They sit at their usual table, tucked away at the back. The food comes, piping hot and delicious – pilau rice and buttery naan, creamy spinach and spiced potatoes, fried aubergine and chilli-coated okra, followed by *kheer* topped with nuts and honeyed *jalebis* dripping syrup – the proprietor making small talk.

Janaki can't eat for nerves.

'Aren't you hungry?' Prasad is bemused.

'I thought I was.' She pushes her *thali* at him. 'Will you finish it for me? I don't want to waste it. This is heaven compared with the food we had growing up. I know how lucky I am to be able to eat like this now.'

'I really enjoyed the trip to the orphanage. Thanks for taking me. I respect you even more now I see where you've come from, how hard you've worked to be where you are.' His gaze is earnest.

The other tables are populated by regulars, heads bent, concentrating on their food. Nobody is paying any attention to them.

The potpourri of aromas, sweet and savoury, usually so appetising, is making her nauseous.

If he doesn't love me, she tells herself as she looks at him, his eyes glowing as he talks about the orphanage, *I'll settle for friendship.*

In her head Sister Shanthi's voice: *He's completely besotted with you.*

'I had parents who pushed me and sent me abroad for my Masters,' he's saying. 'You've had to fight to achieve everything.'

His earnest voice. His gaze radiant as he looks at her. *Perhaps he does love me after all. Perhaps Sister Shanthi is right. Please God.*

'You're a marvel.'

'Stop!' she says. 'You're always saying I'm big-headed as it is.'

'Well, I would be too if I had so many newspaper cuttings about me displayed all over the orphanage,' he teases, eyes twinkling.

'I wondered when you'd bring that up.' She takes a deep breath. She *has* to say it, has to know how he feels. 'Look, at the orphanage, while sharing my childhood with you, I… I realised something.'

'Yes?' Eyebrows raised, a query in his eyes. He appears, for all the world, like an eager young boy.

What is she thinking? He's younger than her, he'll want someone younger, prettier. He… *Stop thinking this way, just get it over with. This way you can know and move on.*

'I…'

'What is it? I've never known you to fumble.' Worry creases his forehead. 'Have I upset you? Was I over-familiar with the nuns?'

'No, it's not that at all. In fact, the opposite. I…' She swallows. Then, in a rush: 'I've begun to care for you.'

'Care?' He says the word wonderingly. 'You mean…?' He looks stunned.

She holds up her hand. 'I'm sorry, I just… Let's forget…'

He takes her hand in his. A thrill starts at her fingertips and reverberates through her entire being.

'Janaki.'

Her name on his lips. It's the first time he's said it. She realises now that while in the hospital he calls her 'Doctor'; elsewhere, he doesn't call her anything at all. But now her name is on his lips, so tender and full of awe; it's the sweetest sound.

'Do you mean to say…?'

'I love you,' she says.

He beams, tears shining in his eyes. 'Oh, Janaki, I… I've loved you since that first day when you interviewed me, lobbing questions at me one after the other without pause. So fierce and yet, when you stopped and rubbed your beautiful eyes with the back of your hand, so fragile.'

Relief and overwhelming joy spreads through every part of her. *He loves me too. Sister Shanthi was right.*

'Some more sweets for you – freshly prepared just now.' The proprietor sets a plate of luminescent *gulab jamuns* swimming in a pool of golden syrup in front of them.

Prasad retrieves his hand, leaving her bereft, although she understands he's only looking out for her, being correct and proper. It doesn't do to hold hands in public. But she's not bereft for long, for he reclaims her hand as soon as the proprietor leaves:

'I'm going to do this properly. Janaki, I've loved you since I first set eyes on you. Will you marry me?'

'Yes,' she whispers. 'But first, I have something to tell you.'

And then, haltingly, she tells him about her adoption, the love she experienced, glorious but too brief. Tears roll down his face unchecked even as he gently, with the hand not holding hers, wipes her tears away.

She tells him of Arthy, her best friend, who had stood by her through it all, cajoling her, loving her out of her depression after she came back to the orphanage – and of how she lost her.

His voice when he speaks is roiling and fathomless as the sea, marinated in salt: 'I cannot believe how you are still standing, still smiling, going on despite all that has happened to you. I admired you before but now I—'

'This isn't why I told you—'

'I understand why you did. You're afraid. Of loving then losing.'

He understands. His gaze is gentle, infinitely soft and tender, so full of love. Nobody has looked at her quite like this before, not even her adoptive parents. It warms her, makes her feel she's not alone. Wrung out as she is with sharing her burden of pain for the first time, she also feels hopeful.

She has lost so much. Surely she has paid her dues, in that giant balance sheet God must keep? Surely she'll be allowed to cherish this man, who is saying – with his loving-and-assurance-filled gaze not leaving hers – 'I promise you, Janaki, that I will love you always. I will never do anything to hurt you. I will never leave you.'

She cannot speak, as emotion overwhelms her, so she nods instead. Their shared tears fall onto their joined hands.

'So much about you makes sense now. Why you volunteer at the orphanage and the refuge, why you are so relentless, so focused upon saving lives.' He smiles, his wet face, shiny eyes, crinkling. 'Janaki, you're everything I've ever dreamt of. I'll make sure you're happy always, my love.'

She smiles, tasting happiness, sweet as *gulab jamun* in her mouth.

Chapter 48

Alice

1935

River of People

Alice is shopping in Jamjadpur when she sees him. She is in the textile-and-fabric section of the market, looking for material for a new dress to wear at the upcoming commissioner's ball. 'This one, Memsahib, or perhaps this one?' the proprietor of the tent she has entered asks, spreading a selection of rainbow-hued silks before her, shimmering and cascading, soft as a lover's caress.

She cannot decide between the maroon of heartbreak and the velvet navy of darkest midnight. She is hot in the close tent, the odour of perspiration and cloth sharp and tangy. Sweat trails down her back. Her throat is dry, she's desperate for a cool drink: tender coconut water, perhaps, or mango *lassi*? Buttermilk spiced with green chillies and crushed ginger? No, she wants tea. Hot and sickly sweet, skin of milk floating on top, liberally seasoned with cinnamon.

'Keep these aside,' she says, pointing to the two fabrics. 'I'll be back in half an hour.' She parts the beaded curtain that serves as a door to the tent and emerges into mayhem. Peanut and *bhelpuri* vendors are calling out; a man is frying *bondas*, the seasoned oil sputtering; another is selling carpets, the multihued stacks dwarfing the vendor and tilting dangerously when people walk past; there are saris, bangles, utensils, flower garlands, wilting vegetables, and snacks attracting flies.

Alice walks briskly towards the tea stall she favours, the vendor greeting her with a wide grin, 'Welcome, Memsahib. I've put extra ginger and cinnamon in your tea just the way you like it. And here, two samosas with coriander chutney.'

Someone cuts in front of her and she tuts, annoyed. She's about to admonish them when her gaze is captured by a man at the other end of the road, haggling with a hawker of what appears to be scarves. Something in his manner, the way he has inclined his head... *It can't be, can it?*

There is a seething river of people between them, moving, talking, pushing, but she stands still, frozen for a quicksilver moment, her gaze fixed on him. Then she is running towards him, ignoring the tea vendor who calls, 'Memsahib, where're you going? Come back, I'll give you the samosas for free.'

But she cannot hear him through the pounding in her ears, the thunder of her disbelieving, agitated, excited, hopeful heart. She is unaware of the people she is pushing aside, the vendors who move their wares from under her feet, shouting, 'Look out, Memsahib!' All she is aware of is the man, all her focus on him.

He stops talking and looks up, towards her, as if somehow aware of Alice running towards him. As if an invisible voice has whispered in his ear; as if the thread that, Alice believes, has always bound them has been tugged.

Their eyes meet.

He startles and for one brief moment, his whole face lights up, eyes aglow. Those eyes, that gaze, so familiar, beloved, filling her heart, which had persisted in refusing to believe he was no more, infusing her soul with exhilarating, overwhelming, exultant, glorious joy.

Then the veiled woman by his side nudges him and their gaze is broken, leaving Alice bereft. The woman says something to him and he turns, and then he is moving away.

Away from her. No!

'Raju!' she calls.

She is still half a road away and they are surrounded and blocked by a surge of people, but he stills for one heart-stopping minute. He doesn't turn, but she sees his back go rigid.

Again, she cries, 'Raju!' All her love, her missing, her ache, her emptiness at the loss of him, her angst in that one name.

He stops and she knows he's heard. And then… and then instead of turning and running towards her, bridging the gap between them, he walks away. *Turn back. Look at me.* But he walks *away*, the veiled woman keeping pace at his side.

Alice tries to catch up, running after them, angling to keep sight of them through alleyways, and down side roads. She overturns baskets of fruit, scatters piles of spices. 'Memsahib, watch out!' the outraged hawkers call, as she leaves in her wake the scent of consternation, cumin and crushed fruit.

She does not hear. Her heart is pounding with anticipation and panic. *I cannot lose him, I cannot. Raju, why are you going away from me instead of towards me?* But she knows why. Of course she knows. He is meant to be dead. Dead to her, she understands now, noting her father's reach and how far it goes. *Who knows what he has threatened Raju with?*

'*Raju!*' she calls, her heart panting, fear and hurt in her chest. But he has mingled among the crowds.

He has gone.

Nevertheless, he is not dead. *Her Raju.* She has spent years trying to live with the knowledge, which never felt like truth, that he was no more. *Years of trying to love another man. Years of trying to* live…

It was just a glimpse, but she knows it's him. For when their eyes met, for just the briefest of moments, she saw the recognition in them, quickly masked as he turned away, towards the veiled woman by his side, and disappeared into the crowd.

Her father must have paid Mali to lie while on his deathbed, knowing his daughter would go searching for her lost love. All those years, in all those letters from England, Alice had tried to convince her mother of her love for Raju; to show her that it was just as strong as Mother's love for Father.

But it was *Father,* Alice sees now, who understood just how much Alice loved Raju; it was *Father* who knew that when she returned to India, she would try to find her love.

She recalls thinking, when Mali told her that Raju was dead and she was struggling to comprehend it, *I'd rather you were alive and married.*

Look at us, eh, Raju? Both married, not to each other, as I once hoped naively; dreamt about. You to that veiled woman by your side, who must be the girl you were betrothed to. Me to Edward, because of the promise I made to my mother on her deathbed. Edward is gentle and patient. Over the years, as the heir he longs for has not materialised, he hasn't complained. He's exactly what my mother, who died soon after we were married, promised. But…

He's not you.

Her Raju has come back from the dead. How fitting that she should find him again in the very city where she'd kissed him during a riot and then lost him. But not forever as she feared and tried to accept after Mali's false pronouncement.

And even though she is married, even though she knows better, that she should leave well alone, she cannot allow him to slip through her fingers again.

You walked away from me, but I know you didn't really want to. I lost you once when we were teenagers. Again, when I thought you were dead.

I cannot lose you now.

Chapter 49

Alice

1935

Everything

Alice paces the courtyard, up and down, up and down.

Everything has changed.

Nothing has changed.

Raju is alive. He's alive, her heart sings.

You are married. Raju is too.

I only want to see him once. Talk to him, say goodbye properly, like I never got to do, she soothes her hectoring conscience.

How to find Raju? She cannot risk her father knowing she's cottoned on to his subterfuge. She shudders, thinking of his reaction, her cheek throbbing with phantom pain from when he slapped her after he caught her kissing Raju.

Father must have paid Mali to lie to her – perhaps he made sure Mali was in the village when she went there asking after Raju – to mislead her. He had sent all the other servants packing, why didn't she think it suspicious that Mali was there waiting for her? 'I've come home to die,' Mali had said. Perhaps that was the truth but she also sees her father's hand in it.

And Edward… He's kind to her. In his own understated way, she believes he cares for her. But not enough to go against her father. Never that. If she is to find Raju, she needs to be very careful that neither Father nor Edward discover what she is up to.

In any case Father and Edward are very busy trying to contain the terrible discord between Hindus and Muslims, which erupts every so often into violence. And there's the Independence Movement; Indians wanting freedom from centuries of British rule.

At the balls she attends as Edward's wife, steeped with the scent of rose water and wine, intrigue and gossip, the ladies say, 'Self-rule is well and good but how the Indians will manage is another matter.'

'I expect they'll end up killing each other without us to calm the *junglees* down, bring order.' The tinkle of sharp-edged laughter fills the air.

Alice fingers the pearls on her throat, which threaten to choke her. She hears Raju's voice from that long-ago afternoon, in the toasty kitchen scented with roasted chillies, sugar syrup and love, clamorous with Ayah and Cook debating whose *methi* chicken recipe was better: 'My da says we managed quite well before you came along and we will manage again when you leave…'

Chapter 50

Janaki

1967

The Best

Janaki and Prasad are married in the orphanage, among the family they have chosen and who chose them: patients and fellow volunteers at Mother Teresa's refuge, doctors and nurses from the hospital, the children of the orphanage, whose illnesses Janaki has tended, and of course the nuns, beaming, ecstatic.

Janaki imagines Arthy looking on from the afterworld, saying, *I wish I could be with you to meet the man who has won your heart and celebrate this wonderful occasion. He must be one in a million!*

In her heart, Janaki replies to her friend: *He is.*

Somu, proprietor of the eatery in the alleyway behind the hospital, which played its part in bringing them together, supplies the wedding *thali*. Everyone agrees it is the best they have tasted.

Afterwards, in Prasad's home, bequeathed to him by his parents, Prasad takes her in his arms: 'I love you, Janaki. I cannot believe you are my wife.'

She kisses him, understanding why people do it, take the plunge, fall in love. Firstly, they have no choice; she had loved almost without knowing that was what it was. Secondly, no matter how vulnerable giving of yourself so completely to someone else might make you, it is worth it.

If she didn't love, she would be happy in a sedate, careful way but not enraptured, enchanted. Not like this. For this, she is willing to risk pain again despite all that has gone before. 'I love you,' she says to Prasad when they come up for air. After that there is no talking. Only loving.

Chapter 51

Alice

1935

Taut

Jamjadpur is even more crowded than usual, tension taut as a stretched string, the throb of danger, a hum in the air as if poised for, on the cusp of something. Alice ignores it, her own heart aquiver with anticipation, thrill. She's so close to finding Raju.

It *was* Raju she'd seen. He had stilled at the sound of her voice. He had recognised her. Those eyes…

Madness, what you're doing, her conscience chimes, as it has taken to doing.

She ignores it, defiant, speaking to the chauffeur instead: 'Please stop here. I need to look at fabric.'

'Memsahib, not a good idea. Looks like trouble's brewing.'

Exactly what Edward had cautioned that morning.

'What are your plans for today?' Edward had asked over breakfast. They were on the veranda, the air stroking Alice's face cool and redolent with roses and jasmine. Edward was eating kedgeree and scrambled eggs, while Alice snacked on mango and pineapple from their garden, scarcely able to contain her excitement.

'I thought I'd go to the city, choose fabric for a dress to wear to the ball.'

Edward looked up at her then. *Did he suspect?* 'I thought you'd been already.'

'I couldn't decide between the navy and the maroon. Upon reflection, I've decided to go with navy.'

'There's unrest, my dear. Tempers are running high between the Hindus and Muslims.'

She let out the breath she'd been holding. *He didn't know, of course he didn't.* 'Nothing will happen in *our* city surely?'

'It's happened before,' he said and Alice was transported instantly in her memory to the riot during which she and Raju had kissed.

Edward was saying, 'All it takes is one unwise comment, one spark, and it will light a fire that will consume everything in its path and will be very hard to douse.'

'I'll be quick.'

'I'd rather you didn't go at all, but if you must, be careful. And head for home the moment there's any hint of trouble.'

He will not take lightly to being cuckolded and you know it, her conscience chided. Fear and guilt ambushed her, even as she promised her husband, but not enough to change her mind.

'Memsahib, I'll come with you,' the chauffeur says now.

'No, I'll be fine.' Anticipation and eagerness lend an edge to her voice, rendering it sharper than she intended.

Chastised, the man nods. 'I'll be waiting right here.'

Alice ignores the vendors thrusting bangles and trinkets at her, barely registering the scent of spices, the myriad colours and fabrics. There's an underlying thrum of menace; men are gathered in huddles, eyeing other groups of men and Alice herself with suspicion and hostility.

She walks single-mindedly to her destination, pushing through the milling throngs, the atmosphere so charged she can taste its zany electric blue.

Her favoured fabric vendor, who's standing outside his tent, urges, upon catching sight of her, 'Memsahib, I've several new fabrics, very beautiful, that have just come in. Have a look.'

But she rushes past him, her heart crooning a melody, *Please let him know Raju.*

The vendor Raju was talking to is standing at the other end of the road, hawking sequinned scarves and bangles, vests and hair clips.

His eyes light up when she approaches. 'Memsahib, what can I do for you? Would you like this beautiful scarf?' He holds up a patterned scarf the dazzling turquoise of a sun-splashed stream. 'It will go so well with your complexion.'

'I'm here to ask about a man you were talking to yesterday.'

His eager expression closes up. 'Many men talk to me.' He is sullen now.

'His name is Raju Kumar.' She sees a flicker of recognition in the man's eyes. It's enough to make her flush with happiness. *It* was *Raju I saw.*

The vendor busies himself with the scarves. 'I don't know…'

'Here.' She whips out a few of the notes she has brought with her. 'I'll only give you these if you tell me where he lives.'

'Why do you want to know?' His gaze is greedy as he stares at the money, his voice both curious and suspicious.

'He used to work for us. I have something of his I need to return.'

His eyebrows shoot up. 'Memsahibs generally do not return stuff belonging to their servants.' A sly note creeps into his voice. 'They don't care…'

'Do you want the money or not?'

The man sizes up the notes, licking his lips in anticipation. 'Is he in trouble? I just… His wife does all the sequins and beading for me, we have a good business going; they collect the scarves and she sews on the sequins every month.'

His wife. The veiled woman. Alice's heart sinks, but at the same time it is singing. *This man knows where Raju lives!* 'He's not in any trouble, I promise. There's something I need to give him.'

'If you say so, Memsahib…'

'Well? Where does he live, then?'

'At Ambalgiri, the village to the south of—'

He is interrupted by a loud voice: 'Watch where you're going!'

A few paces from where Alice is standing, one man is shoving another rather rudely.

'What do you think you're doing, you Hindu dog?'

'Don't you dare…'

In a matter of moments, a mob has formed, shouting insults, hitting and cursing one another, more men joining in…

'All it takes is one unwise comment, one spark, and it will light a fire that will consume everything in its path and will be very hard to douse,' Edward had cautioned.

People are lifting anything to hand and chucking it at one another. There are screams and cries of pain. It is utter mayhem.

Ambalgiri, Alice chants in her head, *Ambalgiri.*

The vendor starts throwing his scarves and bangles haphazardly into a box. Alice thrusts the money at him and runs through the crowd, dense with body odour and spitting rage, righteous anger and manic upset.

Ambalgiri.

There is chaos everywhere. She dodges an aubergine that is flung at her, and a vehement hand glancing her cheek, recoiling from the hot, clammy shock of it.

Ambalgiri.

People are pushing, sobbing, yelling, running, hurting.

Ambalgiri.

The chauffeur, worried eyes scanning the crowd, beams with relief when he sees her. He helps her in, and they are off, narrowly avoiding the mob's violently hurled stones, sticks and insults.

Ambalgiri.

As they escape the city she is transported to another time, another riot, when she found love and simultaneously lost her love. Now in the midst of this one she has located his whereabouts.

'Do you know where Ambalgiri is?' she asks the chauffeur, once they have left the rioting behind and reached the relative quiet of the country lanes leading up to their compound.

'It's across the city on the other side, Memsahib.'

Raju is near enough to touch.

'It's very small, Memsahib, and there's nobody… I mean, there're no Sahibs there, only—'

'That's fine. I...' She roots around for a reason and it comes to her, 'I need some sequins sewed onto my dress – my tailor is not good at that sort of thing, he ruined my dress last time. I enquired at the market and they recommended a seamstress who lives in Ambalgiri.' It amazes her the ease and fluidity with which the lies arrive.

The chauffeur nods assent, his eyes on the road.

'Can you take me there tomorrow?' She cannot wait, she will not. Not when she has waited all this time to find Raju; when she was told he was dead and tried to live with the terrible knowledge even though she didn't quite believe it.

He's married and so are you, her conscience warns again.

I just want to see him once, that's all. Then I will return to my life, leave him to lead his.

'There is no need to tell Sahib,' Alice tells the chauffeur now. 'He's worried enough about the riots, I don't want him to have to worry for my safety.'

'Yes, Memsahib.'

She rests her head against the back rest and closes her eyes, her heart aflutter with eager, impatient anticipation, tasting the sweetly intoxicating memory of the kiss she'd shared with Raju before they were rudely torn apart.

Chapter 52

Alice

1935

Lies

Ambalgiri is a tiny outcrop of hunched, dust-drenched huts rising from the mud. As their car approaches, instead of the occasional bold monkey, which had danced out of the road just in time to avoid getting crushed by the car's wheels, now it's scantily clad children, playing on the road with stones and twigs, who jump out of the way and abandon their game to follow the car, curious.

Alice has hardly been able to sit still; she cannot contain her excitement and anticipation, trepidation and hope, a bittersweet cocktail in her parched mouth.

'What are your plans for today?' Edward had asked as usual that morning.

He'd looked tired, dark circles haunting his eyes. He'd been extremely busy lately, out till all hours, sorting the problems arising from India's fight for independence and the unrest between the Hindus and Muslims, leaving directly after breakfast and coming home after Alice was in bed.

'Oh, nothing much,' she'd said, reaching for the papaya, the rich sweetness exploding in her mouth masking the bitter taste of her lies. *I have to do this, meet Raju, see him just the once. Then I'll be able to move on, face my future when I've said goodbye to my past.*

But will you be able to move on? her conscience chided. *You're lying to your husband but worst of all, you're lying to yourself.*

People come out of their huts to watch the car's approach: women in worn saris, with children clinging to them; old men with hard eyes, leathery skin.

The chauffeur stops the car. 'I'll find out where the seamstress lives, Memsahib.'

But Alice is not listening. Looking at the gathered spectators, not a single young and able man among them, something that should have been obvious, had she been thinking straight, occurs to her: *Of course he's not here. He's working in the fields we passed on our way here.*

She had clocked the men, scattered among the fields, urging their buffaloes on, but had not really paid them any attention, her mind set on getting to Raju. She hadn't planned ahead, with only one thought occupying her mind: wanting to see her childhood companion and love.

You've been extremely reckless, her conscience remonstrates now, *coming here, like this. If word gets back to your father, to Edward, what will you do then?*

She opens her mouth to call the chauffeur back, ask him to turn the car round, but he's saying, 'Memsahib, it's that one over there.' He is pointing to a hut in the middle of the scanty row flanking the road; around fifteen in total that make up the village.

It's too late to come up with an excuse or say she's changed her mind when the entire village seems to be waiting and watching to see what she'll do next.

Mali lied about Raju being dead so he must have lied about Ayah dying too. I might see Ayah. Her disappointed heart warms at the prospect. *And I can always stop at the fields on the way back…*

Alice gets out of the car, clutching the fabric that is her excuse, with curious gazes spearing her. Even as she averts her eyes, she is taking everything in, her heart beating an anticipatory rhythm in her chest. *This is Raju's village. Where he's lived, presumably, since he and Ayah were let go by Father.*

Raju's hut – *Raju's* hut – is indistinguishable from the others, except there's nobody standing outside gawping at the unexpected visitor. An omen? Good or bad? *Does this mean he has no children?*

Yet… her conscience adds. *No children yet, if, indeed, that is the case.*

A sari has been draped in place of a door. She pushes it aside, even as she thinks, *Raju has touched this. I am standing where he does when he enters his home, at the threshold into his life without me in it.* There's a catch in her throat; fear and excitement all mixed up. Expectation and apprehension suffuse her. She swallows, then calls, 'Hello?' Gawking villagers have gathered behind her; a pressing crowd exuding the scent of sweat and curiosity.

Alice blinks, her eyes adjusting to the sudden darkness inside the hut after the blinding sunshine outside. There's movement from within, accompanied by the sound of chiming anklets. A woman comes into view, her face framed by the veil that she has draped around it. Alice sees a round, pretty face, eyes wide with surprise at her visitor.

Is this the girl Alice had once glimpsed from her room? The girl sitting on the well beside Raju, stealing shy glances at him? She feels a stab of jealousy as she takes in the vermilion *bindi* on this woman's forehead, the mark of a married woman. *You can lay claim to him in a way I cannot.*

'Memsahib?' The woman's forehead is puckered, questioning.

'I… I… Raju…' His name, spoken out loud; the beautiful taste of it; honey and chocolate.

The woman's eyes widen even more. 'You know my husband?'

Husband. Again, a lance of bitter, hot jealousy. *I wish I did. I wish I knew him like you do.* And in its wake, the last lingering shred of doubt chased away. *I was right. He* is *alive. This* is *his hut.* 'His mother was my ayah.'

Even as comprehension dawns in the woman's beautiful, almond eyes, a wavering voice calls from within the dark depths of the hut: 'Jyoti, who is it?'

She looks uncertain, worry and confusion warring, her eyes a mirror to her every thought. She's young, beautiful, Raju's. The crowd outside the hut is chattering; a child laughs, a baby wails. Alice draws in the scent of dust and heartache, the lime-blue taste of what might have been.

Then, as Ayah calls again, in a voice tremulous with age, 'Jyoti?', the woman seems to arrive at a decision.

'Come, Memsahib,' she says, inclining her head and pulling the sari door closed to prevent the crowd behind Alice from entering. But Alice doesn't notice. Her heart is conducting a wild and violent symphony in her chest as she walks into Raju's home.

Chapter 53

Janaki

1969

A Million Pieces

Janaki is at the orphanage, attending to a child who is, according to the nuns, 'not quite right', and whom she suspects of suffering from type 1 diabetes, when there is a pounding on the orphanage door.

'I'll answer it,' she calls. She's nearest the door, on her way to hospital to confirm the diagnosis. In her distended stomach, her baby somersaults. She strokes it, smiling, as she reaches for the door handle.

'I don't want children,' she had said to Prasad just before their marriage when the subject, inevitably, came up.

He'd flinched, his smile wavering, but recovered his composure almost immediately. 'Is it because you're afraid?'

She nodded. 'I can do more for the children at the orphanage, hospital and refuge as a doctor. I think of them as my children, I care for them.'

'I know you do,' Prasad had said, his eyes soft.

'But having children of my own, I... Before you came along, I'd thought about adopting children from the refuge and orphanage. I had a flat of my own, I felt privileged and lucky and I wanted to share that. But I knew it would be impossible to make a choice when they're each perfect in their own way and I couldn't take all the children. Given that I didn't want to subject those that I didn't pick to the feeling of rejection that I'd experienced at the orphanage, when prospective parents chose other children over me, given that I…'

How could she put into words what she wanted to say?

During her time as a practising doctor, she'd been unable to save the lives of a couple of children and the devastation of their parents, the way they went to pieces, was harder to bear than the guilt that she inevitably subjected herself to, despite knowing she'd done all she possibly could for the children. Being party to the naked, flayed-alive grief of those parents had reinforced her decision to stay away from emotion and to keep love and its messy vulnerabilities firmly at bay, thus protecting her already broken and battered heart.

But, looking into the soft gold eyes she had fallen in love with, all the reasons she had prepared – emotions and how they broke you, made you hurt – seemed inconsequential. After all, Prasad had got under her skin, stamped himself upon her heart so irrevocably that she was preparing to marry him, she who had decided that she would stay away from love and the pain it inevitably subjected you to…

When she had opened her heart to him, why not do so again for his, for *their* children?

Prasad, understanding what she couldn't voice, said tenderly, 'My darling, I know you've been hurt and you worry about losing those you love. I understand, I do. But should that be the reason not to have a child when there is a very high possibility that everything will be just fine?' His eyes were glowing. 'Don't you want to pass on those formidable genes? I would be only too delighted to have more versions of you.' His voice was trying to be facetious but was actually quite serious. Then his gaze became soft, his voice earnest. 'It would be my greatest privilege to have children with you. But if you don't want any, it's fine.' She knew he meant it, that he would give up his desire for progeny if that was what she wished.

Months had passed, during which she had looked at him and imagined children bearing his beloved, beautiful likeness. Finally, she had said, 'I did not want to marry. You changed my mind, my life. I always thought I did not want children, but now I want *yours*.' He had beamed then, drawing her into the haven of his arms.

Her body announced her pregnancy by reacting violently to the scents that were part of her working life: blood, gore and disinfectant. As her body changed, adapting to the new Iife growing within, she found herself revelling in all of it: the nausea, the irrational cravings, the sore nipples, the exhaustion.

'My pregnancy,' she said to Prasad, 'is making me more attuned to my patients. I understand them better.'

'You're abloom,' he said, smiling tenderly at her. 'You look positively gorgeous.'

When she first felt the baby move, the barest hint of a flutter inside her womb, like cool raindrops pattering onto warm skin, she was at work, reviewing case files. For a minute she wondered if she had imagined it, and as if the baby knew she'd think this, it did it again.

A hello from within the womb.

She had sat there, in her small, cramped office at the hospital – she was the only one who had an office – knowing there were a hundred things she should be doing but unable to do any of them, with one hand cradling her stomach and tears running down her face, as a sudden yearning made itself felt. It was the desire to see her birth mother, to know her, talk to her, and ask, 'Did you feel this too? Were you as awed, blown away, amazed, humbled, as I am?'

And another part of her whispered, 'Who knows what circumstances she was in? Perhaps she was too upset and worried at yet another baby growing in her womb, which meant another mouth would require feeding when there wasn't enough food to go around, to marvel.'

What did you feel, Ma? I wish I knew you, I wish I could talk to you. What made you give me away?

'Janaki, didn't you hear the pager?' Prasad was in her office. 'Darling, what's the matter? Are you okay? The baby?' In response she took his hand, held it against her stomach and urged their baby to talk to its father just as it had done to her.

And as if understanding its mother's unspoken communication, their child had obligingly fluttered a hello. Prasad looked at her, eyes shining, overwhelmed, and this is how Nurse Smita found them both.

Some nights, during the later stages of her pregnancy, Prasad would wake to find Janaki sitting by the window, her face angled to the moonlight, while the city went about its business below: there might be a man leading his bicycle wearily home; a cow mooing in the weak, fly-infested yellow halo cast by a lamp; a dog howling; a drunk, weaving between the ruts on the deserted road, singing off key; street dwellers fast asleep inside makeshift tents.

Prasad would gently kiss her tears away. 'What is it?'

'My parents… did they give me away because they didn't care? Didn't want me?' It was her deepest, most secret worry, unspoken until now yet festering in that clandestine part of her where she shoved her darkest terrors. It would raise its sinister head in the pressing hours of deepest night, trapping her, leaving her loose-limbed with upset, rife with the insecurities that she successfully kept at bay during daylight hours.

Much of the time she chose to believe her parents had given her to the orphanage because they had loved her and had wished for a better life for her than they could provide. But what if she was wrong?

'Of course not. How could anyone not want *you*?' Prasad would say with great conviction, taking Janaki in his arms, his warm body anchoring her, as the city slumbered below them. In the distance, the hospital's lights would be glowing and twinkling; beyond lay the sea, a great undulating shadowy swell, while above them the sky, foggy and smoke-stained, would be pricked by stars.

'What if I cannot bond with this child?' Another of her unvoiced fears would find release in the comforting anchor of her husband's embrace.

'Of course you will. You do already. I've heard you talking to our child, singing to it when you think no one's around.'

'But I'm scared too.'

'It's only natural. And, Janu, your parents loved you. They wrapped you in a hand-knitted cardigan the bright green of budding shoots. That shows caring. It shows you were precious, loved.'

His certainty would seep into her, easing her worry. 'Yes,' she'd mumble into his chest, wet with her tears.

'Come to bed, my love.'

Prasad is at the hospital.

Sister Nandita had called this morning, asking if one of them could pop round to the orphanage on their way to work to look at a child she was worried about. Janaki is still working, having decided she would work until the last two weeks of pregnancy; at almost thirty-seven weeks, she was nearly there.

'I could go,' Prasad had said, but she'd noted an unaccustomed creasing between his eyebrows.

'What's the matter?' Janaki asked, recalling that he had tossed and turned the previous night, even more so than Janaki in her final stages of pregnancy.

'It's just a headache.' But Prasad was wincing, shrinking from the light as she drew the curtains.

'Do you want to stay at home?' she had asked him.

He'd pulled her into his arms and she'd breathed in his smell: mint and comfort and love. She was so happy with him. He was everything she'd wanted and more. Now she couldn't think why she'd decided that not loving, not getting married, was the only option for her and was so glad that he'd changed her mind.

'I'd love nothing more than to stay here like this with you,' he'd whispered in her ear, 'but I've two Caesarean sections scheduled today and there are a couple of new mothers I need to check on.'

'But you don't feel—'

'I'm fine. I'll rest when I get home this evening,' he'd said firmly. 'Shall I stop at the orphanage first?'

'I'll go there,' she'd said. 'I'll meet you at the hospital.'

He'd kissed her deeply and then kissed her bump. 'You and this child are my whole world,' he'd said, throwing his arms around her for one more hug – he was given to making declarations like these, more so as the baby grew within her – his eyes shiny, glowing, reflecting the emotion in hers.

Now she smiles at the memory as she approaches the door of the orphanage, stroking her stomach, her baby dancing in response to her touch, even as she hopes Prasad's feeling better.

And in that moment, she is happy in that ordinary way of ordinary folk. Mundane worries niggling – Prasad's headache, hope her labour will go well and not start while she's still working, worry about the child she's just tended to and suspects of having diabetes – but happy all the same. Content.

It doesn't take much for your world to splinter, to disintegrate into a million pieces.

For your life as you know it to change.

She will, in the days to come, try in vain to recall how it had felt, that perfect, precious, ordinary moment. If she had known what was to come, she would have stayed like that forever. Paused that moment. Prolonged it at least.

But she didn't. And so, she opens the door and her life as she knows it shatters.

Chapter 54

Alice

1935

Shrapnel

Ayah is a shrivelled version of her vibrant self. She reclines on a mat in the corner of the room, with its mud floors and walls, its baked-earth smell of poverty and desperation.

'Jyoti, who was at the…?' she is saying, but she blinks rapidly as Alice comes into view, words dying in her throat. Alice watches as Ayah's expression lights up in that familiar, longed-for way; the way it did for years at the sight of her, for every day of her childhood.

This woman who was more of a mother to her than her own, at whose breast she learnt to speak Hindi before English, and whose milk suckled her. 'Missy Baba…' That name she has longed to hear from this woman's mouth.

She squats beside Ayah, takes her hand, wrinkled and papery now, but familiar. Beloved. The hand that nurtured her. 'Ayah.'

'Look at you! So beautiful.' Then, her gaze becomes shuttered. 'You shouldn't be here.'

'I…'

Ayah looks up at her daughter-in-law and her face shines with love; the love Alice, reduced to a child again in Ayah's presence, wants, *needs* from Ayah. Jealousy flares bilious-yellow in her throat.

Ayah's eyes soft, the mask that has come down lifting again when she addresses her daughter-in-law: 'Jyoti, can you go to Anju and ask her for more of that herb paste for my hip?'

Raju's wife nods, smiling pliantly, and then she's gone, her anklets chiming a cheerful melody, leaving Alice alone with Ayah.

'Ayah, I've miss—'

But Ayah is squeezing her hand, her gaze hard. 'Missy Baba, you shouldn't have come here. Does your father know?'

'No… Ayah…'

'I thought as much. But he *will* find out.' Then, urgently, 'He sacked us without references, threw us out. It was too much for Raju's father – he had a stroke, suffering for months, bedridden, unable to speak or eat, before we lost him.' Ayah's voice stumbles, then rights itself, 'The hand-to-mouth existence – we were destitute for a while – led to Jyoti's miscarriage.' Again, her voice breaks.

A miscarriage. Raju's child. Envy once again stabs Alice's heart, followed almost immediately by guilt and recrimination. *Jealous of a child that is no more! Can you stoop any further?*

'We've endured hard times but we've finally come through, found a community here, a way of life. Raju is happy as can be in his marriage even given that Jyoti hasn't quickened with child since her miscarriage. Please don't spoil it for us.'

Ayah's last few words lancing, destroying Alice from inside out. *Raju is happy as can be in his marriage. Please don't spoil it for us.* This woman who Alice thinks of as her *real* mother, her words pleading, bitter. 'Ayah, I…'

A cockroach, the glossy black of malice, scuttles past the old sari upon which Ayah is lying. Ayah's rheumy eyes spear into Alice's. Alice tries to stop the tears stinging her eyes from spilling down her face. This is not how she imagined her reunion with Ayah.

What did you expect? You almost ruined them. Her husband is dead because of you.

It hurts to think of Ayah and Raju destitute. Raju losing his father and his unborn child. She can see why Ayah blames her. Does Raju too? She thinks of how he walked *away* when she recognised him, called his name, that day in the city. *I've been so foolish,* she thinks. *Worse, I have been selfish. I should have left well alone.*

Yes, you should have, her conscience, never missing an opportunity for chastisement, hectors. *You're exposing Raju, his wife and Ayah to your father's wrath again by being here. And what of Edward? What would he do if he found out?*

'I'm asking as an old woman who looked after you once. Leave us alone, let us be. Let *him* be.'

Ayah's words batter Alice as much as they must surely hurt her to say them. She hates that it has come to this, but still she cannot help asking, loathing the naked hope in her voice. 'Raju… How is he?'

'He is happy, as much as can be, living here, working very hard,' Ayah spits, the sour scent of desperation. 'We get by. Please don't destroy it, I beg you.' Tears tremble in Ayah's bleary eyes, settling into the grooves of her creased cheeks, lending them a salty sheen.

'Ayah, I never meant to cause trouble.' *Believe me.* Her words an entreaty to the woman who had surely loved her once.

She thinks again of how Raju clutched his wife's hand and turned away when she called to him. Would she have done the same had she been with Edward? No, she would have run *towards* Raju, regardless of the consequences.

'Leave, Missy Baba! And don't come back. Whatever you're looking for, you won't find it here. Look for it among your own people.'

And it is *Ayah* saying *your own people*, that is the final straw. *I thought you and Raju were my people.*

The tears come, relentless, even as she pushes them away, as Jyoti returns, breathless, saying, 'I got the paste. I'll…' Then, seeing Alice, 'Memsahib…?'

'Let her go,' Ayah says and her voice is cold, hard, not the Ayah Alice remembers.

What was she thinking? Everything has *changed.*

Alice rubs her eyes with the piece of fabric that had been her excuse to visit this village and, specifically, Raju's house. She pulls her hat down so it covers most of her face, casting the rest in shadow so her swollen eyes aren't visible, and leaves the hut, Raju and Jyoti's home, Ayah's abode, where she is not welcome.

She walks to the car and climbs into it.

'Take me home.'

She does not look out, not when they pass the fields where Raju is, not even when her heart beats a thrumming, *Raju, Raju, Raju.* She stops it, angry with herself, angry with her heart, angry with the world for pronouncing their love unacceptable.

Why is one type of love right and another wrong? Who makes these rules? Aren't we all human, with the same emotions, the same blood coursing underneath the different colours of our skins, notwithstanding our different circumstances? Why was Mother's love for Father celebrated while mine for Raju is unacceptable?

Ayah, who was more of a mother to her than her own mother, saying: *Look for it among your own people…* her words leaving shrapnel in Alice's heart.

Chapter 55

Alice

1935

Trouble

Edward comes home earlier than usual the following evening. Alice is in the hammock slung between coconut trees in the garden, the fronds fanning her with a perfumed breeze. Her heart bleeds; it has done so since seeing Ayah. She is mourning the ending of a dream, the crushing of hopes she had stubbornly told herself she didn't nurture.

'Alice,' Edward says, 'look who's here.' As if Father's visit is something of a surprise rather than an almost daily occurrence.

Father stares pointedly at the glass she's holding: 'Isn't it a bit early for that?'

Alice holds his gaze, her own gaze hard: 'Now that you're here, you can join me.'

She has given up trying to please Father. Gradually she has come to the realisation, hard to accept though it is, that he does not *see* her. She thought he had, for a brief, glorious while after she married Edward, and before Mother's death, but no longer. He is an inherently selfish man who will only give time to people who are of any use to him, and Alice is, after all, only a daughter. And a barren daughter at that; unable, as she has been, to provide him with a grandchild.

The only person Father really cared for, other than himself and to a certain extent Edward in recent years, was Mother. But even there he was selfish, insisting she stay with him, despite knowing how unhappy she was in India; not even allowing her to go to Shimla with the other wives during the scorching summer months.

The men discuss the troubles, the rioting, the violence between the Hindus and Muslims, the implications of the Government of India Act that has recently been passed in the British parliament.

'What are they thinking, giving in to the coolies like this? The coolies cannot even make peace among themselves. They're intent upon killing each other and yet, now, thanks to this Act, they've been awarded a louder voice in government. It's madness,' Father growls.

Then, Father turns to Alice, 'We think it best for you to go away for a while, far from all this violence spilling into the streets, lest you suffer an inadvertent mishap.' His eyes glitter malicious onyx sparks from within their icy cerulean depths.

He knows.

'*We* meaning *you?*' she asks coolly.

Edward takes her hand. 'I know you don't want to leave me here alone, my dear, and that you will worry, but I'd rather you were safe.'

Over her husband's bent head, her father's gaze meets hers: 'I heard you just escaped a riot, having travelled to the city and beyond…' His eyes are charged with warning.

She understands then for sure that Father knows: 'I'd rather stay here.' She looks at Edward.

'My dear, right now there is so much anger and hatred, directed at us, and between the Hindus and the Muslims. I don't want you caught in the crossfire.'

'It's agonising when people we care for, innocent people, are hurt,' her father says. Alice understands that this is a threat. He's saying he'll make sure to hurt Raju and Ayah if she doesn't agree to go away. 'Huts are being set on fire, fields and livelihoods destroyed.' His every word is slow and deliberate, imbued with warning and ultimatum, his gaze never leaving hers.

She knows this is what will happen to her love if she does not do as she's told. She feels anger, potent red, at herself most of all. *Why was I foolish enough to go to Raju's home and so put him in danger? How could I have been so selfish?*

Rage, the pulsing vermilion of a throbbing wound, is directed at her father. *He has manipulated Edward, using my safety as excuse.* Desperation, salty black, viscous with bile, is ambushing her throat. *Raju… so near and yet he might as well be on the moon.*

Her father raises his hand and brings it down hard – a resounding slap that echoes into the mild evening, which is noisy with the nightly chant of crickets. Alice flinches and her father laughs, flicking at the navy-speckled drop of blood on his arm; all that's left of the mosquito he's squashed.

'Where?' she asks, ignoring her father and looking at her husband.

'You can go to my Aunt Lucy in Shimla. She's been wanting to meet you but finds travel difficult. I know you'll like her. I've been meaning to take you up there to visit, but you know how busy it's been here, Alice. I'll make arrangements.'

'But that's so far away.' Her voice is a whisper.

'Which is the point,' her father says.

'It will set my heart at rest, my dear, knowing you're safe,' Edward says gently.

'And out of trouble,' Father adds, his lips rising in a smirk that doesn't quite reach his eyes.

Chapter 56

Janaki

1969

Tally

It is Nurse Smita from the hospital at the door, her hand raised to knock again. It takes Janaki a moment to place her, a familiar face, out of context. Her two worlds, orphanage and hospital, carefully separate, suddenly colliding with no warning.

'Nurse, why are you…?' But the words catch in her throat at the expression on Nurse Smita's face; as she sees that look of pity and sorrow, shock and loss.

No.

Beyond the front steps, all is heat and colour. Dust-stained trees are waving in the already hot and humid breeze, although it's only mid-morning. There are scents of frying oil, roasting spices, caramelised onions, sweetened milk. A little girl is watching the world around her, propped up on her mother's hips mesmerised by the noise, the chaos, one of her chubby hands tangled in her mother's hair, the other waving.

In Janaki's stomach, her baby cavorts, the warm weight of its presence anchoring Janaki as she leans, slack, against the door jamb. She is tempted to shut the door in Nurse Smita's face but instead she closes her eyes, an obstruction catching in her throat even as she prays, *Please.*

'Janaki.'

Her eyes, tightly shut against whatever it is she has to face, open almost of their own accord.

In all their time working together, Nurse Smita has always called her Doctor, although she's old enough to be her mother. But now there's an unaccustomed gentleness, the use of her first name.

Please, no.

The sun is in her eyes, inciting tears. A gaggle of women in glittering saris in all colours of the rainbow, a wedding party, are passing by. Jewels sparkle in their ears and necks, catching the light and singing in golden brilliance, in stark contrast to Nurse Smita's ashen pallor.

Please don't say it.

She shuts her eyes again, imagining Prasad's arms around her, remembering his familiar smell of mint and love. Recalling now how he had looked that morning as he'd left for work; his unusually creased forehead. Why didn't she insist that he stay at home? He had winced, flinching from the light.

'Just a headache,' he'd said.

Not my husband. Please.

In her stomach her baby tumbles.

Not the father of my child.

'Dr Prasad, he… he collapsed.'

Collapsed.

'I'll come at once.' Her voice. Unrecognisable. A subdued whisper. 'He's in surgery?'

Please.

Nurse Smita shakes her head, her eyes huge and hopeless, fixed on Janaki's face. Her mouth opening, spouting words. Irrevocable. Final.

Snatches come as if from afar, even though Nurse Smita is right in front of her.

'...fatal brain haemorrhage...'

No.

'We tried all we could, but...'

No, no.

'So sorry.'

No, no, no, no.

As if picking up on her distress, perhaps intuiting something is wrong, her baby agitates, Janaki's stomach cramping, waves of pain seizing her womb in a vice.

In the street, a siren keens in place of the sob Janaki is withholding, sudden and high-pitched, sundering the thick, stunned silence, soupy with shock, numb with incomprehension, paralysed by dawning, dazed grief.

It takes so little to change a life.

The whisper-soft sigh between one breath and the next – that's all it takes to devastate the life you have so carefully constructed. All it takes to pay for the happiness that is more than your due; all it takes to balance the giant account sheet monitored by a punishing God who keeps a tally.

Janaki's stomach spasms, her body reacting to what she has just heard before her mind can make sense of it.

Around her the world goes on: the sound of a woman's low, throaty laughter clashing discordantly with the plaintive mewl of a kitten; two men arguing, each louder than the other; a child sucking the juice from a mango, his chin spattered yellow with syrup, attracting flies; a woman carrying pails of water, one in each hand, while balancing another expertly on her head, the bangles adorning her wrists chiming a merry tune, glimmering saffron and marigold in the dancing sunshine, which falls in

gilded streaks on the dust by the doorway against which Janaki
is slumped.

All it takes is one moment for happiness to transform into
tragedy, for everything to go to nothing, for life to never be the
same again.

All it takes is one moment.

Chapter 57

Alice

1935

Goodbye

The night after her husband and father have decided that she must go to Shimla, Alice tosses and turns, unable to sleep. The air is fragrant, jasmine-infused, moonlight-tinted; the rustle-and-shadow-populated night stretching and undulating, calling gently in its soft, secret voices outside the window.

Just beyond the city, under the same star-pricked sky, the only person in all the world who had once loved Alice completely and for herself sleeps with his wife, while his mother lies on her mat on the other side of their one-roomed hut, two arm lengths away.

Alice looks at Edward, snoring softly beside her. She had hoped for a child to love, but it has not happened. As the years have passed, she wonders if the doctors – and she has consulted many – are wrong when they assure her that she is fine, that it will happen. She is coming to the conclusion that something *is* wrong with her, that it must be connected with her irregular bleeding. For why else has something that should be so natural and commonplace eluded her?

At other times, she muses whether it is not her alone who is the cause of the problem, but the two of them – herself and Edward. When, very occasionally nowadays, and not for months recently (he's usually tired after long days of sorting out uprisings), Edward has moved inside her, mechanically, cursorily, Alice has wondered if perhaps this is why they are childless. For a child to be created, there should be love; more so than they can conjure for each other.

Now she thinks, *Perhaps it's for the best. A child would only complicate matters now that I've found Raju.*

You cannot do anything, despite having found him, her conscience counters. *You're going to Shimla. He is married – happily – and doesn't want to see you.*

But… Is this it, then, her life? Are her days to be spent longing for something more, something other, wondering, *What if…*? Will the emptiness inside her yawn bigger and wider until it swallows her whole…?

As morning kisses darkness goodbye with soft pink caresses, she makes up her mind. She is leaving for Shimla as soon as Aunt Lucy has confirmed her stay but she cannot go without seeing Raju first.

Just once. To say goodbye.

She'll be careful; she's doesn't want Raju placed in any more danger from her father's wrath than he is already, thanks to her rash visit to his mother and his home. And she doesn't want to hurt her husband. She cannot begin to imagine what her perfidy would do to Edward, or how he would react if he found out.

But she *has* to see Raju. She cannot go away without doing so when he is this close. When, after trying to live with the knowledge that he's been dead for years, she now knows he's alive and well. She wants to know if he feels the same way as his mother. Her heart will break – again, even more than it has already – if Raju agrees with his mother, but at least she will have seen him, said goodbye, put her mind and her heart at rest. She will have tried; she will have done everything she can possibly do.

She will have tried.

*

The next morning, as soon as Edward leaves, she asks the chauffeur to bring the car round.

'Take me to the city,' she says.

Once they reach the textile-and-fabric section, where they usually park, she tells the chauffeur, 'I won't need you until this evening, I have a lot of shopping to do for Shimla.'

'You don't want me to accompany you, Memsahib?'

'No. And please don't tell Sahib about this. He's anxious enough about the trouble and rioting and I don't want to add to his worry.'

'Memsahib, I could come—'

'I'll be fine. Please wait for me here at half past four.'

She walks confidently away from the protesting chauffeur, into the market that once again is thrumming, electric with danger and that eerie sense of something about to happen.

She buys a sari, not from her usual stall, but from a vendor who does not know her and is gratified by her custom.

'A sari?' he says, grinning widely, displaying a jaw lacking in teeth, diseased gums. 'For you?' Looking at her dress, the deep navy of the sky at midnight, dark with secrets.

'For a friend.'

'I give you silk sari.'

'I want this one.' She holds out a plain cotton sari like the ones she's seen the peasant women wearing, the tawny sienna of toil.

'But, Mem—'

She holds out notes, much more than she knows the sari is worth, and it shuts the man up.

Alice slips into one of the alleyways in the textile-and-fabric section, usually busy with vendors but now blessedly deserted because everyone is milling about in the main market, waiting for the impending storm of dissent that is threatening to break at any moment.

She recalls another deserted alley in this same city, and a shared kiss that finally made her acknowledge what she'd always known: that the boy she'd shared it with was her soulmate, completing her. She drapes the sari around herself, taking care to cover her hair and most of her face, so that she passes for an Indian woman.

As she dresses, she recalls Raju's voice, when they were little more than children, as clear as anything: 'Here, let me help. I think you do this.' He had expertly pleated the sari skirt into folds. 'Now, tuck this into your waist, Missy Baba.'

'How do you know how to wear a sari?' she'd puzzled, scrunching up her nose.

They'd been in the courtyard under the banana trees, the gilded caramel scent of banana and adventure, and Alice had been practising donning Ayah's sari, pilfered by Raju for her to wear to the city for Gandhi's visit, which they'd overheard Mali and Dhobi talking about.

'I've watched Ma adjusting her sari a million times. And it's not that hard, surely?' Together they had figured it out, to the tune of birdsong, the aroma of ripening fruit and roasting spices, with the honey-gold taste of friendship and happiness sweet in Alice's mouth.

'There, you look just like a native, Missy Baba,' Raju had said, laughing, when they had finally mastered the slippery yards of cloth. He had clapped his hands with delight when Alice had smiled demurely from beneath her veil and had swayed her hips when she walked, in the way she had seen Cook's maids do in the presence of Mali's boy and the new groom.

*

Now, she pulls the veil down over her head and walks out of Jamjadpur, taking the mud road to Raju's village. She is drenched in sweat and faint from the sun, the dusty road undulating into the horizon, when a bullock cart trundles past. She puts out a hand to stop it.

'Are you going near Ambalgiri?'

'Yes.'

'Can I ride if I pay you?' She does not look at the driver, and masked by the veil of her sari, speaking proficient Hindi, deliberately imitating the accent of the labourers, she passes as one of them. The man allows her to sit amid the hay at the back. The bullock cart makes its lumbering way towards Raju, the musty odour of hay mingled with dung, the tang of fear and excitement, her conscience chiding, *What on earth are you doing? What if Father finds out?*

He won't. All he will know, if he is keeping tabs on me, is that I'm in the city. Then, the other worry she's trying to keep at bay: *Raju walked away when I called to him that day. What if he doesn't want to know me?*

The dust flung by the bullocks' hooves is stinging her eyes. *Then at least I'll know that he doesn't care for me like I care for him. But how can that be? How can he not feel the same way?*

The fields come into view, with farmers tilling the land and coaxing buffaloes on.

'I'll get off here.' Alice pays the man and climbs off the cart, her heart jumping as she walks between the fields, trying to seem nonchalant, her face hidden, but her eyes peeled. Hot air tasting of earth and anticipation caresses her face. Nimbly, her feet barely touching the ground, she navigates the narrow path. Her hopes rise in each new field, then fall again when she sees that the man tilling the land isn't the one she is looking for.

Until she comes to a field at the edge of the forest. Here, her heart leaps. It doesn't fall. Instead, it climbs to her throat. The gait of the man straddling his plough is as familiar to her as her own. Muscles ripple in his shoulders as he coaxes the bullocks on. He sits back, raises an arm and wipes his face, which is gleaming with sweat. Suddenly, he turns his head as if aware that he is being watched, and his gaze finds her eyes.

Her face is covered by her sari, only her eyes visible. She does not take off her veil. She waits instead, and it is as if everything inside her is still, expectant, as she locks eyes with him. His eyes, curious, questioning at first, then puzzled and, finally, blinking once, twice…

His eyebrows rising up his forehead. His nose scrunching in that way he had when he was befuddled. *That beloved way.* She had forgotten – *how?* – but now it comes back to her. The expression on his face. As if he cannot quite believe what he is seeing.

The sun beats down, relentless. And all this time, his gaze never leaves hers. They are connected, across the expanse of the field. The bullocks are getting restless. He places his hands on their flanks. And to her, he mouths, 'Missy Baba?'

Her eyes sting. Slowly, she nods. He shakes his head, as if disbelieving. Then he pats the buffaloes and gets off the plough, walking *towards* her. *He is coming to her!* The field has never felt longer. Every instinct in her wants to run towards him but instead, she waits. The air smells of dust and toil, heat and anticipation, thudding excitement, unbearable tension.

And then he is there, in front of her. In the flesh. Her Raju. He is taller than she remembers – he must have grown after they were separated. He is more muscular, chest gleaming and rippling, chocolate brown, under his vest. His jawline is more defined. His face, oh, that beloved face, even more handsome in real life than in her dreams; his eyes are shining with wonder and disbelief as if she is a mirage.

She has imagined this moment a thousand times, but now that it is here, she cannot move. She is rooted to the spot, suddenly shy, awkward. This person standing in front of her is a man, not the boy she remembers. Exquisitely familiar and yet so different.

The sun beats down. The other men continue to work in their fields, oblivious to the reunion taking place in the field at the edge of the forest. Raju's buffaloes wait patiently for their master. He's trained them well.

In Jamjadpur, tempers that have been stretched to breaking point erupt in violence. Edward and Alice's father try to orchestrate peace by wielding violence upon the rioting natives. In Ambalgiri, Raju's wife tends to her mother-in-law, Alice's one-time Ayah. But here, now, in this moment, it is just the two of them, Raju and Alice, standing in front of each other, their adult selves bound by their joint childhood, and the affection, adoration, friendship and love they once shared.

She grew up with him, her every childhood memory coloured by his presence. He was her best friend, confidant and soulmate. Gently, very gently, he reaches out. His hand trembles even as he touches her veil and pushes it back. It falls away and she is standing before him, clad in a sari the sienna of dried blood, old memories, her golden hair and face on display.

He takes her in, greedily, reading her every feature as if committing it to memory, just as she is doing with him. *Does he like what he sees?*

'Missy Baba,' his voice is soft, awed.

His voice. She has heard it in her dreams, woken up with the taste of it in her mouth.

'Raju.' Her own voice sounds rusty with emotion. 'They told me you were dead.' And now her voice breaks.

'Ah, Missy Baba, don't cry.' Then, softly, 'We might be seen. Your father…' He pulls the veil back gently over her head. 'Come.' He walks into the forest.

She follows.

Chapter 58

Alice

1935

Symphony

Once they are in the forest, tucked within the trees' resinous green bosom, where they are carolled by birdsong, while golden shafts of light angle in through the dense canopy of branches, Raju says, gently, 'Missy Baba, you shouldn't be here.'

'Don't you think I know that?' she snaps, hurt.

'You haven't changed, Missy Baba.'

Her sudden petulance – just as when she was with Ayah, being with Raju has made her regress to her adolescent self – is chased away by the glow of his smile, the affection in his voice. She breathes in his scent, so heady, addictive, familiar, and missed. Mingled together are sweat, musk, a hint of ginger and something rich and spicy, all uniquely him.

She is here beside him, the two of them alone in this dappled gold-and-emerald fecund world. Almost involuntarily, she leans into him, wanting to touch him, kiss him. Startled, he steps back, the smile wiped from his face, which is now unsettled with shadows, making him as much a stranger to her as he was familiar and known, a moment ago.

'I'm married, Missy Baba.'

She bites the inside of her cheek, hard, until she tastes blood. The briny ammonia tang briefly masks the overwhelming, enervating, shocked blue cloud of desperate hurt.

'I know. I saw you in the market that day, you walked away from me.'

'But you found me.' He sounds tired, not happy; defeated, not pleased. 'You visited my home. Ma didn't tell me, but my wife did.' *My wife.* The words are like stabbing knives, making her soul bleed.

She wants to lie down right there on the cushion of leaves under her feet and shut her eyes. She wants to wake in a different world, one where he is *happy* to be with her, not resigned. One where he takes her in his arms, kissing her, not rejecting her.

'Do you remember,' she says softly, through the flood of bitter hurt, the brine-and-blood taste of a crushed heart dashed of all hope, 'that day you found me crying among the mango trees? I was upset, overcome. I had knocked on Mother's door and been ignored. Father had not even glanced at me as he left for work. I had wanted to show them something, I forget what now—'

'An egg, tiny, speckled blue, whole and perfect, that must have fallen off the nest in the banyan tree and which you'd found nestling in the mulch beneath,' Raju says, his voice wistful, eyes alight with the shared memory.

'"They don't love me," I cried and you put your arms around me and said, "I do. Whatever happens, Missy Baba, I always will."'

His eyes are glowing now, shining with tears. He remembers. 'Missy Baba, I *will* always love you.'

How she has longed to hear these words! But not like this. Standing so close and yet apart. His voice wary, heavy with restraint.

'But you knew, didn't you, that we could never be together?' And, seeing the expression on her face, 'Oh, Missy Baba!' At last, again, a glimpse of the Raju she knows: gentle, his eyes shining with affection.

'But that kiss…'

The shutters come down on his face and he is a stranger once more. 'I got carried away, in the heat of the moment, having survived that mob which was out to get you. It was terrifying, standing up to those people. I was convinced we'd be lynched. And then, after the uproar, to come to the quiet, deserted alley… the contrast, holding you in my arms. I forgot myself and who I am; who you are; the difference between our worlds. It was a moment's lapse, for which we paid dearly…'

A moment's lapse. That's all it was for him. She didn't think her heart could be broken further, but she can feel it shattering. Raju is saying, 'How could you even entertain the thought that your parents would allow us to…?'

'I didn't care. I *don't* care. For me you are Raju, the man I love, have always loved…'

Raju ignores her heartfelt declaration. It doesn't seem to register with him at all. He says, 'You always had everything you wanted, had all of us pandering to your every whim, so it did not occur to you that you couldn't have me.'

She flinches from his harsh words, imposing wound upon wound with devastating hurt. This man who knows that as a child she didn't have the one thing she yearned for above all others: parental love and approval. This man who was once the boy who comforted her when her parents failed her, again and again.

He is saying now, 'But, Missy Baba, it is I who have had to pay.'

'I had to pay too, I was exiled to England.'

'Oh, what a dear punishment, staying in comfort with an aunt!' Anger is throbbing in Raju's face, pulsing in his voice.

This bitter, sarcastic man is not the open, warm Raju she remembers.

'For a very long while we suffered a hand-to-mouth existence,' he continues. 'My father died. My wife lost our baby. We have forged a life for ourselves now, but it is precarious, easily lost. Which is why Ma sent you away from our village.' He shudders. 'If your father were to find out you came here, I'd lose everything.'

Alice had believed that *she* was his everything. How naive she has been. Her great love... It never was. Except in her mind.

'Remember the prophecy? That guru with the cobra?' Raju asks her now. 'For a long time I wondered what he meant. I *never* considered that he might be warning me against you. My mother had to point it out, when my father died, when we were on the streets, trying to eke out an existence; when my wife lost our child due to malnutrition. It messed up her insides; she has not been able to become pregnant again...'

Even now, despite everything he has said, and all the heartache, the thought of Raju with his wife manages to stab her afresh.

'"Do what you're supposed to, and you may just be able to avert the fate that is your destiny," the guru advised. I forgot myself once. I kissed you. And I'm *still* paying for it...'

'Did you feel anything at all for me, Raju?'

'Missy Baba, you were my world. You were the sun around which I revolved. A smile from you was enough to sustain me. You shaped me, you're part of who I am.' His voice is a lament and a love song. 'I... I've tried to forget you, but even now I find myself wanting to talk to you, wanting to share things with you. I miss you. You'll always live in my heart. I... I...'

The hope, which Alice thought was crushed, rears its head again. She looks at this man, struggling for words, and she knows that somewhere he loves her still. That all they shared, all they were to each other, cannot be wiped out so easily. That she has not been pining for him in vain. That the feeling is *not* all one-sided.

She thinks of how Raju's face lit up when he saw her. How he recognised her despite the veil, the sari covering her head. She takes a step closer to him.

'Raju.'

'Go, Missy Baba! Back to your life. Let me live mine…'

But his eyes are shining, his voice is shaking and, impulsively, like she did once before, she moves closer and kisses him. It takes a moment, two, and then he's kissing her back.

It is just as she remembers. The flailing, restless part of her is finally settling. The empty corners of her soul are filling, replete. This is what she has ached for, yearned for, all these years; what she has longed for every moment since she was wrenched from his embrace. Then they are lying on the bed of leaves, together at last, the two halves of one soul merging in love.

She has risked everything to be here and it is worth it. Tears are seeping from her eyes onto the carpet of leaves beneath them, for as beautiful as it is, and as right as it feels – a culmination of what was started in the midst of a riot all those years ago – it is also goodbye. She knows, with certainty, that this is the first and the last time she will lie in the arms of this man, who is the love of her life.

A few beautiful moments, treasured and cherished and pro-longed, have been stolen from fate, kidnapped from the reality of their separate lives. They are serenaded by a symphony of birdsong as the sunlight streaming through the branches arching above them lays gold bars on the forest floor and dances upon their entwined bodies.

PART 11

India

Strength

Chapter 59

Alice

1936

Pensive

'Alice, what's the matter? Are you not feeling well?' Aunt Lucy asks.

Alice has been in Shimla for a few months now. Shimla is beautiful. Picturesque houses, populated by the wives of anyone who is anyone, snuggle together on verdant hilltops. It is British suburbia, the England from before the war, a place of high teas and card parties, transported to India.

It is not like the India that Alice knows. It is cold. Mists shroud the hills, as pale as lace from a lady's veil. It is dreamy, like her fantasy world, filling her with ache and yearning.

Mother would have loved this, she thinks, as she accompanies Edward's Aunt Lucy to masquerades and dances. *Mother, you should have come here during the summer months. You would have thought you were back in England. Yet, you suffered the heat in the middle of nowhere just to be with Father, for those few nights of the week when he was home.*

Here, it is as if the communal riots – India divided, collapsing from within, indecisive about its future – the fighting and the killing in the name of freedom and religion is not happening at all. The women talk of fashions and shopping and what they miss about home in England. They shy away from discussing the ominous rumbles in Europe, as Hitler annexes land which is not rightly his, causing discord. They refuse to wonder and worry about whether there will be another war. They do not talk of what is going on in the country they are in; of how it is literally breaking under the burden of trying to be free from British rule; how it can't make up its mind about what it wants, with each faction fighting for identity and neighbour turning on neighbour.

Alice spends most of her time at the window of the morning room at Aunt Lucy's, looking out over the hills at the colourful people going about their lives.

India, where she was born, the place she loves and thinks of as home, never ceases to surprise her. This country, so vast and diverse, which has suffered through so much and is still standing, still functioning, still managing to be beautiful while also being torn apart.

Her heart feels that way: it is torn, wrenched, devastated by heartache.

'Look at you, pining for Edward,' Aunt Lucy says, when she comes upon Alice, pensive and broody.

She writes dutiful letters to Edward and, secretly, she writes to Raju, letters that she will never send: *Did you ever love me, Raju, like I have loved you?*

That afternoon, after those too brief, poignant, exquisite moments together, stolen from time, he had said, not looking at her, 'Please don't come back, Missy Baba.'

'Did this mean anything at all to you, Raju?' she asked.

He had not replied.

Sitting by the window, Alice knits what she thinks of as their motif (hers and Raju's) – a water lily, the symbol of their friendship within heart-shaped entwined leaves – over and over, the wool seasoned salty with her tears.

Aunt Lucy, in her well-meaning attempts at cheering Alice, takes her on a whirlwind of social events. She's Edward's aunt, but she reminds Alice, with her kindness and gentle caring, of Aunt Edwina, although Aunt Lucy is more openly affectionate.

'My dear, I've been wanting to meet you since Edward wrote to tell me about his marriage – I wanted to attend, but with my knees playing up, travelling is difficult and I'm quite settled here. When Edward wrote to ask if you could come to stay, I was quite delighted! And you are even more lovely than I imagined,' Aunt Lucy said, enveloping Alice in a warm embrace when she first arrived. 'Now, you must make yourself comfortable here. Don't hesitate to ask if there's anything at all you need, my dear.'

Aunt Lucy has been good as her word, allowing Alice time to herself, or providing quiet company, but when Alice is in danger of becoming too melancholy, she tucks her arm in hers, saying, 'Come, let's wander into town. Dame Holmes-Davies says the afternoon tea at that new place, I forget the name, is divine and I've been meaning to try it.'

And again, Aunt Lucy's kindness reminds Alice of Aunt Edwina, who had also cajoled her out of her homesickness and her angst, when she had been exiled to England after her kiss with Raju.

'Oh, what a dear punishment, staying in comfort with an aunt!' Raju had mocked when Alice told him she had had to pay a price for their kiss too. At the time, she'd been shocked by how much her childhood friend had changed and unable to reconcile the bitter, angry man with the gentle boy she had known. But now she understands. She did then too, but the cornucopia of emotions at seeing him again meant she did not quite process it. Raju has every right to be angry: he and his family have suffered, while she has been lucky. Very much so. She may not have known the love of her parents but she has had Aunt Edwina and Uncle Bertie, and now Aunt Lucy, to offer her gentleness, affection, caring.

*

This evening, they are at Lady Severn's card party. Alice is feeling distinctly ill. The room is overheated, all the windows closed.

'I can't bear the dust,' Lady Severn says, shuddering. There is no dust in Shimla. The air is clean and cool, flavoured with mountains, tasting of the heavens. But Alice doesn't have the energy to contradict her.

'It's nice to have young people here.' Lady Severn smiles kindly at Alice. 'But you look ever so peaky, my dear, whatever's the matter?'

Although Alice says, 'I'm fine,' as the evening progresses, she feels anything but.

And so, when Aunt Lucy asks, 'Are you alright?'

'I need some air,' Alice admits.

'I'll come with you.'

They walk in the lush grounds, where the scent of *gulmohar* and evening perfume the air wafting from the valley, and Alice feels colour returning to her cheeks.

The next morning, the doctor visits, at Aunt Lucy's insistence: 'Edward would think it remiss of me if I didn't take good care of you, my dear.'

After his examination, the doctor smiles warmly, broadly, 'Congratulations, Mrs Deercroft, you're to be a mother.'

Mother...

'You're around thirty weeks pregnant by my calculations.'

'Oh, my dear, how delightful! It's a wonder you didn't notice!' Aunt Lucy exclaims.

'A surprising number of my patients don't, especially if it's their first child,' the doctor is saying.

But Alice has tuned out, amazement overwhelming her. The sudden flutters, like a tiny mouth blowing bubbles inside her, in her stomach, which has hardened and tightened – which she'd attributed to misery – are a baby!

Chapter 60

Janaki

1969

Complacent

He collapsed. Fatal brain haemorrhage. The pain is clawing at Janaki, breaking her. She shuts her eyes tight against it, closes her mind to it. She will not accept what she's heard. *She will not.* But it is insistent, urgent, wanting her to notice. Coming in waves, tearing away at her, grasping, clenching, seizing, wrenching. Physical.

'You've already given your heart to Prasad. And, my child, you cannot live your life being afraid, shying away from love. What happened to you was terrible, yes, but that doesn't mean it is the norm, that it will happen again,' Sister Shanthi had promised.

Sister Shanthi, whose words she took to heart. Sister Shanthi, who had died a year ago, leaving Janaki bereft. Prasad had cried, along with Janaki. 'She was amazing,' he'd whispered. Sharing her grief had made it bearable.

Prasad…

That sound, long and low and keening. An ululation. Keeping time with the explosion of agony rending her. Coming from her mouth, her throat hoarse with it.

These past two years have been the happiest of her life. *For this, I will risk pain,* she had thought, smug in her bubble of joy, and, as time went on, convinced tragedy couldn't touch her – after all, she'd paid her dues twice over.

She has been careless. Taking happiness for granted. Daring to think she was now like other ordinary people, living their mundane, uncomplicated, happy lives and thinking nothing would go wrong. She had dared to presume, becoming complacent: *I cannot lose everyone I love. Surely I cannot?*

'I promise you, Janaki, that I will love you always. I will never do anything to hurt you. I will never leave you,' Prasad had reassured her, over and over, and gradually she had believed him. She had stopped fearing the worst when he was away. When he was late. When he was ill. She… she had even agreed to have his child.

Child.

Her hand goes to her stomach, which is pulsing and contracting, throbbing and tensing.

'Push, Janaki!' she hears. 'Push!'

The child is coming. Now. The shock… It must have started her contractions. Pain. Sorrow. Grief. Desperation. Fear. A cornucopia of mourning. *Will she lose the child too?* Her pregnancy is of nearly thirty-seven weeks' gestation. Thinking clinically, with the doctor part of her brain, the child has a good chance of survival, she knows.

'I'll be with you every step of the way,' her husband had promised when she told him she was pregnant, his face alight, eyes glowing. 'We're a family now, Janu.' Gathering her in his arms, kissing her stomach where the zygote created by the fusion of their cells multiplied to create their child. A baby made from their love.

I'll be with you every step of the way.

She had believed him. Forgetting, in her happiness, that everyone she cares for, she loses. That everyone she loves, dies. Perhaps it is a curse. Perhaps her birth parents divined the bad luck emanating from her, which is why they abandoned her to the orphanage.

Isn't it better that she loses this child now, before she bonds with it, loves it? *No!* her heart cries.

'Push!' she hears.

I cannot lose you, my babe. I will not. I love you. All those nights she spent worrying if she'd bond with her child, Prasad convincing her she would, that she loved it already.

And now, here, in this agony of pain and sorrow, she is discovering her love, fierce, raw, for her child. The one thing of Prasad's she can hold onto. *Please,* she prays despite her faith being ground to dust, scattered into the humid, mourning-drenched air. *Please be safe. You have a good chance. Survive.*

'One last push, Janaki!' And despite everything, despite lost loves and broken promises and a devastated heart, Janaki gathers strength she didn't know she had into her tragedy-buffeted body and she pushes.

Chapter 61

Alice

1936

Plan

'How capital!' Aunt Lucy beams, throwing her arms around Alice, her kind face glowing with delight, her scent of rose water and lavender. 'Edward will be so very pleased.'

Edward.

Alice's heart, still trying to come to terms with the fact that she is pregnant, stops for a long moment before drumming a staccato lament of fear. Edward *cannot* know. For Alice hasn't shared his bed in the way a wife should for too many months now for the baby to be his.

'Did you not guess at all, my dear?' Aunt Lucy asks, summoning Alice from her urgent ruminations.

'No. I just… I put it down to feeling under the weather…' How could she have been so naive?

Perhaps because, although she desperately yearns for a child, she had all but given up hope, thinking it would not happen, assuming there was something wrong, despite doctors' assurances to the contrary. She has been so miserable, missing and pining for Raju, and for that sense of completeness she felt only with him. She thought she was sickening because of it, that her sadness was manifesting itself physically as a hard ball in her stomach.

Her bleeding has always been irregular so she didn't set much store by the fact that she hadn't done so for a while – in fact, she hadn't even noticed, preoccupied and upset as she has been. She never dared to imagine that her one perfect encounter with Raju would leave a tangible stamp in the form of a child, *their* child, when she and Edward have been trying fruitlessly for children all these years. Her hand snakes to her stomach and she cups the baby nestled there, strokes it.

'What a wonderful surprise it will be for Edward when he receives your letter,' Aunt Lucy is saying.

And again, panic forms a hard knot in Alice's chest, squeezing her heart so she feels out of breath. Edward had been busy sorting the communal riots in the months leading up to her dalliance with Raju, coming home later and leaving earlier every day, too tired to do anything but fall asleep beside her each night. There is no way this child is his and he will know it as soon as he hears of her pregnancy.

She cannot bear to imagine what the knowledge of her infidelity and, worse, the resulting child will do to him, for Alice knows he cares for her in his own reserved way. And, although she knows he's wanted a child and heir, Edward has never pressured her when it hasn't happened, all these years.

The understanding of how much her husband will be hurt, when/if he finds out, reverberates through her, a melancholy, throbbing hurt even in the midst of flaring joy at this miracle, the boon of this unexpected child. Edward cannot know, at least not until she has talked with Raju.

While she is in Aunt Lucy's embrace, a plan forms frantically in Alice's head.

'Aunt Lucy,' she says, 'I have to return home.'

Aunt Lucy peruses her anxiously. 'But why?'

'I'd like to tell Edward in person.'

Aunt Lucy smiles gently. 'He sent you here to be safe, child.'

'I know, but I…' She swallows, then forges ahead with the lie. In the grand scheme of the things she has done already – the betrayals and deceits – this is much the smallest. 'I've missed Edward so much and I can't bear to stay away when…' She cradles her stomach.

'I understand.' Aunt Lucy's eyes shine. 'But he'd rather you were safe, even more so now.'

She grasps Edward's aunt's hand. 'I miss him so much.' She is able to sound sincere, for she is thinking of Raju. 'I'd like to leave as soon as I can. Please don't write and tell him, I'd like it to be a surprise.'

She takes some convincing but, eventually, Aunt Lucy agrees.

'Please don't come back, Missy Baba,' Raju had said that afternoon, his last words to her.

But now she *has* to. She strokes her belly, hope rising again from within her battered heart, mirroring her stomach burgeoning with child. Alice has always believed that a child is created from love. She had wondered whether this was why she hasn't been pregnant all these years with Edward. And now, the first time, the *only* time with Raju, creates a child.

This is proof if anything that Raju loves her, even though he will not admit it, even though he is determined to be true to his new life. She will go to see him, the Raju she used to know – and he *is* there, though masked by the new, distant Raju; the old Raju is the one who made love to her, he is the one she will appeal to.

And he will be thrilled with this news, won't he? *'My wife lost our baby. We have forged a life for ourselves now, but it is precarious, easily lost,'* he'd said that afternoon, both as a plea and a warning.

Oh, Raju! I did not mean for this to happen. I have nothing against your wife but you and I were always meant to be together.

Together, they will come up with a plan. They will have to make sure Alice's father doesn't find out, and that Raju's wife, Jyoti, and Ayah are safe and provided for.

She is terrified; the future is suddenly desperately precarious. But with this child, spawn of their love, like the water lily sprouting from the two heart-shaped leaves, there's hope.

Chapter 62

Janaki

1969

Determination

'You have a healthy baby girl,' Janaki hears.

Prasad. We have a baby girl! Prasad?

'I'll be with you every step of the way,' he'd promised.

Someone places the slippery bundle on her chest. She shuts her eyes tight. She will not look at her baby for if she does, she knows she will love her… *She loves her already, her heart, her body flooding with the desire to gather this little cherub to her, to protect her, to love her with all her might...* But to what end? To lose her like she has every other person she's loved?

Janaki feels a small tug near her breast and despite herself, she opens her eyes. She is a squirming little thing, so devastatingly precious, so incredibly fragile. Scrunched-up features, wispy tendrils of dark hair, rooting for her breast. *How can I protect you? I who have not been able to protect or save anyone I have loved. How will I look after you?*

The rosebud mouth rootles around with determination. Finds her breast, latches on after a couple of blind tries. This tiny new being, trying its hardest to gain sustenance, to live. She watches the minuscule mouth suck. The fragility and yet the resolve.

Prasad appears before her eyes, his face glowing with joy and wonder, 'You did it, my love. We have a little girl!' She pictures him handing their daughter to her, like he has done so many times before, with so many brand-new mothers but now, it is *his* child that he is handing to *his* wife.

The exquisite joy and devastation of this fantasy.

The pain. Oh, the pain!

'We'll name her Deepa if it's a girl,' he'd said, the taste of love and dreams. 'Our little light.'

At her breast their babe, born just as she lost her father, suckles, oblivious. Then her eyes flutter open, her gaze rheumy amber-gold meeting Janaki's.

Love – protective, all-consuming – overwhelms Janaki, for this small, heartbreakingly tenacious darling of a child. Just as it did with Prasad, love has crept up on her without her noticing or knowing. It is too late not to love her child, for she is committed. She loves this babe too much already. All those nights spent tormenting herself, wondering if she would bond with her child, if she would love it...

'What did I tell you?' her husband whispers in her ear. The baby's lips, puckered around Janaki's nipple curve upwards, her eyes winking and glowing. Janaki's heart stops, then lifts, ache and love. She knows babies cannot smile, not this early.

The logical part of her, the doctor, knows they only really smile at between six to eight weeks of life. And yet... Her daughter *smiled*. She *did*. Her heart tells her so. And in her daughter's first smile, Janaki's husband is returned, devastatingly, gloriously to her.

Janaki understands something then. She might have lost Prasad too early, too soon. He will not be there to see his child smile, walk, talk, or to see her grow, but in *her*, Janaki will always see *him*.

Chapter 63

Alice

1936

Premonition

The day before Alice is to leave Shimla, Aunt Lucy, always an early riser, is not at breakfast.

'Where's my aunt?' Alice asks the maid, who is peeling mango before cutting it into cubes.

The maid looks worried. 'Memsahib is not come.'

'Have you checked in the garden?'

Some mornings Aunt Lucy sits on the bench that she's installed under the apple trees in memory of her husband. Here, she can watch the valley slowly coming into view as the mist, delicate as a bride's veil, lifts, revealing snug hamlets tucked into lush vegetation, which rejoices in the new day in shades of gold and emerald, when lit by the rising sun.

The air smells zesty, thrumming with anticipation and trepidation, as Alice wavers between anxiety at Raju's reaction – surely he'll be pleased? Deep down, he *does* love her, why else did he make love to her? And it was so beautiful, the coming together of souls… surely that couldn't be one-sided? – to sheer, boundless panic at what Edward and Father will do if they find out.

Assuming Raju leaves his wife – and he will, won't he? – how will they escape the reach of Father? Where will they make a home for themselves and this child they have created? They will also have to make sure Ayah and Jyoti are safe from Father's wrath as well, Alice worries. Guilt at the havoc their love has inadvertently caused is stabbing and prodding at her.

She strokes her bump, whispering to her child: 'Whatever happens, we'll protect you, I promise. You are the fruit of our love, the water lily in our motif.'

She will not imagine Raju's expression when she reveals the mound of her stomach for fear of expecting too much and being disappointed. But she prays, wishes, yearns that he will be accepting and even, dare she hope, happy, after the initial surprise. Her conscience has given up on her – it stopped hectoring when she slept with Raju, throwing caution and her wedding vows to the wind – shocked into distressed muteness.

'She's not in the garden.' The maid is breathless.

Alice feels a tendril of worry shiver at the base of her spine, which undulates into a thick, all-pervasive and insidious vine when she finds Aunt Lucy in bed, her face flushed. The fug of fever.

Oh no!

Aunt Lucy's eyes fluster open at Alice's approach. Her gaze, when it lands on Alice, is curiously blank. Her eyes are red and swollen. 'Ah, Reginald,' she whispers, smiling. Alice is chilled to the bone at Edward's aunt addressing her by the name of her husband, who has been dead since the war.

'Fetch the doctor,' she instructs the maid, her voice aquiver, even as she thinks back to the previous evening – Aunt Lucy had retired early to bed, claiming exhaustion. Alice remembers thinking that the old lady had looked a little flushed. Why hadn't she checked up on her when she herself went to bed? Would it have helped if she had called the doctor then?

'She's suffering from a nasty strain of virulent fever spread by infected mosquitoes,' the doctor says. 'Don't worry, it's not contagious. But don't sit outside after dusk, don't open the mosquito screens and always use the mosquito net.'

'Would it have helped if you had attended to her last night?' Alice, wracked with guilt, queries.

'It wouldn't have made a jot of difference,' the doctor says, firmly. 'With the medicine I've prescribed and plenty of rest, your aunt should be fighting fit in a few weeks.'

A few weeks. It is only then that Alice, distressed by Aunt Lucy's illness, recalls her plans, her hand going to her stomach. How can she leave now, when Aunt Lucy is like this?

But equally, how can she stay? She cannot have the baby here – for Lucy is Edward's aunt, not hers, and when the baby is born, the truth will out – and Raju needs to be informed about his child...

Looking again at Aunt Lucy's fevered face and her unfocused gaze; at this woman who has shown her nothing but kindness, Alice knows that she will not abandon her now.

But all her careful plans have gone awry. Is this an omen? A premonition?

Chapter 64

Alice

1936

Burden

As soon as Aunt Lucy is on the path to recovery, Alice makes renewed plans to leave. The fever had floored the old lady and it had taken her nearly seven weeks to recover.

Alice had been worried about Aunt Lucy as she had watched the illness sapping her energy, leaving her listless and delirious. Her sickroom had brought back painful memories of Mother's last days. Alice had insisted that the doctor visit daily, but she had begun to doubt his assurances that Aunt Lucy would get better, as the days bled into each other with Edward's aunt showing no signs of improvement.

Alice was also acutely, desperately conscious of each passing day, wanting to get to Raju, to inform him of his child, but in a panicked limbo about what would come next. As she'd tended to Aunt Lucy, she'd fretted and schemed, making and discarding increasingly frantic plans. She'd knitted a cardigan and booties for her child with yarn the sparkling emerald of spring – budding leaves and new beginnings – hoping, wishing and praying this would herald good things for Raju, herself and their child.

She knitted the symbol of their friendship – hers and Raju's – two heart-shaped leaves holding a water lily within, right where their babe's heart would be when he or she was wearing the cardigan.

*

'I'm so sorry to have kept you, Alice.' Aunt Lucy is mortified when she recovers enough to understand that Alice had not left when she'd wanted to, but instead stayed to care for her. 'You wanted to be with Edward and I've detained you here.'

'Aunt Lucy, I couldn't leave you. But now that you're better, I'll…'

'Edward still doesn't know?'

'I'll surprise him.'

'Are you sure you want to leave now, in your condition?'

'I really do, Aunt Lucy.'

She has *to get to Raju.*

'Alice, I don't feel right letting you leave. The communal rioting and the fight for independence is widespread and I…'

Once the babe is born, Aunt Lucy, you won't want me to stay, no matter how much you care for me, Alice replies silently.

'Edward sent you here to be safe and now, it's not only you, but his child as well that I feel responsible for—'

Not his child.

'Aunt Lucy, you're still weak, still recovering from your fever. I don't want to burden you with the baby when it…'

'It will be no burden.'

'But…' All these weeks of desperation, urgency and anxiety manifest in tears that she is unable to hold back. 'I… I just want to see him, to be with him when we bring our first child into the world.'

Aunt Lucy's demeanour softens and she puts her arms, frail and smelling of the last, lingering vestiges of her illness, around Alice. 'I understand, my child, of course you must go if you feel that way. But please promise me that if you feel unsafe on the journey, you will come back.'

'I promise,' Alice says, sniffing, feeling ashamed and embarrassed for deceiving Aunt Lucy, even as relief, sweet as mango juice floods her.

She has grown to love this woman, who's been so openly welcoming and giving. During the weeks of worry and despair, as her babe grew, and Aunt Lucy slowly got better – no longer hallucinating, seeing Alice for herself and not as her dead husband – she had been tempted to confide in her, to share her predicament. But she has stopped at the last moment, the words dying bitter blue in her mouth. How could she open herself up to the judgement of this woman she has come to adore? The thought of Aunt Lucy's kind, loving eyes clouding over with anger, turning hard with upset, looking at her with hatred and scorn, was more than Alice could bear.

When she had been caught kissing Raju and was about to be exiled to England, she had appealed to her mother, but she had been cruelly thwarted, her mother judging Alice for loving a man from a walk of life far removed from the one that society deemed right for her.

She couldn't bear to have the same thing happen again. In any case, Aunt Lucy was not *her* aunt but Edward's. Her sympathies would lie with her nephew and not his cheating, devious, unfaithful wife, who had so brazenly flaunted her wedding vows and was carrying a native's child...

*

They will run away. She has money that she has spirited from the housekeeping allowance over the years and her inheritance from her maternal grandparents – Aunt Edwina is the executor, which is a blessing as Father need not know. Alice, Raju and their babe will go far, somewhere Father will not find them and where they will not be judged – *there surely has to be such a place?* – and they will live a quiet, happy life with their child.

It will be hard at first, their new life coming at the cost of upsetting, thwarting so many people. Edward will be desperately hurt by her betrayal, her father smarting, wanting revenge. It will be difficult for Raju to leave his mother behind, and abandon his wife...

Will he? And even if he does, and agrees to move with Alice and their child far away, out of reach of Father's wrath, what if Father unleashes his rage on Raju's wife and Ayah instead? How will Alice and Raju live with that knowledge? Is there a compromise that can be found whence they can *all* be safe?

These thoughts go round and round in her head, prodding her and making her ache. She strokes her stomach where their child is growing and prays: *Please*.

PART 12

India

Hope

Chapter 65

Alice

1936

Chaos

Alice steps out of the train in Jamjadpur – this city and its surrounds that house her husband and her lover, her present, her future and her past – into slapping, scalding heat and the stench of fire. Buildings are burning. Dissenters throwing stones and spears shaped from tree trunks at each other. Agonised screams, tortured cries and plaintive, heart-wrenching wails pierce the scorched air.

Alice clutches her bag close and looks around her in dismay – she has only brought a small bag with her, containing the cardigan and booties she's knitted for her child and a change of clothes, not wanting to burden herself with cases when she needs urgently to meet Raju and decide upon their future. She'd told Aunt Lucy that Edward would send for her cases once she reached home and in this, Aunt Lucy was in agreement: 'You can't be worrying about luggage, not in your state. Just get home safe to Edward, my dear, you and the babe.'

Smoke agitates Alice's eyes. Her body, her baby, are both tired and stressed from the journey and she is anxious about what is to come. Somehow, in the confusion of utter chaos, she manages to find a carriage to take her to the textile and fabric section of Jamjadpur market, which she takes as a sign that everything will turn out well.

Please.

*

The textile and fabric section is also on fire, a mess of smouldering tents, littered fabric, ash and smoke. The wounded are everywhere, their limbs missing or mangled, festering sores attracting flies and eyes the raw, weeping rose-red of devastation. Alice ducks as a stone sails through the air.

Rioters are looting the shops and stealing fabric, their wrists jangling with jewellery. Alice follows their example and boldly pinches a sari the colour of earth. She's ashamed and regretful but the vendors are nowhere to be seen. Clad in the anonymity of the sari, its veil pulled low over her face, she starts walking out of Jamjadpur in the direction of Ambalgiri. The sun beats down, hard and uncompromising.

Alice is exhausted. Her body, her unborn baby, are crying out for sustenance and rest. But she has only one thought in her head: *Raju*.

Chapter 66

Janaki

1986

The Letter

The letter is propped up beside her book when she wakes up.

'Ma' is written on the envelope in her seventeen-year-old's confident, cursive hand. Misgivings overwhelm Janaki, a boulder that threatens to crush her. She gathers the letter to her with trembling fingers and brings it to her nose. It smells of her daughter: rose and sandalwood, a clash of strong scents. She is bright and vibrant, headstrong, beautiful and vivacious.

Deepa, her bright, shining light. Deepa, who makes her heart twist over with love. *Deepa,* she thinks, even as she brings the letter to her lips, imagining she is kissing her daughter, anxiety and fear performing a war dance upon her chest, cavorting in time to the drum of her agonised heart.

Her daughter has not written to her before. And then there is the dream. More vivid than usual. Almost… portentous.

Janaki hadn't been able to sleep much the previous night. She had tossed and thrashed, while the ceiling fan had drearily churned humid air around the room. The windows had been open but the air that came in was heavy and sluggish. It was pregnant with humidity, waiting for the weather to break.

The sounds of the night had been loud and noisy: crickets chanting and owls hooting; dogs barking and cats mewling;

horns honking and drunks singing. The bed had seemed too big and she had felt keenly the absence of her daughter beside her.

When she was ten, Deepa had declared, 'I'm old enough to sleep on my own.' And nothing could persuade her otherwise.

For the first few weeks after Deepa moved into her own room, Janaki had hardly slept. She went to check on her daughter every hour, worrying about fevers that ambushed during the night, laying claim to best friends; agonising about headaches that manifested overnight, stealing husbands before the morning was out.

As always when she wakes, there's a moment of utter panic to discover that Deepa is not beside her. Then her heart settles again when she realises her daughter is in her own room. The first thing she does every morning is to go to her room to watch her sleep.

Deepa is restless even in repose, her eyelids twitching furiously, limbs tussling with the bedclothes. Her daughter, so fiercely independent, so clever and introspective. Sometimes Deepa surprises Janaki by throwing her arms around her, saying, 'I love you, Ma.'

But those moments are rare.

Mostly she is fighting Janaki, asking, always, 'Why?'

'Why not?'

'Why can't I?'

'Why is it for my own good?'

'Why is your favourite word,' Janaki had cried, exasperated, once.

'Why?' Deepa had asked and they had both burst out laughing.

Her daughter, who makes her so proud and also worries her; who is so difficult and so intelligent.

Who is her everything.

And now this letter.

Deepa, my love, what do you want to tell me that requires to be written down and can't be said aloud?

Chapter 67

Alice

1936

Mad

Raju, Alice thinks as she walks out of the city, gagging on the bitter orange stench of fire and loss.

Raju.

His name is her mantra, her lucky charm. And in the next breath, to her child she whispers: *I'll protect you,* even as her stomach turns at the sight of the many dead, emaciated hands stretched out, pleading; at eyes still open, with shock and incomprehension, pain and desperation, captured forever in death.

A farmer pulls up in his cart. 'Are you mad, woman? What're you doing out? And in your condition too?'

She cannot hide her bump, not even in her sari. It is evident in her waddle of a walk.

'Get in! Where do you want to go?'

'Are you going towards Ambalgiri?'

'I'll be passing through the village, yes.'

She peruses him through the disguise of her sari veil. He looks kind, his eyes worried.

'Don't worry, I've a wife and four children safe at home – I hope.' He looks up to where smoke, the dense swirling grey of impending doom, billows into the sky. 'I won't hurt you.'

She climbs into the cart, breathing in the sweet scent of hay and ordinary life. Her throat, raw and rough with smog and ash, finally loses that gasping, breathless feeling of being choked. It is only when she sits down and rests her head against the soft cushion of the bales that she realises how tired she is. Fear and worry are still warring within her.

I hope Raju is unhurt. I hope he takes to my news once he comes to terms with it. I hope together we come up with a plan for the future.

The farmer talks all the way out of the burning city. 'What is happening to this country, eh? Freedom is well and good, but *this*? We want the British out, but at what cost? We are breaking apart at the seams. It doesn't matter if we are Hindu or Muslim, we're all Indians. Why can't they see that?'

Tears run down his face, mirroring Alice's. He swallows. 'Gandhiji does not want this. I went to one of his rallies. He's a small man, but when he spoke everyone fell silent.'

She cannot speak, tasting Raju's kiss in her mouth, that day when they listened to Gandhi. That very first kiss when their love for each other, finally acknowledged, burning bright, a flame, was immediately, brutally crushed.

As they approach the fields, the smell of burning recedes. The scorched ruins of violence are not in evidence here. The cycle of work in the fields goes on, whether or not India is being torn apart in its quest for independence; whether or not friends are turning on and killing one another in the name of religion.

It is quiet and peaceful. It could be yesterday or a hundred years ago. Men are tilling their land in the way that they always have, urging their buffaloes on. All around is the earthy brown scent of churned earth. This is their livelihood. They will not riot. They cannot afford to, for they have to feed their families.

Alice strokes her bump and sends up a prayer.

Please.

*

'Are you sure you want to get down here?' the farmer queries, his voice gentle, when she asks him to stop.

'Yes,' she says, eyes averted.

'You take care,' he says. 'Hope it all goes well for you.'

With a nod at her distended stomach, he's off, the cart trundling away, churning up a blowsy balloon of dust.

Alice walks between the fields, as quickly as she possibly can – not fast at all, because of her baby – full of anticipation and anxiety, thinking back to the last time she made this journey. Her sari clings to her as sweat beads her face, falls down her back and collects on the ball of her stomach.

She is breathless now, panting, exhausted, and yet she keeps determinedly putting one step in front of the other until she is almost at Raju's field. At first, she thinks it is empty, so her heart sinks, tears stinging her eyes.

Then, at the other end of the field, she sees Raju's beloved profile: those shoulders, muscles rippling in his arms, that familiar gait as he urges the buffaloes on. For a moment, she stands there, taking him in. This man, who was once the boy who had coloured her earliest memories; who had been with her nearly every single day of her childhood.

Part of him now growing within her.

'Please don't come back, Missy Baba,' he had said.

She's shared her childhood with him, she knows him intimately, yet this version of him, grown up, someone else's husband, is essentially a stranger. The worry, fear and anxiety that has plagued her since she found out about her pregnancy overwhelms her, so the determination that has brought her here suddenly falters. Light-headed, dizzy with doubt, she wants to sink to the ground and not get up. She is afraid to face what comes next.

What if he doesn't want her and this child? There was a time when she would never have needed to ask this question of Raju, knowing, without even having to think about it, that he would put her first. But now... Now she cannot predict what he will do.

Chapter 68

Janaki

1986

Overpowering

Janaki sways on her feet, her daughter's letter clutched tight in her hand, feeling faint with anxiety.

I have had seventeen years. Is it now time to lose Deepa?
Stop thinking like this.

A shaft of morning light, fluid honey-gold, leads the way to her daughter's room. It is empty. Bed neatly made. Not a thing out of place. Pristine. Alien. So unlike Deepa's room usually, which would have a tangle of sheets upon the bed, clothes strewn everywhere, the stamp of occupation.

Although Janaki complains, she likes the mess. It mirrors her daughter's lively personality. But now this clinical tidiness gives the impression that Deepa was never here. Janaki breathes deeply to stem the panic that is threatening to overcome her.

She's fine.
She's come to no harm – please let this be so.
She's left a letter.

The letter. She's clutching it so tightly that it's crumpled. She smooths it out. Looks at her daughter's bold, flamboyant writing on the envelope: '*Ma.*'

Nothing's happened to her. She took the time to write you a letter.
But she must have left in the night.
She might think she's grown up at seventeen but she's still only a child.

Where is she?

Her heart is pounding, threatening to explode out of her. She recalls the dream last night. *Prasad. Her beloved.* Looking just the same as he had that last, fateful morning.

'How is our daughter?'

'Feisty.'

'Like her mother, then.'

She'd smiled at that. The scent of roses, cloying. Overpowering.

'She's just like *you*, Prasad. Bright, beautiful and passionate. She takes my breath away. I'm so afraid I'll lose her too. I keep telling myself not to love her too much but I can't help it.'

Prasad had waited patiently, knowing she had more to say.

'She wants to go *away*, study medicine at AIIMS, the best medical college in India. But it is in Delhi – so far – and I can't let her go, Prasad. I cannot.'

'Love, my darling, involves letting go. You of all people know that.' Prasad's smile was poignant.

'But I've lost so much…'

'If you hold onto her too tight, you'll lose her anyway.'

She had jerked awake. Bereft. Her husband had seemed so real. She had felt his arms around her solid, anchoring. She had tasted his kisses, peppermint, comfort and love.

When she had fallen asleep, the night had been still, the air heavy and sluggish. But now, wind swirled wildly into the room, fresh and sharp, redolent of roses, imparting stormy caresses flavoured with rain, while arcs of light branded silver tattoos onto a sky the blue-black of a nightmare. Water droplets, arching through the open window, whipped her face, smelling of wet mud and roses, lost loves, old wounds and fresh scars.

She had lain there, still savouring the taste of her husband's kisses on her lips and trying to hold onto the sensation of Prasad's arms around her, which had felt so exquisitely real. She clutched the bedclothes tightly, her face washed with tears mingled with rain coming through the window, cleansing, smacking of rinsed earth and nostalgia for a time long lost, salty brine.

She did not go to check on her daughter even though the urge to do so was overpowering. Deepa hated it when Janaki checked on her. She once startled awake when Janaki was standing at her bedside. Still half asleep, she had flinched and then screamed.

It had jolted Janaki to have scared her daughter; to have seen her look at her as though she was an intruder, a stranger she couldn't recognise. Guilt overwhelmed her for causing her daughter distress.

'Go *away*,' Deepa had yelled, when her conscious mind overrode her unconscious fear. 'And don't do this again, Ma. Please! I'm fine. I'll come to you if I need anything, if I'm frightened or feel unsafe – although the only instance I felt like that was just now!'

The letter had not been there when she woke in the night after her vivid dream of Prasad, she's sure of it.

She fingers it now. It isn't wet. Had it rained at all last night or was that a dream too? It was an especially evocative and haunting one, if so.

She had these dreams all the time. She took them as signs that her loved ones who had passed on were watching over her, maintaining contact, offering advice, letting her know they were with her. She was not superstitious, yet she clung to those small comforts.

The previous night, after the dream, with her heart mirroring the storm outside, she had stood at the open window breathing in the scent of freshly churned earth. She had perused the newly washed, refreshed night sky scudding with shadows. The clouds now relieved of their burden of moisture were pierced here and there by beacons of stars.

She'd waved at the one in the far corner, shining brightest – her Prasad. It glittered back, dazzling silver gold. 'Look after her for me,' she'd whispered. 'I cannot lose her too. She is all I have of you.' And then she had slept, deep and long. Dream-free.

This morning she had woken to humidity, dry earth, powdery mud. Not a drop, hint nor rumour of rain. The sky was white bright and cloudless. Starless.

And her daughter was missing, the letter in her stead.

Chapter 69

Alice

1936

Responsibility

Alice stands in the strip of road beside Raju's field, watching him, sending up a prayer.

Please.

Just as she is garnering the strength to call his name and alert him to her presence, he turns and, just like last time, across the field, their eyes meet. And again, despite the disguise of a drab sari, he recognises her. Again she sees that instinctive, involuntary joy upon seeing her, that wide-open, heartfelt smile, reminiscent of childhood.

It warms her heart, which blooms with hope. In her stomach, her child jumps, as if recognising its father. And then… Those shutters come down on his face. His mouth is now set in a grim line as he gets off the buffaloes and comes towards her, shoulders hunched, each step dragging, defeated.

She stands where she is, barely aware of the humid, sun-sizzled breeze, which is flinging grit upon her face. Her babe somersaults in her stomach, as if knowing its father is approaching.

'Missy Baba, I told you not to…' he begins.

Then stops.

Eyes wide. Alarmed. His whole body seeming to shrink.

He takes a step back.

Alice's heart shatters once again. And yet she gathers saliva in her dry throat and says, softly, 'It's yours.'

His eyes leave her stomach and settle on her face. There's fear there and shock too. No joy. He opens his mouth and crushes her with his words: 'How can you be sure?'

'I haven't slept with my husband in months. The last time was long before this child was conceived.'

He seems to regress then. Becomes a boy again: frightened, caught out doing something he shouldn't have done. Alice sways, light-headed from exhaustion and upset. She thinks of the hopes she'd had, despite everything… The fantasy that they'd run away together is crumbling into the saffron dust at her feet.

'The prophecy,' Raju is whispering almost to himself. 'The guru warned me. I didn't listen. I… I should have stayed well away…'

And now rage, chasing away the exhaustion, the defeat that was dragging her down. 'I'm telling you, we've created a child together and all you can talk about is some prophecy from a fake guru from many years ago?'

'Missy Baba, I…' Now, his voice softened by shame and apology, he sounds more like the Raju she remembers. 'This is so sudden…'

'It's what happens when you are intimate with someone.' Then, before she can stop herself, for she is still yearning… She still longs for him to tell her that he loves her; that he cares: 'Why did you?'

'I… Missy Baba.' And now he's gentle. 'For all we once were.' There's nostalgia in his voice and wistfulness. Even… love?

'We were everything to each other,' Alice says. 'Weren't we?' *Please say we still are.*

'Yes.' And as if he has read her mind, 'But it was a childhood infatua—'

'Don't say that.' She cannot bear to hear those words.

'Missy Baba, it was a fairy tale. It could never have been our reality.'

'Then what,' she asks, a hand on her bump, 'is this?'

Again, his face collapses, fear taking him captive.

'Raju, listen,' she is again the bossy leader from childhood of their daring duo, taking charge of their greatest adventure yet. 'I have money saved. We can go far away…'

His eyes are shocked, his face blanching. 'Missy Baba, there's no *we*. I cannot leave my wife.'

Those words, flooring her, making her soul bleed.

'She… she's… we've been trying for a child.'

Alice didn't think she could be hurt further, but she can. *She can. Each word a blow.*

'This… this would destroy her.'

And finally, finding her voice, 'Raju, *I'm* carrying your child. What am I to do?'

'You said you have money…'

'It is *your* child.'

'Missy Baba, your father would never allow us to be together.'

His words make her distressed heart rise with fresh hope. 'We could go where he cannot—'

'And what of my wife and my mother? Your beloved Ayah? I cannot abandon them without a backward glance. What if your father punishes them in my stead? I couldn't bear it.' Raju shudders.

All through the weeks of uncertainty and worry, after realising she was pregnant, the thought of informing Raju of their child, the two of them figuring out what to do together has sustained her. Although she had entertained doubts, she had never *really* believed that Raju would spurn her; not once he found out she was carrying his child.

But now… 'What will I do alone?' Her voice is a lament infused with despair as the reality of her situation sinks in. 'My husband will not have me, knowing this child cannot be his. I will be ostracised. How will I manage?' Her voice collapses as it gives in to the fear that is ambushing her.

'You said you could go away…' Raju's voice, too, is floundering.

'I meant *we* could. I would face anything if you were with me.' Even as she pleads with him, undone by torment and heartbreak and crushed hope, the gravity of the predicament they find themselves in, despite the wonder, the miracle of their child, ambushes Alice afresh. There is no winner here. Whatever the outcome, someone will be hurt.

'Missy Baba, I *cannot* be with you. It's madness to think we can create a family together when we are both married to others, when we have our own families,' Raju cries.

Our own families.

I've always considered you and Ayah as my family.

And again, she hears Ayah's cutting words that afternoon in Raju's hut: *'Whatever you're looking for, you won't find it here. Look for it among your own people.'*

She tastes terror in her mouth, wild and bitter blue as it comes home to her that she is completely alone. In her stomach her child, *their* child, somersaults, demanding notice.

'Raju, what will I *do*?'

He is wringing his hands, his voice coated with the same salty helplessness she feels.

'Missy Baba, I'm not some hero. I'm just an ordinary man.'

Tears are shining in his eyes.

Anger swamps Alice as she sees his self-pity and the tears that are for the situation *he* finds himself in. 'You're worse,' she spits. 'You're a coward.'

He doesn't contradict her. Instead, the little boy she grew up with is evident in Raju's wounded whine: 'I didn't mean for this to happen.'

Her hands automatically go to her stomach, protectively cupping their child. 'But it *has*.' All the frustration she feels, the upset, the worry and the fear bleed into her voice, as it is once again brought home to her, by Raju's reaction, that she is on her own. And yet, Alice tries one more time: 'And we need —'

'I'm sorry, but I can't,' Raju says. 'I cannot.'

And it is then, standing on the strip of mud road beside Raju's field, weaving from exhaustion, her child tumbling in her belly, that the scales finally fall from her eyes. *He doesn't love me. Not really. Not the way I love him. Perhaps he never did.* Heartbreak, terror, wretchedness shred her bruised, wounded and devastated heart. *What am I to do?*

'Raju, can't you see how desperate I am? I don't know what to do, who to turn to if you won't—'

'Missy Baba,' he says, 'this is a desperate situation. But I have no power, no means of helping you.'

He's washing his hands of her and their child. This is goodbye. He doesn't care, not the way she wants him to, not the way she cares for him.

'I'm just trying to get by, day to day. I…' And again, Raju's voice trembles with self-pity.

And now, finally, she breaks. Anger, white-hot, at this man she has loved with her all; in whom she has invested such hope, and who has let her down so very badly; and desperation, making her voice sharp and clipped: 'If you'll not take responsibility, I'll just have to tell my father.'

He flinches, taking a step back from her. Shocked hurt clouds his eyes. She cannot bear to see his expression with the stunned hurt at her betrayal.

But then, he has hurt her too.

'Are you threatening me?'

'Yes,' she says, 'if you'll not step up—'

'Missy Baba, this is not a childhood game where if I won't do as you ask you run to your parents complaining.'

'How dare you! Yes, this is definitely not a childhood game. This is a new life you and I have created, for which we have equal—'

Her words, cloaked in ire and despair, are interrupted by a cloud of dust approaching rapidly towards them.

'Alice!' she hears above the crunching of wheels, the sound of an engine.

She turns, shock and panic thudding in her ribcage. She's imagining it, surely? Who could have recognised her in this sari, the colour of mud, which covers her face?

The cloud of dust is looming closer. 'Alice!'

She recognises that voice. It strikes terror in her chest. Is she dreaming? Has mentioning her father, threatening Raju with him, conjured him up? But how? It's too soon for a letter from Aunt Lucy, letting Edward and Father know that she's left Shimla, to have reached them.

So how could Father know she's returned? How could he know she's *here*? Has he been keeping an eye on her all this time? Would even *he* go to such lengths? These thoughts torment her, going round and round in her head. Although not even a minute has passed, each agonising second is stretching and flexing into a nightmarish, tortured eternity.

'Alice!' The faceless voice booming from the cloud of dust is chilling, despite the relentless sun beating down, and too close to ignore.

Raju has heard it too.

'You've told him already?' His eyes are wild, his voice raw and afflicted.

'*No!* What do you take me for?'

But he's not paying heed, his gaze is shiny with the same dread that is pulsing through her, as both stare, petrified, at the fast-approaching dust cloud.

Somehow she finds her voice. 'Go, Raju! Run!'

'Missy Baba—'

'Run!'

He takes her hand and squeezes it. There's so much in his eyes, his gaze encompasses everything they've been to each other. All they've shared.

'I'm sorry,' he says.

'Just go, Raju. Leave!'

She watches him turn and run, climbing onto his cart, urging the buffaloes away.

She watches the only man she has truly loved sprint away from her.

And then, although broken and devastated by heartbreak and exhaustion and undone by fear; although she wants nothing more than to run, as her lover is doing, ideally *with* him, or, failing that, to sink into the coppery earth and lament her crushed dreams; she stands up as straight as she can, to face what is to come next.

Chapter 70

Janaki

1986

Star

When Janaki left the orphanage where her daughter was born – the nuns had insisted that she and Deepa must stay on for at least eight weeks, and were loath to let them go even then – bringing her two-month-old baby to a home that was just as she and Prasad had left it that fateful morning, when she had lost a husband and gained a daughter, she was terrified, suddenly understanding just what being a mother entailed.

A part of her had, despite everything, irrationally hoped that Prasad would be waiting at home – after all, hadn't he promised to never leave her?

And it was easy to believe when evidence of her husband's occupation was in every room. His teacup and plate dusted with stale toast crumbs. She couldn't understand how these things could be there when her husband was not.

She wanted to bury her head in his shirts that were waiting to be washed; in the pillow that still carried the indentation of his head; to breathe in his smell and sob. But their daughter, so fragile and defenceless, needed her. And so she had, resolutely and with immense effort, pushed her grief aside, her daughter saving her from drowning in the morass of sorrow that called to her.

*

That first night with her daughter in the home she'd shared with Prasad until so very recently – Deepa would not stop crying, even when Janaki had fed her, changed her, paced up and down with her – it was as if her daughter was bawling the grief that Janaki was trying to contain. Perhaps Deepa wanted her father, having decided her mother was not nearly enough.

'Where are you when I need you, Prasad?' Janaki had shouted into the empty rooms, rife with shadows, pulsing with loss. 'You promised you'd be with me every step of the way. You promised to never leave me.' Panic was maintaining a stranglehold on her chest. 'I'm not cut out for this. I don't know how to look after a child. She's so precious. So perfect. And entirely dependent on me. What if I… I mess her up?'

She had stopped then, realising suddenly that her daughter was silent. That her eyes, the liquid gold of innocence, were open and fixed upon her face. As she watched, her daughter blinked, her gaze moving from her mother to the window beyond. Below Janaki and her daughter, the city slumbered. Above them, the sky was a smoky, cloud-strewn canopy and Deepa's gaze was riveted by the lone star piercing it; twinkling down at them. As Janaki watched, Deepa's lips lifted in that heart-stopping smile that so recalled Prasad. Janaki had stared at the star, with tears running down her face, and she had smiled too. Prasad had always had that effect on her.

'Hello, my love,' she said.

The star winked and dazzled, incandescent, at Janaki and her daughter, who were framed in the window of a house crowded with memories but bereft of their loved one; who were lonely and yet suddenly reassured that they were not alone in the whispering, seething darkness.

*

Janaki and Deepa had stumbled through the days and nights together after that.

Soon, Janaki discovered that Deepa loved the sound of her voice, so she shared with her daughter the stories that Sister Shanthi used to tell her under the mango trees in the jasmine arbour of the orphanage on somnolent afternoons, while the other orphans and nuns slumbered. She could still recall the scent of baked earth and sweet jasmine and the taste of stewing tea and over-ripe fruit in the air.

When she narrated tales to her daughter, Janaki listened for the ghost of her husband and that of the beloved nun who had seen just how much Janaki loved Prasad even before Janaki herself had seen it.

At night, when Deepa wouldn't settle, mother and babe would go to the window, Janaki with Deepa in her arms, and commune with the brightest star in the vast horizon, which sparkled and shimmered directly at, and, Janaki imagined, *only* at them.

'Ma,' Deepa announced when she was four – Janaki was thrilled and gratified in equal measure, as always, to hear herself addressed so, while part of her was immeasurably sad that Prasad would never hear his daughter call him 'Baba' – 'I want to have a brother like the Pandavas.'

Janaki stared open-mouthed at her daughter, who had been brought up on a diet of tales from the Mahabharata and Ramayana, suddenly deciding she wanted a sibling, not knowing whether to laugh or cry.

What do I tell her, Prasad?

Deepa was eating a takeaway *thali* from the eatery that had been instrumental, in its way, in bringing Prasad and Janaki together. Her buttercup mouth was stained orange with remnants of the *paneer masala* she loved, grains of rice clinging to the edges of her lips.

'Ma, can I have a brother?' Deepa asked again.

Janaki cleared her throat. 'To create a child, my love, one needs to have both Ma and Baba. But your baba is in heaven, the star we wave at every night.'

Deepa had scrunched up her little nose. 'Can't he come down from heaven to create a brother for me?'

Janaki had gathered her food-smeared daughter close. 'I wish he could. I'd like nothing better,' she'd whispered into Deepa's curry-stained hair, which was now also wet with Janaki's tears.

At night, after dinner and before bed, it was their ritual to sit on the veranda as day gave way to night in a bleed of colours, her daughter's warm weight on Janaki's lap anchoring her. Glow-worms: heartbeats of gold punctured the grey curtain of evening. Mosquitoes circulated, buzz and whine. The scent of waning day and cooling earth infused the air.

'Tell me about my baba,' Deepa would command, eyes shining.

'Your father had a great capacity for joy. He was so looking forward to your birth…' Anecdotes of her absent husband perfuming the darkness, tangy with nostalgia, moist blue.

'Do I look like him?' her daughter would ask, gazing at Janaki trustingly with her father's eyes.

'You're the very image.'

'And he's over there, yes, looking down at us?' Deepa waving to the brightest star in the canopy above their heads.

Janaki had thought that talking about Prasad would hurt. But it eased, briefly, the constant ache of missing him and brought him back to life.

*

'My baba is in heaven. You stay at home. So, who goes to work? How do you make money?' her perceptive daughter asked, almost as soon as she was old enough to grasp how money worked.

Janaki never went back to work properly after Prasad's death and her daughter's simultaneous birth. She wouldn't let her child, born at the orphanage under the capable hands of Nurse Smita and the nuns, out of her sight. 'Although countless babies have grown up here, you're the first baby to be *born* here,' the nuns liked to declare when Deepa visited the orphanage with Janaki and Deepa would beam with delight.

Sister Nandita, Sister Malli and Mother Superior (when she had been alive) had urged Janaki into going back to work at the hospital: 'We'll look after Deepa, you have so much to offer.'

Although she couldn't bear to be away from her daughter, Janaki had given in to the nuns' coaxing; she had left Deepa at the orphanage and trialled a half-day at the hospital. But every time the phone rang or a pager beeped, her imagination went berserk. Every sick child was her child. Every emergency involved Deepa. She couldn't even last half a day.

She collected her daughter from the orphanage, took her home and never went back to work at the hospital. With careful budgeting, she managed to get by, bringing Deepa up on the savings she and Prasad had squirrelled away, Prasad's legacy from his parents and the proceeds from the sale of the flat that she had bought and had been living in before she married.

Over the years she has revelled in her precious gift of a daughter and has wondered how the women who left their children at the orphanage – including her own mother – could bear to give them away. The women Janaki used to watch gently placing their beloved bundles on the steps of the orphanage, ringing the bell, its brassy echoes shattering the slumbering humid nights.

It scares her sometimes, the sheer strength and depth of her love – fathomless, heart- wrenching, gut-tearing, fear and protection and heartache – for Deepa. And she finds herself talking to her absent mother: *Ma, I cannot imagine ever being parted from my child now she is here. Giving me away must have hurt so much, like removing a limb, leaving a vital part of you missing. It must have shaped you, defined you. What happened to make you give me away?*

Although she didn't return to work at the hospital, Janaki never stopped tending to the children at the orphanage and volunteering at Mother Teresa's refuge, taking Deepa along with her. But if one of the orphans or the patrons at the refuge suffered potentially infectious diseases, she stayed away.

'You cannot protect her forever,' the nuns echoed.

'I can and I will.'

When, inevitably, her daughter fell ill, Janaki panicked. She prayed, despite not believing in God. She asked the nuns to pray.

'We *are* praying, all the time, child. For you and for her.'

'Then why did I have to lose Prasad?' was her anguished cry. 'And those dearest to me?'

'It's all part of God's plan. He works in mysterious ways.'

'I don't want mysterious ways, I want my loved ones here with me.'

'They're looking down from above.'

'Why can't they be here?'

'His plan…'

'I don't care for it.'

She stayed vigil by her daughter's bedside when she was ill. She made bargains with gods, Hindu and Christian. *Please don't take her. Take me instead if you must. Please.* She shed tears of relief when her daughter – a fighter if there ever was one – recovered.

As she grew older, Deepa, always curious, became more questioning. She railed against being taught at home: 'Why can't I go to school?' she asked, a wistful expression on her face.

Janaki shuddered as she considered all the dangers her daughter would be facing if she did so. 'I'm teaching you all you need to know.' *And this way I can protect you, look out for you at all times, keep you safe.*

'You can go to work at the hospital, I'll go to school.'

'No.'

'Why not?'

'Because I can teach you better.'

'But…'

'No buts.'

Her daughter sulked and the next day asked to move into another room, not wanting to sleep with Janaki, as if to punish her.

Deepa was nothing if not persistent when she wanted something: 'I understand that you're worried about sending me to the government school, but why can't I go to school at the orphanage?'

How could she explain to her daughter that this way Janaki was not only protecting her from harm but also from hurt? If she did not make friends, she would not miss them. There wouldn't be the constant, stabbing lance in her heart of loss. Of pain… She was doing what was best for her daughter.

At night, Sister Shanthi appeared and after Mother Superior passed, she did too, nagging from the afterworld: 'Is it really for the best, Janaki? Are you doing it for her, or for you?'

Each came with her own aura: Mother Superior bright blue and Sister Shanthi vivid mauve.

'I'm doing the best I can.'

'You're doing a great job. She's wonderful. But you can't protect her forever. She's lonely.'

'Better to be lonely than hurt.'

Janaki knew her daughter was lonely. She saw Deepa watching the orphans and noticed her envying them their easy companionship. *It comes at a price,* she wanted to say.

Prasad, in her dreams, his aura the honey gold of love, says: *'Perhaps it is a price she is willing to pay, my darling. You have to allow her to make the choice. Give her the freedom to do so.'*

She wakes from these dreams wrung out, her pillow wet with longing and ache and hurt. Prasad, gentle as always, is saying what needed to be said. She acknowledges the truth of this and yet… And yet, she cannot put the advice from her loved ones, communicated via dreams, into practice.

The older Deepa grew, the more she rebelled. When she looked at Janaki, her daughter's expression had lost the admiration and adoration it had once held for her. The softness had now been wiped away by resentment, anger.

Was there any love left, beneath the disgust and the fury? And yet, Janaki still told herself, 'I'm doing what's best for her.'

On those nights after her daughter had fought with her, Prasad always appeared.

'You're pushing her away.'

'She's all I have and I will protect her with my everything.'

'But if you hold on too tight, you'll lose her anyway, my love.'

*

Now, standing in Deepa's room, bereft of her daughter and fingering the letter from her, Janaki, her heart thundering with worry, her mind frantically tabulating everything that can go wrong – all the dangers her daughter might be exposed to – whispers, 'You were right, Prasad, as always. Keep her safe, please. Watch over her, won't you?'

Chapter 71

Alice

1936

Reality

The dust haze takes the form of a car careering across the fields.
'Alice.'

This time, her name is spoken by a different voice, which, although distorted with anguish and incomprehension, is instantly recognisable.

Her husband. Alice's hands instinctively, protectively, encircle her bump.

The car careens to a stop and Edward and her father emerge. Edward's face is disfigured by torment. Her father's is impassive, only a muscle jumping in his cheek gives away his anger.

Even as Alice tries to contain her panic, she flicks a quick, sideways glance in Raju's direction. He's at the very edge of his field, almost but not quite out of sight. *Please disappear.* Her father has followed her gaze and, although she looked away almost immediately, it is too late.

Far too late. Her father's eyes when they meet hers are knowing, dark and glittering with venomous fury.

Edward comes to a stop in front of her. They stand like that, on the pebble-encrusted mud path, fields stretching on either side, Alice facing her husband, while her lover, the father of her child, a heartbeat away, disappears out of her life.

A crow calls plaintively, somewhere above her in the wide, white, cloudless sky.

Edward speaks first: 'Alice, why are you *here*?' The question an agonised gasp.

Alice looks into her husband's tortured face and knows she owes him an answer. Yet her mouth is dry. Her legs tremble and shake, unable to hold her up, and it is a wonder her voice is steady when she finally locates it: 'How did you know to find me?'

'We've been following you from the city. Your father and I... we'd been watching the train station, having received word that rioters would target it. We saw you get off, which was a surprise in itself, for I do not remember asking you to come home...' His every word is weighted, heavy and throbbing with hurt, anger and upset. 'And when I saw you like *this*...'

He is looking at her distended stomach. Is that hope flaring in his eyes? Perhaps he hasn't kept as close a count of the times they've been together as she has. Can she convince him this child is his? But even if she did, what if, when the child is born, it looks like Raju? Wouldn't that make her betrayal worse?

Right now, caught in this impossible situation – her mouth tasting bitter with despair and hopelessness; her body pulsing with fear; her mind frantically working to concoct some way out of this dilemma – looking at her husband, whose gaze is fixed upon her stomach, she is ready to try *anything*.

Edward is upset, hurt and puzzled. He's trying to make sense of why she's returned from Shimla, pregnant, and has travelled to fields in the middle of nowhere. If she can come up with a plausible excuse, perhaps he will believe her?

She flicks a glance at her father, who knows *exactly* why she is here. Will he give her away? Surely, it's in his best interests to keep Edward in the dark? Wasn't this why he conspired to have her packed off to Shimla when he found out she'd been to Raju's village?

Alice takes a gamble, her mouth dry, her voice hoarse, as she addresses Edward, who is still looking at her bump. 'I... I wanted it to be a surprise.'

He laughs then, harsh and mirthless, and Alice flinches. It is jarring, his sudden, sharp cackle. She realises, as fresh panic ambushes her, taking her body captive, that she has miscalculated.

Her husband knows *precisely* when he was last with her and that the child isn't his. What she took to be a flare of hope in his eyes was, in actual fact, fury.

'You have cuckolded me, humiliated me. You have taken my trust and thrown it in my face. You have lied to me. And you are *still* doing so.' Every word flung at her, bitter onyx with rage.

'Edward—'

'I married you because I looked up to your father, admired and respected him.'

Although swamped by despair and terror, Alice understands, when she hears her husband's words, why she has always felt as though something was missing from their marriage: passion, true love. Each of them had married the other for the wrong reasons. It is ironical – both she and her husband had competed for her father's affection. But the ultimate irony, surely, is that her father has no affection to spare for anyone but himself.

'I am from a lower class to yourself, Alice, as you know. I... For me, it was a great honour that your father was willing to overlook the lowliness of my birth; that he was happy for me to marry his only child. It was only when it was far too late and we were already wed that I heard the rumours about your scandalous kiss with a coolie...' He pauses, takes a breath.

And suddenly, in her mind's eye, Alice sees the insides of the watermelon spattered into the mud, smells the charred reek of smoke, pictures the gardener and his boy hovering beside it. Somehow, although it has been years since the incident, the image is now seared in her mind, as fresh as if it had happened yesterday in all its gory glory. The gardener and his boy had been gossiping about her and Raju, Alice realises now, which Edward overheard and because of which he sacked them...

'Your father foisted you upon me not because he valued me, but because I was a much better prospect than a coolie.' Edward looks at her father and he at least has the grace to look ashamed. 'But...' he swallows, rubs his chin, struggling to find words. 'I... I grew to care for you, Alice, more fool me! I was able to forgive your dalliance with a coolie for it was in the past, or so I thought.' Hurt is seeping into the anger in his voice so that it bleeds with pain, stabbing her.

This reserved man's obvious emotion and his declaration that he cares for her, which it clearly takes a lot for him to admit, torments Alice more than his anger.

'This morning, when you stepped off the train, and I saw you... your condition... I...' There is raw hurt, utter devastation and abject humiliation in his voice. 'I thought I was moving up in life by marrying you. I thought I'd gained respectability and cemented my place in society.' He swallows. 'Instead you've brought me down. You've ground my name into dust and undone everything I've worked so hard to achieve.'

How foolish she has been.

How naive to think she could leave her marriage behind, shrug off all ties and start again, far away. How stupid to think that Edward would get over her betrayal, eventually. She never fully considered the emotional toll her actions would exact. She did not properly think ahead.

'I wanted to confront you at the train station but your father advised me to wait and see what you would do,' Edward is saying.

Alice is taken aback. She'd thought her father would not want his son-in-law to find out about his daughter's indiscretions, but…

Her father meets her gaze with a flinty one of his own, the muscle jumping markedly in his cheek.

She understands now. She's gone too far. He wants her punished, to pay for her actions.

'We were right on your heels,' Edward says, 'but unfortunately, we were waylaid along the way, having to intervene and bring some rioters to order.'

When he says those words, vehement and furious, Alice shudders, knowing what bringing those rioters to order would have involved; wondering what her punishment will be. Terror manifests itself in a sudden, sharp pain in her stomach.

'Is this where you meet him, Alice? Who is he? How long has this been going on?' His voice is raw, laid bare. Naked hurt pulses in every word.

'Edward,' she tries, 'it's not what you think—'

'I will *not* be lied to any more.' Now, his voice is cold, stripped of emotion and all the more terrifying for it. 'Whose child are you carrying?'

'*Edward.*' A plea.

'And don't you dare insult me by trying to pass it off as mine. I can't have children, you see, owing to an infection I contracted as a child.'

A sudden gust of capricious breeze flings dirt into Alice's eyes as she stares, shocked, at this man she has lived with for years and is now finding out she never really knew.

He had watched her hope for a child, month after month. He had allowed her to consult one doctor after another, had clocked her yearning, her disappointment, her pain, her gradual loss of hope. He knew she had blamed herself for their lack of offspring and yet not once had he said anything.

Father is looking at Edward as if seeing him for the first time. *So,* he *didn't know either.*

'You allowed me to think it was my daughter's fault,' he says softly, but each word ringing with anger.

'I couldn't bear to have you think less of me,' Edward is saying to him. 'I looked up to you. Marrying your daughter, becoming your son-in-law was the ultimate prize, despite the fact that you kept your daughter's dalliance with a coolie from me. I… It was never the right time to tell you.'

Alice is stunned, still trying to process what she has heard. Her marriage to Edward is a sham. It is also irrevocably over – they can never come back from this.

She has cheated Edward, true, but *he* has cheated her too. He says he has come to care for her, but he had allowed her to hope, month after month, for a child, knowing all the while that there wouldn't be one. She understands why he did it: he was ashamed, embarrassed, afraid that her father would shun him. But he stood by and cruelly allowed Alice to blame herself when she didn't get pregnant, to think *she* had failed him. He remained quiet when her father needled her, blaming *her* for not giving him a grandchild.

Alice has lied but so too has Edward. All those years he allowed her to believe she was barren. That there was something wrong with her; that she had failed in her primary duty as woman and wife in not providing him with an heir.

Swaying now with exhaustion, dread and upset, she can see it: the truth about all the men in her life. Her father is uncaring and selfish, thinking only of himself and loving only himself. Her husband is a liar, whereas her childhood friend, the father of the child she's carrying, is not the man she thought him to be.

In her quest for love, she has got it all so wrong… so very wrong.

As if in physical manifestation of her distress, her stomach clenches in pain. The feeling is impossibly violent, just as she imagines angry fists would be. She feels faint with agony and horror. 'You lied to me,' she tells her husband.

'*You* are the liar,' Edward spits. 'You *whore…*'

Despite everything she's learning about him, this loss of control shocks her. The sight of the spittle flowing from his mouth as he swears; the word jarring her, coming from her sedate, usually impassive husband, as it does. With one flick of his hand he pulls her sari away, revealing her travelling clothes, her straining bump. It is as if he has stripped her naked.

'Edward,' her father snaps, 'get a hold of yourself! And you,' Father's voice is black, pulsing rage as he turns on his daughter, 'you're a disgrace to your mother, to all of us.'

You're supposed to love me unconditionally. To love me. Have you ever?

And finally, now, at this, her lowest point, she finds the courage to stand up to her father, properly, for the first time in her life: 'You wanted a grandchild. Well, now you have one!' She steps forward so her bump is almost touching him.

Her father flinches, taking a few steps backward, his face grey with shock at her unprecedented riposte. For the first time, in the harsh, unrelenting sunshine, he looks his age. But it is only momentary, his slack expression soon replaced by steely venom: 'I'd rather die than accept the child of a coolie,' he spits.

'Whether you want to or not,' she says, cupping her stomach, which is throbbing with pain, 'your blood runs in this child's veins…'

'Don't you dare…' her father begins at the same time as Edward seethes, 'Alice, have you no shame?'

And then, before she understands what he means to do, Edward lifts his hand, casting the sun – white gold, beating down all this while, mercilessly upon them, a silent, burning witness – in shadow, and hits her, hard, across her face.

The shock of her husband's hand connecting with her cheek, and the stinging heat, makes her lose her balance and she crumples, blessed blackness obliterating the nightmare that is her reality.

PART 13

India

Ghosts

Chapter 72

Alice

1936

Effort

Alice opens her eyes with effort. Her head feels too heavy to lift. The room is dim, window closed, curtains drawn… Something is not quite right.

This room… She is in her father's house, in her childhood room, where every morning she would be woken by…

Raju…

And then the events of the afternoon come back to her in a roiling rush, the taste of terror pulsing violet in her mouth, her cheek throbbing with the remembered shock of Edward's slap.

Raju, their baby…

As if replying to her unspoken question, her stomach contracts in a throbbing wave of pain. *Her baby.* It's too early for it to be wanting to exit but it seems intent on doing so. She tries to endure the agony, suppressing the scream rising in her throat, but it escapes her mouth in a wounded whine.

'Memsahib.' A maid comes into the room. She must have been waiting by the door and heard Alice. 'You're awake.'

'Yes, I…'

'There's a message for you from both Sahibs. They said they have urgent business to attend to in Ambalgiri… Memsahib, where are you going? Memsahib, you're not well… Memsahib?'

Chapter 73

Alice

1936

Cold

Jamjadpur is as razed as her mind. As tortured as her soul. As ravaged as her stomach is by agony, heralding a baby who wants out early and whose birth she is not ready for.

Will I ever be ready? What am I bringing this child into?

Terror throbs in time with her contractions.

What will I find when I reach Ambalgiri?

What have I done?

Alice approaches the outskirts of Raju's village, her stomach clenching with pain at regular intervals. The baby is coming – too soon – but she cannot think about that. Not now.

Hold on, please. The taste of desperation is in her mouth, rotting yellow. Her throat is coated with fear, her body shaking with it. For somewhere deep within herself she is aware of an emptiness. A devastating understanding that she will not acknowledge.

Raju's village is littered with ghosts.

Wailing women in widows' whites are keening beside shrouds. A body is laid on the ground outside every hut.

The villagers look at her with dead eyes before they go back to mourning.

The sight of her does not incite any reaction at all.

Please.

Not Raju.

Her feet are faltering. She clenches her fists, chanting, *Please*, like a charm to ward off misfortune, snatching at hope that is elusive at best, as she puts one shaking, reluctant foot in front of the other. Until…

No.

Please no.

She will not believe the evidence in front of her own eyes, the lament of her heart. Raju is draped in a sheet. His wife is beside him, sobbing, clad in widows' whites. No *bindi* or bangles.

Ayah. Drained. Old. Hunched. Devastated. Made small by grief at the loss of her only son.

Flies are congregating around Raju's beloved face, daring to squat on the lips Alice has tasted, the eyes she has traced with her fingers and lips, the nose she has kissed. She stumbles forward, hands raised to shoo the flies away.

'You don't have the right.' Ayah's voice is as cold as death itself. Her eyes are as lifeless – *lifeless* – as her son's.

The father of Alice's unborn child.

'Happy now?' Ayah says, her gaze drifting emotionlessly over Alice, grazing her bump. Settling there a moment. But grief saps the question even before it forms.

Should she answer anyway? Inform Ayah that she is to have a grandchild very soon, the grandchild she has been yearning for, although *not* from Alice.

Alice's gaze snags upon Raju's widow, who is lost to the world as she mourns her husband. If she has noticed Alice, she doesn't give anything away. Her face is bare – without its adornment of *bindi* and *kumkum*, the accoutrements of a married woman – awash with tears, stunned by loss.

'We've been trying for a child,' Raju had said, the words stabbing Alice – was it only a few hours ago? 'This… this would destroy her…' Nodding at Alice's bump.

Alice cannot do it. She cannot devastate this woman by presenting evidence of Raju's infidelity at his deathbed, when it is she, Alice, who is responsible for his death.

'Is this what you wanted?' Ayah is saying. 'Your father, your husband and their cohorts came and ruthlessly, single-mindedly, destroyed this village. Every single man. Said they had caused the riots. Are you happy now?'

I can believe it of Father. But Edward… Edward wouldn't do this. Her last vivid memory of her husband: his raised hand briefly blocking the sun before it connected with her cheek.

I drove Edward and Father to this.

I killed Raju.

I destroyed his village as surely as I… I loved him.

She looks at Raju's unresponsive body and remembers the guru's prophecy.

I should have stayed away but I wilfully ignored Ayah's warning, your pleas, Raju, all the signs.

I thought Father was selfish in love, making Mother stay with him in a country she hated, where she was unhappy. I have been even more selfish, persisting in loving you, Raju, despite you wanting to get on with the life you had made for yourself, having suffered at Father's hands once before, because of me; I foolishly pursued you, while, once again, blithely disregarding the danger I was putting you in.

She is cold; so cold. The chill of Raju's inanimate form taking up residence within Alice.

'You take and you take, without asking, refusing to heed those who know better, to think of those who will be hurt by your actions. You help yourself, carelessly to what is not yours, thinking you're entitled to it. He never was yours. *Never.*' Ayah's venomous words, directed at Alice, slice the grief-choked air with the hissing potency of a poison-tipped whip.

Raju's wife, who has been almost catatonic until now, rocking by her husband's motionless form, her face frozen in an expression of shocked incomprehension, lets out a wail and throws herself across the body of her husband: Alice's lover and father of her child.

Ayah raises her hand and strikes Alice hard across the cheek, just as her father had done, all those years ago, during another riot, and just as her husband had done, only that afternoon but a lifetime away – when this village was unmarked by violence; when Raju was alive.

Alice doesn't flinch.

I deserve it.

'I should have done this years ago. Perhaps then things would have been different. I rue the day we came to work at your house. I bemoan the day I agreed to be your wet nurse.' Ayah's voice is reverberating through the village so the other grieving women fall silent, raising their heads and staring at Alice through their mourning veils with their uniformly dead eyes.

Alice concentrates on Raju's cheek – so very still – for a beat, two. Then she walks away, Ayah's words echoing around her and inside her; the frigid iciness of her lifeless lover possesses her body, taking root in her heart, while her stomach cramps urgently as her baby, Raju's baby, wants out, too soon.

Chapter 74

Janaki

1986

Storm

At fifteen, Deepa topped her matriculation exams, her name appearing in all the newspapers. 'Just like your mother,' Sister Nandita told her, now old and rheumy-eyed, bringing out the yellowing, frayed newspaper cuttings cataloguing Janaki's achievements again.

Every time Janaki and Deepa visited the orphanage *all* the cuttings came out. 'They showed them to your father too, when he first visited. It's a wonder he didn't run away,' Janaki would say, laughing.

'Was he bored?' young Deepa would ask.

'Far from it, he was entranced. Said of your mother, "Our girl's amazing," as I recall,' Sister Nandita would insist.

'Tell me more.' Deepa, when younger, had never tired of hearing stories of her father.

'You're famous,' she'd say, wowed by the newspaper cuttings, running her hand over the faded photos of her mother, looking at Janaki wide-eyed with awe.

As she grew the awe dulled, replaced by boredom, indifference, anger. 'What use are all those headlines when you gave up practising medicine at the hospital and stayed at home to look after me?'

'I don't regret it.'

'*I* do,' Deepa retorted, getting the last word.

*

'Have you decided what you want to be?' Sister Nandita asked, when Deepa came first state-wide in her matriculation exams.

'A doctor.' She did not hesitate.

Janaki was ambushed by pride. Her daughter had never confessed what she wanted to do to *her*, saying vaguely, when Janaki had posed the question: 'I haven't decided yet.'

'Following in your mother's footsteps, eh?' Sister Nandita smiled.

'No. I actually *will* practice. I won't give up, I'll make a difference.' Deepa's eyes were flashing.

'Just like your mother,' Sister Nandita said calmly, deliberately obtuse. 'She *is* making a difference, working at the orphanage and the refuge. She has saved countless lives. She has set a good example for many, including her daughter.'

'I will not put my career on hold for a child.' Deepa's tone was cutting.

'One day you'll appreciate what your mother has done for you and the sacrifices she has made.' Sister Nandita's voice, though tremulous with age, was crisp and sharp.

'I did not ask her to make sacrifices, I will not carry the burden of her choices.'

'Nobody is asking you to. And you will not talk about your mother like that, do you hear? You should be grateful for what she—'

'I'm tired of being grateful,' Deepa snapped and flounced out of the room.

'She's young,' Sister Nandita said, patting Janaki's hand.

'I'd never have dared to speak to you like that.' Janaki laughed shakily.

'Ah, but everything's changing, child. This generation...' And as Sister Nandita launched into her usual bugbear about the current generation, Janaki tuned out, thinking of her daughter.

'I understand why you feel you—'

'You *don't*!' her daughter shouted. 'You promised that if I got full marks in all my subjects, I could attend pre-university college instead of being home-schooled. I don't know why I expected you to keep that promise when you have reneged on all your previous ones…'

Janaki had not expected her daughter to get full marks in *all* of her subjects. She'd thought it impossible and yet her determined daughter had achieved it.

Janaki had won that particular battle; her daughter had stayed at home, being tutored by her in her pre-university subjects. But now, two years on, having topped her pre-university exams and her medical entrance tests, Deepa wanted to study at the All India Institute of Medical Sciences in Delhi – AIIMS, the best medical college in India – and Janaki could not bear to let her go.

They rowed about it again and again. 'I've obtained a place, and a *full* scholarship, which is like gold dust. You can't complain about the cost of fees – everything's covered by the scholarship. It's the best college in the country, one of the best in the world…'

'What is wrong with the medical college in this city? I went there and I did just as well as the graduates from AIIMS.'

'Ma, I'm seventeen…'

'Still but a child.'

'Old enough to live by myself. I want to be independent and experience life, make mistakes, find my way. Let me go.'

'I… I cannot.'

'*Please,* Ma,' her daughter had begged, just the previous night, with no trace of the anger she often wore like a shield. She had surprised Janaki with her pleading, her desperation. But the thought of Deepa going far away, to live by herself in a strange city with all its attendant dangers, sent Janaki into a paroxysm of anxiety.

'If you want to go so badly, I'll come as well.'

'No. *I* want to go. You can go back to work, increase your hours at the orphanage and the refuge.'

'But I… If something…'

'Nothing will happen to me, Ma.'

'I…'

'You cannot live my life for me.' Her daughter spoke uncharacteristically gently, giving Janaki pause.

'*Please.*'

Janaki had shut her eyes and tried to stem the panic, but it had persisted, her mind harking back to that morning when her husband complained of a headache and she had let him go to the hospital, to his death.

'I… No, Deepa. Just… No.'

Her daughter's shoulders had slumped. She had gone to her room and shut the door.

That night – was it just last night? – Janaki had dreamt of a storm.

In the midst of it, there was Prasad, advising her to let their daughter go.

And now, in the bright clean light of morning, her daughter is missing. In her place, the letter.

Deepa's room is neat but some of her clothes have gone. The bag in Janaki's wardrobe has gone. The money Janaki keeps for emergencies has been taken. Her daughter is clever: she has planned this very carefully and in advance.

Now that the worst has happened, what she has worried about and fretted over, Janaki feels curiously numb. She realises that she's been expecting this since Deepa became a teenager and started to rebel against her.

Sitting on her daughter's bed, she picks up Deepa's pillow and brings it to her face, breathing her scent in deeply: coconut shampoo, sandalwood, roses, and something uniquely Deepa.

I spent her life protecting her from illness, from getting too close to other people, from hurt, from pain, from every danger I could conceive of. How was I to know, Prasad? She speaks out loud to her husband, just as she used to when Deepa was a baby. *How was I to know that the person I would need to protect her from most was myself?*

Chapter 75

Alice

1936

Punishment

Alice is being torn apart with a wrenching pain of a kind she hasn't experienced before. *I deserve it. It is punishment for what I have done.* But no amount of physical agony can match the torture in her mind and the image of Raju's still body: *my fault.*

As suddenly as the pain has seized her, it is gone and in its place she hears a mewling wail.

'Memsahib, you have a baby girl!'

A baby girl. Ours, Raju. Raju...

She had waited for this child with a mixture of hope and trepidation; had weaved such fantasies involving this babe. She had wished that she and Raju could start anew with this proof of their love.

The baby came too early. It will be just punishment if she's... No. Please. Let her be alright.

Alice's voice is just a whisper, tentative, reluctant. 'Is she alright? Healthy?'

'She's beautiful, perfection itself. See for yourself.' The maid places the child gently on Alice's chest.

Alice shuts her eyes, turns her face away. She will not look at the child. If she does, she won't be able to look away. She keeps her hands fixed by her sides although she wants to throw them around her babe, gather her close and hold on tight.

'Take her away. I don't… I can't…'

The warm, scrabbling weight is lifted from her chest and she feels bereft. *I deserve this.* The chill that had infused her upon seeing Raju's unresponsive, still body – *my fault* – briefly lifted by the child being placed upon her, takes possession of her again.

'I found a cardigan and booties in your bag. Shall I dress her in…?'

'Do as you wish.' Alice had knitted her hopes and prayers for a future with Raju into the cardigan, with yarn the fervent green of new beginnings. She had knitted the water-lily motif, *their symbol*, right where she imagined her baby's heart would be.

'It's beautiful, this design,' the maid says. 'And the colour suits her so.'

Alice keeps her eyes shut tight. 'Take her away,' she says.

'Shall I bring her to you later? When you've had a rest?'

'I don't want to see her again.'

'Memsahib…' – the maid is trying to hide her shock – 'you'll feel differently later.'

'I won't.'

'I'll bring her to you tomorrow?' The maid is hesitant now, her last words rising in question.

'I don't want her. Tomorrow. Or ever.'

It's for her own good.

My love is selfish, poisonous. It takes and it destroys. If the baby is removed far away from my horrible influence, she will, hopefully, thrive.

This innocent young babe, Raju's child, his legacy, is perfect, precious, untouched as yet by harm. She deserves a new start somewhere she will not be defined by the horrible circumstances of her birth: created because her mother selfishly wanted what she couldn't have, her actions leading to her father and all the menfolk of his village being killed by her mother's father and husband.

*

Alice's father comes to see her.

'I hear congratulations are in order. You've given birth to a mongrel child, half coolie.'

'Get out of my room!'

'This is my house and I'll enter any room I like,' he says, coolly.

'I'll leave,' she says.

'Good, it appears we're on the same page! For that's just what I came here to tell you – you are not welcome here and neither is your coolie daughter. You're only here now because I couldn't turn you away, since Edward didn't want you and you were about to give birth. There would be talk if I turned my birthing daughter onto the streets and even more if they found out just whose child she was carrying.'

And now she knows for sure what she has suspected all her life, but persisted in refusing to believe. The answer to the question of whether her father loves her: No, he loves only himself. His status. His position.

And I am just like him, selfish like him. Wanting to possess Raju, to claim him, regardless of the consequences.

Oh, what have I done? Self-loathing, bilious blue, crowds out her hatred for her father.

I loved you once, so very much, Father. I admired you. I wanted you to love me. I never stopped trying to please you. I don't want my daughter to feel the same. To try to please me, yearn for love from me, when I am empty inside and have nothing to give. She'll be much better off without the mother whose selfishness and unthinking possessiveness brought about the death of her father.

'Just out of interest,' her father is saying, 'where will you go? To the husband you betrayed? He doesn't want you and I can't say I blame him.'

'I'll go to England.' She hasn't planned this, she is just saying the first thing that comes to mind. But even as she says the words she realises that's just what she will do. She thinks of her aunt and uncle, who took her in as a young girl of sixteen, mourning her lost love and homesick for India. They had offered uncomplicated affection, kindness and succour. They made her feel welcome and, in their quiet way, had showed her the love that she had always yearned for, futilely, from her own parents. She will write to Aunt Edwina to ask if she can stay with her and Uncle Bertie.

'You think your coolie child will be welcome there?'

'I'm not taking her with me.' *I hurt those I love, my child. I destroy them and I don't want to do that to you.*

'Ha! Not planning on leaving her here, are you? You're not welcome here and she is even less so.'

'Don't worry, whatever I do, I'll not leave her with you. I would not subject *anyone* to that fate.'

'Good!' her father says again and turns away.

PART 14

....

England

War

Chapter 76

Alice

1936–9

Quest

Alice sleepwalks through those first few years back in England, trying, in vain, to shut out memories of the man whose death she caused and his child, who she willingly, purposely, gave away and left behind. And yet those memories persist: images of Raju and his child stamped onto her soul, haunting her, asking, *What have you done?*

She is reminded, when she is unable to find the energy to do anything but sleep, of her mother, who would while away her unhappy life in bed, except for a few hours each evening knitting with her daughter or socialising with her husband when he was home. Alice shudders, shying away from thoughts of Father.

Aunt Edwina was once again waiting for Alice when the ship docked. She did not say a word, just opened her arms – this woman who was not overly effusive – and enveloped Alice in them, offering her niece the unquestioning comfort she didn't deserve.

How can this woman be so maternal when my mother wasn't? Alice thought then and at the same time, pining for her child. She wondered, for the umpteenth time, if she had done the right thing, undone by the missing of her.

Perhaps I should have kept you. If so, would I have been kind and loving to you like Aunt Edwina is to me, instead of distant, like

*my mother was? But… Raju. Ayah. No, I am like Father. Selfish.
I hurt those I love. Destroy them. You are better off without me, my
perfect little one.*

When she had decided to come to England, Alice had written
to Aunt Edwina, informing her of her failed marriage and asking
if she could stay with her and Uncle Bertie. But she hadn't been
able to bring herself to tell her aunt about Raju and the child
they'd made together. Her broken marriage was scandalous
enough.

Alice knew that her aunt and uncle cared for her and that
Aunt Edwina loved her in a way her parents never had. Edwina
and Bertie had taken Alice in when she was exiled to England
following her kiss with Raju, which she suspected they knew
about – her mother must have written to her sister about it and
asked her to keep an eye on Alice, which must be why Aunt
Edwina had insisted on taking Alice to all those balls and dances
(after she'd finished school) and had encouraged eligible suitors
her way. But even her kind, accepting aunt had her limits. Would
she not spurn Alice if she knew *everything* she had done? Alice
judged herself; she could not forgive herself, so how could she
expect her sedate and respectable aunt and uncle to do so?

'It is I who have had to pay,' Raju had said, when she foolishly,
stubbornly, went to find him, disrupting his life once again,
destroying it, this time for good.

'I had to pay too, I was exiled to England,' she'd insisted.

'Oh, what a dear punishment, staying with an aunt in
comfort!' Raju had mocked, and she had been shocked, taken
aback by this bitter, hard Raju that she did not know.

*You fool! You made him that way – he became tough and disil-
lusioned because of all he endured in the wake of that kiss, which
you instigated – and yet you did not learn from it. You persisted in
pursuing him, despite Ayah and Raju himself warning you off, and*

your unthinking, selfish actions destroyed not only Raju but all the men in his village. And now here you are, having killed your love and his fellow villagers and having given his child away like a piece of unwanted clothing, once again living in comfort in England, where your mother would have given anything to be.

'It is I who have had to pay.' Raju's words reverberate in her aching head.

I am so sorry.

What use is it being sorry now? Here you are, no better than your parents, giving birth to a child and abandoning it. Worse than your parents, for they at least kept you. You have given your child away.

She will be better off without me. At least she'll not be scrabbling for love, yearning for it, making mistakes along the way in her relentless quest for it, destroying lives. She will know that, from the start, her mother did not want her.

That is a bare-faced lie! her heart screams. *I* do *want you.* Alice resolutely stifles the funereal keen of her heart; she buries its lament – *I love you, I miss you, my babe* – into her soggy, salt-stained pillow.

Alice had taken her child to the best orphanage in Jamjadpur. Through the fighting, she'd journeyed to the gates.

She'd allowed herself to kiss her child, just once: damp, sweet new skin; the heart-stopping fragility of ten perfect little fingers and toes; long eyelashes curling like question marks over eyes the colour of sun-warmed pools of water. Then, before she could change her mind, she'd placed her baby, so defenceless and alone, wrapped in a hand-knitted cardigan the green of spring shoots and matching booties, on the steps of the orphanage as the city rioted around her. She was surrounded by mayhem and violence, heartbreak and unimaginable hurt.

'You're better off without me,' she'd whispered to her child even as she laid her on the steps leading to the orphanage, before pounding on the gate and running away to hide; a coward to the last. Her child had opened her eyes, the blue of a blameless conscience, the aquamarine of innocence, and looked a question at her.

'Believe me, you don't need me in your life.'

As she left, her babe had let out a wail that rocked her heart. She almost went back to gather her in her arms and not let her go. *Almost.*

She had secreted herself behind a wall, suffused by the scent of fear and grief, the taste of dashed hope and mourning and prayer. The chant she'd been repeating to herself since her daughter was born was loud in her head: *She's better off without me, the selfish mother who brought her into this tearing-apart world, because of whom she lost her father.*

She'd watched as some Hindus and Muslims, so recently intent on killing each other, had stopped fighting and gathered around her babe. She looked on as they'd tried to soothe her, as they called out to the nuns. She'd watched as the gate to the orphanage had opened and a nun appeared, smiling at the men, gathering Alice's daughter into her arms, ever so gently.

She'd fought the impulse to run and snatch her babe from the nun's arms.

You're better off without me.

She'd watched as the orphanage door had closed with finality, shutting her out of her child's life, when the Hindus and Muslims went back to fighting each other to the death. The cries wafting from the wounded Hindus, the tortured Muslims giving voice to the anguished ululations of her splayed heart.

And then, her whole being scoured and numb, she went back to her father's house to pack her bags and leave for England.

You're better off without me, you surely are.

*

Her first evening back in England, at supper, her uncle had smiled warmly at Alice. 'It's good to have you stay, my dear.' Then – reverting to his favourite topic of conversation: politics – 'Unrest on the Continent. I daresay there'll be another war.'

Her aunt shuddered. 'Oh, Bertie, must you? The country has barely recovered from the last war.'

'That's neither here nor there, my dear. Hitler's forces have entered the Rhineland. If he doesn't stop, then, well…' Her uncle sighed long and loud.

War.

Alice thought of bodies laid out in a village of newly widowed women, the devastation instigated by her actions.

'Excuse me,' she said and left the table, sleepwalking through the next few years, all Aunt Edwina's efforts to coax and cajole her out of her angst – fresh air, tea at Lyons Corner House, lunch at the Grosvenor, visiting with friends – failing.

Alice stumbles through her days, suppressing the part of her that aches for her child, telling herself, over and over: *This way is best, this way she knows what she's getting rather than yearning, always yearning for love.*

You are like your father and your child does not deserve that. And, when she longs and misses and mourns her child and Raju: *You deserve it. It's punishment.*

But then, just as her uncle predicted, on 1 September 1939, Hitler invades Poland. Two days later, Britain and France declare war on Germany and Alice wakes to the reality of it.

Chapter 77

Alice

1939–44

Malaise

It is Aunt Edwina who jolts Alice out of her malaise. Uncle Bertie, despite being almost too old, signs up to do his bit for the war effort, blusteringly patriotic. Aunt Edwina waves him off and sweeping into Alice's room, opens the curtains, saying, 'Alice, you're *young*. Only thirty-four. I know the break-up of your marriage was terrible, my dear, but you cannot wish your life away. That's enough of moping, now. There're people much worse off than you.'

And then, Aunt Edwina, stiff-upper-lip, practical, sits on Alice's bed and bursts into tears. Alice, shocked into action, hands her aunt a handkerchief from her bedside table.

When she can speak, Aunt Edwina tells her about women she has seen at the railway station – wounds of the last war still stark in their too-bright eyes and etched onto the lines in their faces – smiling bravely, determinedly, at their enthusiastic offspring, knowing it might be the last time they see them – saying goodbye to their sons, who have no memories of their fathers who died in the First World War; these sons who have given their mothers a reason to go on living, while mourning their long-dead husbands.

'Bertie… He came back from the last war, but this one… I… To have to go through it again, waiting, wondering…' Aunt Edwina sniffs into Alice's handkerchief. Then, she blows her nose and looks at her niece with purpose in her eyes. 'I cannot sit through another war doing nothing but worrying. I want to be useful. They're asking for women to help. I'm signing up, will you?'

Once again, I have been so selfish, Alice thinks. *Yes, Aunt Edwina doesn't know the whole truth – that I am grieving for Raju and for the child I gave away – but she is right, I am far better off than countless others. I've been so self-indulgent and Aunt Edwina and Uncle Bertie, in their loving kindness, have allowed me the luxury of wallowing. I should be out there doing my bit, like my brave uncle.*

'I will,' Alice says.

Aunt Edwina smiles through her tears. 'That's my girl.'

Alice cringes as she hears the warmth in her aunt's voice.

I don't deserve it.

'You'll find that doing something useful will help, my dear.'

Impulsively, Alice throws her arms around her aunt, shocking them both, and they stay like that, stiff in an unaccustomed embrace, for a long moment before drawing apart. 'Aunt,' Alice says, 'I'm so grateful to you and Uncle—'

'Not another word.' Her aunt offers another watery smile. 'Now then, let's decide exactly what we will do over a nice cup of tea. What do you say?'

Aunt Edwina, brave and determined – 'She wanted to see the world and have adventures. She'd never be content to sit at home and knit,' Mother had said of her sister, when she and Alice would knit together on those innocent summer evenings from another life – joins the Women's Auxiliary Air Force (WAAF).

Alice signs up for the Voluntary Aid Detachment (VAD) and after her initial training, begins work at St Thomas' Hospital, London, in late summer 1940 when the Battle of Britain is in full swing and the Blitz begins, wreaking terrible havoc and destruction. The suffering, the overflowing wards – injured civilians, policemen, firemen and soldiers stoic in the face of missing limbs and body parts, and in unimaginable agony, sometimes dying; doctors and nurses alike tending to the wounded in the grimmest of conditions, working in converted basements, sterilising equipment on stoves, when the hospital itself is bombed in September 1940 – puts Alice's own loss in perspective and makes her ashamed of the time she has spent wallowing.

In her fourth year of volunteering with the VAD, Alice is teamed with Doreen, a stout, cheerful woman about her age, who introduces herself with a bright, 'Hello, you must be Alice, I'm Doreen. I just *know* we're going to be great friends', and proceeds in the next few months to make good her word.

Doreen is undoubtedly the bravest person Alice has met. She is able to talk naturally with the injured soldiers, whereas Alice flounders. She convincingly lies to them that all is well, and with the ones who are confused from pain and driven out of their mind by loss of limbs and blood, even goes so far as to pretend to be their fiancée or wife.

'Honey, it's me, Linda.' Doreen affects an American accent for the dying serviceman who's been asking after his wife and children even as his breath fades away. 'Betty and Charlie are doing fine. They are so very proud of their daddy, as am I.' The soldier dies with a smile on his lips.

Doreen is deftly bandaging an American serviceman's wound, with Alice seeing to another, surrounded by the lemony scent of antiseptic and distress and the ammonia-and-rust tang of blood, when Doreen sighs and clutches her stomach.

That is when Alice notices the just-visible, tell-tale curve of her belly.

She closes her eyes, starkly reminded of her own child.

You're better off without me.

She gathers saliva in her dry mouth and asks Doreen, 'Are you okay?'

'This babe is giving me a funny turn, that's all.' Doreen fondly strokes her burgeoning stomach.

'The father?' Alice ventures before she can stop herself.

She wishes she'd kept her mouth shut when she notes the sheen of tears that Doreen cannot hide. 'His father did not know of him. I got the telegram before I found out.'

'I'm so sorry…'

Doreen blinks, then shrugs. She nods at the wounded and the injured around them. 'Puts it all into perspective, eh? At least I have something of Billy to remember him by.'

I had something of Raju but I gave her away.

Doreen smiles at Alice. It is a brave smile, sadder than anything Alice has seen, making her stomach hollow with hurt. 'I hope Billy was looked after in his last moments, I hope someone was kind to him.'

'Like you are to these men.' Alice sweeps her hand to indicate the American servicemen they're tending to.

Now Alice can see how Doreen is able to lie to these men, pretending to be their loved ones when they are delirious with pain and calling for their fiancées or wives. It is because she's wishing, hoping, that someone was there to do this for *her* love; she is picturing her Billy in every one of these men.

Doreen tucks her hand in Alice's. 'We're all doing the best we can in horrific circumstances.'

I didn't. I gave up. I ran away and came here.

'My mother lost her husband to one war and her son to another,' Doreen continues. '*She* is the brave one. And there are so many women like her.'

What I lost, and the ache I feel when I think of my daughter, Alice thinks then, *is insignificant in the face of all this suffering.*

'What's your story, Alice?' Doreen asks now.

Her friend, who confessed in a rare moment of vulnerability when Alice came upon her retching in the toilet after a soldier had died in her arms: 'Every time one of our patients dies, it's like I lose Billy all over again.'

'Something happened to you. I can see the pain in your eyes,' Doreen says now.

'I…' Alice flounders. How can she tell this brave woman about her cowardly actions?

'When you're ready, my love.'

I never will be. I finally have a friend. I do not want to see her eyes dim with disappointment when I tell her of what I have done, of all I have done.

Chapter 78

Alice

1945

Safe

'There you are.'

Alice is waiting outside Doreen's apartment. It is completely dark, owing to the blackout, but her eyes have almost adjusted to the way things look, because she makes this journey regularly when working the night shift.

This evening the air is stinging, sharp and frosty, with a hint of snow. Sounds drift down from different apartments, cooking pots clang, and there's the pungent odour of boiled cabbage. A baby wails plaintively. As Doreen slips out of the door, in the patchy sliver of light she looks pale and not her usual, determinedly cheerful self. Her hand, when she tucks it into Alice's, is clammy.

'Are you alright?' Alice asks.

'Not really,' she admits.

This is shocking. Normally Doreen is quick to pretend everything's okay.

'What's the matter?'

In the near-darkness, the whites of Doreen's eyes shine and her face is pallid, dotted with perspiration, although the night is cold, verging on freezing.

'I've been having pains on and off,' she whispers.

'Labour?' Alice stops, turning to face her friend.

Two boys run past, chuckling and shoving each other. There's the click-clack of footsteps across the road; a giggle wafts on the snow-sprinkled air.

'It's too early,' Doreen says, looking worried. 'This babe…' She swallows. 'He's given me the strength to carry on despite losing Billy. If only he'd hang on for a few more weeks…' Her voice breaks. Her breath is coming fast and heavy, as if they're running, when in actual fact they're standing still in the middle of the road.

'He *will* hang on,' Alice says brightly, pushing thoughts of her own child, who also arrived early, firmly away. 'We'll ask Dr Merritt when we get to the hospital, but I'm sure it's all okay.'

Doreen flashes a quick smile, seeming almost her old self. 'Thanks, Alice. You're a good friend.'

They're nearly at the hospital – their progress has been slower than usual, because Doreen has needed to stop every so often. Alice is trying not to panic as she takes in her friend's pallor when the air-raid siren goes.

People spill out of their houses and move towards the tube station, which is the nearest designated shelter. The air-raid warden shepherds Alice and Doreen towards it.

'I need to get to the hospital,' Doreen's voice harsh with panic.

'She might be going into labour,' Alice pleads.

'This is *safe*,' the air-raid warden insists.

'But the hospital's just round the…'

Alice's words are interrupted by an almighty bang, which reverberates through the ground beneath them, almost throwing them off their feet. The dark world around them explodes into a bright-orange fiery glow. They are aware of shrapnel, rubble and screams all around them, and their mouths fill with the acrid tang of smoke and the vermilion brand of fear, red hot. The rumble of aircraft overhead warns of another imminent strike. Now there's a taste of fire in the air.

Alice squeezes her friend's hand. 'You and the babe'll be fine, I promise.' She is grateful that her voice is steady.

Together, they stumble down the tube station steps alongside dozens of other people.

Doreen is panting by the time they get down to the bottom of the stairs, where the smells of exhaustion, sweat, fear and body odour assail them. The darkness is punctuated by lanterns and furious speculation, from the people hiding underground, about the air strike going on above them. Despite the crush, Alice manages to find a corner by a wall.

'Will this war, this senseless destruction, ever end?' an old woman cries, eyes rheumy with sorrow and ringed by despair. 'How much longer will this go on? I was widowed in the last war and my daughter has been widowed in this one. I've lost a son to each war. And the fighting still goes on, swallowing our young men, taking and taking… What will be left?'

A group of women take her in hand, brisk and comforting: 'We've got to be brave now. Keep going for King and country…'

Beside Alice, Doreen emits a small moan of pain.

'Lean back, nice and gently,' Alice tells her friend, who's looking distinctly peaky.

The woman next to Alice pauses in the act of trying to shush her wailing baby to exchange glances with Alice. Doreen has closed her eyes, but her face is still alarmingly pale and moist with sweat. She doesn't look at all well.

Alice tries to fight the panic taking her hostage; tries to quash the memories crowding in of giving birth herself: the pain, grief and guilt. The image of Raju's too-still body is branded into her soul. *She needs to be strong for her friend.*

Beside them, people have settled down. Some are on the station floor, some on the rail tracks, all with accustomed resignation. Women knit, crochet and rock babies to sleep. There's a crinkle and rustle of paper as a mother unwraps sandwiches for her children.

One old man drinks from a flask, while another has fallen asleep and is snoring long and loud. A group of children has collected around him, watching his stomach rise and fall with each breath, giggling every time his mouth explodes in a sputtering exhalation.

Doreen bites her lower lip hard when waves of pain overtake her. 'Here, hold my hand,' Alice says, willing her voice not to show her fear and anxiety.

One woman sings lullabies to her infant, while another tells her children stories in a quiet voice.

To get her friend's mind off her pain, and also because she wants to reassure Doreen, who she knows is worried about her baby coming early, that everything will be alright, Alice says, 'You've always asked me for my story. I…'

And then, haltingly, she pours out her whole sorry tale: 'So, you see, I had a baby early too, but she was fine. We'll get you to hospital but, even if we can't, there's no need to worry.'

'Oh, Alice,' Doreen says, tears sparkling in her eyes.

Her friend is not repulsed or shocked by Alice's past actions. Instead there's love shining out of Doreen's eyes, and caring. All these years Alice has been desperate to find love and, just as she did with Aunt Edwina and Edward's Aunt Lucy, she has found it again in the most unlikely of places.

'Oh, my dear,' Doreen says, racked with pain and yet feeling for her, 'I think it is very brave to give the child you longed for away in the misguided belief that she'll have a better life without you.'

Alice looks at her friend, stunned.

'Yes,' Doreen says, correctly reading the question in Alice's expression, 'it *is* misguided, for whatever you think of yourself, Alice, your daughter's place should be with you, her mother.'

Alice thinks of the years that she had slept away, like her mother used to, trying to ignore the pain, the ache, the desire to run back to the orphanage and grab her child. How she has kept telling herself all these years – when she has seen mothers sobbing at their sons' deathbeds, and mothers gathering their children with limbs missing, and bloodshot eyes that have endured the horrors of war, to them – that her child is better off without her. How when she sees mothers waving goodbye to their sons and daughters, knowing they might never see them again, she thinks, *That's what I did too, in a way.*

'Alice,' Doreen's voice is urgent, 'you love your daughter. That makes you a good mother. You will not be, you are *not* like your parents.' A contraction rocks her and, when it passes, Doreen says, 'Life is short. Too short to spend it without the ones you love. Promise me you'll go to India to find your child. She needs her mother, and you need your daughter.'

And, as Alice hesitates, Doreen squeezes her hand, insistent: 'Promise me?'

'I promise.'

A young girl squeals. 'A rat just walked across my leg.'

'That's the least of your worries, my girl,' a man tells her, laughing, while a boy asks, with awe in his voice, 'How big was it?'

A little later, Doreen says: 'Alice.' She's panting hard, as though walking uphill. 'The baby is coming.'

Alice turns to some of the other women. They come together, helping quietly, efficiently, children kept away, entertained by the men – one doing magic tricks, another telling jokes, yet another fantastic tales of gruesome adventures – designed to keep curious eyes away from what is taking place in the corner, inside the closed circle of mothers, sisters and grandmothers.

The coterie of women supply towels they've brought along for their own children, urging Doreen, 'You can do this. Calmly now, push.'

They give her water from flasks, wipe her sweaty forehead with flannels they'd carried for their babies. Through it all, Doreen keeps a tight grasp of Alice's hand.

'I don't think I'll make it,' says Alice's usually optimistic friend.

'Of course you will.' Alice's voice is steady, although she's howling inside.

'If anything happens to me, make sure Billy is—' Doreen pants.

'*Nothing* is going to happen to you. You and little Billy are going to be fine.'

'I have a feeling it's a little boy. I'm going to call him Billy, after his father,' Doreen had confided in Alice some weeks ago.

'What if it's a girl?'

'She can be Billy too. Short for Billy-Anne. But I just know this is a boy,' Doreen had said, fondly stroking her stomach.

When the pain takes her, Doreen squeezes Alice's hand. She does not cry out. 'The children... Babies sleeping... Don't want to disturb...' Even suffering intense pain, in the midst of premature labour in a tube station during an air raid, Doreen is thinking of others; Alice's extraordinary friend.

'Push,' the women urge. Doreen does so, holding onto Alice.

Outside the circle of women, children giggle as they are regaled by stories and jokes by men sitting on the train tracks, among the rank reek of dirt and sweat, iron and rust.

The women tending to Doreen look at each other wordlessly as they watch the blood gushing out of her along with her baby, a steady stream they cannot stop.

'It's a boy,' the women say. Then, 'Oh…'

'He's not crying,' Doreen whispers.

Alice is beside her friend, holding her hand, so she is unable to see the baby clearly, only the lake of blood spreading around Doreen, soaking into the towels, bright crimson. The women shake their heads slightly, their faces blanched.

'Doreen,' Alice says, softly.

'Please can I hold him?'

Her friend's face is pale as mist clinging to the edges of a waning day.

The baby is placed in Doreen's arms, while the women try to stem the blood that keeps on coming.

'He's the image of Billy.' Doreen's gaze is soft with love. She kisses the child. *Cold. Blue.* But she doesn't seem to notice. As she holds him to her chest, tears are falling down her face. She closes her eyes, still clutching her child.

PART 15

India

Legacy

Chapter 79

Alice

1945

Future

India. Home. Bittersweet. Longing and pain, lost love and heartbreak.

Father is not here in Jamjadpur; he's not anywhere. Just before Alice left England for India, she'd received a telegram, addressed to her, care of Aunt Edwina. The words 'DEEPLY REGRET TO INFORM… ROBERT HARRIS… CONFIRMED KILLED…' had blurred before her eyes. She hadn't known that Father had signed up. She hadn't written to him, or kept in touch.

The telegram had fluttered from her suddenly slack hands. In her head she could hear his infectious rumble of laughter, which she had been party to only twice in her life, both times before she had disappointed him by loving a coolie.

An image of her father appeared before her closed eyes: the father she had admired and tried to please, whose eyes would soften when he looked at his wife.

I loved you once, Father, and looked up to you, she'd thought. For the next few nights she'd dreamt the same dream, of Father carrying her high in his arms, so she might see if she could touch the sky.

Now, as she feels a pang of loss for the father she had feared and in the end loathed – yet still somehow always loved – she understands how enduring family bonds are; how deep they run and how much they matter, despite everything. When she had discovered what Father and Edward had done to Raju and the menfolk of his village, she *hated* her father, but now, with the passing of time, she is able to see beyond his actions to the person he was and the reasoning behind what he did. In his own stilted and selfish way she understands that he cared for her, but that he could never forgive her association with a coolie.

Yes, there are ups and downs in families – in the case of her relationship with Father, mostly downs, but she is grateful for the few happy memories she has of him, which ever so slightly redress the bad times.

I wasn't thinking straight when I left you here, my dear… In her head, Alice talks to the child she hopes to meet and lay claim to in a few minutes as she walks up the steps of the orphanage. *Forgive me, my love, if you can.* Laughter comes drifting from the compound – the happy abandon of children at play – as she waits for the door to be opened. *I was grieving and angry with myself. I was a mess. I thought I was doing the right thing by leaving you here.*

As she waits to see Mother Superior, she tastes regret and desperation, yearning and unbearable anticipation. *I'm sorry. I've made so many mistakes but I've learnt from them. I'm here now. I will be the best mother possible. I've lost all this time with you but no more, my child. No more.*

'How wonderful,' Mother Superior says, beaming, 'that you've just learnt of your friend's child, who was brought here nine years ago, and would like to adopt her.'

Alice can hardly sit still on her seat. She's like the little children who Mother Superior must see in this very office: excited, nervous, anxious. In her mind she's going over what she will say to her daughter. Who will she look like? Herself? Raju? Are her eyes still blue or have they changed colour?

Since Alice made the decision to come here – keeping her promise to the friend she was not able to save, who had died with her stillborn child nestled in her arms – she has been desperately impatient, wanting to see her child *now*, to gather her into her arms. Since she gave herself permission to want her child, it's as though all the longing contained for so many years is spilling out.

She takes in the boxy little room, with the cross hanging behind the desk, and wonders how often her daughter has been in here and for what reason. She looks at this woman with her wimple and her kind eyes, and she wonders how her daughter feels about her, this mother figure in lieu of herself.

'You say she was left here during the nineteen thirty-six riots?'

'Yes.' Alice's heart is thrumming in her chest.

Mother Superior turns to the bureau beside her and pulls out a ledger labelled 1936–7.

'She was wrapped in a green cardigan and matching booties,' Alice whispers. She's so close to her daughter, who is going about her life just beyond this room. *We are sharing the same space after nine long years. I love you so much but all these years I have forced down my love, pushed it away.*

I tried to sleep away the first few years after I gave you away. Then I signed up for the war effort, all the while hoping, praying you were alright, trying to convince myself you were better off without me. Ignoring my longing. Telling myself I didn't deserve you.

All these long, barren years my imagination has supplied images of you. And in a few minutes, I'll get to see you in person, my love. You are so close, so very close.

My child.

*

Mother Superior leafs through the book on her desk. She stops at a page, her fingers running down it, halting at an entry.

She leans back, crosses her arms, a closed-off expression on her face. 'Ah, you mean Janaki.'

Janaki. Such a beautiful name. Alice repeats it in her head. Three perfect syllables.

'She's not here.' Mother Superior says, but she is smiling.

What is she saying, what does she mean?

'Janaki has recently been successfully adopted into a very good family. I've just heard from her and she is very happy there.'

Alice sits there, stunned.

'Her parents love her very much and are taking good care of her. She doesn't want for anything.'

Her parents… I am her parent.

'If you're interested in adoption, there're many other children here who would benefit from someone…'

But Alice is standing up, then she's stumbling outside the walls of the orphanage into the crowded street. *Adopted into a very good family. Her parents are taking good care of her. She is very happy there.*

She is happy. That's all I wanted. She has two parents now. Who will look after her, care for her, give her what I cannot, Alice tells herself, as she stands in the middle of the street, ignoring the honking traffic, the shouts to get out of the way.

Alice walks the streets of Jamjadpur, her face wet, awash with salt and memories. *She is happy.*

Her feet lead her almost without thinking to the textile and fabric section of the market, happily chaotic with tents, where all manner of colourful cloth, silks and bangles, deep-fried snacks and *bhelpuri,* spiced tea and milky coffee are on sale. Alice wades through the crush of people, the hot, sweet scent of busyness, bustle, and crisp new clothes.

She can almost believe that if she looks up, she will, in the distance, spy a familiar profile, as she did on that fateful day when everything changed. She recalls the disbelieving exultation of that one blessed glimpse...

She wanders the streets, unable to settle, wondering if her daughter has walked here as she is doing. Street children tug at her clothes, their palms stretched out for alms.

And it is then, as she sees the street children, emaciated and hungry, looking at her with pleading eyes, that Mother Superior's words come to her, 'If you're interested in adoption, there're many other children...'

She hears her friend Doreen's voice in her head, saying, as she tended to dying American servicemen, pretending to be their wives, their beloveds, 'I hope someone is doing the same for my Billy...'

And Alice understands what she can do, *must* do to pay for all the wrongs of her past, and to face a future without her daughter in it...

Chapter 80

Janaki

1986

Unique

Dearest Ma…

Janaki reads the first two words in her daughter's firm handwriting, as tears, tasting of love and worry and fear for her beloved child, fall. She has tried – and failed – to find the balance between loving and yet not loving too much; tried – and failed – to barricade her own heart from the loss that she knew would one day come.

> *Dearest Ma,*
>
> *First of all, I want to say I love you.*
> *It may not have felt like it, especially recently, but I do. Very much so.*
> *You are the most important person in my life.*
> *I look up to you and admire you, Ma.*

She sits on the bed in Deepa's room. The room that is bereft of her daughter, and of any signs of her occupancy. And yet, although Deepa's vibrant mark is not in the room, it is now in Janaki's heart.

Her words. These words that her daughter has never said before. All her actions as a teen designed to convey just the opposite.

The breeze that wafts in through the open window tastes of amazement. It is cool on her stunned cheek, perfumed with roses and jasmine, creamy yellow, whispering in Prasad's voice, 'She's quite something, isn't she? Our girl?'

She is. She *is*.

I know your life has been hard. That you have suffered. What you didn't tell me I gleaned from Sister Nandita and Sister Malli. For a little girl yearning for love, a family, belonging, to be adopted and then to lose her adoptive parents, and, after, the best friend who made her life bearable...

And yet to rise from this, make the most of her circumstances, win a place at medical school. It is amazing. Inspirational. And then... To find love in Baba and lose him too... The shock of his sudden, unexpected demise starting labour. My being born the day of Baba's death.

I cannot begin to imagine how you must feel. For you have done an amazing job, saving me from the hard knocks of life.

Ma, I can understand why you want to protect me. I do.

But I feel suffocated. Stifled. I want to live. *Not just drift through life.*

Do you remember when I was younger I would pester you for stories about Baba?

Your eyes would glow when you spoke of him. 'I had made up my mind not to love anyone but your baba stole my heart. Wrenched it from right under me.'

'Why did you make up your mind not to love anyone?'
I asked.

'Because love hurts,' you replied.

'But Baba came and you decided to love him.'

'I had no choice,' you whispered.

'And do you regret it?' I asked.

'No, never,' you said. 'Never ever.'

'Because Baba gave you me?'

'That too.' You laughed through the tears in your eyes.
'And also because before that I was just living but loving
him, it was an explosion. It was incredible. I wouldn't
exchange it for the world.'

'Do you love me like that too?' I asked.

'More,' you replied.

'Does it hurt to love me?'

'Yes.'

'How?'

'I'm scared for you – I don't want you to be hurt. I want
you to be happy, always. I want to give you the best, do the
best by you. It hurts, but my darling, I love you anyway
and I always will. With my all until the day I die.'

'Whatever I do.'

'Whatever you do.'

'Even if I hurt you?'

'Whatever you do,' you repeated, your voice soft against
my ear, bright with conviction, thrumming with intensity.

I believed you, Ma.

And yet, I couldn't help asking, 'Do you regret loving me?'

'Not for a moment,' you said fiercely. 'Not at all.'

'Is it because you have no choice?'

'We chose to have you, my love. Your baba and I chose
together. And if he was here, he would be so proud.'

I remembered that conversation, Ma. I wrote it down. It was because you were so unguarded, so transformed when you spoke of love and of Baba. After that and before that too, you were always careful about what you said, thinking things through before you spoke. But that one day you let your guard down, opened yourself up to me and for that, I am grateful.

I understood something that day. That to love someone like you did Baba, even briefly, is worth it, regardless of the pain that is its twin. I want love like that. I want to live life to the full, grab it with both hands.

Baba was like that, I gather, from what you've told me. Experiencing everything life had to offer, not afraid to take risks: like standing up to you, his superior, even though he admired you, even knowing it might put you off him.

And in the time he was with you he taught you to be like that, I think. In those few years with him, you lived more fully than you ever had before and after – that's what I've gleaned from listening to Sister Malli and Sister Nandita's stories of you.

Ma, I think this is what it is to live: it is experiencing glorious highs and devastating lows. It is joy and sorrow, agony and comfort. It is exquisite and soul-destroying. Loving and hurting.

What I have done so far is watch life play out from the sidelines. I want to immerse myself in it. Get hurt and recover – or not. Make mistakes and find out how to set them right. Learn from them.

I want to love and lose. To embrace everything life has to offer. Baba lost his parents at a young age. It shaped him but it did not stop him. It did not take away his capacity to love and he showed you that you could love too; that accepting that love hurt but doing so anyway was the only *way to live.*

Ma, you must think me mad, crazy, to willingly want to experience the pain you've tried to shield me from. You who have lived all your life with hurt, with unimaginable pain, with the gnawing ache of missing. You who have known love to slip through your fingers, who are on intimate terms with loss.

But Ma, don't you see how very different you and I are? You, growing up in an orphanage, have yearned for love and family; I've never had to.

The very reason I want to experience life in all its complicated, messy, fragile, whimsical and evanescent brilliance is because I am loved so very much.

I have always known this. There hasn't been a single moment in my life where I haven't had the security of your love to fall back on.

I can confidently forge ahead, taking risks, loving and losing, for I am assured *of one love I will never lose, of one love that is constant, that will always sustain me: Yours.*

Janaki wipes the tears soiling her daughter's beautiful words, blown away by Deepa's wisdom. Her love for her.

I have wanted to tell you all this for a long time. But when I am with you, when I try to talk to you, I cannot find the words. They are absorbed into the wall of anger that slams me hard, that pushes rational thought away. I feel smothered, your love, possessive and protective, choking the words out of me.

I understand your need to protect me. I know you worry something might happen to me, but I'd rather live a short but full life than a long, boring, unfulfilled one. You cannot give me everything even if you want to. Give me this instead: Let me go, Ma. Let me live my life.

But I know you find it almost impossible to do. It's what all our fights are about, after all. And so, I've decided to take matters into my own hands.

Ma, I've thought long and hard about what to do. I do not want to hurt you. If I leave you to try and live my life, I'll always harbour guilt with regards to you.

So she has not left me. Janaki feels a sudden surge of hope.

Ma, I believe the reason you hold onto me so is because you believe I'm all you have. But what if that's not the case?

What does Deepa mean?

What if your parents, who left you at the orphanage, are alive? Perhaps if, through them, you were able to make sense of your past; if you understood why they gave you away, you would be able to let me go? It was worth a try so I set out to find them.

Janaki drops the letter, shocked. Of all the possible scenarios she imagined, she never expected this!

Her daughter the romantic. When Deepa first understood that the orphanage had been her mother's home, she was full of questions.

'You don't know who your parents are?'

'No.'

'You were brought up by the nuns?'

'Yes.'

'But they're scary.'

'Sometimes.' Janaki laughed.

'And strict?' Deepa scrunching up her nose.

'I'm afraid so.'

'Who loved you? Cuddled you good night? Soothed you when you had nightmares?'

'The nuns and the other children at the orphanage.'

Arthy. And for a brief while my adoptive parents.

'But didn't you miss your parents?'

'I didn't know them.' *I missed my adoptive parents so very much, I still do.*

'Your parents must miss you very much.' Deepa's face was solemn.

Janaki had gathered her inquisitive daughter into her arms, revelling in her rose-and-sandalwood scent. 'They must do.' Wondering: *Do you? Where are you?*

A crow cackles just outside the open window of Deepa's room. The breeze that wafts in and brushes Janaki's hot, flustered face carries the hint of pineapple and tamarind. Janaki picks up her daughter's letter, her hands shaking so much that it flutters as if being blown away in a squall.

Thinking, *Deepa, my love,* even as she reads her daughter's next few words.

> *I dug out the cardigan you were wrapped in when you were left at the orphanage. I knew where you kept it.*

'Show me exactly where you were found, Ma,' her daughter would ask, when they visited the orphanage.

'Right here by the steps.' Janaki would point out the nook where desperate mothers used to leave their babies. 'I was wrapped in a cardigan the bright green of monsoon-bathed fields and given matching booties.'

'Where are the cardigan and booties now?'

'The booties were misplaced but the cardigan is at our house.'

'Will you show me where?'

Someone knitted that cardigan by hand, Ma. It is beautiful, unique, the water-lily pattern so distinctive. I knew there wouldn't be many of its kind so I took photographs of it with the camera I asked for my birthday and wrote to all the tailors in the city, then to others whom they suggested might know more.

You thought all those letters part of my medical college applications…

Anyway, the long and short of it is…

I believe I've found your mother!

Chapter 81

Janaki

1986

Mother

I believe I've found your mother, her daughter's letter says.

> *I've gone to meet her, check if she really* is *your mother. If so, I'll bring her to meet you.*

> *I'm coming back, Ma.*
> *And when I do, you'll see that letting me go isn't so hard after all.*
> *I will always come back to you, Ma.*
> *But you have to let me go first.*

Chapter 82

Alice

1986

Cardigan

The photograph is of an infant's cardigan.

She recognises it; she knows it. She *made* it. In yarn the green of new shoots, and bright budding hope. Knitting into it her hopes, her dreams for the future.

'Do you recognise this cardigan? Know anything about its creator? It's home-made, the pattern distinctive. I asked around, and the only instance I could find of similar cardigans was here. The children in your home wear them, so I was wondering…' the girl is saying.

Alice looks up at her, filled with wonder and thrill. Incredible, marvellous joy is overwhelming her. Now she knows why this girl is familiar. Even before the girl speaks, before she says, 'My mother was left at the doorstep of St Ursula's Orphanage for Destitute Children in Jamjadpur during the riots of nineteen thirty-six. She was wearing this cardigan and I…'

My mother…

Alice traces her features with her eyes: that honest, open face, that shy smile. Her heart sings. All these years, she has showered all the love in her heart – she who had believed she would be a bad mother, a selfish one – on children who are not hers, in the hope that one day she would find her own daughter.

And now this beautiful girl, young and determined, has come to find *her*, and is looking at her with Raju's gold eyes.

'Hello, granddaughter.' Each word is spoken in marvel and wonder; her heart, her whole body alight with happiness, with love.

Her granddaughter beams.

'I *knew* it,' she cries, in laughter and awe. 'But your colouring… it threw me. Although it shouldn't have done, given Ma's blue eyes...'

So, her daughter's eyes didn't change colour after all… Alice's heart dances with barely contained exhilaration. She has hoped for this – *a reunion with her daughter* – imagined it in those velvet, navy hours of night when nagging doubts cripple and secret desires overwhelm…

Alice had been tempted over the years to try to search for her daughter. But then she would think: *She's happy. She has a family, a life crafted for herself without me in it. Is it right to disrupt that life? Will it be in her best interests? Won't it be selfishness, wanting for my sake rather than hers? I will be repeating the same mistakes I made with Raju by barging into the life he had fashioned after he and Ayah were sacked by Father, destroying the life they'd had...*

As the years have gone by, Alice has contented herself with living in the same country and breathing the same air as her daughter, praying for her, loving her from afar and sending best wishes to her in her thoughts… And now this. *Thank you… to the gods, to destiny, to the universe.*

The girl – *her granddaughter!* – suddenly shy and curiously formal, holds out her hand.

'Hello, grandmother.'

Alice takes her hand and pulls her into an embrace. 'When you get to my age, you dispense with formalities,' she says, holding her grandchild, beautiful perfection, in her arms. 'Will you tell me your name?'

Her granddaughter laughs, a kaleidoscopic cascade of flowers, a choir of voices raised in song.

'I'm Deepa. And I'm so happy to meet you.'

Chapter 83

Janaki

1986

Wise

It's been two days since Janaki woke to find her daughter gone – two whole days spent pacing and worrying, chastising herself: *I've done this: goaded her, fought with her, pushed her away*; making promises to gods, both Hindu and Christian, and railing at them; railing at herself: *Why did I tell Deepa about being left at the orphanage, wrapped in a cardigan, knowing what a romantic my daughter is? Why didn't I destroy that cardigan?*

In her mind, she scolds her daughter: *You foolish girl, why on earth did you want to find my parents? What sort of mad idea is this? Do you know what a dangerous world it is out there? But you* don't *know and that's because of me!* She turns on herself again and then, in desperation, turns to the gods again, any, all: *Keep her safe, please.*

It's been two days and nights, during which she couldn't sleep, couldn't eat; two days of imagining and preparing to accept the worst; two days of reading and rereading her daughter's letter, trying to decode it, trying to find clues as to where she has gone. It's been two days of talking wildly out loud to Prasad in the empty house bereft of her daughter, which is ringing with the silence and the missing of her; two nights of communing with bright stars in the sky; two days of asking long dead and hopefully sainted Sister Shanthi and Mother Superior to bargain with the gods on her behalf.

Then a knock on the door and there she is.

Her daughter. Standing on the doorstep, grinning sheepishly, looking none the worse for wear.

Janaki breathes her daughter in, unable to believe she is there, in front of her, whole and hale. Then she is throwing her arms around her daughter, crushing her to herself. Deepa allows Janaki to hug her – something she hasn't done in a very long time – only murmuring, after a while, 'Ma, I cannot breathe.'

But there is laughter in her daughter's voice. Her daughter, who is already smelling different. Not quite like *her* Deepa. A tinge, a whiff of something other. But her daughter all the same. Returned to her.

'See, I'm back like I promised. I'm safe.'

'You gave me such a fright.'

'I'm sorry I couldn't tell you. But if I had, you wouldn't have let me go.' Deepa gently wipes the tears from Janaki's cheeks. 'Nothing happened to me, Ma.'

Janaki looks into her daughter's liquid gold eyes and scours her face for lies. Deepa holds her gaze.

'I took an auto rickshaw to the train station, the overnight train to Delhi, and the same back. And here I am.'

'The overnight train!' Janaki whispers, closing her eyes, terror gripping her.

'I'm fine, unmolested. I booked a first-class cabin.'

Unmolested. Janaki sways on her feet.

'I promised you I'd come back and here I am.'

Her daughter gently wipes Janaki's tearful eyes again, her expression tender.

'I will always come back to you, Ma, no matter how far I go.' And then, 'Did you read my letter?'

'I know it by heart.'

Deepa laughs, a beatific symphony. 'I thought as much. The small matter of it being so long wouldn't have deterred you. I got a bit carried away; you can say things in letters you never will face-to-face.'

'It's beautiful. You're so wise.'

'You agree with what I say?'

Janaki cups her daughter's cheek and looks into her suddenly vulnerable eyes. 'Every word. I'm so proud of you. You've taught me so much. Deep down, I always knew I couldn't hold on to you. Your father, he told me so, again and again.'

Deepa raises her eyebrows.

'He visits in my dreams. No need to look like that, I'm not crazy.'

Again, her daughter laughs, music and delight. 'That's debatable.' Then, softly, 'Ma, the last part of the letter?'

'Yes?' Wary hope colours Janaki's voice.

Deepa's voice is gentle: 'I visited your mother.'

Janaki lowers herself into a chair and rests a shaking hand upon her heart. 'You did?' Her voice a barely-there whisper. 'Is she…?'

'You can find out for yourself. She's waiting at the new branch of the *thali* restaurant you used to frequent with Baba.'

'She… she's *here*?'

'She came with me, but I thought it would be best if you met somewhere neutral.'

When did her daughter become so wise?

'Go! She's waiting,' Deepa says.

'You…?'

'I need a wash.'

'But…'

'Ma,' Deepa is firm, 'you can leave me. I will not run away, I promise. At least not without telling you first. And, to be fair, even this time I did leave a letter.'

Janaki closes her eyes.

'Just teasing. I'll be here when you get back. With, or without your mother, whatever you decide.' Then, 'And Ma…'

'Yes?'

'Don't look so scared. She's your mother!'

'Are you… are you sure?'

'She definitely is. Do you think there are women lining up out there to claim as their daughters crazy women who do *not* take advice – delivered in dreams – from their long-dead husbands?'

Startled laughter escapes from Janaki, briefly displacing the terrified anticipation reverberating through her being.

Her daughter chuckles. Then, serious again, says: 'Ma, you need answers. You've been waiting all your life for this.'

'I have.'

'Go and see her. Ask her why.'

Her bright, perceptive, wonderful daughter.

'Thank you, Deepa.'

'Ma…'

'Yes?'

'I love you, you know.'

Janaki's eyes are overflowing, her heart is overwhelmed. 'I love you more.'

'Don't I know it!'

As Janaki leaves to meet the mother she doesn't know, for the first time since she was given away, the waterfall of her daughter's giggles reverberates in her ears.

Chapter 84

Alice

1986

Magnificent

Alice looks out of the window at the bustling street outside – she deliberately chose the table by the window at the restaurant where she will meet her daughter – *meet her daughter!* – trying to settle her racing heart even as she peruses every passing woman's face, wondering if this one will be her child.

She is elated, excited and incredibly nervous. She doesn't know what to do with her hands. The restaurant is busy, filled with chatter and laughter, families and friends, parents smiling indulgently at their children; there's the scent of spices and coffee, of roasted coconut and caramelised sugar, and the taste of fried onions and cinnamon-milk in the air.

How this city – near to the compound where she grew up; where she found love and lost it, once and then again – this city, which houses her daughter and granddaughter – this city, which is witness and caretaker to her past, present and future – has changed. And yet in many ways it is the same. It is busier – cars, rickshaws, overcrowded buses and packed lorries have replaced carriages – but there are still bullock carts jostling with dogs and cows, and even the occasional pig and chicken.

Humanity, in all its complicated glory and pathos, is here. Beggar children, with emaciated faces, hands stretched out and pleading eyes, pester besuited men and beautiful women, who, in their glittering saris, with their necks and arms choked by jewellery, dazzle the eye.

Alice is almost overcome by the thrill of being here again, and with the excitement of waiting to meet, at long last, the daughter she gave away, but came back to claim, only to find that she was too late...

After Alice found out that Janaki had been adopted, she had walked the city, aching with loss, yearning for her daughter.

She's happy, she told herself. *She's been adopted into a wonderful family, with two parents who dote on her.*

Her heart awash with anguish and a thousand regrets, she was in danger of sliding into the depression that had taken her captive after she had first given her daughter away, when she came upon the children of the slums, playing by the side of the road with sticks, scavenging in rubbish, their wide, sudden smiles like rays of sunlight after a winter storm.

The sight had pulled her up short. *You are lucky, blessed. Your daughter is happy, loved, leading the life you wanted for her. And you... you've got so much compared to these children and yet they find something to smile about while you wallow in despair.*

Being here in India compelled Alice to count her blessings; its flaws made its small perfections shine more brightly and made her small, bleak life seem magnificent. Encountering those children and others had shown her a way forward. But...

She couldn't bear to be in Jamjadpur, with its poignant reminders of her lost loves, of the mistakes she had made, which had led her to this point. *Be happy,* she told her daughter. *Be loved.* And then she had climbed into the first train leaving the city. It was going to Delhi.

So that was where Alice stayed. She bought a home with the inheritance left to her by her maternal grandparents and gathered children, who had been caught in the crossfire after the partition of India, who were broken and hurting, to her.

All her life she had yearned for love. She had wanted so much; wanted everything. Now she gave instead and, in giving, she found healing, the damaged parts of her becoming whole again.

In giving, she found she was able to forgive herself for what had happened to Raju.

In giving, she forgave herself for giving away her daughter.

She loved the street children and hoped that her daughter never wanted for love. That she was loved. She gave of herself and hoped her daughter was reaping the rewards.

'Excuse me.' It's a woman's voice. Alice looks up, heart thudding.

But it's just the waitress, nodding at her empty cup, asking, 'Would you like another?'

'I'm okay, thanks. I'm expecting someone.' *My daughter!* 'I'll have another when she arrives.'

When she arrives…

By the side of the road, a woman bends down and drops a coin into the plate of a beggar. As if from nowhere, a crowd of beggar children materialise and she distributes coins to all of them. Her slender shoulders, that elegant stance; there's something familiar about it.

The woman looks up, straight at the restaurant, her gaze meeting Alice's. *That gaze. Vivid blue, like a stormy lake. Burnished with the undertone of sorrow, the pulse of ache, the burden of loss.* Alice recognises it – she faces it in the mirror every day.

*

The woman walks towards her. She's wearing a salwar, owning it, her head held high, her hair in a bun at the base of her neck, auburn with chestnut streaks that glint gold-red in the sun. She walks confidently, hands swinging, looking right at Alice; heart-shaped face, bow lips, inquisitive gaze, soft and beautiful, tempered with sadness.

It is like looking at Raju. *Raju.* The man she loved and lost once and again, returned to her, but with *her* eyes, starburst sapphire, reflected back at her.

She is standing up, she is smiling, even as one hand finds her heart, which is beating to an insistent, joyful rhythm: *Janaki. My daughter. My child.*

Chapter 85

Janaki

1986

Incandescent

Janaki walks towards the restaurant where her mother awaits her, nerves at meeting this woman who gave birth to her, then gave her away, who is essentially a stranger, keeping time with joy and relief at the safe return of her own daughter.

Deepa – delight and wonder, so mature and wise beyond her years and yet, in many ways, still such a child. Janaki's heart is overwhelmed by fierce, wild love, the urge to rush back home, gather her daughter to her and not let go.

Curb that impulse! her conscience chides. *It is that which prompted Deepa to run away.*

Well, she *didn't run away exactly. She went to find my mother for me, wanting to give me what she had; what I didn't realise she knew I yearned for – a parent!* Deepa, who has been so tight-lipped about this woman who is waiting to meet Janaki.

Oh, Deepa, why didn't you tell me something, anything, about her? Prepare me? What do I say? What if we run out of words? What if I don't feel any connection to her at all? What if I get angry? What if she—

Janaki, Prasad says in her ear, his steadying voice arriving, as it is wont to do when she needs it most, *she is your mother. You can get angry with her, rail at her if that's what you feel like doing. She gave you away so you can walk away if that's what you decide after meeting with her. You're not under any obligation to her. Deepa said this too; that she'd be at home, waiting, regardless of whether you decided to return with your mother or without her.*

She's amazing, isn't she, our child? Janaki communes with her husband in her head.

Well, she takes after her brilliant mother. There's a smile in her long-dead husband's phantom voice before it disperses into the sandalwood, sunshine and spice-flavoured breeze.

As Janaki nears the restaurant, the children and beggars whom she encounters at the Mother Teresa refuge crowd her: 'Doctor!' Although she tends to their illnesses, she feels a sham hearing herself called this when she hasn't practised at the hospital in years.

She digs in her pockets, distributing the coins she finds there, and they grin with delight. 'Thank you, Doctor!' Perhaps she should consider going back to work, like her daughter has suggested over and over again.

Janaki's heart warms with pride when she thinks of her daughter's kindness, her magnanimity, her love, which propelled her not only to find Janaki's mother – *her mother!* – but to travel across the country in order to bring her here to meet Janaki, even if it has scared Janaki right out of her wits.

These last two days have been torture, sheer torment, but they have taught Janaki that she can let her daughter go; that she *has* to let her go, or she will lose her. Deepa will study at AIIMS in Delhi and she will stay at the hostel there, by herself, without Janaki.

In a city many times the size of this one; big enough to get lost in. Janaki tries to quell the tsunami of panic that threatens to drown her. *Deepa went to Delhi to find your mother and she didn't get lost. She didn't get hurt. She came home, whole and hale, back to you.*

Janaki will manage; she will have to. She has to let her daughter go. This is the only way she will keep her. She will go back to work at the hospital while continuing to help at the refuge and the orphanage. In this way she will fill her days while her daughter is away.

She is thinking this when she looks up at the restaurant where she knows her mother is waiting. Her thoughts are on her daughter as she meets the eyes of a woman sitting by one of the windows. An older woman, her face is stamped with lines of experience, which only serve to make her elegant features more defined, enhancing her gentle beauty, lending it gravitas.

Her gaze, hopeful and eager as it peruses Janaki, is intensely familiar. It is only as she bids goodbye to the children and beggars, not breaking eye contact with the woman, and enters the restaurant, that she realises why the gaze is familiar. Because it is *her* gaze.

Her eyes that she is seeing in this white woman's face.

She has been anxious and unsure about this meeting and yet now all residual doubts are disappearing as she speeds up her pace, compelled by the gaze of this woman who looks as familiar as her own reflection.

Her eyes have that same haunted expression that stares back at Janaki from the mirror. She has never met this woman but she *knows* her. She is drawn to her and feels, as the woman stands, a hand going to her heart, as if she has waited all her life for this moment, as if she has known, always, that it would happen.

Thank you, Deepa, she thinks even as the woman says, in a voice rich and sweet like vintage wine, 'You look like your father,' her lips tilting upwards in a grin so incandescent, it is as if her whole body is smiling.

Chapter 86

Alice

1986

Nothing More

'Ma,' her daughter says. For five decades, Alice has tried to resign herself to the fact that she would never be called so. And yet, this beautiful woman, this strange, hypnotising image of Raju, but with *her* eyes, comes right up to Alice and it is the first word she says.

Despite it taking fifty years, it feels like no time at all, as she opens her arms and her daughter steps into them. And her heart, finally, after years of ache and yearning, is settling, filling, replete.

After a bit, her daughter gently extricates herself, leaving Alice bereft.

'Shall we sit down?'

Once they do, Janaki looks across the table at Alice: 'Why did you give me away?'

Her daughter is unflinchingly direct, like her granddaughter. They both have that slender strength to their features. But while Deepa's eyes were open, inquisitive, innocent, Janaki's are haunted, carrying the burnished, melancholic undertone of loss.

'It's a long story,' Alice manages.

'I've waited a very long time to hear it.'

And so Alice tells her. She does not spare herself, laying bare all, including her part in Raju's death. When she has finished, she waits for her daughter's judgement; her anger at her mother's selfishness.

There is none. Her daughter's gaze steadily meets Alice's, although her eyes shine brightly with tears. She says, 'I was born when my father died. Like my daughter—'

'Oh?'

'I… I lost my husband to a brain haemorrhage.' Pain is stark in her daughter's eyes. Pain that Alice has not been part of. Pain that Janaki has endured and is suffering still. 'I was nearly thirty-seven weeks pregnant with our daughter and went into premature labour. Deepa was born that evening.' A pensive sigh, her gaze far away. Then, 'How history repeats itself. But while you gave me away—'

'I thought it was for the best. I worried I'd be selfish, like my parents. Or that I'd hurt you, destroy you, as I had done Raju. I wasn't thinking straight. A part of me thought I didn't deserve you, that I should have this punishment for all the wrong I had done.'

'Whereas I have kept my daughter close. *Too* close, stifling her with my overprotectiveness,' Janaki says softly, her voice tinted purple with regret.

'She knows you love her. And she thinks the world of you. She loves you so much that she came to find me.'

Alice is rewarded by Janaki's smile, her face glowing. 'Yes.'

My daughter, Alice thinks. *My child.* 'I came back for you.'

'When?' Janaki's eyes widen with surprise.

'After I gave you away, I went to England, you see. I worked in a hospital during the war. I had a friend…' Her eyes are tearing.

Her daughter lays her hand on hers. It is calming. Gentle. 'Tell me.'

Alice does. She tells of the promise she made to her friend, Doreen, just before Doreen died giving birth prematurely to a stillborn Billy, in the tube station air-raid shelter, while bombs were destroying buildings above ground.

'When I returned for you, Mother Superior told me you had been adopted into a good family. That you were happy.'

Shadows crowd her daughter's eyes, rife with pain, drenched in loss. 'I was.' Janaki's voice is the stark navy of melancholy. 'Until I wasn't.'

'What happened?'

'My adoptive parents died,' her daughter says simply.

And now it is Alice's hand that squeezes her daughter's, even as she wishes, fiercely but in vain, that she could go back through the years, gather her in her arms, spare her the agony, the stabbing knife of loss.

'If only I'd known…' And a thought crashes into her, bitter violet, full of pain and remorse. 'I left the city after I found out you'd been adopted. If I had stayed…' Now comes the acrid, burnt-orange taste of regret. 'So much time wasted. Lost. Time I could have spent with you.'

'We just missed each other,' Janaki says softly. 'When you came for me, I had left to be with my adoptive parents and when I came back, you had moved to Delhi.'

'After I found out you'd been adopted, I walked the streets of the city obsessively, hoping to see you, staring into the face of every child, wondering if it might be you.'

'Oh.'

'And when I looked at the street kids, that's when I had the idea. Something your Mother Superior had said. I had pretended that you were a friend's child whom I'd come to adopt, too ashamed to tell the nun I'd willingly given you away.'

'I understand.'

Her daughter is magnanimous. Alice takes a breath, gathers her thoughts. 'Mother Superior told me you were already placed with a family, but, "If you're interested in adoption, there're many other children…" Those were her exact words; I still remember them. I looked into the faces of the street kids, their despairing, hungry, hopeless gazes. They were desperate and so was I. They wanted love, I had so much love to give…' She swallows. 'I had money. My maternal grandparents had left me a legacy. I decided to set up a home where street kids would have the love of a mother. Love like I never got from my own mother, but did have from Ayah.' She pauses, lost in the memory. 'I couldn't stay in this city. I kept seeing your face everywhere, yearning for you, wanting you. But I couldn't have you. So I moved. I took the first train out of the station and I went to Delhi, where I offered a home to children displaced by partition and orphaned, destitute.'

'The nuns never mentioned that someone had come looking for me while I was with my new family,' Janaki muses softly, her eyes wet. 'But I suppose when I returned to the orphanage, devastated after the loss of my adoptive parents, I was in no state to be told. It took me a very long time to get over their loss…'

Alice takes a breath, tasting regret, coloured bitter blue with what-might-have-beens. 'If I'd stayed put, if I'd revisited the orphanage, I would have found you…'

'Ma, it has not been in vain,' her daughter says, squeezing Alice's hand entwined with her own, where their tears fall and mingle.

'All these years, I thought you were happy,' Alice tells her daughter. 'That you were loved, part of a family unit. It is why I didn't try to find you again, although I was tempted to, so very much, over the years. But I worried I would be doing it for me, that it wouldn't be in your best interests. I didn't want to march into your life, disrupt it, for fear of repeating the same mistakes I had made before by bulldozing my way into Raju's life… I couldn't bear it if anything happened to you, if I became the architect of your ruin as I did with your father. So I loved you from afar; I cared for the children in my home and hoped you were cherished by someone, loved... If only I had known... All this time...' Alice's voice bleeds with the pain and remorse she is experiencing, knowing now that her daughter didn't have the family she had very much hoped and wanted for her.

'All this time, you have helped so many children and changed the course of so many lives,' her daughter interjects, softly. 'It's what I want to do, now that Deepa is leaving home to study. I will return to work at the hospital, while also continuing to volunteer at the Mother Teresa refuge and the orphanage.'

Although lamenting all the lost years, Alice is grateful to her daughter for pointing out the bigger picture: 'Yes, over the years I've learnt that giving of oneself eases the pain. All my life, I longed for love, and when I gave of it unselfishly, without expectation, without wanting anything back, I got more love than I thought possible.'

Her daughter's gaze steadily meets Alice's, shining with... is it love? Alice asks the question she has been afraid to ask since she shared the circumstances surrounding Janaki's birth: 'Aren't you upset with me, angry, for what I did?'

Her daughter pats Alice's hand; such a simple gesture that feels so right, but has taken so many years to accomplish, with such heartbreak along the way. 'You paid.'

'Missy Baba, it is I who have had to pay,' Raju had said, his words reverberating down the years and now pulsing at this table as she meets their daughter for the first time since she gave her away.

She takes a breath. 'But your father's death was my fault.'

Janaki's hand is on Alice's, steady. 'You didn't kill him.'

The generosity of her daughter humbles Alice. 'But if I hadn't pursued him—'

'I wouldn't be here,' Janaki says, smiling gently. 'You've been doing penance all your life.' Then softly, 'Tell me about my father.'

'Ah, now,' Alice begins, sniffing and fumbling with a tissue, even as she breathes her daughter in, her coconut-and-sweet-vanilla scent; this elegant, grown woman the image of Raju – older than Raju was when he died – leaning in towards her, her sorrow-ringed eyes fixed upon her. 'Your father colours my earliest memories.'

She shares Raju with their daughter, the flower created by their love. She tells her the stories she has saved and savoured, from her book of memories, all flavoured with nostalgia and seasoned with yearning, scented with sorrow, spiced with love. That is all she has left of Raju, other than this woman herself, his greatest, most precious legacy.

It is relief and release; it is sheer joy to relive those days; the simple innocence and unparalleled happiness of her time together with Raju, when with the foolish, heady optimism of youth, Alice had believed anything was possible. And who better to tell it to than their daughter, who is listening, eyes wide, giving Alice a glimpse into the child she must have been, bright-eyed and eager.

'You never really lose the ones you love,' Alice says tenderly when she has finished, reaching across and cupping her daughter's face in the palm of her hand, revelling in the exquisite joy of this simple action, which should, by rights, be a mother's privilege, but which has taken fifty years to actuate. 'Your father lives on in you.'

Her daughter smiles back, eyes aglow. 'Come home,' she says.

Outside the sun shines, people banter, argue, chatter; vehicles honk and stall in the stop-start traffic, dogs bark, cows moo and children play in the winking, glimmering puddles of muddy water filling the potholes and overflowing from the rubbish-strewn ditches beside the road.

Inside the restaurant, families are conversing and friends are catching up over food and laughter. Alice beams at Janaki, as her daughter reaches across the table and tenderly wipes away the tears that well and flow from a heart alive with gratitude, 'I'd love nothing more.'

Chapter 87

Janaki

1986

Anchor

'Come home,' Janaki says to her mother.

And when Alice smiles, her eyes shining, Janaki feels the part of her that has been rootless since losing her adoptive parents find anchor. Her mother, who also lost the man she believed she loved on the same day that she gained a daughter, who then gave her away in the misguided notion that it was for the best.

Her mother who lost her daughter again when she came to claim Janaki and discovered she'd been adopted. Her mother who, like Janaki, has suffered loss. But, unlike Janaki, she didn't have a daughter to tide her through.

Her mother who has forged a life by creating a home for abandoned and abused children, so needy of the love she has to give. Her mother who has loved Janaki without knowing her, in this way. Her mother, who by giving of herself to others, has found herself and made peace with her life.

For the first time, Janaki is able to see just how much she has had instead of what she's lost.

She has had love, so much love. She had adoptive parents who loved her; a mother who still does; nuns who were surrogate parents and wonderful mentors. She's had friends who adored her, who supported her, who consoled her and loved her: Arthy, Shali, Bina, to name a few.

She has a daughter who loves her so much she found her mother for her. She had a husband who transformed her life; who taught her not only to love but to live. She has had so much but she has been blind, just as Sister Shanthi once warned her not to be.

She has always looked at the wrong thing. But now, thanks to her daughter and her mother, she has opened her eyes to the truth; appreciating just how very blessed she is.

Her daughter will go to AIIMS, she will become a wonderful doctor. And Janaki will refresh her skills and return to work at the hospital. She will help at the refuge and the orphanage and she will open up her home to children who need love, just as her mother has done in Delhi. She hopes that Alice will guide her with this.

Janaki can see the future unfolding and instead of dreading what it might hold, she is looking forward to it, in the way that she had when Prasad was alive.

Once, right after she shared the loss of her adoptive parents and Arthy with Prasad, he had read her Tennyson's 'In Memoriam'. They were in bed together, surrounded by the musk-and-ginger taste of love. It was a long poem, but he'd read it all, his voice, melted chocolate, echoing in the velvet dark.

Afterwards he had very gently kissed her tears and tenderly made love to her again. It is only now, with the salt-and-caramel taste of that memory, coated with nostalgia and wistfulness, that she fully understands; the last couplet reverberating through time in Prasad's melodic voice:

> 'Tis better to have loved and lost
> Than never to have loved at all.

A Letter from Renita D'Silva

I am hugely grateful to you for choosing to read *The Orphan's Gift*. If you enjoyed it and would like to keep up to date with all my latest releases, just sign up at the following link. Your email address will never be shared and you can unsubscribe at any time.

www.bookouture.com/renita-dsilva

What I adore most about being a writer is hearing from readers. I'd love to know what you made of *The Orphan's Gift* and I'd be very grateful if you could write a review. It helps new readers to discover my books.

You can get in touch with me on my Facebook page, through Twitter, Goodreads or my website.

Thank you so much for your support – it means the world to me.

Until next time,
Renita

Acknowledgements

I would like to thank all at Bookouture, especially Maisie Lawrence – you are amazing and I feel incredibly lucky and privileged to have you as my editor. Thank you for your advice, kindness, patience and insight. You are the absolute best.

Huge thanks to Jenny Hutton, editor extraordinaire. I am so grateful to you for homing in on the story I want to tell despite the convoluted mess of words that I send across. I cannot thank you enough.

Thank you, Anne Jenkins, for your eagle eye and wonderful suggestions during copy edits for this book. Thank you, Jane Donovan for proofreading this book.

A million thanks to Lorella Belli of Lorella Belli Literary Agency for your untiring efforts in making my books go places, for your friendship and support, and for being all-round wonderful and brilliant. Thank you also to Laura, Milly and Eleonora.

Thank you to my lovely fellow Bookouture authors, especially Angie Marsons, Sharon Maas, Debbie Rix, June Considine (aka Laura Elliot), whose friendship I am grateful for and lucky to have.

Thank you to authors Chris Babu, Janet Rising, June Arnold and Manuela Iordache for your wonderful friendship and support.

Thank you to all the fabulous book bloggers who give so freely of their time, reading and reviewing, sharing and shouting about our books. I am grateful to my Twitter/FB friends for their enthusiastic and overwhelming support. An especial thanks to Jules Mortimer, Joseph Calleja and Sandra Duck, who I am privileged to call my friends, and who are the best cheerleaders one could wish for.

A huge thank you to my mother, Perdita Hilda D'Silva, who reads every word I write; who is encouraging and supportive and fun; who answers any questions I might have on any topic – finding out the answer, if she doesn't know it, in record time – who listens patiently to my doubts and who reminds me, gently, when I cry that I will never finish the book: 'I've heard this same refrain several times before.'

I am immensely grateful to my long-suffering family for willingly sharing me with characters who live only in my head. Love always.

And last, but not least, thank you, reader, for choosing this book.

Author's Note

This is a work of fiction set around and incorporating real events and people.

Jamjadpur and Ambalgiri are imaginary places. I have taken liberties with regards to the Indian setting, picking characteristics, such as food, vegetation and customs, from different parts of India to fashion my fictional villages and cities; the areas I have set them in may not necessarily have places like the ones I have described.

The communal riots between Hindus and Muslims did take place in India, becoming more frequent in the lead up to the Indian Independence Act of 1947. The riots described in this book are imaginary.

Mother Teresa established many hospitals and refuges for the destitute in India, but I have imagined the refuge in Jamjadpur and also her visit to the slums of that city.

Similarly, I have imagined Gandhi's visit to Jamjadpur.

I apologise for any oversights or mistakes and hope they do not detract from your enjoyment of this book.

Printed in Poland
by Amazon Fulfillment
Poland Sp. z o.o., Wrocław

57450382R00287